Praise for Enchanted, Inc.

"With its clever premise and utterly engaging heroine, Shanna Swendson has penned a real treat! *Enchanted, Inc.* is loads of fun!"

—JULIE KENNER, author of *Carpe Demon*

"A totally captivating, hilarious and clever look on the magical kingdom of Manhattan, where kissing frogs has never been this fun."

—MELISSA DE LA CRUZ,
author of *The Au Pairs* and *The Fashionista Files*

"Light and breezy, but not without substance . . . a bit of the sense of a screwball comedy, only updated for these times that we live in . . . with a hint of *Sex and the City* and maybe a dash of *Bridget Jones*."

—CHARLES DELINT, *Fantasy & Science Fiction*

"Lively . . . a pure and innocent fantasy . . . a cotton candy read."

—*Publishers Weekly*

"This is a witty, unique approach to the familiar story of a young woman working in modern Manhattan, and the laughs are plentiful."

—*Romantic Times*

"Swendson offers a quirky twist on supernatural powers, suggesting that not having any can actually be an asset. This appealing novel offers a charming cast of characters and a clever premise, and readers will hope that Katie's skills will be needed in New York City again soon."

—*Booklist*

"A totally fresh approach to chick lit that's magical and fun."

—freshfiction.com

"From the moment that you pick up *Enchanted, Inc.*, you know that you will have fun. . . . A marvelous world populated with the most interesting people."

—aromancereview.com

"Ms. Swendson does a marvelous job of bridging our world with the world of fantasy, in such a way, as to be completely plausible. . . . This book, if you'll pardon the pun, enchanted me from the first page."

—romancejunkies.com

"Light humor, a bit of magic, a dash of danger and adventure, and an engaging heroine add up to a recipe for a really enjoyable novel."

—BooksForABuck.com

"Lots of likeable characters (and potential romantic interests) that leave you wanting more."

—*Locus* magazine

"[Katie is] like the Harry Potter of adulthood. Author Shanna Swendson pens a delightful, whimsical tale about an unlikely heroine who saves the day against all odds—and oddities. *Enchanted, Inc.* offers a wonderful escape from the ordinary."

—*Dark Realms*

Damsel
Under
Stress

Damsel Under Stress

A Novel

Shanna Swendson

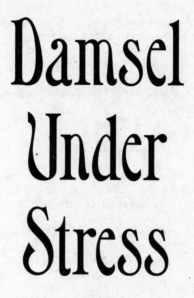

Ballantine Books
New York

A Ballantine Books Trade Paperback Original

Copyright © 2007 by Shanna Swendson

Published in the United States by Ballantine Books, an imprint of The Random House Publishing Group, a division of Random House, Inc., New York.

BALLANTINE and colophon are registered trademarks of Random House, Inc.

ISBN 978-0-345-49292-0

Library of Congress Cataloging-in-Publication Data

Swendson, Shanna.
Damsel under stress : a novel / Shanna Swendson.
p.   cm.
ISBN 978-0-345-49292-0
I. Title.

PS3619.W445D36 2007
813'.6—dc22   2006052635

Printed in the United States of America

www.ballantinebooks.com

2 4 6 8 9 7 5 3 1

Book design by Katie Shaw

*Dedicated in memory of my friend, Rosa Vargas,
who helped me find the courage to write the first book,
who gave me feedback along the way as I wrote the first
two books, and who, sadly, never got to see this one*

Acknowledgments

Thanks to my agent, Kristin Nelson, my editor, Allison Dickens, and the whole team at Ballantine who helped me make this book the best it could be.

Thanks to my friends and family for being understanding when I fell off the face of the earth for a while when I was writing, and who put up with all the insanity when I made brief return trips to this reality.

And special thanks to all the readers who wrote to me, commented on my blog, or came to book signings. The readers have to be the coolest part of what I do, and you have no idea how much your support helps, even during The Dreaded Chapter Five.

Damsel
Under
Stress

One

The last thing I expected to see when I stepped through the door of the coffee shop was a fairy godmother. Not that fairy godmothers are normally high on the list of things I expect to see, even as weird as my life is. I work for a magical company, so running into fairies, gnomes, elves, wizards, and talking gargoyles is something that happens every day. But I'd never yet seen an honest-to-goodness fairy godmother, and I really wasn't expecting to see one that morning because, for the first time in my life, I really didn't need one.

As of the night before, I had my Prince Charming. At the company Christmas party, Owen Palmer, the wonderfully handsome, brilliant, powerful wizard who also happened to be an incredibly nice guy, had kissed me like he meant it and told me he'd always had an interest in me. Yeah, the guy who was the magical world's answer to a movie star liked plain old nonmagical Katie Chandler, the ordinary small-town girl from Texas. That Saturday morning was our first official date as two people who'd admitted that we had feelings for each other. We were meeting for brunch at a snug little coffee shop on Irving Place, possibly the most romantic New York setting I could imagine for a casual first date.

Which meant, of course, that the fairy godmother had to be waiting for someone else. At least, I assumed she was a fairy godmother. I know making assumptions can be dangerous, but I was pretty good about seeing the truth, and she looked like Central Casting's idea of a fairy godmother. She looked older than the eternally youthful fairies I knew, and her wings were a fairly good sign that she wasn't just another eccentric New Yorker. A star-topped wand lying on the table in front of her was yet another clue. None of the other magical folk I knew used wands. Anyone else would surely have made the same assumption, if they saw what I saw.

I almost felt sorry for whoever her Cinderella was because she didn't exactly look like the top-of-the-line fairy godmother. Unlike most of the fairies I knew, she was squat and round, but I couldn't tell if that was flesh or if it was her clothes. She looked like instead of taking off the previous day's clothes and putting on something new each morning, she just put on a new outfit on top of the old one—and she'd been doing that for centuries. In all the layers of clothing I caught glimpses of calico, tulle, patchwork, satin, and velvet. The top layer was old, dusty rose velvet, worn threadbare in places. A rusty tiara missing a few stones sat haphazardly on top of her gray sausage curls, and one of her fairy wings was bent.

Of course, no one in the coffee shop seemed to notice that there was anyone odd among them, and it wasn't simply because they were all distracted by their newspapers and conversations or because the caffeine hadn't yet made it to their brains. I'm immune to magic, so the spell she used to hide her magical appearance didn't work on me. I saw what was really there, while I was sure the rest of the patrons probably saw only an elderly woman wearing a tweed suit and sensible shoes.

But as I said, it wasn't any of my business. I was about five minutes early because I knew Owen was relentlessly punctual and I was sadly overeager, but I figured I could use the time to stake out a table. Unfortunately, the shop was crowded, and there weren't that many tables to begin with. I lingered near the doorway, waiting either for Owen to show up or for someone to vacate a table.

"Yoo hoo! Katie!" I turned when I heard my name and saw the fairy godmother waving at me. I waved back halfheartedly, and she pointed her wand at the empty seat across from her. With a shrug, I went over and took the seat. There was always a chance I could talk her into leaving, and then I would have managed to snag a table before Owen got there. "Oh good, you're right on time," she said as I sat down.

"On time for what?" I asked.

"Our meeting, of course." She gave a tinkling little laugh. "But silly me, I haven't introduced myself. I'm Ethelinda, your fairy godmother. I'll be managing your case, helping you find true love."

"There must have been some kind of mix-up then. I don't need any help right now. You would have really come in handy for the past ten years, but now things are finally working out for me."

She waved her star-topped wand over the table and an elaborately decorated china tea set appeared. As she poured two cups and dropped in lumps of sugar, she said, "We don't make mistakes. You probably need more help than you think, and that's why I was sent your way. Milk or lemon?"

"Milk, please. But I'm actually meeting someone for a date here in a minute or two. So, you see, I don't need help right now, for probably the first time in my life. I've found Prince Charming, he's found me, and all's right with the world."

Frowning, she waved her wand again, and a battered, dog-eared book appeared on the table. She took the pair of spectacles that hung on a cord around her neck and brought them up to rest on her nose. One of the earpieces was missing, so they hung lopsided on her face. "Hmmm," she murmured as she flipped through the book. "Oh, yes, I see what you mean. I haven't seen such a sad case in a very long time. You really could have used a helping hand or two, couldn't you?"

I cringed at her description of what I assumed was my dating history.

A lot of other people's dating histories would also have had to be in that book, though, for it to be that fat. My relationship history wouldn't have required much more than an index card. "That's putting it mildly. So you can see why I'm confused. If you weren't around all those years when almost every man I met acted like I was his little sister or thought I was too boring and nice, then I don't see why you're here now."

"We don't waste time with the little things. We only step in when destiny is at stake, when it matters in the grand scheme of the universe whether or not you find your fated true love."

"Fated true love" sounded like something out of the worst kind of romance novels. It also sounded like something out of my wildest fantasies. Fate sure would make finding Mr. Right and knowing he was Mr. Right a lot easier. If Owen and I really were meant to be together, then I could relax about whether or not a super-powerful wizard could stay interested in someone like me. Then a doubt struck me. "Um, we are talking about Owen Palmer here, aren't we?" It would have been just my luck if she'd shown up at this particular time to hook me up with someone entirely different.

She consulted her book again, flipping through pages and making little humming noises to herself as she did so. At last she said, "Most definitely. And, my, he seems to have needed even more help than you did with his past romances. He's awfully shy, isn't he? But then, we only work for women. The men are on their own." She gave a tittering laugh. "After all, you don't hear much about Prince Charming getting any help from a fairy godmother, only Cinderella."

"Yeah, but isn't Cinderella a—" I almost said "a fairy tale," but then wondered if that might be considered offensive. "—fiction?"

She raised one eyebrow above the frame of her glasses, giving her face an even more lopsided appearance as the glasses dangled precariously off one side of her nose. "Then how would you explain the fact that almost every human culture has some variation of the classic Cinderella story?" She sniffed disdainfully. "That was one of my biggest triumphs. I even won an award." She fished around her neckline until she hooked a finger on a golden chain, then pulled on the chain to raise a star-shaped medal from somewhere deep within the layers of clothes. "See? My claim to fame."

"Very nice," I said, even though the medal was so tarnished it may have been an award for best apple pie at the county fair, for all I could tell. I tried to remember all the fairy tales I'd read and heard—beyond the Disney versions. "But aren't there also a lot of stories about fairies helping out good-hearted younger sons on quests?"

"Those are fairies, not fairy godmothers," she said with an exasperated sigh, like she got that question a lot. "There is a significant difference, you know. We have our own kind of magic, very specific powers and all that. Now, about your case."

I heard the door open and turned to look, hoping it wouldn't be Owen, not yet. Fortunately, it wasn't. He'd picked a very good time to break his punctuality habit. The last thing I wanted was for him to catch me consulting a fairy godmother. It would give him the totally wrong impression. I turned back to Ethelinda. "Not that I don't appreciate the offer, but I really don't think I need help right now. I'd like to try to work things out on my own."

Her glasses fell off her face, bouncing once on their cord against her ample chest. She looked positively heartbroken. "Whatever you think is best," she said, her tone chilly, but with enough breaks in her voice to make it clear that she'd put on the ice as a way of covering her hurt.

I couldn't stand to make an old woman—fairy godmother or otherwise—cry. "I suppose if it starts to be a total disaster, then maybe I could give you a call."

She brightened immediately. Her book disappeared, and a golden heart-shaped locket appeared in her left hand. "You can contact me through this," she said, handing it to me across the table. "Open it when you need me. You'll know what to do from there." And then before I could ask any questions, she was gone, vanished into thin air, along with her tea set.

As I dropped the locket into my jacket pocket, I felt a gust of cold air and thought for a second that it was an aftereffect of her vanishing spell, but then I realized the door had opened. I looked up and saw Owen entering the coffee shop. I wasn't the only one gazing at him. He looked like a celebrity heartthrob, he was so ridiculously handsome. I could practically hear the other patrons trying to remember what movie they'd seen him in as he spotted me and hurried across the room to fall into the seat Ethelinda had just vacated.

On this particular morning, he looked like something out of a paparazzi photo of a celebrity in his off-hours. His nearly black hair was still slightly damp, as if from a shower, and it curled up a little around his ears and at the back of his neck. There was a faint shadow on his strong jaw, and his dark blue eyes were hidden behind wire-rimmed glasses.

I might have been put out that he hadn't made at least some effort on our first official date if he hadn't appeared so flustered. "Sorry I'm late," he said, slightly out of breath. "There's been a bit of a crisis."

"What is it?" I asked, immediately concerned.

A paper cup bearing the shop's logo appeared between his hands, and he picked it up and took a long sip. I noticed then that a similar cup had appeared in front of me, so I got a little caffeine into my system while I waited for him to answer. Cups appearing out of nowhere were practically normal in my life, especially around Owen, so I'd long since gotten used to it.

"Ari got away last night," he said at last, sounding like he'd finally caught his breath and settled down some. Ari was the wicked fairy—and my ex-friend—who'd been helping our company's enemy by spying and sabotaging from within Magic, Spells, and Illusions, Inc., the company where both Owen and I worked. We'd exposed her at the company party the night before, and she'd been taken into custody by the company security forces.

"How'd she escape?" I asked.

"I don't know. But I'm going to have to go to the office and see if I can detect any remnant traces of spells that might have been used. I'm sorry to have to bail on you like this."

"Don't worry about it," I insisted. I'd never been the type to stamp my feet and demand that a man make me his number-one priority in life, so I certainly wasn't going to start now when my date's other priority happened to be saving the world from bad magic.

"I'll make it up to you," he promised. Then he tilted his head and gave me a smile that would have made me agreeable even if I had been throwing a hissy fit about his priorities. "Care to walk me to the subway?"

"Sure." I picked up my paper coffee cup. "Good thing we got these to-go, huh?"

His cheeks went pink. "I usually wouldn't do that, but I didn't have time to wait in line." We took our cups and headed to the exit, then went up the steps to the street level.

Away from the crowded coffee shop, we could talk more freely about Ari and Phelan Idris, the guy who had to be behind all this. "I guess Idris's calm exit last night should have been a sign he had something up his sleeve," I said. "He usually wouldn't give up that easily."

"Maybe. But he's never struck me as the type to care all that much about a damsel in distress. He'd be more likely to forget about her and move on to the next person he thinks he can use."

"Unless she knows too much about what he's up to, and if she was willing to betray us to him, it stands to reason she could be persuaded to tell us about him."

"Oh, I'm pretty sure that was the case. And I'm not sure 'persuasion' is the right word." He sounded so cool about it, practically icy, that it sent shivers down my spine.

"You weren't going to torture her, were you?" I asked.

He choked on the sip of coffee he'd just taken, and I had to pat him on the back until he caught his breath. "Torture? No! You didn't think we'd do that, did you? But there are other methods for getting information out of people."

"Good. I'm mad at her, but I wouldn't want to go that far. If she got away, does that mean someone else in the company is working for Idris?"

"That's what I'll have to find out. Did he pull this from the outside, or was it an inside job?"

"Our work is never done, is it?"

"*My* work is never done. I don't think you'll have to worry much about this one—at least, not yet. We've got some immunes doing verification work on the security force, and they'll be helping with this initial sweep."

I probably should have been stung by the implication that I wasn't needed, but what I actually felt was a great sense of relief. I had my own job to do, and I liked my little corner of the company. I was looking forward to returning to what passed for normal during the holidays. Christmas was barely a week away, and the last thing I wanted to do was take on a big new project with only a few days left in the office before the holiday.

We reached the Union Square subway entrance, and Owen paused before heading down. "I'll call you later, and I will make it up to you."

"I'll hold you to it," I replied, giving him a little wave. Only when he was out of sight did I realize that our first real date hadn't gone any differently from almost any other time we'd spent together up to that point. We'd walked to the subway station and talked about work, like we did every weekday morning. Nothing had changed. He hadn't kissed me good-bye, and there had been no affectionate physical contact while we'd walked—no hand-holding, no arm around me.

I couldn't hold back a disappointed sigh as I turned and headed toward home, away from the red-and-white-striped stalls of the holiday market that seemed made for browsing hand in hand with someone special. This certainly wasn't the way I'd imagined this day going not much more than twelve hours ago. I smiled to myself as I remembered the night before.

· · ·

I'd still been floating on air as we left the office party, giddy not only with my success in exposing Ari as the company spy and saboteur, but also with the fact that Owen Palmer had kissed me and told me how he felt about me.

We took a cab back to my place, and I invited him up for some hot cocoa and a chance to rehash the events of the party. Although the shabby little apartment I shared with two roommates was a far cry from his comfortable town house, he hadn't looked like he felt at all out of place there. I had to restrain myself from doing a happy dance in my kitchen while I made the cocoa. All I could think was, "Owen Palmer is sitting at my kitchen table, and he kissed me!" A lot of strange and wonderful—and some not-so-wonderful—things had happened to me in the last couple of months, but this was the one I had the most trouble believing.

I was almost afraid to leave the kitchen and return to the dining alcove, for fear he wouldn't be there, that I had imagined the whole thing. But there he was, looking so very handsome in a tuxedo. After all the kissing and other displays of affection not too long before, a kind of goofy awkwardness had developed between us. We didn't quite meet each other's eyes as we sat at the kitchen table, drank cocoa, and ate Christmas cookies. I wondered if inviting him up had been a bad idea, after all.

"That was a nice party," I said at last, when I couldn't take the silence anymore.

"Well, aside from a few disruptions," he replied with a crooked smile.

"Yeah, I guess. Are our office parties always that interesting?"

"It depends on how you define 'interesting.' They're probably not anything special to us, but most people would find them a little odd."

"Oh yeah. I can see that if you worked for a brokerage firm you might find this party kind of different." Argh! I was alone with Owen Palmer, and all I could do was make small talk about the office party.

Then to make the situation even more awkward, a key turned in the front door. At least one of my roommates was home. I'd hoped I'd be able to solidify things with Owen a little bit more before subjecting him to my roommates, but I guessed I should have thought of that before inviting him up. Why, of all nights, did they have to come home early on a Friday night?

And, just my luck, both Gemma and Marcia stepped through the door. Then they both froze, their mouths hanging open, when they saw who was sitting at the table. They didn't have to say a word; I could read their faces quite clearly: "So, this is the guy you've been talking about? What took you so long to make a move?"

I glanced at Owen, and the beet-red color of his face was a good sign that he'd read their faces as easily as I had. He stood, like a good gentleman, and I hurried to make introductions. "Gemma, Marcia, this is Owen. We work together." I left out the "And he kissed me! He likes me!" part for decorum's sake. Besides, I was sure we'd get to that the moment he left. "Owen, these are my roommates, Gemma and Marcia."

He came around the table and approached them where they still stood frozen not too far inside the doorway. "It's nice to meet you," he said, shaking their hands. They managed to respond, but they looked like something out of a zombie movie. I thought I detected a hint of drool on Gemma's chin. Then he turned to me and said, "I'd better get home."

As I helped him collect his overcoat from where we'd draped it over one arm of the sofa, I said, "I'll walk you out." I went with him as far down the stairs as the first landing, then he paused.

"Thanks again for a nice night," he said.

"And thank you."

"Do you want to get together tomorrow? Maybe for brunch, and then we can spend the day together?"

It sounded like heaven to me. "Sure. That would be great."

"Okay. How about we meet at ten at that coffee shop on Irving Place near my house? I'd pick you up, but I'm not sure your roommates could deal with that right now." Although his tone was teasing, a flush shot up from his collar to his hairline, and I suspected that he was the one who wasn't sure he could handle my roommates.

"Sounds good to me," I said.

"Great. I'll see you then." And then he placed his hand on my cheek and bent forward to kiss me, a soft, warm, firm, gentle kiss that somehow felt like a hug at the same time.

Even the next day, the memory of that kiss made me almost warm enough to have to unbutton my coat, although it was a raw December day. If I thought about it, I could still feel the touch of his hand on my face.

I doubted much had changed in those few hours. He was just being Owen, utterly dedicated to his life's work. That was one of the things I liked about him. If he'd blown off the crisis at work because he wanted to spend the day with me, he wouldn't be Owen and I wouldn't have liked him nearly as much.

I got to my apartment building, unlocked the front door, and went up the stairs, pausing only briefly on that landing where the last kiss had taken place. Then I went the rest of the way to my apartment, which was more crowded than I expected it to be. Not only were Gemma and Marcia there, but Connie, the former roommate who'd married and moved out soon before I came to New York, was there, as well. They were gathered around the kitchen table, looking like they were having a summit meeting.

"Katie! You're back early," Gemma said when she noticed me. "What happened?"

"He had an emergency at work, so we just had coffee," I said as I took off my coat. I left out the part where we had coffee while we walked to the subway station. Gemma and Marcia, in good girlfriend form, weren't inclined to be forgiving toward what they perceived as my dates' missteps.

"What did you say he did?" Marcia asked.

I hadn't said anything about what he did. It was kind of hard to explain without bringing up the concept of wizards, and if I said he worked in research and development, it didn't sound important enough to warrant the kind of emergency absences I could expect from him. "He's an executive with the company I work for," I said. That was probably vague enough and sounded important enough to cover a lot of bases.

Marcia nodded. "Yeah, that's the downside of dating powerful men." As driven and career-oriented as she was, she was the most likely to understand someone else who made work a priority. I was surprised, though, at how wistful her voice sounded.

"When you've got one who looks like he does, you can make the occasional allowance, but don't let him get away with it too often," Gemma said. She turned to Connie and added, "You should have seen this guy. He seemed pretty nice, too, what little we saw of him. Our little Katie snagged herself a good one."

"What brings you down to this end of the island?" I asked Connie.

"Minor relationship crisis," Gemma answered before Connie could speak. "And you're just in time."

"For what?"

"Ice skating at Rockefeller Center."

While I was still trying to figure out what ice skating had to do with a relationship crisis, Gemma handed me a piece of paper. "What do you make of this?" she asked.

The paper was stiff and heavy, the kind used for formal correspondence. I unfolded it to see a handwritten note in a flowing script. The note invited Gemma and her friends to go ice-skating this morning at Rockefeller Center, and specified a time that Philip would call for us. "It looks like an invitation to me," I said with a shrug.

"You don't think it's odd?"

I had to bite my lip to keep from laughing. Saying there was something odd about Philip, Gemma's boyfriend, was putting it mildly. Although she didn't know it, he was a magical person who'd been living under a frog enchantment for decades before he was freed a month or so earlier. You couldn't expect a guy who'd been living near a pond in Central Park and existing on flies to be anything approaching normal. I thought he was coping pretty well with adapting to modern times and re-adapting to life as a human, but it wasn't as though I could tell Gemma all that. She didn't know anything about magic, and there's no way to explain the frog thing without getting into magic.

"A handwritten note is unusual," I admitted. "It is kind of charming, though. It's sweet."

"It was hand-delivered, by someone else. It's like he's avoiding me, or something. Hasn't he heard of text messaging? Or maybe this nifty new invention called the telephone? I always have my cell with me, so he has no excuse for not being able to reach me directly. And what's with inviting all my friends? What kind of date is that?"

"It's a date where you're getting no action," Marcia said drily. "And let's face it, that's the real problem. He hasn't slept with you yet."

Gemma actually blushed, which may have been a first. "Well, there is that. But it's not the only issue. He's started to be 'busy.' " She made air quotes with her fingers.

In adherence to the universal law that the person you're talking about will show up while you're talking about him, the buzzer from downstairs sounded. Gemma got up and ran to the intercom. I felt that Philip was lucky the intercom only worked from our end when someone pushed the button. He'd have probably keeled over if he'd heard this conversation. Gemma pushed the intercom button and said, "We'll be right down."

"I'll come up to meet you," Philip's voice replied, scratchy over the speaker.

"You don't have to do that," Gemma insisted, then released the button and turned to us. "Well, come on. If I have to have chaperones for my date, you may as well be the ones. Then you can tell me if I'm imagining things."

We all collected purses and coats and trooped downstairs. I had to admit that this arrangement was a little odd. Even Owen, as shy as he was, hadn't come up with anything like this for a date. Though, come to think of it, we hadn't yet had a real date, so I couldn't compare.

When we got downstairs, Philip presented a red rose to Gemma with a bow. Then he bowed to the rest of us. "Ladies, thank you for joining us today. Now, I believe public transportation will be the most effective way of reaching our destination." He offered his arm gallantly to Gemma, and the rest of us fell in behind them as we walked to the subway station.

We hung back just enough to be able to talk about them. "Okay, I've gotta admit, this is kind of on the weird side," Marcia said. "The note was one thing, but bringing us along?"

"Maybe you were onto something when you said she wasn't going to get any action on this date," Connie mused. "It's like we're chaperoning them."

I almost shouted, "That's it!" before I turned it into a cough. Depending on how long he'd been a frog, he may have come from a time when men and women were seldom allowed to be alone together before they were married. I couldn't recall if he'd ever let himself be alone with Gemma when they weren't out in public. But that would have been hard to explain without getting into the magic thing. Instead, I said, "Well, he is kind of old-fashioned. If he's not ready to get that involved, then he might be coming up with ways to put the brakes on while still seeing her."

"That makes sense," Marcia said, but then we had to stop talking about Gemma and Philip because we were almost at the subway station and too close to them to take the risk of them overhearing us.

I tried to watch Philip and Gemma for clues, but I didn't notice anything particularly odd, other than the fact that Philip probably would have looked more at home wearing an Ascot tie and spats. Gap khakis were just wrong on him. He definitely acted interested in Gemma. He never took his eyes off her, he appeared to listen to everything she said, and he was incredibly attentive in every little gesture toward her. Unfortunately, she didn't seem to notice that and acted more and more put out toward him. It looked like she was in danger of losing a great guy simply because they were from different eras and had different ideas of what made a good courtship. If anyone needed the help of a fairy godmother, it was them.

But if I protested the interference of a fairy godmother, I knew Gemma would reject it outright, if she even let herself believe in such a thing. Meanwhile, I didn't exactly have a lot of time to be meddling in my friends' relationships, not when my enemies were at large and, come to think of it, I had the distinct impression that I was being watched.

Two

If it had been summertime, I'd have suspected that a bumblebee was hovering nearby. There was definitely a buzzing sound, like tiny wings flapping at high speed. Since it was below freezing, I could be fairly certain that it wasn't any kind of insect that was stalking me. I immediately went through my mental catalog of magical creatures. The problem was that my exposure to magical creatures was still pretty limited, and besides, Idris seemed to have a fondness for creating new ones.

I lagged behind the others at the entrance to the subway station, pretending to have to search for my MetroCard, so I could get a better look at something I was sure they couldn't see without being too obvious about it. It took me a moment or two to spot the tiny thing hovering over my shoulder, and when I did, I relaxed considerably. It was a male fairy—or sprite, as they preferred to be called, as they had issues with being called "fairies." Go figure. I hadn't realized they could shrink that small, but then I remembered Tinkerbell. Yeah, that's fiction, but I was learning that a lot of things I thought were just stories were real, so why not that, too? The sprite saluted me, and I figured he must have been my current magical bodyguard. With the threat from Idris and his people, I was almost always tailed by someone in the MSI security force.

That made me hesitate about going out with my friends. With my enemies on the loose, did I really want to put myself out there in public around my friends? I didn't think Idris or Ari would hesitate to try to at least embarrass me, if not outright harm me or them. In the middle of Rockefeller Center, there were all sorts of magical disasters that could happen. "I just remembered something I need to do," I said. "Y'all go on and have a good time. I probably wouldn't have skated anyway. I've never been on skates before in my life, since we don't have a lot of ice in Texas that's not in drinks, and I'd rather not spend Christmas in traction."

"I bet I know what you have to do," Connie said. "You have to find a gift for the new boyfriend. That's the problem with starting to date someone so close to a major holiday. You suddenly have to come up with a gift that's meaningful as well as appropriate for where you are in the relationship."

I was perfectly willing to use the excuse to get away from them, but thinking about what Connie said set off a panic attack. I'd already given Owen a gift, but that was only because I was his secret Santa at work. I hadn't considered that I'd now need to come up with a gift for him on a personal level. "What is appropriate this early in a relationship?" I asked.

"Well, it needs to be personal enough to show your feelings, but not so personal that it presumes something that may not be there yet. Nothing too expensive, but possibly something that will go on to be meaningful if the relationship lasts."

"No pressure there," I said with a snort. "I guess this is where you'd give a girl a cute stuffed animal or a pretty candle set. But what do you give a guy?" I thought I heard a high-pitched, faint burst of laughter and turned to shoot my sprite bodyguard a glare. He immediately moved out of range, hovering somewhere I couldn't see him anymore.

"That's one of the great mysteries of life," Marcia said. "Everything they like is expensive and, therefore, inappropriate this early in a relationship. Maybe you should have waited until after Christmas to hook up."

"What kind of music does he like?" Connie asked. "You could get him a CD."

I hadn't noticed any CDs or even a CD player in the one time I'd been in Owen's house. All I could remember seeing was books everywhere. If he had a stereo, it was probably buried under piles of books. And when someone had that many books, it was hard to find a book you could be sure he'd like that he didn't already have. Besides, that's what I'd given him as a secret Santa gift. With a groan I said, "I'd better get going. I have my work cut out for me."

I did a little window-shopping in the general area around Union Square, but no modest yet meaningful—but not too meaningful—gifts perfect for a man I was just getting to know jumped out at me. No enemies popped by to make veiled threats or cause magical havoc, and I wasn't sure if that was good or bad. It would have been really nice if I could have tackled Ari, turned her in, and ended this whole thing. After a while, I gave up on either finding the perfect gift or having the bad guys show themselves. Instead of doing more intense shopping, I went home, hoping I'd have word from Owen about how things were going. Alas, the "message waiting" light on the answering machine remained unblinking and unlit.

I'd underestimated Owen's abilities, for I'd barely hung up my coat when the phone rang. The timing was too perfect for it to be a coincidence. "Katie?" a voice on the other end said when I answered. "It's Owen."

Like I didn't recognize his voice almost instantly, even though we'd only ever spoken on the phone at work. "How are things going?" I asked, grateful that he'd called when I was at home alone, so I could talk freely.

"It's tedious," he said, but I could tell from his tone that it was the kind of methodical, painstaking, analytical work he enjoyed. "She definitely had help, but I'm not recognizing the fingerprints. Something's odd about it all. We've got the security team searching the city, and I'll probably be here all day. How's your Saturday going?"

"Not bad. One of my friends dropped by, and I did some shopping, so it all worked out."

"I'm glad to hear that," he said. "Do you have dinner plans tomorrow night?"

"Not at all."

"How does six sound?"

"Works for me."

"Good, then I'll come by and get you. I told you I'd make it up to you."

"I believed you," I hurried to assure him.

"I just hate to start on the wrong foot."

"You didn't."

"Well, I'd better get back to work," he said, and I could practically hear him blushing over the phone.

"I'll see you tomorrow night. Don't work too hard today."

"I won't." But if I knew him, he would. I'd have bet money that he'd have dark circles under his eyes when he came to pick me up for our date.

By the middle of the next afternoon, I was in serious danger of having some dark circles, myself. I hadn't slept much as I'd continued to worry about what to give Owen for Christmas—if I should give him anything at all so soon after starting to date him—and, of course, what I should wear to go to dinner with him.

After church and a quick lunch, I'd headed out shopping, presumably to consider gifts, but in large part to look for ideas of something to wear. I'd lectured Owen on not worrying about making a good first impression on me, but I was doing the same thing as I fretted about this first real date.

As I walked up Broadway in SoHo, looking more at the shop windows than at where I was going, I bumped into something soft. I yelped and jumped backward. I hadn't exactly been paying attention, but I surely would have seen another person that close to me. When I got my bearings and realized who the person was, I knew I hadn't lost my peripheral vision. It's easy to bump into someone who's just materialized right in front of you.

"Didn't mean to startle you, dear," Ethelinda said. "Just popping in where and when I'm needed."

"I don't really need you right now."

"Don't you? You're having quite the dilemma at the moment." She tilted her head to one side. "I know you don't want my assistance with your affairs, but could I offer you one gift?"

Suspicious, I asked, "Like what?"

"A little wardrobe advice. For your dinner tonight. Wardrobe is part of my job."

Looking at her and her weird, mismatched layers of clothes—today with an outer layer of dark green washed silk trimmed in yellowed lace, yesterday's rose velvet peeking from underneath—I wasn't so sure she was qualified, but what could it hurt? I could always ignore what she said, and I did desperately need wardrobe advice. "Okay, sure. What should I wear tonight?"

She tapped her wand against her lips and pondered. "Based on his profile, I believe you'd do best in something classic, not showy. He appreciates function over form. Good material, good workmanship, that's what impresses him, although he won't be consciously aware of it." I had to admit, she had Owen pegged. Not that I owned anything like that or could afford to buy it. I supposed I could borrow something from Gemma or Marcia.

"Thanks, that's good advice," I said, but then before I could react, she'd waved her wand at me. I felt a tingle all over, then I looked down and saw myself wearing a red satin dress with a hoop skirt. I couldn't say anything in protest because the corset was so tight I couldn't breathe.

"Oh, no, that won't do at all," Ethelinda said, shaking her head. "Wrong century, and possibly the wrong season." She waved her wand again, and I gasped to catch my breath once the restriction around my chest was gone. Whatever she'd put me in this time, at least it was more comfortable, although it scratched my neck. I looked at my reflection in a nearby shop window and saw that I was wearing a high-necked, starchy Victorian blouse and long skirt. "Now, that is fetching on you," Ethelinda said, "but I don't think it's quite right for the occasion." This time when she waved the wand, I went back to the outfit I had been wearing. I glanced around worriedly, even though I was pretty sure nobody could see me changing outfits while standing on the sidewalk. Then again, in that neighborhood, it might not even raise an eyebrow. They'd think it was a photo shoot for a fashion magazine.

"Oh, I know just the thing," Ethelinda said, her eyes lighting up with delight. She waved her wand, and suddenly my coat was a lot nicer. It fit me perfectly, it was made of fine material, and it didn't have that stain on the lapel that came from trying to drink coffee while walking to work. Intrigued, I unbuttoned the coat and saw a beautiful silk jersey dress underneath.

"Wow, thanks, this is gorgeous," I said, still reeling slightly from the rapid changes of wardrobe. I probably would have gone through just as many outfits at home as I tried to decide what to wear, but I wouldn't have gone through such extremes or ultimately found anything so nice. Then I remembered the way these things tended to go in the stories. "Does this outfit have an expiration date? Am I going to turn into a pumpkin at midnight or suddenly be nude, or anything like that?"

"It's supposed to last until the next day, though to be honest, I'm not sure if that's defined as midnight or sunup. You'd probably best be home by midnight, to play it safe. Not that you should be out later than midnight on a first date," she added with a "tsk-tsk" gesture from her wand.

"I wasn't planning on it. I have to work tomorrow."

She studied me critically. "I wish I could do something about your hair and face, but your magical immunity makes that problematic. I can change your clothing, but I can't change any part of you. Make sure you powder your nose and brush your hair before you go out."

I gave my hair a self-conscious pat as I wondered what was wrong with my face. She sounded like she was channeling my mother, who never stopped telling me to put on brighter lipstick. "My roommates will help me get ready," I assured her. "Thanks again for your help."

I turned to go, but before I got very far, she called out, "Your shoes!"

I looked down and saw that I was still wearing the comfortable flats I'd worn shopping. She raised her wand, but I held up a hand to stop her. "I've had a bad experience with magical shoes. I have some shoes at home that will go with this, if you don't mind."

"Oh yes, I remember seeing something about that. Quite understandable, though I do recall that it worked out rather well for you."

"In the long run, yeah, I guess." You'd think that a pair of shoes that made you utterly irresistible would be a good thing, but in reality it's a totally different story. They had sent me running into Owen's arms, which turned out to be good eventually, but along the way the enchanted shoes had caused me plenty of woe before I got the happy ending.

"Have a good time tonight, dearie, and you know you can call on me if you need help." She vanished in a puff of sparkly dust, and I headed up Broadway toward home, already trying to think of a way to explain to my roommates how I came home from a shopping trip in obviously expensive designer clothes, with no sign of my old clothes. They'd know I was too practical to just throw away what I'd been wearing.

I'd barely made it a block before I nearly bumped into someone else. This time it wasn't because the person had just popped into existence, but because he'd suddenly come to a dead stop in the middle of the sidewalk. It was none other than Phelan Idris, the rogue wizard who was the reason Owen was having to work so hard. I barely sidestepped him and kept moving so that no one behind me would bump into me, and he hurried to turn around and fall into step beside me. I couldn't quite stifle a groan.

It would have been easy to underestimate Idris. He looked like a geek with inflated ideas as to his own power and intelligence, and I knew I was immune to any magic he wanted to use on me. I would have bet I could also take him in a physical fight because he didn't look like the type who had ever learned to fight with anything other than magic, while I'd grown up with three older brothers, so I knew a thing or two about scuffling. But I'd also been through some really frightening attacks by all kinds of creatures controlled by Idris, so I didn't take his presence lightly. He was either up to something or passing on a message. If I handled this well, I might come away with some useful information.

"You look nice today," he remarked. He sounded almost normal, which immediately made me suspicious.

"Thanks," I replied automatically. I couldn't seem to turn off my old-fashioned Southern manners.

"I guess you've got a hot date tonight with the boyfriend."

"That's none of your business. What do you want?" When I didn't get an answer, I turned to see that he was no longer beside me. He was standing in front of a shop window, staring openmouthed at a mannequin in a slinky dress. Idris was notoriously short in the attention span department. It didn't take much to sidetrack him. I debated with myself for a moment: Did I want to take advantage of this opportunity to get away from him, or would I get anything useful out of him?

While he was captivated by the shiny object, I tried to glance around without looking like I was glancing around. I was fairly certain I had a magical bodyguard or two. The problem was that they wouldn't know I was chatting with the enemy. They'd see whatever illusion he was using for disguise. We needed to work out a set of signals so I could let them know that there was something magical and freaky going on. It would have been nice if I'd had a way to know that magic was in use so I'd know if others were seeing what I saw. I could usually sense a bit of a tingle when a lot of magic was being used, but even with Idris right next to me, I didn't feel anything obvious.

I thought I saw Rod Gwaltney across the street, looking in a shop window that reflected the street behind him in its plate glass, and I let myself relax. Rod was director of Personnel at MSI and Owen's best friend. Although he was stylish enough to be out shopping in SoHo, it was more likely that he was my designated magical guard. With Rod there, I felt like I ought to take advantage of the opportunity to subtly interrogate our chief suspect.

I had to suppress a sigh as I retraced my steps to go back to where Idris had stopped. "That's not your color," I said.

He blinked at me like he'd totally forgotten I was there. "Huh?"

"The dress you're looking at? It would look lousy on you."

"I was looking at the shopgirl. I think I know her from somewhere."

"Well, before you get on with your reunion, would you mind telling me what you wanted?"

"Wanted?"

I counted to ten before replying so I wouldn't yell at him. "I presume you wanted something. We're not friends, so you usually don't pop by just to say hi. Weren't you going to threaten me or intimidate me or give me a message to pass on to Owen, or something like that?"

He got a vacant look, like his brain was rewinding the tape. If Owen hadn't assured me that this guy was actually competent, and if I hadn't seen him in action myself when he was focused on something, I'd have felt pretty secure that the world was safe. "Oh, yeah," he said at last. Then he ducked his head and stared at the toes of his high-top sneakers. "I wanted to see if you could tell me how Ari was doing. I guess I shouldn't have left her there to take the heat."

It was my turn to blink and look vacant. If he was asking after Ari, then he didn't know she was free, and it meant he wasn't the one to free her.

"Funny you should ask," I said. Then I trailed off with a sigh as I realized I'd lost Idris again. A trio of model types, looking like they'd just emerged from their coffins after a night of partying, walked past. His head practically snapped as he turned to watch them. He moved as though to follow them, but I caught the belt on his black trench coat and tugged him back to me. "You did want to hear about Ari, didn't you?" I reminded him.

"Oh yeah, what about her?"

"As I was saying, it's funny you should ask because she's no longer in our custody."

"You let her go?"

"She got away. Someone got her out."

He grinned widely. "Excellent. I knew she was a sharp one."

"You really didn't know? I'd have thought you'd be the one to rescue her."

"If I could get in there and get into secured areas, do you think I'd have been relying on flighty fairies to do my spying? But you're saying Ari's free? Wow." Before I could respond, he vanished.

As I turned around to head back toward my apartment, Rod ran up to me. "Are you okay?" he asked. "Was that guy bothering you?"

"That guy was Idris."

"Really? Isn't that rather bold of him to walk right up to you on Broadway in the middle of the afternoon?"

"That's what was weird. He didn't see any reason he shouldn't be talking to me. He didn't know Ari escaped."

"Very strange. But you're okay?"

"Yeah, I'm okay. He just wanted to know how Ari was doing. He didn't even make his usual threats." Then I noticed something different about Rod. It took me a moment to figure out, but then I grinned. "I like your hair," I said.

Rod wore an illusion that made him appear incredibly handsome. As a magical immune, I saw the real thing, which wasn't quite as attractive. It wasn't that he was really ugly, though he did have some unfortunate features. But when you can make almost everyone see you as a dashing heartthrob, you aren't going to waste much time in front of a mirror in the morning, especially when you can also use magic to make hearts throb.

Today, though, Rod had done something with his hair. Normally he just slicked it back, but now it looked more natural. Without all the pomade, his hair turned out to be thick and wavy, and a rich, dark chestnut color. The wave in his hair as it framed his face softened his angular features, and the lack of grease in his hair also made his face look less shiny. When he smiled, he was actually cute.

"It looks good?" he asked, sounding a little unsure.

"Yeah, it looks great. You should do it like that more often."

He looked pleased. I couldn't help but wonder what had brought this on. I'd been planning to attempt a makeover on him, if I could figure out a way to do it without hurting his feelings, but if he was going to do it himself, I could provide positive reinforcement. "You look good, too," he said. "Is that for your dinner with Owen tonight?"

I didn't need to ask how he knew about our date. Gossip flew at light speed around MSI, and Rod and Owen were best friends, so it was a given that Rod already knew, and I knew he approved of the two of us. I couldn't help but wonder, though, what the rest of the company would think about our office romance. "Thanks, and yeah, it's for dinner," I said. "I just, um, borrowed it from a friend and was going to look for some accessories. I needed to be sure whatever I got would match."

"It's a perfect choice. He'll love it. Have fun tonight."

Fortunately, my roommates weren't around when I got back, so I was able to give them an almost-true story about borrowing the dress from a co-worker when they arrived as I was doing my hair.

"You look great," Gemma assured me. "Your co-worker has fabulous taste. Maybe you should invite her shopping with us sometime."

Oh, I could see that happening. "Maybe," I hedged. The buzzer from the front door downstairs kept me from having to come up with an excuse. Owen was right on time, in more ways than one. I got to the intercom before Marcia had a chance to interrogate him. "I'll be right down," I said, making it sound as decisive and final as possible. I wasn't in the mood to have to shelter him from my roommates.

"You're no fun," Gemma pouted, but she couldn't stop herself from smiling. "Have a good time and remember it's a school night."

"Yes, Mom," I promised as I grabbed my purse and headed for the door. When I stepped out the front door downstairs, I was immediately glad that I hadn't invited Owen up. He looked even more handsome than he normally did. He was clean-shaven, the glasses were gone, and he wore a silk suit with an open-collared shirt that made him look like a photo spread from *GQ*. My roommates might have fought me for him. I was glad Ethelinda had worked her magic on me. Otherwise, I would have felt awfully frumpy next to him.

A slow smile spread across his face when he saw me. "Wow. You look amazing. Not that you don't always look nice, but you look really nice tonight." That was my Owen, absolutely adorable and delightfully awkward.

"You're not so bad, yourself," I said, feeling my face grow warm. Giving compliments like that wasn't as easy as it looked.

He stepped toward me and gave me a gentle kiss that more than made up for the lack of a kiss Saturday morning. Up close to him, I could see I was right about the dark circles under his eyes. "Did you get any sleep at all this weekend?" I asked.

"Some." He didn't meet my eyes and instead turned toward the street. "I'll get a cab." That was an area where magical powers really came in handy in this city. He barely waved one hand, and suddenly a taxi practically jumped the curb to get to him.

He took me to a Village restaurant that was upscale in a classy, unobtrusive way. It was different enough from the kinds of places we'd gone together when we were going out as friends to make this very clearly a special date, but not so fancy that it looked like he was trying too hard. The prices on the menu were almost high enough to make my eyeballs bleed, but the food was described in plain, unpretentious English.

We spent several minutes discussing the menu and deciding what to order, then after we'd given our orders and the waiter had brought our drinks, an awkward silence descended over the table. We'd never had trouble talking to each other before. What had we talked about before we were officially dating? Oh yeah, work. Well, whatever it took to get the ball rolling.

"How did things go this weekend? Did you find anything interesting?" I asked.

He looked so relieved and grateful to have a topic of conversation that it was almost funny. "Interesting, yes, but I'm not sure how valuable it was. I'm now certain that someone I don't know broke her out magically. I'm not sure yet how they got past our defenses."

"You don't think Idris was involved?"

He shook his head. "No."

"He doesn't seem to know anything about it." I told him briefly about my earlier encounter with Idris. "So now in addition to having a rogue wizard with a short attention span to deal with, we also now have his girlfriend, who has more than enough reason to have a vendetta against both of us, and who's capable of staying focused on one thing for more than five minutes at a stretch. Plus, maybe another player entirely who's capable of getting past all our security. Fun."

He made a rueful face. "You said it. We're trying to track them down, but I'm also curious to see what they do next. I imagine we'll know soon enough."

"I guess it's too much to hope that their big plan is running away to Fiji and leaving us alone."

He laughed at that. "It would be nice, but I doubt it."

I had something incredibly witty and clever to say in response, but before I could say it, there was a scream from the back of the restaurant, followed by a whooping alarm and a burst of cold water as the sprinkler system came on.

"Fire!" someone yelled, and I somehow doubted they were testing their First Amendment right to yell "fire" in a crowded restaurant.

Three

A stampede to the exit began immediately, with people knocking over chairs and tables in their haste to escape from the restaurant. Fortunately, our table was against the wall, so we weren't in the traffic pattern to be trampled. As usual, Owen remained calm in the crisis. "Get your coat," he reminded me. "It's cold outside." Meanwhile, he put on his own coat. I threw my coat over my arm and grabbed my purse, then we plunged into the melee. Owen kept a protective arm around me as we moved through the crowd. The real holdup seemed to be the front door, which was so narrow only two people could get through at a time. It created a bottleneck as people pushed forward in a panic. All the while, the sprinklers drenched us.

"This isn't good," Owen muttered. He waved his right hand and whispered something in a mystical language under his breath, and the glass in the front floor-to-ceiling windows vanished. Another wave of his hand and the tables and chairs in front of those windows relocated to another part of the restaurant. "This way!" Owen called out as he guided me toward one of those open windows, but he was so soft-spoken by nature that his voice didn't carry over the noise of the crowd, the fire alarm, and the approaching sirens.

I put my fingers to my lips the way one of my brothers had taught me and gave a piercing whistle. "This way!" I bellowed. The crowd split off and followed us as we stepped onto the sidewalk. The police and fire engines had arrived by then, and the police officers directed everyone to the sidewalk across the street from the restaurant. Nobody questioned the glassless windows without any shards on the ground below. "Are you going to put those back?" I asked Owen, my teeth chattering as the cold outside air hit my thoroughly soaked hair and clothes.

"Oh, sorry, I can't believe I forgot," he said, but when he waved his hand, the window glass didn't come back. Instead my clothes suddenly became dry. Then he helped me with my coat, which was drier because it had been folded over my arm, but he worked his magic on that, too. His clothes were suddenly drier, as well. "I'd do something about drying your hair, but that's more difficult with your magical immunity, and besides, it might be suspicious if we both suddenly looked blow-dried in this crowd," he said with a rueful grin. I looked around and noticed that all the other escapees from the restaurant looked wet and miserable. "And the glass should come back in an hour or so."

He pulled me against him, holding me inside his coat with his arms tight around me. That made me a lot warmer, in spite of my damp hair. He wasn't a big guy, but he had a fair amount of muscle packed onto his slim frame, so being held by him made me feel safe. "My dating luck strikes again," I said with a sigh. "Normally it only affects me, but now I can ruin the evening for everyone, just by being there."

He chuckled and hugged me a little tighter. "I don't think you can take the blame for this. It just happened." Then he paused and said, "Or maybe . . ."

"Maybe what?"

"Take a look at the building and tell me what you see." I turned my head to look at the building where the restaurant was, and while I saw flames, those flames didn't appear to be actually doing anything. The structure of the building wasn't changing at all. I also didn't smell smoke. Nobody who'd been in the supposedly burning restaurant was coughing or wheezing.

"It's not a real fire," I said. "Magic?"

"More than likely. Come on." He released me from his arms and took my hand, then led me to the side of the restaurant building. He put his palm against the building, closed his eyes for a second, then said, "Yep, it's a magical fire. Do you think it would raise too many questions if I killed the spell now?"

"Could you make it fade away, so the firemen'll think they put it out? It's not hurting anyone, is it?"

"It shouldn't be. I think I even know which spell they're using. If it's what I think it is, countering it will be easy. I can't actually undo it, but there are plenty of spells to stop it."

"I don't suppose they left a trail we could follow."

"I'm already on it," a rough voice said. I looked up and saw a small stone gargoyle perched on the bottom rung of a nearby fire escape ladder.

"Hi, Sam," I said to the gargoyle. Sam was MSI's chief of security.

"You didn't see anything, did you?" Owen asked.

"Nope, but my people are on the case. We're fanning out in a search pattern."

Owen nodded his approval. "Good."

"We're sure to catch 'em before long," Sam assured us. "Now, you two kids probably ought to find someplace warm and dry to finish your dinners. We've got the situation under control."

"You heard what the gargoyle said," Owen said, holding his arm out to me. I took it, and then we made our way down the street with the rest of the restaurant crowd that was milling away from the scene. About a block away from the restaurant, I felt a warm breeze ruffle my hair and turned to look at Owen. He shrugged and said, "We shouldn't be walking around with wet hair." I couldn't help but wonder what my hair looked like after it had been wet and then dried like that, but I felt much warmer.

We found a bakery a few blocks away that was about to close and bought the last two chocolate cookies in the display case, along with a couple of hot coffees, then we wandered through the West Village, sipping coffee and eating the cookies. The smell of Italian food wafting through the cold air made me glad we'd found that bakery. I hadn't quite been done with my dinner. "This wasn't the way I planned things to go," Owen said after a while.

"I should hope not, or I'd worry about you." Then I sighed. "If it was who we think it was, then it was about me, or us, after all. See, my dating luck holds true." I finished my cookie so I'd have a hand free, then ticked my recent dating disasters off on my fingers. "Let's see, on my last date we were affected by the enchanted shoes that made us do crazy things. And before that I was attacked by a bunch of magical creatures on the way to a party. The date before that, we got caught in a magical scheme to swindle people. Then there was the guy who thought he used to be a frog who showed up during the date to serenade me. Are you sure you want to go out with me? This kind of thing is normal for me."

"And you think my life is what anyone would consider normal?"

"Good point."

"Look on the bright side: We can only go up from here. We can't have a worse date than this one."

I cringed. "Don't say that. Whenever you say that, it's like asking the universe to prove you wrong."

The dry clothes and hair and the hot coffee had warmed me considerably, and I got even warmer when Owen finished his coffee, threw his cup in a nearby trash can, then put his arm around my shoulders. This was turning out to be a pretty good date, after all. We were together, we'd had chocolate, and we were walking through something that felt like a fairyland, with all the Christmas lights twinkling from windows above us.

The Christmas decorations jolted my memory. The holiday was almost upon us, and I'd been too busy to notice it other than as a gift-giving occasion to worry about. "I can't believe Christmas is right around the corner," I said. "Why is it that when you're a kid, it seems to take forever to come, but when you're an adult, it's on you before you realize it?"

"We have been pretty busy," he pointed out.

"Yeah, and I sort of already had Christmas when my parents were here for Thanksgiving, so the day itself is something of an anticlimax for me this year."

"Do you have anything planned?"

"Not really. I'll probably do something with my roommates. You're still going to visit your foster parents?" He was an orphan who'd been brought up by foster parents who'd never adopted him legally, and he'd always had a somewhat distant relationship with them. That explained a lot of his personality quirks.

"Yes, they even invited me. I'm looking forward to it, but I'm trying not to get my hopes up. We're never going to be the Waltons."

"Nobody is the Waltons, not even my family, which may be as close as you get."

We reached the Avenue of the Americas, where cabs came by often enough that it didn't even require any of Owen's magic to hail one. Once we were in the cab, the taxi wheels weren't the only ones turning, as I could tell Owen was already furiously pondering the current puzzle with every cell of his powerful brain. He paid off the driver in front of my building and walked me to the front door, his attention clearly elsewhere. "Thanks for the evening," I said. "It was certainly memorable."

"It was, wasn't it? And thank you for making it pleasant in spite of everything." He bent forward to give me a quick kiss, then said, "I'll see you in the morning." He was gone down the sidewalk before I even had a chance to kiss him back or to turn it into a proper kiss good night, and I was left standing there with my lips slightly puckered.

"I'll see you in the morning, too," I muttered under my breath to the thin air where Owen had just been before suppressing a sigh of disappointment. I reminded myself that this sort of thing came with the territory when we had so many other distracting priorities. And, after all, it was only the first date. We'd have plenty of opportunities to intensify things.

When I went down the stairs Monday morning, I felt a familiar flutter in my stomach. Owen had been commuting with me almost every morning since not long after I'd gone to work at MSI, and every morning I'd found myself all atingle with the anticipation of seeing him again. This morning, the first since we'd gone beyond being just friends and co-workers, the tingle was even worse. I'd always known that the main reason he escorted me to work in the morning was that we made a good team for keeping each other safe from our enemies. My magical immunity meant I could spot the bad guys even when they tried to disguise themselves or make themselves invisible. Owen, as a magical person, could be affected by magic and might not notice the danger, but once I alerted him, he could do something about it. He lived a few blocks away from me, so he didn't have to go too far out of his way to meet up with me, but I'd always hoped that he might have really wanted to spend that time with me in the morning. That had turned out to be the case.

I opened the front door, and the flutter in my stomach became a full-scale hurricane. You'd think that going out with him the night before would have made the anticipation a little less intense, but I was learning that I couldn't predict my reactions when it came to Owen. He really put me off-kilter.

I couldn't hold back a huge smile as I emerged onto the front steps, knowing he'd be waiting on the sidewalk. Then the smile slid right off my face, for he wasn't there. I checked my watch to make sure I wasn't early—I had been a wee bit eager to see him—but it was the same time we usually met, and even when I was off-schedule one way or another, he always managed to adjust and still be there to meet me. I was beginning to wonder if I should wait for him and for how long when I heard a rough voice say, "You're the Chandler gal, aren't you?"

I looked up and down the street, seeing plenty of people on the sidewalk, but nobody who seemed to be talking to me. "Psst, up here," the voice said. I stepped forward, turned around and craned my neck to see a gargoyle perched on the fire escape above me. It wasn't Sam or any other gargoyle I'd run into before, but he was probably on the MSI security force.

"I'm Katie Chandler," I said.

He spread his wings and glided down to sit on top of a nearby parking meter. "Mr. Palmer said to meet you here. He had something come up and had to be at the office early. I'm supposed to make sure you get to work safely." He spread his wings once more and took off in the direction of the subway station.

I hurried to follow him. "Did something happen?" I asked, out of breath from having to keep up with a flying gargoyle.

"Hey, I'm just a messenger. All I know is what he told me."

I was worried and disappointed, all at the same time. It had to be something big for him to abandon our daily routine, but it was the second time in just a few days that duty had called him away from time with me. I knew I could expect more of that in the future because of what he was up against, but that didn't entirely erase the disappointment. At least he'd sent word instead of standing me up, and he'd made sure I'd be protected.

Owen wasn't chatty, but he was a far better conversationalist than this gargoyle, who didn't seem to be making much of an effort. He was strictly doing his job. Fortunately, there were no threats. The morning commute was as uneventful as you can get when you're being escorted to work by a taciturn gargoyle.

Once I reached the office, I faced my next ordeal: dealing with all the office gossip about Owen and me. If I'd had my choice, I would have preferred to date secretly until our relationship was more secure. But we'd already been pretending to date to help flush out the bad guys, and then we hadn't dropped the act once the crisis was over. I was pretty sure that, as shy as Owen was, if he'd thought about it, he wouldn't have kissed me in public the way he had, but parties and excitement have a way of short-circuiting the brain. Plus, it was a very nice kiss and I wouldn't trade it for anything.

Trix, the fairy who served as receptionist in the executive suite, greeted me with a flutter of her wings and a wink. "Hey, you! How was your weekend?"

"It was good."

"Good? Is that all? I did notice what was going on at the office party, and you didn't seem to need any mistletoe."

"We didn't run off to Vegas over the weekend, if that's what you were wondering. We just got together a couple of times. You know Owen, this thing isn't going to move at light speed." Then it was my turn to tease. "And anyway, I wasn't the one who spent a good portion of the party in a broom closet with someone."

She immediately looked down at her desk and gave her wings a little flick. "That wasn't our idea. Ari and that Idris guy put us there."

"But you did take advantage of the opportunity."

"Hey, I'm no dummy." My turning the tables seemed to have worked, for she quickly became businesslike. "The boss wants you for a meeting at ten. His office."

"Thanks. I'll be there," I said before heading to my office.

"This isn't over!" she called after me. "You're going to have to give me the full scoop sometime."

I ignored her and settled in at my desk to catch up on messages and e-mail before the meeting. I was the assistant to the boss, who was otherwise known as Ambrose Mervyn, CEO of Magic, Spells, and Illusions, Inc. If you did all the translation into and out of Welsh, Latin, and probably a few other languages in between, that came out as Merlin. Yes, the Camelot wizard. He'd founded MSI, in a noncorporate form, as a way of fine-tuning and regulating magic way back then, then had gone into a self-imposed magical hibernation until he was needed again. Our current problems with a rogue wizard trying to undercut our efforts to keep magic safe and on the good side of things had brought him back to lead the company.

Just before ten, I gathered my supplies and headed for Merlin's office. As I went through the doorway, I almost missed a step even though I was walking on an even surface. Owen was already in there, sitting at the conference table and twirling a pen between his fingers. I wondered if there would ever come a time when seeing him didn't take my breath away. I should have known he'd be at any executive meeting since he usually represented the research and development department, but I still wasn't prepared to see him again. He looked very nice dressed for work, as he always did, but he appeared even more tired than he had been the night before.

"Oh, good, Katie, you're here," Merlin said, waving a hand to shut the door behind me. Owen looked up, saw me, gave a half smile, then turned bright red and looked down at the notebook that lay in front of him on the table. It seemed I wasn't the only one feeling a little taken aback by seeing each other here.

I took my usual seat at Merlin's right hand, ready to take notes on the meeting so I could write up a report and note the items for follow-up. A moment later, the office door flew open and Sam the gargoyle soared inside to land on the back of the chair across from Owen. Merlin waved the door shut again. I wrote the date and time of the meeting on the top of my notepad while I waited for the rest of the department heads to arrive, but before I could start listing names of the attendees, Merlin spoke.

"Katie, I'm sure by now you're aware that the prisoner we apprehended Friday night has escaped."

"Yes, sir," I said, wondering if this meant the meeting had already begun. Apparently, this wasn't the meeting of department heads I'd expected.

"And I'm sure you realize how important it is to find her again."

"She might make Idris even more dangerous. He's not necessarily evil, and even if he was, he's not focused enough to really do anything about it. But she's vindictive, and though I used to think she was flighty, she does seem to be capable of following through on something."

"Exactly. And that's why I want you and Mr. Palmer to work together to either find her or learn what Ari and Mr. Idris are doing. You'll be working closely with Sam on this, since a security breach was involved."

There went my idea of being relatively stress-free for the holidays. "You want me investigating?" I asked.

"You were the one who figured out she was the spy," Owen said. I wondered if he'd been the one to suggest working together. If he had, we'd have words about that later.

"You're also the perfect investigative combination, with your magical immunity and Mr. Palmer's abilities. I believe you also have an excellent personal rapport." I detected a definite twinkle in Merlin's eyes. Great, now even the boss was getting involved in our relationship. "Of course, I don't expect you to work during the holidays, but I would like you to be thinking about it. Sam, you'll have security personnel at their disposal."

"But what about my other work? I got pretty far behind when I was working on the last investigation." Not that I was trying to weasel out of this assignment, but it really wasn't in my job description, and I wasn't getting most of the stuff that was in my job description done.

"I'll have someone else take on your more administrative and clerical duties. Anyone can take notes in a meeting, but you've proved you have the special skills for this task." There was an edge of finality to his voice, like what he'd said had been carved into stone tablets on top of a mountain.

"That'll be a big help, sir," I said.

The meeting adjourned, and Owen caught my elbow as we left Merlin's office. "Maybe we should strategize for a while. Are you free now?" He said it with a totally straight face and no hint of a blush, so I got the impression that he wasn't finding a convenient cover for other kinds of activities. I suspected that while we were in the office, it would be strictly business between us, and that was fine with me, even though my elbow was already tingling from his touch. I'd never dated someone I worked that closely with, and had never worked this closely with someone I was dating. It seemed that the boss didn't mind our personal relationship, but I wished there was a handy rule book for how to make this sort of thing work.

"Your office or mine?" I asked.

"Would you mind going to mine? I have more whiteboard space for thinking."

"No problem," I replied. As we passed Trix's desk, I said, "I'm going to be down in R and D for a while."

She gave us a sidelong look that said she thought she knew what we'd be doing down in R&D. "Okay. Want me to forward calls or send them to voice mail?"

"You can forward them, if I even get any calls. Thanks." I didn't bother correcting her assumption about us because I had a feeling that would only fluster Owen, and the more I protested, the more convinced she'd be.

Owen ran the theoretical magic lab in R&D. His job was finding old magic texts, translating the spells, figuring out what they did, testing them to see if they actually worked, and then finding a way to apply those spells to modern situations. His lab was full of old books, most of them shelved around the perimeters of the room, but a good number of them scattered around on tables, chairs, and even the floor. A couple of whiteboards on wheels were covered in textbook-perfect handwriting that was still unreadable because almost none of it was in English. Owen's office, which opened off the lab, looked like it belonged in an English manor house. Being in his office always gave me an overwhelming craving for hot tea.

When we reached the lab, he erased one of the whiteboards and picked up a marker. I boosted myself up to sit on the big wooden table that filled the center of the room. "I guess we should start with what we already know," he said. "I know Idris well enough to know some of his habits and patterns. You know something of Ari, and you know her friends. Let's each see what we can come up with to analyze places where they might go or be found." He wrote "Ari" on the top of one side of the board and turned to me.

"Well, let's see," I said, thinking out loud. "She's kind of boy crazy and will chase just about anyone, but I think she's in it more for the conquest than for any real romantic leanings. In fact, she seems to lose interest as soon as she catches one, but she manages to spin it so she's the wounded party and she has an excuse for revenge. She has a lot of stamina when it comes to fun, knows all the hot spots and stays out all night. She never seems to go home alone after an evening out."

He stared at me, his mouth hanging open. "What?" I asked. "That's what women talk about. We tend not to get into our world domination plans on your typical girls' night out or office lunch. Sorry, that's all I've got."

"No, I was actually surprised you knew that much. I've known Rod since I was little, and I don't think I know quite that much about him."

"That's because you're guys. You talk about things, not how you feel about things. I take it, then, you don't have a lot of scoop on Idris."

"Not like you've got on Ari. I usually tried to avoid talking to him about anything, if I could help it. I know he likes testing the limits to see what he can get away with. He never liked taking the accepted path. If he'd been willing to stay away from darker magic, he could have been a real asset here, but he got bored easily by the usual things and wanted to try something as different as possible."

"Sounds like Ari and men," I quipped. "They're a match made in heaven."

"Why do you think she's with him?" From the expression on his face, I couldn't tell if he was baffled by Ari being with Idris, or by Idris being with Ari.

"It's hard to say. I can't be sure how much of what she told me was real and how much was part of her act all along. I suspect he gives her an outlet for her less admirable qualities. She can take revenge and use people, and he considers it a good thing. I doubt she set out to find him and join the side of evil. He probably recruited her gradually, and then she got in too deep."

"Which might mean we could recruit her back. She's sure to have a falling-out with him, if what you've observed about her dating patterns is accurate."

"If we could find her. Which brings us back to the initial problem. Idris was worried about her and didn't know she was free. I think he might actually like her, when he isn't being distracted by something else. He took off pretty quickly when he found out she was free, so he might have had an idea where she'd be. Meanwhile, who's that other person who may or may not be working with Idris? Think about who he was close to when he worked here. I know he and Gregor were tight. Anyone else?"

He looked intensely uncomfortable, and when he spoke, he dropped his voice to little above a whisper. "He got along really well with my boss."

"You mean the frog guy?" I asked, barely remembering to keep my own voice low. The head of R&D had been turned into a frog in an "industrial accident" years ago and seldom left his office. "You know, there are a lot of industrial accidents in this department, what with the frog thing and Gregor's ogre problem." Gregor, now head of Verification, wasn't always an ogre, but he tended to turn green and sprout horns and fangs when he was angry. That actually made him easier to deal with than my boss at my old job, who didn't have such obvious physical clues when she was in evil mode.

"They used to take a lot of risks in experimentation under the former management."

"Do you mean former as in before Merlin?"

He nodded. "But I never got the sense of anything dark from it, just pushing the envelope."

"What happened to the former boss?"

"He retired. I don't recall any hint of scandal associated with him." I took that statement with a large grain of salt. Owen was so clueless about the company rumor mill, they could have tarred and feathered the former CEO and chased him out of the building with the staff brandishing pitchforks and torches, and he might not have noticed. Until he found himself the point man in the fight against Idris, he'd apparently stayed hidden away in his lab, happily translating ancient spells and oblivious to anything happening elsewhere in the company.

On the other hand, I'd been picking up a lot of the corporate grapevine, thanks to my last task of finding a mole, so I was sure I'd have heard about it if there had been any breath of scandal associated with the former boss. It was yet another dead end.

"You didn't recognize the magical fingerprints, did you?"

He shook his head wearily. "Unfortunately, that doesn't always work. You can only figure out who did a spell if you have a basis for comparison. I guess it works like real fingerprints—just finding one doesn't solve the crime unless you have a copy of the criminal's prints and can put the two together. All I can say is it wasn't someone whose magic style I've worked with before."

"Can people change their style, kind of like wearing gloves hides fingerprints?"

"It would take some effort, almost like learning magic all over again, and even so, there would still be hints if you knew where to look."

"I guess if you didn't recognize the style, it can't be someone who works here."

"I don't work closely enough with everyone in the company to recognize each person on sight. But I am working on a process to compare the style against what we have on record. It'll just take time."

"It sounds like we've got the makings of a plan," I said with a mock salute. "Now I'd better get back to my office and get things as settled as possible before the boss sends someone to fill in."

But I realized as soon as I got upstairs that my temporary replacement was already there. Kim, the overly ambitious verifier I'd met when I first joined the company, the one who had made no effort to hide the fact that she wanted the job I'd been given, was sitting at my desk like she owned it.

It looked like I'd better solve this case quickly or I might find myself backstabbed out of a job.

Four

Kim gave me a smug smile. "I thought it would be easier for me to pick up your tasks if I worked from your office. You don't mind, do you? I assumed you'd be officing with your little task force, or whatever it is that you'll be doing."

"We hadn't really talked about moving my office," I said, trying to catch up with the situation. There was some sense to her working in this general office suite, since she would be handling my clerical tasks and would need easy access to Merlin and Trix. But did she have to sit at my desk to do it?

"Well, it wouldn't be moved permanently, but I have to work some-where, don't I?" This was more chipper than I'd ever seen Kim in the short time we'd worked together. She didn't really do cheerful. She was aggressive, focused, and determined, but never chipper. That made me nervous and suspicious, but there wasn't much I could say, given that all of her arguments made total sense, in a way.

"I guess I could take my computer and some of my things down to R and D," I said.

"I probably need your computer. I don't have one of my own, and don't a lot of the appointment requests come through your e-mail?"

That was one step too far. My desk I could take or leave, but I didn't want her having access to my e-mail. If she took my computer and e-mail account, she'd be one step away from becoming the office version of *Single White Female* and stealing my entire life. "I'm sure we can set you up with a computer, and I'll forward you any e-mails that are pertinent to your duties." I mentally scored a point for myself. I thought I'd handled that situation rather professionally.

She glared at me, but it would have been unreasonable for her to insist on taking my computer, so there wasn't much she could say. "I put all of your other things together here, so I wouldn't get them mixed up with my stuff," she said. My desk calendar, planner, and coffee mug had all been shoved to one corner of my desk. She already had a potted plant and a few photos set up on the bookcase. I got the feeling that the paint color would be different the next time I dropped by.

"Oh, thanks," I said halfheartedly. "Let me get those out of your way." I disconnected my laptop from the network and closed it, then put the rest of my things in my tote bag, grabbed my coat, and hauled everything out of the office. "I'll probably be working out of Owen's lab for the time being," I told Trix as I passed her desk.

"You've got to be kidding," she said. "She didn't waste much time, did she? I can't believe you're letting her kick you out of your own office."

"Who would you rather share an office with, Kim or Owen?"

"You've got a point there."

The intercom on Trix's desk buzzed, and Kim's voice said, "I need you to get IT to bring me a computer right away, and I'd like some coffee."

Trix rolled her eyes. "Her majesty calls. She's lucky she's immune to magic, or I'd be tempted to put a good curse on her."

As I lugged my belongings down to R&D, I reflected that what I really needed was a fairy godmother for work. True, my love life wasn't always spectacularly successful, but I didn't necessarily have the skills, experience, or raw material to be a love goddess. When it came to work, though, you'd think I'd know how to handle myself. I'd started more or less running a business when I was still a teenager, I had a business degree, and I'd survived in the New York City business world for more than a year, but I still felt out of my element when office politics came into play.

Why was it that you could only get a fairy godmother to help you snag Prince Charming with a glass slipper? Where was the benevolent soul who provided the killer presentation, the perfect thing to say to the office backstabber, and the fabulous Armani suit to wear to the crucial meeting? Of course, you'd probably have to make sure you got out of the meeting before the stroke of five, or else that Armani suit would turn into polyester separates from JCPenney and your high-end laptop with the killer presentation would revert to being an Etch-a-Sketch.

If Ethelinda really wanted to help me, she wouldn't be meddling in my relationship with Owen. She'd help me find a way to hang on to my job and my place in the company without making unnecessary enemies while I worked on what I hoped would be a temporary and one-time-only project. I wondered what she'd say if I told her she needed to update her fairy godmother duties for the twenty-first century now that women had a lot more on their minds than finding a good husband to provide for them.

The door to R&D swung open as I approached, which meant Owen was expecting me. I still had an access crystal Merlin had given me while I worked on my last assignment, but since my hands were full, I was glad for the touch of magical chivalry.

Owen's eyes widened when I entered his lab with all my worldly office goods. "You're planning to stay awhile?" he asked.

I set the laptop down on one of the lab tables, let my tote bag fall at my feet, and threw my coat over the back of the nearest chair. "Apparently

Kim's been assigned to handle my administrative and clerical tasks, and she's already taken over my office. I figure since we're supposed to be working together, I might as well work down here. Otherwise, it could get ugly."

"Did you talk to Mr. Mervyn about it?"

I hadn't even thought of that. I was the youngest child in my family, so I should have honed the tattletale instinct to perfection. "No," I admitted. "But it does make sense, even if I'm not crazy about her appropriating my desk so quickly. She's even got a plant and pictures."

He gestured around the lab. "Well, if you can handle the mess, you're welcome to claim a spot as yours for the duration. Just don't rearrange anything." Owen's one of those people who looks disorganized but who has everything sorted into piles only he can understand.

"Don't worry about that. I can't read half of what you've got in here, and I'm not sure I want to know everything you're working on."

He looked around the room, as if seeing his own clutter for the first time and suddenly realizing that there was no spot I could take at any of the tables without disturbing his piles, then he waved his hand. A desk appeared in one corner of the lab. "I think there's a network connection near there. And let's see, you'll need walls." He pushed a wheeled freestanding whiteboard over to shield the desk from the rest of the room. "Anything else?"

It wasn't as nice as my real office, the one Kim had usurped, but I reminded myself that my office mate more than made up for the difference. The only amenity missing was a phone, and I didn't mind that so much. It meant I was less likely to be disturbed. "It looks great. Thanks."

I set up my computer, arranged my few office belongings on the desk, and hung my coat on the top corner of the whiteboard. I'd just settled in when Owen stuck his head around the whiteboard. "Telephone call for you."

Surprised, I went to his office and took the phone from him. "This is Katie," I said.

"I thought I'd find you there," Trix's voice said in my ear. "I've got a call for you. I'll put it right through."

A second later, Marcia's voice said, "Katie?"

"Yeah. What's up?"

"Do you have any plans for Christmas?"

"Nothing set in stone yet. I was planning to tag along with whatever y'all came up with."

"Well, I just found this insane bargain airfare to Dallas, in case you want to go home. The catch is you have to leave tomorrow and come back Christmas day, but it's less than half the usual cost. Gemma and I decided to surprise our parents, so we thought we'd let you know in case you wanted to get in on it, too."

"I'm not sure I could do it," I said.

"If money's the problem, I could loan you the cost of the ticket, and you could pay me back."

"It's more time than money that's the issue. I'm not sure I could leave as early as tomorrow. I'm working on a project I just got assigned today, and getting to the airport on Christmas would eat up most of the day."

"Uh-huh, I know exactly what you need time for: that gorgeous guy you've landed. Go back to Texas for a few days and you run the risk of him getting away."

"That's not it at all," I insisted, looking through the office doorway to the lab, where Owen stood in front of the whiteboard, thoughtfully chewing on the end of a dry-erase marker. I lowered my voice and added, "He's going to his parents' house for the holiday, anyway." It occurred to me that if Gemma and Marcia went home for Christmas, I'd be left all alone in the city. Owen would be gone, and Connie'd said her in-laws were coming over. For a moment, I was tempted. How much work would we get done in the next couple of days? But for all I knew, that was when Idris and Ari would wreak havoc.

"Thanks for letting me know," I said firmly, more to convince myself than to convince her, "but I really don't think I can make it."

"You don't mind if we leave you alone, do you?"

"Are you kidding? It'll be the longest I've had the place to myself since I moved in. I may even change the locks while you're gone."

She laughed. "Okay, then. I guess I'll see you tonight."

In spite of my assurances to Marcia, I couldn't help but feel a little lost and lonely as I walked back out into the lab. "Is something wrong?" Owen asked.

"No. It was one of my roommates. They found an airfare sale to go back home for Christmas and were letting me know in case I wanted to go, too."

"Are you going?"

I shook my head. "Nah. It's a weird schedule to get that fare, so I'd have to leave here tomorrow, then come back on Christmas itself. It's several hours to the airport from my parents' house, so I wouldn't even be able to stay for Christmas dinner. My roommates are from around Dallas, so it's a lot easier for them."

"You're going to be stuck by yourself for Christmas?"

"Yeah, but it won't be so bad. It'll be nice to have some peaceful alone time."

"You could come with me." He said it casually as he uncapped his marker and moved toward the board to write something on it.

"With you? You and your foster parents are just starting to work things out. You don't need an outsider there."

"I'd love an outsider there," he said, still facing the board, his back to me. "Think of it as a buffer zone."

"But would they want me there?"

"You've already been invited."

"What?" This was awfully fast to be meeting the folks. We'd only just kissed for the first time when magic wasn't involved a few days ago. Now I was already invited home for the holidays?

"Not like that," he said, finally turning around to face me. His cheeks had turned the shade of pink that meant he was very uncomfortable. He didn't quite look me in the eye as he spoke. "I'd already told them about you—not as someone I'm dating but as a friend from work who's relatively new to the city. When they invited me to come for Christmas, they suggested that I could invite you if you didn't have other plans. Until now, I suspected you had other plans. But if you don't, you're welcome to come."

For Owen, that was a long, heartfelt speech. It also demonstrated that although he was a genius when it came to stuff like magic, research, and translation, he could be a little clueless when it came to women. If he'd talked enough about me for his foster mother to notice and feel as though she should invite me, then she was dying of curiosity about me and wanted to make sure I was worthy of him. And that made this a potentially tricky situation.

"You're sure it won't be really awkward?" I asked.

"Oh, it'll be awkward. But it will be whether or not you're there. It may be less awkward for me with you there."

"But what about me? I have a feeling it'll be more awkward for me there than it would be if I stayed here."

He took a step closer to me and gave me the shy smile that had totally floored me when I first met him. "I'd really appreciate it if you came along with me."

He was impossible to resist when he was like that. I also couldn't deny that I was curious about his foster parents, and I didn't particularly want to spend Christmas alone in this city. "Okay, I'll go," I said. "What's the itinerary, and what should I bring?"

He grinned, and for a second I thought he'd kiss me or at least hug me, but we were at work, and Owen was nothing if not proper. "I was planning to take the train up the morning of Christmas Eve and come back the morning after Christmas. It's about an hour-long trip. Does that work for you?"

"Owen, we work at the same place, so we're on the same schedule," I reminded him.

He flushed slightly, "I didn't know if you might have any other plans. As for what you need to bring, well, they tend to be rather formal, so you can expect to dress for dinner, and a church service Christmas Eve night is mandatory. You won't need to bring anything for the dinner. That will have been planned in detail well in advance."

"I should probably bring gifts. Any suggestions?"

"You were the one who helped me buy my gifts for them," he reminded me. I refrained from telling him that his gifts had been far, far out of my price range. Great, now I not only had to find an appropriate gift for him, but it had to be appropriate enough to give him in front of the closest thing he had to a family. And, I had to find something for them that wouldn't make them hate me on sight. The way he described them, I pictured his foster parents as being very stern and forbidding. Still, they couldn't be all bad for him to have turned out so nice. It wasn't like there was a niceness gene. That usually had something to do with one's upbringing.

"Then we're set," he said, smiling so brightly that I was glad I'd agreed to go. If it made him that happy, I was certainly game. "I'll check the train schedule and let you know what time we'll need to leave from Grand Central. In the meantime, what do you say to spending the day before that together?"

I blinked, trying to catch up. "Huh?" I said, showing how smooth I was at this male-female communication process. He wasn't the only one who had a thing or two to learn.

"Well, we have noticed that the one thing that seems to bring Ari out of the woodwork is us together. What could be more tempting than the two of us, spending the day enjoying all the romance of Christmas in New York City?"

"So you mean we'd be doing this as work?"

He gave me that shy smile again. "We could have fun, too. That's certainly allowed. In fact, it would work even better if we were having fun."

"I guess if we have to do it to get our jobs done, then I'm willing," I said with a wink. "I should warn you, though, I think I've seen every movie that involves any kind of Christmas scene in New York, so my expectations are pretty high."

"I can't guarantee a pretty snowfall—well, I probably could, but altering weather patterns is usually frowned upon—but I'll see what else I can come up with."

I didn't think he was likely to kiss me at work, but he was awfully close to me. Our heads were practically touching, and neither of us would have had to move much if we wanted to kiss. Then the sound of a throat clearing made us jump apart. Of course, that made us look guilty, like there had been something going on. I turned to see Owen's assistant, Jake, who seemed to be trying to look anywhere but at us. "Uh, boss, just bringing your mail," he said. From the way he acted, you'd think he'd caught us undressed and rolling around on the lab floor.

Owen didn't help matters when he turned several different shades of red and took the long way around the lab table to take the mail from Jake instead of walking past me. Looking guilty was a sure way of giving the impression that something was going on. "Thank you, Jake," Owen said firmly, the implied dismissal clear in his tone.

Jake didn't move. "What's this I hear about Ari getting away?" he asked.

"Yes, she got away. Thanks for bringing the mail."

"Wow. I wonder how she pulled that off. That was quite a scene at the party Friday night."

I was pretty sure Jake was talking about the showdown that had taken place among Idris, Ari, Owen, and me instead of Owen kissing me, but I still felt my face turning red. I ducked back into my makeshift cubicle and let Owen deal with Jake. I had enough to worry about now that I was meeting Owen's family.

That evening was consumed by a flurry of packing as both of my roommates got ready for their trip home for the holidays. I got assigned Laundromat duty to help them get some last-minute loads done while they packed.

"I hate to leave you alone like this," Gemma said as she folded and packed the last load I'd brought back.

I continued sorting through the laundry basket for the items of mine I'd thrown into the load. "Actually, I'm going home with Owen."

"You are?" She raised her voice and called into the living room, where Marcia was packing. "She's going to meet the hottie's folks!"

A second later, Marcia was in the bedroom. "Really? He's taking you home for Christmas?"

"It's not like that. They don't even know we're dating. They just know that I'm a friend from work who was going to be alone for Christmas, and they invited me." They looked at each other and rolled their eyes. I couldn't help but laugh. "Yeah, I know. I don't believe it either, but that's honestly what he seems to think."

"They are totally going to be checking you out and trying to see why he's been talking about you," Marcia confirmed.

"Okay, this is a minor emergency," Gemma said, hurrying to the closet. "You may not be meeting the parents in an official girlfriend sense, but you are meeting the parents, and this is your only chance to make a good first impression." She disappeared into the closet, then returned with a small suitcase. "This should do. It's good quality but not covered with designer labels."

"I've got an overnight bag," I said.

"You have a glorified gym bag. Take this. Now, what do you know about them?"

"They live in some village on the Hudson. I think they're rich. And he says they're pretty formal. They dress for dinner."

"Okay, got it." She disappeared into the closet again, then returned with an armful of sweaters. "You have to have cashmere. I'd suggest going with subdued and classy—nothing too obvious, but definitely not bargain bin or trendy. That's the safest bet for meeting any parents for the first time."

"And then I have to come up with some gifts," I said.

Gemma groaned. "Oh, we don't have time to do this right. I wish I wasn't leaving town."

"If you weren't leaving town, this wouldn't be an issue. Don't worry, I'll be fine. I can shop for myself, you know."

She didn't look convinced, but Marcia said, "Yeah, Gemma, she's a big girl now." She went back to her own packing, and I spent the rest of the evening listening to Gemma rattling off ideas for presents.

I was looking forward to some rare private time when I got home from work the next evening, but I'd barely had time to take my coat off before the intercom buzzed. I hit the button, and it was Philip's voice asking for Gemma that answered me.

"Gemma went home for Christmas today," I told him. "Didn't she tell you?"

There was a pause, then he said, "No, she didn't. May I speak with you?"

This was my first good chance to have an honest heart-to-heart, magic and all, with Philip, so I said, "Come on up," and buzzed him in.

He knocked on the door a few seconds later. "Would you like some tea?" I asked as I took his coat.

"Yes, please," he said. He looked exhausted and utterly miserable. "When did she leave?" he asked as I put tea and a plate of Christmas cookies in front of him. He reflexively stood as I moved to take my seat across from him at the table, then resumed his seat when I sat.

"Today during the day. She's coming back late Christmas night. This whole trip was very sudden. She just found out about the last-minute fare sale yesterday, and last night she was so busy getting ready that I guess she forgot to let you know."

He sighed and bit the head off a gingerbread man. I couldn't help but flinch. "Perhaps," he said.

"Look, I don't mean to pry or get into your business, but as you may recall, I do know something about what you really are, and I suspect most of your issues with Gemma have to do with that. You're out of your time, which has to be disconcerting. Things have changed a lot, particularly the courtship rituals. For example, engraved invitations and chaperones aren't really necessary these days."

"Yes, she made that clear to me."

"We have other ways to communicate," I went on, but before I could start on the wonders of the cellular phone, he pulled a tiny flip-phone model out of his breast pocket. It was even fancier than Gemma's. "Okay, you've figured that part out for yourself."

"I suspect she's feeling neglected," he said, snapping a leg off his gingerbread man. "I have been busy, but I can't explain to her why I've been busy."

"What's keeping you so busy?"

"I'm trying to regain my family business. An unscrupulous associate of my father's was the one who enchanted me, and then when my disappearance was never explained and I never returned, he inherited the business upon my father's death. His descendants are still running the business, and I must take back what is rightfully mine."

"Yeah, that would tend to keep you busy," I agreed. "And you're right, it would be hard to explain. But have you told her you're busy at work? She should understand that much."

He reassembled the headless gingerbread man on his plate, shoving the broken leg back into place with his index finger. "I'm not even certain that us being together is a good idea at this time. She came across me when I was feeling very lost, and she was the most beautiful woman I'd ever seen. Now, though, I have business I must attend to, and her association with me could put her at risk from my enemies. I cannot expect her to wait for me, either."

"You know, I work for the big guns in the magical world, so I'm sure I could get you some help if you needed it."

Hope flickered in his eyes. "I could use your assistance with something. As I understand it, you're a magical immune."

"That's right."

"I've scheduled a meeting with the new head of what should be my company. He doesn't know who I am, simply that I'm a potential investor. It might be useful to have a magical immune present to help me determine if underhanded means are being used."

"I guess I could do that. When's the meeting, and what's your excuse for having me with you?"

"The meeting is Thursday afternoon. I thought perhaps you could pose as my wife or lady friend."

"Undercover work sounds like fun, and I get off early that day. Maybe I could be the daughter of a Texas oilman with money of my own to invest."

The blank expression on his face reminded me that he'd never seen an episode of *Dallas*. He nodded politely and said, "Whatever you think is best. The meeting is at two in the afternoon. Shall I call for you here?"

"Yeah, that'll be fine."

"I appreciate your assistance. And I thank you for the tea." He put on his coat and hat and left, and I finally had the apartment all to myself. Talking about Gemma's relationship issues reminded me of my own. While I was looking forward to living out all of my romantic holiday fantasies now that I finally had someone to share them with, I couldn't help but feel nervous. I was about to meet Owen's foster parents, and I knew they'd see this as a big event. I had to find gifts.

If ever there was one, this sounded like a time to call on a fairy godmother. I went to my nightstand to retrieve Ethelinda's locket from the jewelry box I kept in the back of the drawer. I hesitated, though, as I sat on my bed and prepared to open the locket to summon the fairy godmother. I was almost always a hit with the parents of men I dated, even if the men weren't so crazy about me. In fact, back home I'd been the number-one choice of parents for their sons' girlfriend, which was one of the reasons I'd had so few dates in high school (three overprotective big brothers were among the other reasons). It wasn't as though I needed a fairy godmother to help me with that sort of thing.

I put the locket back into my nightstand drawer and closed it. A firework then went off right outside the bedroom window. That window faced a narrow air shaft—so narrow I was sure if the people across the air shaft needed to borrow a cup of sugar, we could easily pass it over. It was unlikely that anyone was shooting off fireworks in that confined space. I went to the window, raised the blinds, opened the window, and leaned my head out to see what was going on.

Five

I jumped back in surprise when I saw Ethelinda hovering right outside my window. "I can't enter your home magically," she said. "Your young man does very good wards. I couldn't find a single chink in them."

"What are you doing here?" I asked. "I didn't summon you. There's no need for you to come inside."

"You don't have to summon me. I've been watching your case, and it seems to me that you're in need of advice."

"No, not really, thanks. I've got it under control."

"Have you eaten?"

"Huh?"

"Tsk, tsk, what kind of response is that, Kathleen? It's better to say, 'Pardon,' or 'Excuse me.' "

"What does me eating have to do with anything?" I clarified.

"It's better to discuss these things over food, don't you think?"

No, I didn't think. Eating meant being in public with a fairy godmother who seemed a bit ditzy. I could never be sure she'd remember to hide her magic from the rest of the world. Never mind the fact that I didn't need her there. "That's not necessary," I insisted.

"Nonsense. You're meeting his family. This is important. If this goes wrong, your future together may be doomed. Put on your coat and meet me outside." She vanished in a shower of silver sparkles before I had a chance to argue. There went my plans for a quiet evening at home alone, but I didn't feel I had much choice. She'd probably set off more fireworks and annoy the neighbors until she got her way. I got my coat and purse and went downstairs to find Ethelinda waiting for me on the sidewalk.

This time, she was dressed like the Sugar Plum Fairy in a really old production of *The Nutcracker,* from back when they wore their tutus almost down to their ankles instead of in a little ruffle around their hips. Her previous outfits, including the rose velvet and green silk, hung out from under the hem, and the blue satin of her bodice was so faded it was almost white. It was missing a few pearls around the neckline, the threads that had once held them hanging free.

I hoped she had a good illusion hiding all that from the rest of the world. If not, I supposed I could pass myself off as a good Samaritan taking a bag lady out to dinner. Speaking of which, I wondered if I was expected to pay for the meal. I wasn't sure how much money I had on me. None of the etiquette lessons my mother had taught me covered how you were supposed to interact with your fairy godmother, and I didn't recall Cinderella ever going to a restaurant with hers in the stories. Technically, Ethelinda had invited me, but she didn't seem like the kind of person who carried cash.

As soon as my feet hit the sidewalk, she turned and fluttered off, glancing over her shoulder and saying, "Well, come along."

She had a distinct advantage with her wings, so I had to trot to keep up with her. This was starting to feel like a big mistake. There were a lot of people I could ask about dealing with Owen's parents, like Rod, who actually knew them. As far ahead of me as she was, all I had to do was stop running and she'd more than likely forget about me entirely, but then there was always the chance she'd pop back into my life at the most inconvenient time to make up for our missed meeting.

I soon realized she was leading me toward Owen's house. She wouldn't, would she? I made up my mind to refuse to go if that was her plan. I didn't want him thinking I was so insecure about him that I'd resorted to consulting a fairy godmother.

Fortunately, she came to a stop in front of a neighborhood tavern around the corner from Owen's house. There was a chance that he'd be there eating dinner, but I suspected if he'd planned to eat out, he would have invited me to join him on our way home from work.

Ethelinda breezed right in and commandeered a table. The waiters didn't even blink, so I suspected magic was involved. Soon after we sat down, steak dinners appeared in front of us. I supposed that took care of the "who pays?" issue.

"Now, let's talk about this holiday with his family."

Before I could open my mouth to say anything, I noticed that her attention had strayed. I turned my head to see what she was staring at and saw a thirtysomething couple sitting at a nearby table. They'd finished their meals and were drinking coffee, apparently waiting for dessert. I didn't see anything about them that might have drawn a fairy godmother's attention. They weren't fighting, and they certainly didn't look awkward. They had an old-married-couple comfort level about them.

"Tsk, tsk. What a pity," Ethelinda said.

I turned back to her. "What's a pity?"

"They've been together so long, but something is missing. They need a boost to get them going in the right direction." She beamed suddenly. "And I know just the thing."

A waiter walked by us, carrying a tray with two desserts on it. As he passed, Ethelinda waved her wand. I turned my head to watch the waiter set the desserts on the table. A second or two later, the woman squealed in surprise—a happy squeal.

"Oh Mike! I love it! I thought you'd never . . . Yes, definitely yes!" She took a diamond ring from her dessert plate and slipped it onto her ring finger, then held her hand up to admire it as tears of joy streamed down her face.

A little choked up myself, I turned back to Ethelinda. "I take it that was your doing?"

She looked smug. "It's very simple, really." For a moment, I halfway expected her to launch into some "Bibbidi Bobbidi Boo" type song about how fairy godmothers work, but before she could explain how simple affecting the course of true love was, there was a commotion from the engagement table.

"Where did you get that?" the man's voice asked.

I turned just enough to watch without looking like I was staring. The rest of the restaurant was also looking, and most of them weren't even pretending to mind their own business. So much for New Yorkers being too jaded to stare. If there was enough potential juice involved, they were as likely as anyone else to take a gander.

"It was on my dessert plate," the woman replied, her voice trembling. "You mean—you mean you didn't set this up to have it put there?"

"Why would I? I thought I told you how I felt about marriage. I'm not looking for that kind of commitment. Are you trying to trap me into something?"

"Mike, we've been living together for ten years. That seems pretty committed to me. What difference would a ring, a ceremony, and a piece of paper make?"

"Exactly my point."

"It would make me happy. It would make me feel secure. That's the difference it would make for me. But I guess making me happy would be too much effort. I wouldn't want to pin you down." She stood and pulled the ring off, moved as if she was about to throw it at him, then thought better of it and put it in her pocket before she grabbed her purse and coat. "I want you out of my apartment before I get home from work tomorrow."

Cringing, I turned back to Ethelinda, who was blissfully eating her dinner. "That went well," I remarked.

"Yes, it did," she replied, completely missing my sarcasm. "She can't find the right man if she's stuck herself to the wrong one. Now she's open for new possibilities."

"You mean, you planned for that to happen?"

She looked enigmatic as she took a bite of her steak. "Now, about your problem."

"It's not really a problem, but if you've got anything in that book of yours about Owen's family, that might help."

"Of course I have something about his family. I have access to all records pertinent to your relationship. That's how I knew you'd been invited to spend Christmas with them." Her book appeared in her hand, and she retrieved her lopsided glasses from within the layers of her bodice. "Hmm, now, that's odd. There aren't supposed to be blank pages in here," she muttered. Before I could ask what she meant about blank pages, she said, "Oh, there we are. The Eatons, Gloria and James. Married late in life, no natural children. Goodness, but it took some effort to get those two together." She looked up at me across the top of her glasses. "They're very stubborn." Turning her attention back to the book, she continued, "Took in an orphaned child after their retirement from the university at the request of an old friend. Hmm, that part's strangely blank, too. Very odd."

She snapped the book shut, it vanished, then she took off her glasses and looked at me. "I'm sorry, but there's nothing here that would be of much use to you."

"That's okay. It was worth a shot." I turned my attention to my dinner. It wasn't often that I got steak, so I didn't intend to waste this chance.

Ethelinda's attention strayed again. There was another couple seated near us. This couple did seem to have a cool emotional distance between them. They were cordial but didn't show any signs of affection. Both of them wore business suits, and that gave me the impression that maybe this wasn't a date. When the woman bent and pulled a folder from the briefcase at her feet, it confirmed my impression.

Before I could say anything to stop Ethelinda, she had waved her wand at another passing waiter's tray. When the waiter placed the woman's plate in front of her, there was a long-stemmed red rose along-side it. "From the gentleman," the waiter said.

The woman went very pale, then abruptly turned red as she leaned across the table, clearly trying to keep her voice low but unable to succeed, as angry as she was. "What is this?" she hissed. "You know I'm married. I never had you pegged as such a sleaze." All the poor guy at the table with her could do was stammer incoherently.

Someone had to deal with this, and since I was the only person around who had the slightest clue what was going on, it looked like it would have to be me. I slipped out of my seat, hurried over to the bar, and fluttered my eyelashes at the bartender. "Can I borrow your apron for a second? I just noticed a friend of mine is eating here and she hasn't seen me yet. I thought it would be funny to pretend to be a waitress and surprise her."

I must have improved my eyelash-fluttering technique, or else it really is true that you suddenly become a lot more attractive to all men as soon as you get a boyfriend, for he grinned at me and untied the apron. I put it on and approached the table where the woman was still teaching a sexual harassment seminar to her shell-shocked colleague.

"Excuse me," I said, hoping neither of them had noticed me sitting at a nearby table. "There's been a mistake. I'm very sorry, but the order numbers and table numbers got mixed up back in the kitchen. You weren't supposed to get this." I grabbed the rose off the table. "I'm sorry if there's been any misunderstanding about this. I hope I'm not too late to get this rose to the proposal that's supposed to happen in the other room!"

The man and woman stared at each other for a moment, then the woman hid her face behind her folder and burst into nervous giggles. "I'm so sorry! I guess I shouldn't have jumped to conclusions," she said.

As I walked away, untying the apron, I heard him say, "Believe me, I'll never make a pass at you. Not that I don't think you're attractive, but . . . Okay, can we just forget all this? There's nothing I can say right now that wouldn't sound like an insult or get me in trouble."

I handed the bartender his apron, then presented him the rose with a flourish. "Thanks! I'll never forget the look on her face," I told him, then I hurried back to Ethelinda before he could say anything. I hoped she hadn't done anything else while I was gone.

"For what it's worth," I said as I took my seat, "there are reasons other than romance for men and women to have dinner together, and you might want to be sure of the reasons before you interfere. You could have ruined that man's career."

She gave a haughty sniff, then summoned dessert. I thought she might have forgotten about my own issues in all the excitement, but just as I dug into the chocolate cake, she asked, "And things are going well for you otherwise? How was your dinner Sunday night?"

I had to blink myself back to my own relationship concerns. After what I'd seen from her this evening, I knew the last thing I wanted was to have her involved. "Things are going great," I said, keeping my voice neutral. "I doubt he'd have invited me home for Christmas with him if they weren't. And we're going out later this week."

"Your dinner, though? It went well? Your outfit was good?"

"The outfit was a big hit, and the dinner was good, too. It started a little awkwardly, but the friends-to-dating transition can be a challenge. We seem to have worked it out, though."

"Nothing happened, did it?"

I instantly grew suspicious. "What do you mean?"

"Oh, nothing unusual?"

"You mean like the restaurant catching on fire?"

"Heavens! Is that what happened?" She seemed so stunned that either she was innocent or she was Dame Judi Dench in costume and makeup, turning in another Oscar-caliber performance.

"Yeah, but it was a minor fire and nobody was hurt."

She fanned herself and looked like she was having heart palpitations. "A brush with disaster! That doesn't happen to my clients!"

I grew suspicious again. She was pouring it on awfully thick. "It's okay, really. Everything worked out."

"It did?"

"Yes, it did, so relax."

"That's good to hear." She finished her dessert, the empty plates vanished from the table, and she said, "Do you need anything else from me?"

I hadn't actually needed that much from her, but I said, "That's it. I hope I didn't waste your time."

She waved a dismissive hand. "Pish tosh. Time spent with my clients is never wasted, and I needed to eat. Are you sure you don't need anything else?"

"Nothing. My roommate's already loaned me her cashmere sweater collection, so I don't need any wardrobe help. I don't need you to turn a pumpkin into a glass BMW. We've got our next date planned, and I think I'll be okay. Yeah, I'm a little nervous, but that's part of the fun of a new relationship. The butterflies only intensify everything."

"Well then, you know how to reach me if you change your mind." She got up, and I followed her out of the tavern, where she abruptly vanished in her usual burst of glitter. I was halfway tempted to sneak around to Owen's street and see if his lights were on. Both his study and his bedroom overlooked the street. But, knowing my luck, his Katie radar would be working and he'd look out the window just in time to catch me, and then I'd feel like an idiot. Instead, I hurried home, wondering what was missing from those blank pages Ethelinda mentioned.

Owen was at a meeting and I was sitting at my desk in the makeshift office in Owen's lab the next morning when Rod stuck his head around the whiteboard. "Hi!" he said. He was still wearing his hair the way I'd seen it on Sunday, and his skin looked better than I'd ever seen it before.

"Are you exfoliating?" I asked without thinking about what I was saying.

Before I could apologize, he grinned and said, "Yeah. You can tell the difference?"

"You look fresh and well rested." I thought that was a diplomatic way to avoid saying his skin usually had pores you could drive a truck through.

"Then I guess getting sucked in by that saleswoman at Blooming-dale's was worth it. I thought maybe she'd give me her phone number if I bought enough stuff. Is Owen around?"

"Departmental meeting," I replied. "It could be an hour or more. Did you need something?"

He patted the fat envelope he carried. "I've got those results on em-ployee magic use for his comparison project."

"Oh yeah, that. I can take them and give them to him when he gets back, unless there's something else you needed to talk to him about."

"No, that's fine. I can leave them with you."

He turned to go, but I said, "Can I talk to you a second?"

"Sure. What is it?"

"I don't know if you know this already, but I'm going home with Owen for Christmas. I was hoping you could give me the scoop on his foster family."

He gave a low, long whistle. "Oh boy. That's a topic for a disserta-tion."

"That bad?"

"I wouldn't say bad, but yeah, there are some things I should warn you about."

That sounded even more ominous than Ethelinda's blank pages. "Pull up a chair," I told him.

He grabbed a chair from the lab outside, then turned around and waved his hand at the lab doorway while muttering some words under his breath. "An alarm, so he can't sneak up on us," he explained before sitting down. "I don't know the whole story because I was a kid when James and Gloria took Owen in. They were good to him. There was never any sign of physical or emotional abuse. But they never really warmed to him. I'm not sure why they agreed to bring up a child when they seemed to have no interest in children whatsoever. I don't even think he was related to them in any way."

"He sounds like he's a bit in awe of them."

"They're the kind of people you tend to be in awe of. They wouldn't look out of place wearing crowns. They're not really all that warm to anyone, to be honest, so I don't think it's all directed at Owen."

"He also makes it sound like they're very clear on the fact that they're his foster parents, not real parents."

"They never adopted him, I know that much, but I don't know why, and they always had him call them by their names, never anything like 'Mom' or 'Dad.' But as foster parents they should have been free of their obligations to him when he turned eighteen. He was even prepared for them to cut him loose then. That's when he went into the custom-spell business at school, so he could stay at Yale even if they quit paying the bills. But nothing at all changed when he turned eighteen. They kept paying his school bills and sending him an allowance even on into graduate school, and they kept expecting him home for holidays until he finished his studies and moved to New York."

"What are they like, other than being very regal?"

"They're proper. They're demanding. They don't use magic at home—they don't believe in shortcuts." He shrugged. "It's hard to say. If they suggested that Owen invite you—and he wouldn't have dared unless they suggested it—I think it's a good sign. They probably think you're good for Owen, and I'd have to agree with them. They might not act like normal parents toward him, but he's been the center of their lives since they took him in."

"So, bottom line, what should I do?"

He shrugged. "Be yourself. Follow their lead. And dress before you go to breakfast."

"What?"

"Seriously. Owen says he's never seen them in their pajamas. They get fully dressed before they leave their bedroom, every single day."

"Wow. Now, that's formal. Hey, do you think they're really something nonhuman, only it's hidden by illusion, and the clothes are somehow part of covering it all up?"

"I have no idea. But if you notice anything unusual, you'll have to let me know."

As he left my office, I realized that I might be in for a very interesting Christmas. I faced either magical royalty or some other kind of mysterious being that had fostered my boyfriend.

My crazy family Christmases from childhood were starting to feel very tame in comparison.

We only had to work a half day Thursday, so when it was time to shut down for the holiday, I stuck my head in Owen's office door and asked, "Are you ready to leave?"

He looked up at me, frowning. "Is it that time already?"

"Five minutes past."

"I still have a few things to wrap up. You don't mind heading out by yourself, do you?"

Not only did I not mind, I was relieved. I needed to do some shopping, and I had that meeting with Philip. "That's okay. I've got stuff to take care of. I'll see you in the morning."

"Okay. See you then." He'd already returned to his work by the time I turned to leave his office, and he didn't seem to notice when I left for the day, judging by the fact that he didn't respond to my farewell as I passed his open office door. He was lost in his project and probably would be for the rest of the day, if not all night.

Shopping for Owen's foster parents looked like it was going to be quite the challenge. Owen himself had to ask me for advice to get them anything more personal than a gift basket or a charity donation in their

name. Their apparent wealth and grandeur made them even more difficult to shop for on my budget.

After looking at and rejecting any number of items as I browsed the
stalls of the Union Square holiday market, I came to the conclusion that
when it came to finding gifts for people like that, it took either a lot of
money or a lot of personal effort. Personal effort I could do. I had a nearly
finished cross-stitch sampler somewhere in the closet, so if I got a nice
frame and buckled down to work, I figured that I could have it done and
offer a truly personal gift. There was an ornate metal frame at one of the
stalls that seemed ideal. I bought Owen a nice wool muffler that would
go well with his coat and that had blue flecks in it that matched his eyes.
It seemed a safe enough gift, personal without being too personal and
demonstrating that I had some concern for him.

Then I had to hurry to transform myself into an oil baron's daughter
before Philip came over. I wore a slim skirt, one of Gemma's silk blouses,
and my own red stiletto shoes, now unenchanted. I made liberal use
of all those Mary Kay makeup samples my mom kept sending me and
teased and sprayed my hair to within an inch of its life. All I needed was
a fur coat to complete the effect, but that I'd have to do without. Philip's
reaction when he came over told me all I needed to know about how effective my transformation was.

"Hi, hon," I drawled. I hooked my arm through his and added,
"Now, let's go find us a place where I can invest all of Daddy's money."

"Is this really what an oilman's daughter would be like?" he asked, his
eyes popping enough to remind me that he once was a frog.

"No, not based on the few I've met, but it's what people around here
will expect from TV shows and movies."

"Very well, then. I propose we take the subway, as it's faster than surface transport."

I didn't think your typical oil baron's daughter would set foot on
the subway, but he was right about the speed issue. The company that
should have been his was located on the far tip of Manhattan, below Wall
Street. Its building looked like it might have gone all the way back to

Colonial days. Philip stood on the sidewalk in front of it for a moment or two, gazing up at it. I tried to imagine what this must be like for him, to see his family business about a century later in a very different world. Then he took a deep breath and opened the front door.

The interior was full of heavy antiques that had probably been new when the building was built. Philip approached the receptionist's desk and said, "I have a two o'clock appointment with Mr. Meredith."

She checked her computer. "Ah, you must be Mr. Smith."

I remembered myself just in time to keep from giggling. I could see why he might want to use an alias when checking out his family business, but he could have found one that sounded a little less like an alias. Come to think of it, I needed an alias of my own.

The receptionist gave me a sidelong glance. "And is Miss . . ."

"Sue-Ellen Hunt, of the Texas Hunts," I drawled, sticking my hand out at her. My alias wasn't much better than Philip's, as Sue-Ellen had been a character on *Dallas* and Hunt was the only family name associated with oil I could think of off the top of my head. If someone Googled the name, they'd certainly get the Texas oil associations.

She eyed my hand for a second before shaking it, then she said to Philip, "Miss Meredith will be with you in a moment."

"My appointment was with Mr. Meredith," Philip said. "I understand he is currently chairman of Vandermeer and Company."

"Mr. Meredith is indisposed. His niece is taking care of the business for him in his absence." She glanced around as if to make sure she wasn't being overheard, then whispered, "He had a stroke last week, totally incapacitating. I'm sure Miss Meredith will be officially installed as chair very soon."

If we were meeting with a woman, I was in trouble. All my preparation had been designed to distract a man, but I was playing the kind of woman other women tend to hate on sight. It looked like I'd have to wing it and see what kind of person this Miss Meredith was.

Soon a frazzled-looking young man came into the lobby. "Mr. Smith? This way, please." He appeared as though at any second he was going to slip a note saying something like, "Help! I'm being held hostage!" into our pockets. I recognized the look; I'd looked much like that in my old job.

The chairman's office was even more lush than the lobby. The desk in the center of it was large enough that you could have held a feast for twenty of your closest friends on it, with room for several courses' worth of silverware at each place setting and space in the middle for a string quartet to provide entertainment. I sank past my three-inch heels and almost up to my ankles in a carpet that could have doubled as a mattress. But what really caught my eye was the thing lurking in the back corner of the office.

Six

It was a skeletal creature much like one that had been stalking me for the past couple of months. I couldn't be sure if it was the same one, since all skeletal magical creatures look pretty much alike to me, but the one I knew had worked for Idris. That made this meeting suddenly a lot more interesting. I had a feeling I wasn't supposed to be able to see Mr. Bones, who stood silent and still in his corner, so I forced myself not to react. That was a challenge, like ignoring the giant pink elephant in the middle of the room.

Then Miss Meredith came into the room and shook Philip's hand. "Mr. Smith? I'm Sylvia Meredith. Thank you for coming in." I wasn't sure which was more dangerous, her or Mr. Bones. She was a shark in human form—sleek, efficient, and deadly, and I wouldn't have been surprised if she had a couple of extra rows of teeth. The ones we could see were white and even, and she turned the full force of them on Philip in a smile I was sure was supposed to be charming but which looked like it might draw blood. Philip turned out to be pretty smart, for he didn't look like he was the least bit taken in by her attempt at charm.

I remembered that I was supposed to be a brassy oil heiress, so I waded through the carpet and stuck my hand out at her. "Sue-Ellen Hunt, of the Texas Hunts," I said, thickening my drawl as much as I could and still be understood. "Nice place you got here. I bet this office runs you about as much as my daddy's whole estate back home. We like things big in Texas, you know." I was beginning to annoy myself, so I was sure this act was like fingernails on a blackboard to a New Yorker.

"Miss Hunt is my fiancée," Philip said, not missing a beat. "When she heard about my appointment with you she thought it would be beneficial for her to meet with you, as well."

"I gotta do something with my trust fund other than buy shoes, right?" I said with as much gusto as I could muster.

"Please, have a seat," Miss Meredith said, gesturing toward a pair of plush wingback chairs. Only the tiniest hint of annoyance showed in her eyes, but I got the feeling that meant she was steaming inside. Nothing but the strongest emotion would get past her icy facade.

I more or less tuned out the financial discussion while I checked out the setting. There was a row of portraits on one wall, going from a modern photograph of a white-haired, stern-jawed man on one end to oil paintings of men wearing powdered wigs at the other end. About five portraits in from the modern end, the look of the people changed abruptly. They went from having Philip's refined features and golden hair to looking coarser and meaner. It was obvious when the company had been usurped. Other than the skeletal creature still lurking in the corner, I didn't spot anything obviously magical. An uninformed person who wasn't immune to magic wouldn't have noticed anything odd.

When I blinked back to the meeting, it seemed to be wrapping up. "Thank you for the information. I shall have to consult with my advisors," Philip was saying.

Sylvia eyed him warily. I hoped she hadn't noticed the resemblance between him and all those portraits on the wall. "You won't find our specialized services anywhere else," she said. "We're one of the only high-level banking houses exclusively serving the magical community." She turned to me and added, "I hope what we have to offer interests you, as well."

"Oh, I let Philip handle all my major decisions," I drawled. "And I'm so sorry to hear about your uncle. I hope he gets better real soon."

A flicker of reaction crossed her face, but before I could decipher it, she managed to tamp it down. "Things don't look good," she said, sounding more determined than sad. I had the strongest suspicion that she had something to do with that "stroke." She walked us to her office door, and I felt the tingle of magic in use nearby. It didn't affect me, but I was worried about what it would do to Philip. I moved to stand between her and him, then caught his arm to make sure I had some sort of control over him as we left the building.

We both let out deep breaths when we were safely on the sidewalk and well away from the building. "Did you notice anything untoward?" he asked.

"Yeah. She had a nasty-looking bodyguard in there that I'm sure was hidden from you. And, oddly enough, it was a kind of creature my big enemy happens to be fond of. Are walking skeletons popular on magical goon squads?"

"I'm not familiar with that kind of creature."

"I thought so. I wonder if she's in league with Idris, then. That would make things interesting. Oh, and she tried to use magic on you when we were leaving."

"I noticed. I'm not certain that it worked, but I will be careful."

"That lady is bad news. And I don't think you can count on her saying, 'Oh, so sorry my ancestor put you under a spell, you should take over.' She probably would have you killed—like I bet she did to her uncle—instead of having you turned into a frog."

He sighed. "I didn't imagine this would be easy, but I fear it may be more difficult than I thought."

"Remember Ethan, the guy I used to date? He's both magically immune and a lawyer, which is just what you need for taking her on. And if she is teamed up with our enemy, you're about to have the resources of

Magic, Spells, and Illusions, Inc., on your side, including Merlin himself."

He smiled at me, then gave me a gallant bow. "Then I must thank you for your assistance."

"Don't thank me yet. We may end up putting you to work."

When I got home, I felt like I was changing out of my superhero costume and returning to my mild-mannered persona as I changed out of my fancy meeting clothes and into sweats. I spent the whole evening finishing my cross-stitch for Owen's foster parents while some pop star's holiday special played in the background on the TV—something I was sure the fictional Sue-Ellen Hunt would never do. She'd wear cashmere sweats, if she even wore sweats, and she'd have people to do her sewing for her. The pop star would be playing live in her living room instead of on TV. Sue-Ellen was so far from my reality that I had a feeling my secret identity was safe.

Concentrating on my needlework was a good way to distract me from worrying about the next day with Owen or the holiday with his family. I'd forgotten what a good stress release this kind of thing could be, but my roommates would tease me mercilessly about being old-fashioned if I started doing it on a regular basis, I was sure. Maybe I should go back to knitting, I thought. At least some Hollywood stars had made that almost cool again.

The next morning, I was eager to get to Owen's house to tell him what I'd discovered. The romantic day in New York was almost secondary. Although I'd been in his home before, I'd never entered by the front door. The last time I'd been there, I'd been magically teleported inside. This time I had to climb a fairly imposing set of front steps and ring a buzzer. Instead of a response by intercom, the door just opened. I went up the staircase in the vestibule to the next floor, where Owen's door was, and it, too, opened for me.

I expected to see Owen waiting there for me, but the entry hallway was empty. A loud "meow!" at my feet corrected me. "Hi there, Loony," I said to the white-and-black-spotted cat that was rubbing happily against my ankles.

"Back here," Owen's voice called from the kitchen. I took off my coat, hat, and gloves while Loony waited patiently for me, then she headed back to the kitchen, her tail giving me a "follow me" flick. I heeded her instruction and found Owen standing at the stove in his cozy kitchen, tending one skillet full of French toast and another full of bacon.

"Wow, you're cooking for me?" I asked.

"I wanted to make sure you knew last time wasn't a fluke. And you're just in time. Breakfast is almost ready."

When he turned to talk to me, I noticed the dark circles under his eyes. I crossed my arms over my chest and said, "Don't tell me, you worked all day yesterday and most of the night."

He deftly flipped a slice of French toast. "There's coffee in the pot if you want some."

"Owen," I warned.

"Yes, I worked late. I wanted to finish before I left for Christmas." He arranged everything on plates, which he carried to the small table in one corner of the kitchen. Unless he'd cleaned house significantly in the last couple of weeks, the dining table was probably too full of books for anyone to be able to eat there. "And breakfast is served," he said.

"It looks great," I told him as I took my seat at the table. Loony immediately jumped into my lap, but Owen snapped his fingers and pointed, and she jumped down again, looking offended.

"I hope you don't mind that we didn't go out to eat," he said as he took his own seat. "It's easier for us to talk this way." He grinned and added, "And you'll need your energy for what I have planned today."

"Now you've got me intrigued." I ate and complimented him on the food, then finally said, "So, what did you discover from all your extra work?"

"Nothing." He sounded discouraged. "It didn't match any of our current employees."

"On the bright side, that does mean we don't have another mole or double agent."

"But on the not-so-bright side, it also means there's an outsider who can get through every layer of security we've got."

"Oh. I hadn't thought of that." I ate some more, keeping my mouth busy with the food so I wouldn't be tempted to say something stupid. After a while, though, I couldn't help myself. "Could it be an ex-employee? I mean, other than Idris. Someone who might not be in your current files but who would know something about how to get past security? I don't know if you could magically change the locks, so to speak, but that would explain someone being able to get in."

"We did change the security wards after Idris was fired. I can't think of anyone who was at a high enough level to have that kind of access who has left between then and now."

"There's the former boss," I reminded him.

He frowned. "No, I don't think so. As I said, he retired on good terms, and he's not even living in the city anymore. It was his idea to revive Merlin, and if he were in league with Idris, that would be the last thing he'd want to do. He was the one to make the final call on firing Idris. If he wanted to delve into that kind of magic, you'd think he would have stayed on board and turned the direction of the company around." He raised an eyebrow and flashed me a crooked smile. "And then I guess I'd have been the dangerous rogue wizard trying to bring down the company."

"I suspect you'd have been a lot more successful than he has been."

"That's because I'd be the good guy."

"Yeah, because the good guys always win in the real world. Meanwhile, I may have found something else." I briefly told him about Philip's predicament and the skeletal creature in the office.

"I haven't heard of anyone else using that kind of creature," he said. "It seems to be unique to Idris. If he's allied with someone like that, then it could mean he's found funding, and it means there are people within the establishment who might support his goals. That widens the scope of our problem somewhat."

After we finished breakfast and washed the dishes, we bundled up against the cold, then headed outside, where we walked side by side down the street. We took the subway and got off at Thirty-fourth Street for a quick peek at Santa at Macy's, then headed over to Fifth Avenue. We worked our way up the avenue, stopping in front of each elaborately decorated store window. I felt like a little kid, back in the days when I'd been utterly enchanted by the tinsel and lights strung around the shop windows on the town square back home.

At one particular store, Owen made a point of steering me to the front of the crowd to get a good look at the window. It was an intricate woodland scene, with fairies fluttering over a toadstool village inhabited by gnomes while snow drifted down from overhead. This wasn't one of the famous department stores, but it was the most exquisite window I'd seen yet, with the figures looking incredibly lifelike. They even had facial expressions. One of the fairies winked as she fluttered past the front of the display window. After we'd watched the window for a while, I realized that the patterns of the figures didn't repeat. They were spontaneous and random. I started to blurt, "These are for real!" but caught myself just in time and whispered it to Owen instead.

He leaned forward and rested his chin on my shoulder so he could whisper back. If it hadn't been so cold, I was sure I'd have melted into a puddle of goo on the sidewalk from having him next to me like that. "Yes. They work in shifts. It's one of the more popular seasonal jobs in the magical world."

"Are any of the other windows magical?"

"I'd say there's a little magic involved in all of them."

"Real or figurative?"

"Ah, that's the big question."

We continued walking up the avenue and enjoying the seasonal sights until we reached the big FAO Schwarz toy store. "Ready to regress to childhood?" he asked.

"Always!"

The doorman dressed as a toy soldier ushered us inside, where we were surrounded by every kind of stuffed animal. "The good stuff is upstairs," Owen said, and I knew what he meant as soon as we reached the top of the escalator. That was where the giant piano kids could play by running around on it was, but that wasn't what caught Owen's attention. He was focused on the display of magic kits, which were being demonstrated by a young employee. I bit my lip to keep myself from laughing. Not only was Owen a genuine wizard, but he also had a knack for stage magic. You had to know your magic to be sure whether he was using sleight of hand or real magic. If the demonstrator picked the wrong audience volunteer, I knew this could get interesting.

We stood near the back of the cluster of shoppers that had formed around the demonstration table, then as the employee finished a trick, that group trickled away and we moved to the front. The next volunteer was a little boy, who could never properly guess which card would be drawn, while the demonstrator got it right every time. The demonstrator then turned to Owen, who guessed correctly. That took the demonstrator aback. He turned to get another trick from his case, and Owen bent to whisper to me, "I've got the same set."

From there, it turned into a game of magical one-upmanship, each of them trying to stump the other. As far as I could tell, Owen wasn't using real magic. I could usually sense the tingle of power in use if I was paying attention. A larger and larger crowd formed as the show grew more and more spectacular. The demonstrator finally pulled out a silk top hat, showed everyone that it was empty, then pulled a plume of feathers out of it. He handed the hat to Owen, who shrugged and reached inside. That time, I felt a tingle. Owen pulled a live rabbit out of the hat, to much applause. While everyone was applauding, the rabbit turned into a stuffed toy, which Owen handed to the little girl next to him.

We slipped away in the commotion as the shoppers surged forward to buy magic kits. The still-baffled employee kept shouting that the rabbit trick wasn't included in the kit. On the way down the escalator, I elbowed Owen. "You cheated."

"I couldn't let a college student beat a real wizard," he said with a grin and a blush. "It would be bad for my reputation. And he's going to sell a lot of magic kits."

"Nice justification. But don't you feel bad that he'll be spending months trying to figure out how you got a rabbit out of that hat?"

"He'd be better off working on his technique so he can fool your average ten-year-old. Ready for lunch?"

I was hungry enough in spite of the big breakfast that I didn't mind him changing the subject that way. We found a deli nearby, and it felt incredibly good to sit down after all the walking we'd done. "How have you enjoyed the day so far?" he asked.

"It's been wonderful. I saw some of these places before when I was with Mom at Thanksgiving, but at the time I was so worried about what else we might run into that I barely noticed them. It was nice to be able to take our time and enjoy it all."

"I'm glad it hasn't been a total waste of time."

"Oh no! It's been great."

"It's not over yet," he said with one of those sly grins of his that woke up the butterflies in my stomach.

After we finished our meal and were leaving the restaurant, he said, "And now, our final adventure of the day."

"What is it?" I asked, feeling like an eager, excited child.

"Haven't you learned by now that I'm not going to tell you?"

I soon figured out that we were heading toward Central Park. He led me down the path alongside the pond, where I'd once kissed frogs with some co-workers on a very wild girls' night out. And then we were at the plaza overlooking Wollman Rink. Skaters twirled beneath us on the ice. We watched for a moment, then he said, "Come on."

I followed, then realized that he intended for us to go onto the ice. "Whoa, wait a second," I said. "I've never been ice-skating."

"All the more reason for you to give it a try."

"But I don't know how."

"You've roller-skated, haven't you?"

"Yeah, when I was in third grade and had Barbie skates."

"Don't worry, I won't let you fall."

I knew he wouldn't, and that he had more than just brute strength to rely upon for keeping me upright. That still didn't make me feel much better. "I'll make a fool out of myself in front of all these people."

"You won't be the only one." As if to prove him right, a girl fell straight onto her behind not too far from where we stood. I knew he was too nice to have done that to her just to prove a point.

"I take it you know what you're doing on the ice."

"Yeah, Rod and I used to play hockey when we were kids on the pond in the village park."

"See, that's where I'm at a disadvantage. Where I'm from it doesn't get cold enough or stay cold long enough to freeze any body of water thoroughly enough for it to support a person's weight, unless it's a really freaky weather year."

"Skating here at Christmastime is one of the most romantic things to do in the city. It shows up in movies all the time." I had to give him that point. How many times had I watched a romantic scene of a couple on this ice rink and sighed, wishing that could be me one day? Here I was a couple of days before Christmas with an amazing guy. It was a scenario right out of a movie. Then he moved in for the final argument. "Who knows, if we're lucky, it might even start snowing."

I knew when I was beat, and besides, I secretly really wanted to do this. "Okay, but if I break my leg, you're carrying me up and down the stairs to my apartment."

"Deal." He paid the admission and skate rental, then we took our skates to a bench to put them on and stowed our shoes in a locker. I felt wobbly getting to the rink, so I could only dread how bad it would be when I stepped onto the ice. Ice was slippery and cold, and that wasn't a great combination in my book.

True to his word, Owen kept an arm tight around my waist as he eased me onto the ice. I was glad he didn't feel the need to show off, but he did seem good enough at what he was doing to keep his balance and support me at the same time.

I was sure I looked a lot like a newborn foal whose legs aren't quite steady and tend to try to move in different directions, but I didn't feel like I was going to fall. Soon I felt confident enough to let myself glide a little, and before long I was actually enjoying myself. A lot of that was probably because of Owen's arm tight around my waist and the way he smiled patiently down at me.

After a full lap around the rink, he eased up on the death grip around my waist, keeping his arm there but not squeezing quite so hard. I was finally able to notice my surroundings—the trees in the park, the tall buildings overlooking us, the other skaters. Christmas music played on the sound system. All we needed to make it perfect was a little snow.

No sooner had I thought it than a scattering of light flakes began to fall. I laughed out loud. "Okay, you're right, this is perfect."

"Isn't it, though?" he said mildly, a glint in his eye.

"You're doing this, aren't you?"

He tried to look innocent and failed. "Maybe. But look how much everyone is enjoying it." He was right. The kids were squealing in delight and the adults were all beaming.

"Thank you," I whispered, smiling up at him. And then I was suddenly falling into something very wet and cold.

Seven

I wasn't surprised to be falling; I'd actually been anticipating a big fall from before the moment I stepped onto the ice. However, I'd expected the ice to be cold and hard. Instead, I was cold and wet, all the way up to my shoulders. If I hadn't known better, I'd have thought I'd fallen through the ice on that frozen pond Owen had mentioned. The only thing keeping me from going under entirely was Owen's firm grasp on my arm.

"Katie!" he yelled. I blinked to see him stretched out on the ice, face-down, as he tried to get his free arm under my shoulders. I vaguely recalled having read somewhere that when you were on cracking ice, you should lie down to spread out your body weight. I wondered if he was doing that instinctively. But then I remembered that this rink was on top of a cement slab, and the ice couldn't have been more than a few inches thick, even if I couldn't seem to feel the bottom of whatever I'd fallen into.

I got my wits about me enough to reach my other arm up and try to get a grasp on something, but my fingers were numb from cold, and the ice kept breaking off around me. Owen grabbed that wrist and managed to pull me a little farther out of the hole. The whole time, he mumbled under his breath, and I could feel the tingle of magic near me. A crowd gathered around us, and soon a couple of men helped Owen pull me up onto the ice. I turned around to see the hole where I'd fallen and caught only a glimpse of the hole freezing over again.

A muddle of voices asked variations on the "what just happened here?" question, only with lots more profanity, this being New York. My teeth were chattering so hard I could only hear bits and pieces. Next thing I knew, something heavy was being wrapped around me and I was being pulled to my feet. Then I felt my feet leaving the ground. My legs were still pretty numb, but I got the feeling they were draped over someone's arm, and I was cradled against something warm and solid. The wind stirred around me, making me shiver even more, and I realized that whoever was carrying me was moving.

Soon I was deposited onto a bench, and I heard Owen's voice barking out orders. "I need someone to bring a blanket and something hot to drink." Then his face was very close to mine. "Katie?" he asked, looking tense and worried.

I tried to tell him I'd be fine, but my teeth were still chattering. He pulled something from around me—his coat, it turned out—then peeled my own wet coat off me. I tried to fight him because if I was this cold already, how would I feel without a coat on at all? He shushed me, though, murmuring so only I could hear, "I'll take care of it, but the last thing you need is to be wrapped in a wet coat." Sure enough, soon my clothes were dry and warm, and I felt much better. He put his dry coat back around me and set my soaking coat, which had ice crystals forming on it, aside on the bench. As the cold seeped away from my brain, I realized what he'd done. He'd managed to dry my clothes magically while still keeping my coat wet, and with his coat around me, nobody would notice that my clothes were dry. They'd only see the wet coat and assume I was still wet, so they'd never suspect anything funny—well, anything funnier than falling through ice that had a concrete slab under it. My Owen was really good at thinking logically in a crisis.

A moment later, someone draped a blanket around me, and Owen held a steaming paper cup to my lips. "Come on, drink," he urged. It turned out to be hot cocoa, and that warmth going into me just about did the trick. Soon my hands had thawed enough for me to hold the cup myself. While I drank, Owen disappeared for a moment, then returned and knelt in front of me. It took me a second to realize he was pulling off my skates and putting my shoes on. My feet seemed to be the last parts of me that remained numb from the cold.

The people around us were still talking. "Must've been a sinkhole," one voice said. "No way," another replied. "Not that deep." "Strangest thing I ever saw, and I seen a lot." I felt the air around me stir, then turned to see Sam perched beside me on the back of the bench. He winked at me, then faced Owen, who gave him a quizzical look. Sam shook his head grimly, then took off again. He coasted in a spiraling pattern above the rink, looking for all the world like a buzzard circling a dead animal out in the country.

Someone wearing a park employee uniform joined us. Owen dealt with him, saying something about how I'd be okay, there must have just been a melted spot. The employee went out on the ice, others leading him to the place where not too long ago there had been a gaping hole full of icy water, but it was impossible to tell that anything had happened there. I almost felt sorry for the guy, who was probably going to have a hard time writing the report on this incident.

He returned and had more words with Owen. There were raised voices, and I wished I could concentrate enough to pay attention to what they were saying because Owen never raised his voice, not even when he was angry. He was one of those people who got quieter and calmer when he got mad, so this was unusual and probably well worth listening to. I did manage to hear him say quite firmly, "I need to get her home and warm. I don't know what happened, but you don't have to worry about us filing a complaint or suing. I don't care about your paperwork. I just need to get her warm."

Then he came back to me, sitting beside me on the bench. "Do you think you can walk?" he asked, his voice soft and gentle, more like his normal self.

"Yeah," I managed to croak.

"Okay, then. Let's go get a cab."

He picked up my ice-covered coat, then helped me to my feet and walked with his arm around me toward the Fifth Avenue side of the park. Once we were away from the crowds, he said, "I'd try the magical tele-portation thing again, but at this distance and with your magical immu-nity intact this time, I'm not sure I could do it, and even if I could, it would drain me completely. I'd rather be ready to face anything else that comes at us."

"That sounds like a good idea. A cab will be fine. They usually have their heaters up to eleven this time of year."

When we got to the street, he did his taxi-summoning trick, and soon I was safe in the back of an overheated cab that smelled faintly of curry and incense. "We're going downtown," Owen told the driver, then he turned to me. "Would you rather go to your place or to mine?"

"Yours," I said without hesitation. "You've got a fireplace and a cat, and I recall that you have at least one sweat suit that fits me."

"Mine it is, then." He gave the driver the address, then he turned his attention back to me. He tugged my gloves off and wrapped his hands around mine, rubbing them to restore the warmth. Of course, since this was Owen, it had far more than the desired effect on me. Soon my whole body verged on uncomfortably hot. Before I had a complete meltdown, I pulled my hands away from his, but then I leaned my head against his shoulder and let him cuddle me so he wouldn't think I was rejecting him. The terrifying memory of falling through a hole in the ice that shouldn't have been there faded rapidly. In retrospect, it was a small price to pay for feeling this cherished.

We reached Owen's place, and a concerned Loony met us at the door, meowing loudly. Owen hushed her with a glare, then in short order there was a fire blazing in the living room fireplace and he was holding an armful of clothes that seemed to have appeared out of thin air. "There should be some towels in the bathroom under the stairs, if you want to finish drying off. I'm sorry, but I was only able to affect your clothes. I couldn't dry your skin very well." As I took the clothing from him, he added, "If you want to warm up with a hot bath or shower, you could do that, too."

I shook my head. "No thanks. I'm not eager to be wet again for a while."

It was the same old pair of sweatpants and sweatshirt he'd given me to wear the last time I ended up cold and damp at his place. This was getting to be a very bad habit for me. I stripped off my mostly dry clothes, toweled off, then hurried to put the dry sweat suit on. A pair of thick socks was sheer heaven to my still-chilled feet.

When I emerged from the bathroom, Owen was waiting for me in the living room with two steaming mugs in his hands. He gave one to me. It proved to be a hot groglike drink, full of spices and probably a bit of something else. It reminded me of a drink my grandmother made when we had colds. I sat on the rug in front of the fireplace, and Owen wrapped an afghan around my legs before sitting beside me.

With the hot drink inside me, the fire, Loony in my lap, and Owen's shoulder to lean against, I finally felt like asking, "What exactly happened back there?"

"I'm really not sure," he admitted. "One minute we were skating along—and you were doing pretty well—and the next thing I knew, you'd fallen through the ice."

"Correct me if I'm wrong, but that really isn't an iced-over pond, right? I've been there in the summer, and that's a concrete slab they set an ice rink up on in the winter. I shouldn't have been able to fall more than a few inches, even if the ice melted or broke."

"It was definitely magic, but I didn't recognize the spell. Not that it's a kind of spell I'd want to spend a lot of time with. Then again, it might be useful if you were in a situation where you needed water, depending on whether it requires ice to make it work . . ."

"Owen," I said, giving him a little nudge to jolt him back to the present.

The tips of his ears turned red. "Sorry. Anyway, when you fell, it pulled me down, too, but I didn't go through the ice. I barely managed to hold on to you, but I couldn't get enough leverage to pull you out. I must have tried every spell I could think of that might have been remotely useful in that situation, but nothing worked. I'm not sure if it was your immunity or something to do with the spell on the ice, or what, but I was getting worried."

"I imagine you're not used to being helpless like that," I mused.

"No, not really," he said softly, staring into the fireplace. I thought I detected the tiniest flicker of a shudder in his shoulders.

"But you did get me out with some help, and you got me warm and dry, and now I'm okay, so it worked out." I left out the part about how spending the rest of the day snuggling with him wasn't such a bad thing. "I guess the usual suspects are behind this, huh?"

"Very likely. I didn't notice anything odd, but then, I often don't when they're using magic to hide. Did you see anything before you fell?"

"Not that I can recall, but I wasn't really looking. I was a little distracted by trying to remain vertical. It does seem like their style, though."

"You have been attacked a few times since you joined the company."

"I think I'd have to take off my socks to count the times, but my feet are too cold for that right now."

"Are you still cold? I could warm the house up a little more or get you another blanket."

I had to fight myself to keep from laughing at his tone, which was so concerned it was almost frantic. "I'm fine, really. In an hour or so, I'll even be ready to go home and get packed for tomorrow. Relax."

We ordered a pizza for dinner and ate in front of the fire, Owen tossing Loony the occasional bite of meat as he briefed me on the upcoming holiday. "I know I make them sound terrifying, but James and

Gloria really aren't that bad. They'll be nice to you. I don't think you have anything to worry about. I did tell you they dress for dinner, though, didn't I?" I nodded. "And they don't believe in hanging around the house in your pajamas. They're fully dressed before they leave their bedroom."

"That's good to know," I said, omitting the fact that Rod had already briefed me on that detail. "Y'all don't have any weird traditions I need to know about, do you?"

"Nothing I can think of, but then I don't know what you might think of as weird." I knew if our positions were reversed, my brothers would be likely to invent traditions to put him through and make him think were a normal part of our holidays, but somehow I doubted his foster parents would do anything like that.

When I couldn't delay getting home anymore, he insisted on walking me to my door, in case the sidewalks decided to swallow me. I was late getting to bed after wrapping up my packing. I doubted I'd get much sleep, anyway, what with my nervousness about the next day and the likelihood I'd end up reliving the day's adventures.

Sure enough, as soon as I tried to shut my eyes, I was right back on that ice rink, enjoying the blissful moment when I felt like I was living a scene from a favorite romantic Christmas movie and then reliving the sudden terror of plunging through the ice. The memory was vividly painful, and as it flashed before my eyes, I could swear I recalled a hint of silvery sparkles in the air just before I fell.

I sat bolt upright in bed, shouting, "Ethelinda!" Fortunately, my roommates were out of town so I didn't have to explain that. I wanted to bang my head against the wall in frustration at it having taken so long to dawn on me. It was the kind of semi-disastrous thing she might try, given what I'd seen from her at the tavern the other night. To give her credit, it had worked, in a way. Me falling through the ice had given Owen the chance to play both rescuer and comforter, and we'd had some quality snuggling time in the aftermath.

On the other hand, it could have been dangerous for both of us, and what was the deal with setting up a situation where I became a victim and he had to rescue me? Besides, hadn't I told her I didn't want her interfering?

I was tempted to get out the locket and call her so I could give her a piece of my mind, but I didn't know if she worked nights, and it would be just like her to answer my summons while I was at Owen's foster parents' home. No, it was best to leave her out of this until after the holiday. In the meantime, I'd keep my eyes peeled for any signs of silvery sparkles.

Late the next morning, after a train ride during which Owen grew more and more jittery, we stepped off the train onto a platform in a bare-bones station that consisted of little more than cement platforms on either side of the tracks. Owen carried our bags down a flight of steps, then paused to look around. In a parking lot across the street, someone standing by a car waved. Owen nodded and headed over.

The car was a Volvo wagon, several years old but in mint condition, without so much as a door ding. Beside it stood a tall, slender man wearing a dark hat and coat. He looked like the Hollywood stereotype of the perfect, proper English butler, the kind who runs the household and keeps his clueless employer out of trouble. Owen hadn't mentioned servants, but I shouldn't have been surprised, as rich as these people supposedly were.

But then Owen reached him and the man shook his hand fondly. It looked like that was as close to a hug as this man ever got. Up close, I could see that he was quite old, with pale, watery blue eyes and skin that looked almost translucent with age.

"Katie, I'd like you to meet James Eaton," Owen said. "James, this is my friend and colleague, Katie Chandler."

James gave me a smile that was warm and genuine, even if it wasn't all that broad. His face looked like it might shatter if he tried a broad grin.

He clasped my hand in both of his own and said, "I'm pleased you could join us for the holiday, Katie." He had a clipped Yankee accent with perfect enunciation.

"Thank you so much for having me," I replied, trying and failing to fight my own accent. So far, this man didn't seem to be a monster, and either he was fully human or a being that looked human because I didn't see anything odd.

James turned to Owen. "I hope you don't mind driving," he said. "My eyes aren't what they used to be."

"Not at all," Owen replied. "Let me get our bags loaded." James handed him the keys, and he put our bags in the back of the car. While he did that, James opened the door to the backseat and got inside. Owen opened the front passenger door for me, then once I was inside, he went around to the driver's side, where he had to adjust the seat before starting the car.

The road from the station into town was so steep I thought I'd have to get out and help push the car up it. It was a good thing there was no ice or there would have been no way to get up that hill. The buildings that lined the road were stair-stepped into the hill, which gave them a quaint appearance. The town itself looked like something out of a storybook, complete with the fairy fluttering down the sidewalk with shopping bags over her arm. Gnomes tended the grounds in front of the gothic town hall, looking very much like those in that store window we'd seen the day before.

"You've got quite the magical population here," I remarked. "Or is it this way in all the towns in this part of the world?"

"This particular village was settled by magical folk," James said. "Almost everyone in town is magical or somehow associated with magic."

I tried not to gawk as we drove through the village center, turned onto a major road, and then turned again to go up yet another steep hill. Most of the homes seemed to be fairly old and fairly large, on spacious, well-groomed lots dotted with mature trees. Owen turned onto a side street, then into a driveway, whose wrought-iron gates swung open at our approach.

The Eatons' home looked like one of those elaborate gingerbread houses hotel pastry chefs do for display during the holidays. It was an ornate Victorian built from warm brown brick, with lots of peaks, eaves, chimneys, and green-painted woodwork. The icing of snow on the roof added to the gingerbread effect. All it was missing was a row of gumdrops along the roof ridges. "Oh, what a wonderful house," I said in awe.

"Yes, it is quite the Victorian pile of bricks," James said. "And in case you were wondering, we're not the original owners." I turned just in time to catch the twinkle in his eye, and I couldn't help but smile back. I decided that I liked him.

Owen pulled into a detached garage that looked like it once must have been a carriage house. It was perfectly neat and organized rather than being the repository for junk that garages tend to be. That was my first sense of what I might be getting into. James's relative friendliness and good humor had lulled me into complacency, but anyone who kept a garage neat enough that you could have a party in there was someone to be reckoned with.

My next hint that this wasn't going to be anything like my visits home came when we went around to the front door to enter the house. Back home, we always came in through the kitchen. Our front door may have gone years without being opened. The entry foyer of this house was wide and floored with dark, polished wood overlaid with an antique Oriental rug. An equally polished staircase with an intricately carved banister twisted its way from the back of the foyer up to the next floor. James took off his hat, revealing a thinning shock of white hair, then took my coat and hat from me as Owen took care of his own coat in a closet under the stairs.

There was a snuffling sound, and soon a black Lab came into the foyer from an adjacent room. It breathed as though it was running full speed, but moved at a snail's pace, its tail wagging feebly. The white around its muzzle indicated that in dog years it was about as old as James was. The dog made a painfully slow beeline to Owen, who moved to meet it halfway, then knelt and scratched its head fondly. "So you do remember me, Arawn," he said.

James sniffed. "Of course he remembers you. When you leave he'll stare out the front window for a couple of days like he's hoping you'll come back. You spoiled him when he was a puppy." It was the first hint of the disapproval Owen had mentioned when he told me about his strained relationship with his foster parents, but I thought James's tone was more fond than critical. Judging by what I knew about how long dogs like that lived—I'd had one very much like Arawn when I was growing up—this one must have been a puppy around the time Owen was in his late teens, maybe just before he went off to college.

The dog finished greeting Owen and came over to investigate me. Even if I managed to screw up with Owen's foster parents, I was pretty sure I could make a good impression on his dog. I bent and patted his head the way my old Lab used to like. This one increased the speed of his tail wagging, which I took as a sign of approval.

Then a voice rang in from another room. "James? Are you back from the station already?"

Both James and Owen automatically snapped to attention. Even the dog moved into the position you'd expect him to assume if you shouted, "Sit!" and faced in the direction from which the voice had come. I started to get a sense of why Owen was so nervous.

Eight

"We've just arrived," James called out, then he said more quietly to us, "This way." Owen followed him, looking like he was heading to his own execution, and the dog trotted faithfully at Owen's heels. I grabbed the tin of homemade cookies I'd brought as a hostess gift from my bag, then brought up the rear, feeling more than a bit nervous, myself. I'd seen Owen in all kinds of scary situations, including an all-out magical battle involving monsters out of my worst nightmares, and I'd never seen him look this anxious.

The woman who stood waiting in the parlor was certainly formidable. She looked like the kind of character Katharine Hepburn played in her later years—the crusty, sharp-tongued, aristocratic octogenarian who turned out to have a warm, gooey center. It remained to be seen how gooey this woman was inside. She was tall—almost as tall as Owen, even with the shrinkage and slight stoop of age—and angular, with almost no hint of softness anywhere on her body. She had the kind of white hair that looks like it once was red, pulled up in a tight bun on top of her head, and her blue eyes were so sharp and piercing that I wouldn't have been at all surprised to find that one of her powers was X-ray vision.

She swept those all-seeing eyes past each of us. I got the sense she was collecting data to analyze later. The whole time, she stood totally still. If it hadn't been for her eyes, I might have thought she was carved from granite. Or maybe ice.

But then she suddenly melted as her face softened into a smile. She stepped forward, took Owen by the shoulders, and kissed him on the cheek. He looked like he might faint at any moment, while James did the kind of double take Bob Hope built a career on. Even the dog made a funny little "whuh?" sound.

Just as abruptly, her eyes focused on me. It took every ounce of will I had not to step backward. "You must be Katie," she said, clipping her words brusquely.

"Yes ma'am," I said, fighting off the urge to curtsy. "Thank you so much for having me." I thrust my tin of cookies toward her and tried to keep my hands from visibly shaking. "These are for you."

"You're quite welcome," she said as she took the tin from me. "And thank you." I wished I could tell if her tone was particularly frosty or if that was the way she always talked. I'd felt warmer right after I fell through the ice than I did with her looking at me like that. She turned back to Owen and softened again. "Did you have a good trip?"

"It—it was fine." He darted a glance at his foster father, and the two of them exchanged baffled looks.

She didn't seem to notice, or if she did, she pointedly ignored it. "You'll want to get settled in. Lunch will be in half an hour." Then she swept out of the room, and Owen gestured with a twitch of his head that we should follow her. Out in the foyer, he picked up our bags and had to hurry to catch up with Gloria, who was halfway up the stairs. Arawn settled himself at the foot of the stairs. I had to step over him to run up after Gloria and Owen. I now knew where Owen had learned his rapid walking pace.

"Katie, you'll be in the blue guest room," Gloria said as I reached the top of the stairs. Without waiting for me to respond, she turned to the right and led me down a short hallway to a room that overlooked the front lawn. "You have your own bathroom through that door. Towels are laid out for you. There are empty hangers in the closet, and you may use the top drawer of the bureau. Let me know if there's anything you need." I was still opening my mouth to respond when she left the room. Owen set my bag down in front of the bureau and then followed her. I could hear her voice in the hallway, sounding softer and gentler now, as she said to him, "You'll be in your old room, of course. I have it ready for you."

The room I'd been assigned was furnished in delicate, feminine antiques, with pale blue floral wallpaper, white lace curtains, and a blue-and-white quilt on the four-poster bed. Because I had a feeling Gloria would check, I unpacked my bag and arranged everything as neatly as possible. Then I freshened up a bit to make myself presentable for lunch.

It was still about fifteen minutes before the appointed lunchtime, so I left the room in search of Owen. His room turned out to be almost directly across the hall from mine, and I noticed that the hallway floorboards creaked loudly. I doubted it would be a factor in this visit, but any nighttime crossing of the hallway would require great caution. We had a similar squeaky spot in our house back home, so I was used to treading carefully.

Owen's room looked less like a showplace out of a bed-and-breakfast in a travel magazine and more like a room someone had actually lived in. There was a twin bed shoved into a corner. Most of the walls in the room were covered in bookcases, some of them with trophies lined up on top of them. Several books were already scattered on the bed and on the floor by the bed. Sometimes I suspected books automatically jumped off the shelf whenever Owen entered a room.

Owen sat on the bed, looking at two of the books as though he was cross-referencing something. His overnight bag stood open on the floor in front of the closet, a shirt hanging halfway out of it, like he'd been sidetracked while unpacking.

I tapped lightly on the door frame, and his head snapped up guiltily.

Then he saw me and relaxed. "Oh, I thought for a second you might be Gloria. I guess I'd better finish unpacking."

He got up to get back to work, and I took his spot on the bed. I glanced at the books he'd been reading, but neither was in English. From inside the closet he said, "I'd tell you not to worry about Gloria because she's not always this way, but it wouldn't be true."

I knew I should tell him that there had been nothing to worry about, but that wasn't true, either. Instead I said, "It seemed like she gave you a bit of a shock."

"A big shock. She may have kissed me one other time in my life, but I can't think of a specific incident." He came back out into the room, his face stark white. "Oh God, you don't think she's dying, do you?"

As old as Gloria seemed to be, that probably wasn't entirely out of the question, but the idea here was to reassure him. "I'm sure it's nothing. You said things were better at Thanksgiving."

He sat heavily on the bed, a necktie hanging from one hand. "Maybe that's when she got the diagnosis."

"Or maybe it's what I said after Thanksgiving, that she knows how to deal with you now that you're an adult."

"You don't know how weird this is."

"I got the picture when James looked like he thought she'd lost it. And if he thinks this is odd, then surely there's not something seriously wrong with her. He'd know, wouldn't he?"

Some of the color returned to his face. "That's true. She might not tell him everything that's going on, but she doesn't drive, so he'd be the one taking her to any doctor's appointments." He glanced down at the necktie he held, as if just realizing that he'd let himself be sidetracked again.

While he returned to the closet to finish unpacking, I decided to distract him. "Your dog seems like a real sweetie."

"Yeah, we got him not long before I left home, when he was only a few weeks old. James is right, I did spoil him then, and they were stuck with a very attention-hungry puppy when I left."

"He's a Lab. He would have been attention-hungry no matter what you did. But he does seem a lot smarter than the dog I had. Cletus was as dumb as a box of rocks."

He came back out into the room, grinning, and sat beside me on the bed. "Cletus? Seriously?"

"Seriously. Remember, I am from Texas, and that name really fit that dog."

Still grinning, he stood and extended a hand to me. "Want the grand tour before lunch?"

I took his hand and let him pull me to my feet. He led me, still holding my hand, out into the hallway and toward the stairs. "Over on that end of the house is James and Gloria's room and the other guest room," he explained. Arawn perked up and started wagging his tail when he saw us coming down the stairs. "You've already seen the parlor." At the bottom of the stairs, the dog joined us as we went to the back of the house. "And this is James's study." The study door was open, and I saw that James was in there, reading by the fireplace. The room looked a lot like Owen's office, cluttered with books and papers.

James looked up at us. "Ah, you're all settled in, then?"

"Yes, sir," I said.

He addressed Owen, a slight twinkle in his eye. "I trust everything was the way you left it at Thanksgiving. I wouldn't let her put away those books because I had a feeling you were onto something."

"I appreciate that," Owen said. "It wasn't anything important, though, just a passing thought."

"Some of the greatest innovations come from passing thoughts."

With great fascination, I watched the two of them talk. They might not have been blood relatives, but they were very much alike. It was a good argument for the "nurture" side of the nature vs. nurture debate. Still, there was something odd about their interaction. James was certainly friendly enough to Owen, but he regarded him more the way he might a work colleague he was on good terms with than he would someone who was the closest thing he had to a son. It was a miracle Owen was as sane as he was, having grown up in a home where he was treated like a guest, even if he was a welcome guest.

James glanced at the clock on the mantel and said, "Lunchtime. Let's not be late." He appeared to struggle a little to get out of his chair, but he shook his head firmly when Owen moved to help him.

Arawn followed us to the dining room, then sat in the doorway without entering the room. "He's not allowed inside," Owen explained. "He used to beg at the table, so he was banished."

"And who taught him that habit?" James muttered with a hint of a smile. I had to bite my lip to hold back a giggle as I recalled the way Owen was always giving his cat food off the table. He apparently hadn't learned his lesson.

The dining room almost took my breath away. It looked like a room on display in one of those historical homes, preserved the way the famous family had once lived there, complete with antique period furnishings and museum-quality china. The china wasn't just in a display case, either. It was set on the table in place settings right out of an Emily Post book. I got the feeling this wasn't going to be a soup-and-sandwich lunch. Rod had warned me that the Eatons were formal, but this was more than I expected. My mom certainly had nice china, but it came out of the china cabinet only on major holidays. I wondered if they ate like this all the time.

"You didn't have to go to all this trouble," Owen said. I could see the struggle in his face as he tried not to sound critical.

"Nonsense," Gloria replied in a tone just short of snappish. "You're company, and you've even brought a guest. I don't get to entertain often these days, so I may as well take advantage of the opportunity." Then she turned to me and I caught myself popping to attention. "Sit wherever you like, Katie. We don't have assigned seats in this house."

I noticed James edging toward a particular chair, so I hesitated and dawdled long enough to get a sense of where the others wanted to sit be-

fore I chose a chair. As I looked at the array of dishes, glasses, and silverware, I was glad my mom had taught me all the table rules. Once we were
all situated, James said a quick grace, and then Gloria began passing serving dishes around the table.

Before I took my first bite of roasted chicken, I steeled myself for the
interrogation I was sure was about to begin. There was a tense atmo-
sphere in the room. In spite of the formal antiques, I had a sense of cold,
bare cement, one of those harsh spotlights, and an inquisitor pacing the
room in jackboots while slapping a riding crop against her palm. I tried to
remain calm and remember the answers I'd mentally prepared about my
background, my family, and my plans for the future.

But when the interrogation started, it wasn't directed at me. "Work is
going well?" Gloria asked Owen.

"Well enough," he replied evenly.

"So Idris and his ally getting away isn't causing you too many problems?"

Owen exchanged a glance with me. "You know about that?"

"We're still in the loop, even out here."

"Then, yes, it is causing us some problems. We're working to track
them down or figure out what they're up to, but leads are scarce at this
time." He looked down at his plate and picked up a forkful of food.

As soon as Owen turned his attention from her, Gloria's face softened. There was real concern in her eyes. "I'm sure you'll catch him soon
enough," she said. "When you do, will you be up to dealing with him?"

Still looking at his plate, he answered, "I believe so. I did the last
time."

"As I recall, you nearly got yourself killed the last time. Didn't you say
it was only because of Katie that you weren't hurt more seriously?"

I could feel my face growing warm at her mention, but none of them
were looking at me. "Katie's still around," James said as he served himself another helping of green beans. "It's her job to notice things like that.
That's why we recruit immunes."

"We've been assigned as a team," Owen added.

I wondered if I should chime in, but before I could think of anything to contribute to the discussion, Gloria was off on another tangent. "And what does Merlin have to say about all this?"

"It was his idea that we work together. We're trying to prepare for any possibility, whether Idris just wants to disrupt us or whether he's really trying to take over the magical world."

"What do you think he's doing?" James asked, his voice calm and neutral, but his eyes keenly focused on his foster son.

"I think he's being used. He's not the real threat. He may just be a diversion." He looked directly at them then. "You were around the last time anyone made a real bid for power. How was that dealt with? There's not a lot in the chronicles."

James and Gloria exchanged a look that made chills go up and down my spine. If I wasn't mistaken, they both looked scared to death. Owen frowned and bit his lip, which indicated he'd noticed that look, as well. They held the look for a while, and then Gloria nodded at her husband.

"The situations don't compare," James said, his voice as cool and calm as before, but with an edge underneath it. "That was a direct, obvious attempt at domination, while this appears to be a more subversive, oblique approach. We were able to take on those rogues with an all-out magical attack. Your enemy is hiding. This appears to have the makings of a magical guerrilla war."

"I doubt there's anything to learn from that particular bit of history," Gloria added, her voice gentler than before. "There's not much point in spending a lot of time studying it. You'd be better off talking to Merlin about Mordred and Morgana if you want to study the past. Would anyone care for seconds?"

It was a clear signal that that part of the conversation was over. Owen and I had barely made a dent in our food, and Gloria hadn't touched hers yet, so I doubted she really felt like she needed to offer seconds. I worked up the nerve to say, "No, thank you, but it's delicious." She then turned her laser-sharp gaze on me, as if just then remembering that I was even in the room. I instantly regretted opening my mouth.

"Katie's a pretty good cook, herself," Owen said. "She does a lot of baking."

I thought that would focus the interrogation on me, so I braced myself to describe what I could cook and how I'd learned, but she turned right back to Owen. "How is Rod doing? Is he coming home for Christmas?"

"I think he's doing okay, but I don't know what his plans are. We haven't talked much in a while."

James and Gloria exchanged another funny look, though this one wasn't as intense as the one before. "Really?" Gloria asked. "Why not?" I could have sworn that there was a hint of nervousness or uncertainty in her voice, but I couldn't imagine why that might be.

"We've been busy. We keep missing each other at the office, and he's got his usual extracurricular activities."

"You two aren't fighting, are you?"

Owen returned his attention to his plate, shoving food around with his fork. His cheeks had gone bright red. "No, nothing like that. Just life, you know?" I knew he wasn't telling the whole truth because he and Rod had fought about what had happened between Rod and me when we were under an enchantment, though they'd since worked that out. Gloria didn't look like she missed much of anything, so I was sure she also knew he was lying, but she didn't press the issue.

"You mentioned you got your hands on that Welsh codex," James said, changing the subject abruptly. Then James and Owen were off once more in an academic discussion. I ate while pretending to listen. Gloria was able to make a few comments, but mostly she just listened, too. Once when I glanced in her direction, I could have sworn her eyes glistened with tears while she looked at Owen. Maybe he was onto something about her getting a scary diagnosis.

After lunch, I overrode Gloria's objections to help clear the table, but she absolutely refused to let me help wash dishes. "You're our guest. I won't let you wash dishes until your next visit. Besides, I like washing dishes. The warm water feels good on my hands, and it helps me think. You and Owen should take Arawn for a walk." In the hallway outside the kitchen, the dog barked in agreement.

We bundled up, then took a short walk up and down the street. Owen didn't appear to be in a chatty mood, and I didn't press the point, so we walked mostly in silence. We returned to the house to find dessert being served in the parlor, with hot coffee and tea in a formal silver service.

When we'd all been served, I discovered it was finally my turn to be interrogated by Gloria. She fixed me with a measuring gaze. "So, Katie, as you can well imagine, Owen has told us next to nothing about you other than that you work together and that you're from out of town. Where were you before you came to New York?"

"I'm from a small town in Texas. I'd lived there all my life, except when I was off at school."

"And what did you do there?" Her tone wasn't nearly as sharp with me as it had been with Owen, but I still felt like I'd been hooked to a polygraph machine and this testimony was the only way I might be able to clear my name and avoid life in prison.

"My family owns a farm supply store there, and I worked in the store. I pretty much ran the business from the time I was in high school."

"Are you planning to stay in New York long?"

"I haven't been considering it a temporary thing. I love the city. I could see myself settling there." She nodded like she was happy with the answer, and then I caught her glancing toward Owen. I knew then exactly what was going on. She was a lioness with a cub. Coddling him wouldn't do him any good in the wild, so she'd be as tough with him as she had to for him to grow up strong and self-sufficient. Meanwhile, she'd defend him to the death against any possible threats, including me. It was funny that, as brilliant as Owen was about so many things, he hadn't seen this.

Then again, she only got that motherly look in her eyes when he wasn't paying attention.

She eased off on the questioning at that point, and I hoped that meant she didn't disapprove of me. I had a feeling it would be awhile before she decided to go so far as to actually approve of me, but as long as I was in neutral territory, I figured I was doing okay with her.

When we'd finished with dessert, Gloria said, "We're attending the early church service this year. We don't like to stay out too late these days. We'll have to leave by four-thirty if we want to get a good seat. That leaves us just enough time to relax a little and change clothes."

It sounded more like an order than a suggestion, so we trooped upstairs obediently. Owen looked like he needed some serious book time, so I left him to his reading and went to prop my still-chilled feet against the radiator in my room.

Just before four, I changed into my planned outfit for the evening, Gemma's cream-colored cashmere sweater and my black skirt. After I was dressed, I figured I'd better head downstairs. I got the feeling punctuality was essential in this household. I took my gifts with me to put under the Christmas tree that stood in the front window. Owen's door was still closed as I passed it, and I carefully stepped over the squeaky spot in the hallway so I wouldn't disturb him.

Downstairs in the parlor, I checked the tags on the gifts under the Christmas tree to find the appropriate piles, then added my gifts. I couldn't help but notice that there were two gifts there with my name on them. Then I sat and communed with Arawn while I waited for the others. James joined me first, and we made stiff small talk until Gloria and Owen came downstairs. Gloria then hustled us outside to the car. Owen drove, and Gloria insisted I sit in the front with him while she and James took the backseat.

The church in the heart of the village looked like something you'd see on the front of a Christmas card. It was built of stone with a snow-dusted slate roof and red-bowed evergreen wreaths on the arched front doors. The congregation, however, was like nothing I'd seen before. It was a mix of every kind of magical person I'd encountered. There was a special raised seating area near the front for the gnomes. Elves and fairies were mixed in among the humans. Gargoyles perched on the backs of pews. I wasn't sure if they were local or if they were part of the MSI security detail. The sense of power inside the church was so strong it felt like my hair was standing on end.

Once we started singing carols, I learned that Owen had a very nice singing voice. It made me self-conscious about the fact that I couldn't carry a tune in a bucket. I fought off the feelings of inadequacy that always seemed to lurk where Owen was concerned. He was so perfect, so good at almost everything, that it was often difficult to imagine him being interested in me. But he was interested and had made that clear, and he wasn't entirely perfect now that I knew him better. For one thing, he was kind of an emotional basket case, for reasons that were becoming increasingly obvious.

But that little vulnerability only made him more interesting to me. What woman could resist a handsome, wealthy, powerful, nice man who was also just a tiny bit broken inside? It meant that in spite of him seemingly having everything, there was something he still needed from me. He might have been ultrapowerful, but I couldn't help wanting to protect him.

The service ended with an announcement that there would be a reception in the church hall. "We'll make a token appearance, but we won't stay long," Gloria whispered to us as we gathered our coats and followed the crowd out of the sanctuary. The hall was in a more modern building that still wasn't very new, and it had fake walnut paneling on the walls and yellowed linoleum on the floor. It looked a lot like most church halls I'd seen. A couple of folding tables with red and green paper tablecloths on them stood down one side of the room. One held trays of Christmas cookies and cupcakes while another held a punch bowl, a tea service, and a coffee urn. As we hung our coats on pegs near the doorway, Gloria hissed, "Now, remember, just greet people, have a cookie, and then we'll go home. Don't spoil your dinner."

"She hates these things, but she feels obligated," Owen confided to me as soon as Gloria had pasted a smile on her face and moved ahead to make a circuit of the room. "She thinks social chitchat is a waste of time."

"I kind of have to agree with her there," I said, but before I could add anything, we were surrounded.

"Look at you, all grown up," said a gnome who stood craning his neck to look up at Owen. "I remember when you only came up to my shoulder."

The other locals then chimed in about how good it was to have Owen back for a visit. He blushed bashfully, but he didn't seem too taken aback. Apparently these were all people he knew and was comfortable with. I caught his eye and mimed drinking a cup of coffee, and he responded with a nod and a smile before returning to his conversation.

I made my way over to the refreshment table, where the cookies sat practically untouched. Back home, that would have been the ultimate insult to the cooks who'd made them, so I took a couple, just to be polite, of course. "And I'd thought we might not have enough," a voice behind me said. I turned to see the minister, still in the black robe he'd worn for the service. "You're a friend of the Eatons?" he asked.

"I work with Owen," I explained. "I couldn't get home for Christmas, so they invited me to join them."

He nodded, and the smile he gave me echoed the disbelief I'd seen from everyone I'd told that story. He knew I must be more than a coworker, and I was being investigated by the folks. "It's nice to see him have friends," he said, putting a funny little emphasis on the word "friends." "He was always a quiet one." He glanced over his shoulder toward the person we were talking about, then blinked. I couldn't blame him. I was pretty sure I'd blinked, too, when I followed his gaze.

The older people and creatures who'd been fussing over Owen were gone, and he was instead surrounded by a gaggle of young women who looked like they'd stumbled onto a rock star. He was backing slowly away from them, but if he didn't escape soon, they were likely to tear the clothes off him. The only thing keeping him relatively safe was the fact that the mothers of all the young women were also involved, running interference to keep the others out of the way of their daughters. Handbags flew with a fury I'd only seen before at a designer sample sale Gemma had once dragged me to.

The mob moved in my general direction, possibly because Owen instinctively headed toward me. I wasn't sure how I could help. It didn't look like that bunch was going to be fended off by me stepping up and declaring that I was his girlfriend. That would probably only make things uglier.

"Ladies, ladies," the minister urged, "this isn't the time or place." A frosted snowman cookie then splatted against his festive purple stole. I couldn't believe it. All these WASPy magical types were starting a food fight in the church hall. I hurried to get on the other side of the food table, out of the range of fire, as the women pelted each other with food. Owen wisely took advantage of the opportunity to duck under one of the tables. If I wasn't mistaken, he'd also gone invisible at the same time. I was sure I felt the tingle of magic in use.

But it was more magic than I'd expect for a simple invisibility spell. The hairs on the back of my neck stood up, and I had shivers going down my spine. That meant a lot of magic was flying around the room. I looked to see if I could find James and Gloria. James was standing in a corner, chatting with some of the other older men while drinking coffee, seemingly oblivious to the chaos—or else pointedly ignoring it. Gloria did not look amused. She was trying to drag one of the mothers away from the melee. I was impressed with the way she managed to avoid being hit by any of the flying cupcakes or cookies.

The scene was right out of a slapstick comedy. I wouldn't have been surprised if the Keystone Kops had shown up to stop the riot. And the Baptists used to accuse the Methodists back home of being wild, I thought with a grin. At least we'd never had a food fight in the fellowship hall. Well, not when it was anyone other than the kids involved. I decided that James had the right idea, so I moved to the far side of the room, well away from the fracas and near enough to the door that I could escape if I needed to.

Then while I was still fighting back giggles, the sense of magic intensified and someone grabbed me from behind.

Nine

At first I thought it was Owen, having made it safely out from under the table and ready to make his escape with me. I went willingly as he pulled me through the door to the parking lot outside. But then he didn't release me, and I realized that something was wrong. I kicked my captor in the shin and pulled away.

It was my old friend Mr. Bones, one of Idris's cronies, and now I was absolutely certain that it was the same skeleton guy I'd seen in that office. He had a bunch of his goons lined up, surrounding me.

He didn't have to tell me that screaming would do no good. The noise from the riot inside spilled into the parking lot. One more female scream wouldn't stand out in all that. Instead, I did what I did best. I bent down and scooped up a handful of slushy snow, packed it into a ball, and threw it. I needed to come up with a new trick for when I got into a tough spot, but I had a good arm and good aim, so I figured I might as well stick with what I knew for the time being. Maybe I'd sign up for a karate class when things settled down some at work.

The snowball hit Mr. Bones square in the face and some of the slush trickled into his eye socket, which couldn't have felt good. While he was still reacting, I made another snowball and threw it in the general direction of the other goons. I'd been in all of two snowball fights in my life, on the very rare occasions when we'd had enough snow to make snowballs back home in Texas, so I didn't have a lot of practice with this. The goons were closing in, and it was harder and harder to keep them at bay with snowballs.

Something came out of the sky, and I instinctively ducked. It had been my experience that some truly scary things could come at you from out of the sky. This time, though, it looked like the air force was friendly. Two unfamiliar gargoyles swooped around, keeping themselves between the goons and me. "You'd better make a run for it, miss," one of them shouted as it flew past me. "We don't got a lot in the way of attack magic."

"Yeah, just staying animated takes a lot out of us," the other said.

"Bein' a gargoyle ain't easy," the first one said.

"Watch it, you idiot!" the other called out when they almost collided in midair. After the near miss, both of them laughed so hard they almost fell out of the sky.

These gargoyles were keeping the goons from getting to me, but I was still surrounded. I wasn't sure how long the gargoyles could hold them off. I made another snowball and took aim at the goon that was between me and the door to the church hall. If I could just create a gap in that circle and make a break for it, I was sure I'd be safe inside, surrounded by Owen, Gloria, James, and a whole bunch of presumably friendly magical people. I could even kill two birds with one snowball by creating a distraction to break up the fight inside and rescue Owen from the horde of matchmaking mamas.

Then the church hall doors flew open and a lone figure tore outside like the hounds of hell were on his heels. It was Owen, and just as I recognized him, so did Mr. Bones and his goons. I shouted a warning, but not before the goons had forgotten about me and turned their attention to Owen. I wondered if that had been the plan all along, to use me as bait to capture him.

I was worried because although he was pretty powerful with magic, it could also be used on him. The air zinged with magic as they threw spells at him and he deflected them. I tried to pitch in by throwing a few more snowballs, and the two gargoyles kept trying to create a distraction, but it was still many against essentially one.

Not for long, though. Owen wasn't going to get away from the mob that easily, and soon the mothers and their man-hungry daughters spilled out of the hall, in search of their quarry. I wasn't sure what they thought was going on in the parking lot, but they reacted as though yet another party was trying to steal Owen from them, and they turned their efforts against the bad guys. Mr. Bones found himself beaten soundly by high-end designer handbags. A few of the women were still fighting each other, but there was enough confusion for Owen to get away from the attackers and catch my arm as we ran for James and Gloria's car.

I was surprised to find James and Gloria already there, wearing their coats. Gloria had our coats over her arm, and she handed them to us when we reached them. "Honestly, Owen," she scolded gently while she helped him with his coat. "That's not the way I taught you to behave in public."

James helped me with my coat, saying, "I hardly think we can blame the boy for all that nonsense."

"It was magic," I said. "It must have been that influence spell Idris likes to use, making them act that way. It created the perfect distraction for his goons to drag me outside."

"But it backfired on him," Owen put in. "Those crazy women saved our lives. If they hadn't been chasing me, I don't know what would have happened."

"I'm sure you could have handled the situation," Gloria said. "Now, get in the car and let's get home. I said we didn't want to stay long, and now you see why. These socials never go well."

Dinner was a lot less awkward and uncomfortable than lunch had been. The events at the church social gave us plenty of conversational fodder. Owen looked like he would have been happy discussing anything other than what a good marriage prospect the women in town thought he'd make, but I was relieved to see that Gloria apparently thought none of those women were good enough for her boy. I couldn't tell how much she approved of me, but at least she didn't have a prospective bride already picked out from among her neighbors' daughters.

When we'd finished eating, I helped clear the table and offered once more to help with the dishes, but Gloria shook her head sternly. "They'll wait until morning," she said. "James and I are ready to turn in, but you two young people are welcome to stay up as late as you like."

"Just don't stay up late enough to catch Santa Claus in the act," James added with a wink. "He doesn't like that."

Owen and I went back to the parlor and sat by the fire, side by side on the formal velvet sofa. It was as good as a chaperone, since it was the kind of sofa that forces you to sit up straight and behave properly. I couldn't imagine snuggling on that sofa. Arawn lay contentedly at Owen's feet and promptly went to sleep. "Well, that was an experience," I said.

"I hope I don't have to tell you that church socials here aren't always like that." He sighed. "And now I'll be the focus of gossip for months. Gloria and James will have to visit me in the city because it won't be safe for me here."

"And the city is that much safer? You know, with our enemies out to get us, and all? Now I'm definitely sure that skeleton guy is the same one I saw in the office the other day."

"So, Idris is teamed up with the descendant of someone who stole Philip's family business a hundred years ago?"

"Maybe. Mr. Bones could be freelancing. These people could be Idris's customers. They probably wouldn't have issues with shady magic. I just find it odd. It's something to think about."

"Yeah. Just what we need, another puzzle piece that doesn't quite fit. Instead of making the picture clearer, it only confuses the issue."

We sat by the fire a little longer, stewing over this new information, then he said, "We should probably get to bed. They're very early risers."

"And like James said, we wouldn't want to disturb Santa Claus."

As we left the parlor, he paused in the doorway. "Hey, mistletoe," he said.

Before I could look up to verify that there was, in fact, mistletoe hanging there, he'd bent to give me a firm kiss. I returned it, wrapping my arms around his neck. "Merry Christmas," he whispered.

"And merry Christmas, yourself," I whispered back. "But I don't remember any mistletoe there."

"Look."

I glanced over our heads and saw a sprig of mistletoe with a red ribbon around it hanging suspended in the air over our heads. "Isn't that cheating?" I asked.

"Are you complaining?"

"No, I'll let this one slide."

We kissed again, then he pulled away. "I have to walk the dog one more time before bed, so you go on up."

"Do you need any company?"

"No, I'll be fine. It'll only take a few minutes. Arawn doesn't like being outside in the cold any more than I do. I'll see you in the morning."

He got his coat and went outside, the dog following happily at his heels. I went upstairs, trying to be as quiet as possible. When I reached the top of the stairs, I heard voices coming from the first room that opened from the left of the stairs. I knew eavesdropping was a bad idea, but I was curious. Gloria's voice carried clearly, saying, "I don't see why we have to continue that way. Things have certainly changed since the rules were established."

James was more soft-spoken, so all I could hear was the fact that he was speaking. I couldn't make any words out. Then Gloria spoke again, apparently responding. "What harm does it do? It's not as though they can take him away from us at this point. He's not even under our control any longer. It's entirely up to him and to us whether we want to remain in contact."

James spoke again, and I caught the word "responsibility," but not its context.

"Well, yes, of course," Gloria responded. "But surely it's too late to have much of an impact, one way or another. He's turned out the way he's going to turn out, for better or worse."

I knew I should move on. This was none of my business. But I couldn't resist lingering at the top of the stairs. I was too curious.

James said something else, far too softly for me to hear anything more than the rumble of his voice. When she responded, Gloria's voice had a strained quality to it. "I simply think that in these times what he needs is to know that he's not alone. You saw what happened tonight. They really are after him. The girl may be able to help, but she could also be a distraction."

That made me even more curious. Was I the girl she mentioned? And what was I supposed to help with, other than spotting disguised magical beasties so Owen could deal with them? The idea of me being a distraction was more unsettling. The voices grew too muffled for me to make out more words, and I didn't think I wanted Owen to catch me eavesdropping, so I went on to my room, puzzled about what I'd heard.

Although it was more than an hour before I usually went to bed, the travel and stress of the past thirty-six or so hours, not to mention the rapidly fading adrenaline from the excitement earlier in the evening, added up to me falling asleep pretty quickly. I wasn't sure how long I'd been asleep when I was awakened by a strange clattering sound and a glowing light coming through the windows.

I didn't recall a Times Square–rivaling light display at the house across the street, and my room had been perfectly dark when I went to bed, so the light was something new. My pulse immediately quickened. Although I'd known the truth about Santa Claus for nearly twenty years, thanks to my older brothers, there was still a childlike part of me deep down inside that wanted to hold on to the belief. I couldn't help but listen for the sound of sleighbells or hoofbeats on the roof on Christmas Eve night, and I always had the sense that if I was awake at the right time, I might see something magical. Now that I knew magic was real, it didn't seem like such a farfetched idea anymore. If there really was something like a Santa Claus who managed to sneak in and out without being detected, I of all people should be able to see it.

As the old poem went, I sprang from my bed to see what was the matter. Away to the window I flew like a flash, and all that. But when I opened the curtains (there weren't any shutters), what I saw wasn't a miniature sleigh and eight tiny reindeer or a little old elf. I saw a hovering fairy godmother dressed like Mrs. Claus in threadbare red velvet with sooty white fur trim along the collar and cuffs.

I wanted to pull the curtains closed again and ignore her, but I was worried that the racket she was making—which turned out to be caused by her shooting silver sparks at my window from her wand—would disturb Gloria and James. Reluctantly, I put on my bathrobe, then opened the window, shivering as the freezing outside air gushed into the room. "What do you want?" I asked, not even trying to sound welcoming.

She shook her head and tsk-tsked. "It's not about what I want. It's about what you want."

"I don't want anything, other than sleep. In fact, things are going better than I expected, aside from a minor magical attack, and I don't think you can take credit for that. I'm getting along with his folks, and Owen and I seem to be doing just fine. You can go off and take a nice Christmas holiday."

"Ah, but I would have thought this visit raised a few questions for you. Such as what it means to him to have the power he has and how that will affect his future."

I had to admit to some curiosity about those matters, especially given what I'd recently overheard. "I'm not thinking about that now, though," I said. "I'm thinking about sleep and not being caught with a fairy godmother. That's not a way to win over the parents."

"They wouldn't see me," she said with a haughty sniff. "Give me that much credit."

"Can we talk about this later, when we're back in the city and it's not the middle of the night?"

"If you insist. I'll be in touch." As she winked out of existence I realized I could have asked her about the ice rink incident, but that could wait for later. It sounded like I was going to have to talk with her, like it or not, if I ever wanted to get rid of her.

I closed the window and the curtains, then turned to head back to bed and nearly bit my tongue in two as I tried to keep from screaming out loud. A small creature with a feather duster in its hand stood on top of the chest of drawers. I managed not to scream, but I did jump and squeak a little. I must have startled the creature, for it, too, jumped and squeaked, and then it froze, as though it hoped I might not notice it.

Keeping my eyes on it, I edged my way back to the bed. "What are you doing in here?" I asked in a whisper.

The creature blinked in surprise. "You can see me?" it asked. I would have expected something that small to have a high, squeaky voice, but its voice was rough and husky, as though it had smoked a couple of packs of cigarettes a day for a couple of hundred years.

"I'm a magical immune," I explained. "Your veiling spell doesn't work on me. But you haven't answered my question. Who are you and what are you doing in my room?" In my dealings with the magical world, I'd yet to run into anything like this. There was something elfin about its features, but it was to the elves who worked at MSI what a raisin is to a grape—shrunken, shriveled, and brown. It had long, wispy white hair and wore a shapeless brown garment with an apron tied around its waist. I might have guessed it was a female, but these days it's dangerous to make assumptions like that based on hairstyle and stereotypical gender roles.

"I keep house for the family," it (she?) said. "But no one's supposed to know. Mistress Gloria would be most upset if her secret were out." She rolled her Rs and had the slightest trace of a Scottish accent. "You won't go tellin', will ye?"

There was something vaguely familiar about this situation, an old story I'd once heard. I had a mental image of sitting in a circle of girls while wearing a brown beanie. "Hey, you're a brownie!" I said. One of the first things we'd done at my very first Brownie scout meeting was listen to the story about the helpful little creatures who worked in the night.

The brownie rolled her eyes. "Of course I am. What would you think, that I was a fairy godmother like your friend there?" Then she looked concerned again. "You won't be tellin', will ye?"

"No, of course not. Though I think it would actually make her son feel better if he knew she had help. He's worried about her."

She frowned in thought—at least, I thought she was frowning; as wrinkled as her face was, it was difficult to tell—then said, "Fine. He can know once you're gone, but he mustn't let on he knows. The mistress couldn't bear that."

"Have you worked here long?"

She went back to her dusting, talking as she worked, "Oh, I lose count of the years. The boy was just a wee thing when I came to this house. I'd known the mistress before, though, and she gave me a home when my own was torn down. This is my way of makin' it up to her for her kindness." She gave the mirror a final swipe. "Well, now, I have dishes to do, and you'll be needin' your sleep." She disappeared before I could tell her good night or wish her a merry Christmas. As I settled back onto the pillow, I wondered what was next. At this rate, Saint Nick would have needed Rudolph and the Grinch with him to be the oddest sight of my night.

Fortunately, I was able to sleep the rest of the night without any magical interruptions. I woke early the next morning, my subconscious too afraid of annoying Gloria to let me sleep late. I dressed in Gemma's red sweater and a pair of black slacks, put on a touch of makeup, then opened my bedroom door and stuck my head out into the hallway to try to get a sense of the situation. Owen's bedroom door was still closed, which made me hesitate to go downstairs. I didn't want to be alone with James and Gloria, and the faint sound of voices downstairs told me they were up. They'd been nice enough so far, but I wasn't sure I was yet ready for a lot of alone time with them. On the other hand, I didn't want to be the last one downstairs.

This looked like a good time to make use of that squeaky board in the hallway. I took a deep breath and stepped outside my room, aiming for the spot that would make noise and hopefully signal to Owen that I was up and about. But just as I hit the squeaky board, Owen's door opened and I found myself face-to-face with him. I didn't have fast enough reflexes to stifle my yelp. Owen caught my arm to steady me when I wobbled. "Sorry, didn't mean to startle you," he said.

"How do you do that?" I blurted.

A flush rose from his collar to his hairline. "I don't know. Maybe it's subconscious. I honestly don't plan it."

"Are you two up?" Gloria's voice called from downstairs.

"We're on our way down right now," Owen replied. He then held his arm out to me. "Shall we?"

Gloria had a light breakfast of sweet rolls laid out on the dining table, which was set with china. I had a feeling the brownie had something to do with that. I couldn't help thinking how great it would be to have one of those.

After we ate, we went into the parlor, where James and Gloria took seats on the sofa. I imagined they'd have a difficult time getting down on the floor, and a more difficult time getting up again. Owen settled himself cross-legged on the floor by the tree, and I joined him. It seemed that their custom was for Owen to hand the appropriate packages up to his foster parents.

"This one's for the two of you from Katie," he said, handing Gloria my package. My heart instantly started beating faster. My humble handmade offering suddenly seemed entirely inadequate.

However, Gloria was more than gracious when she opened it. "This is lovely, thank you," she said, her words almost thawing around the edges. "Did you do this yourself?"

"Yes, ma'am. It's one of the ways I work off stress, other than baking."

"It's very nice. I used to do needlework, but my hands and eyes aren't quite up to it anymore."

Owen's gifts to his parents, which I'd helped him pick out, were big hits, and he even gave me credit for helping with the selection. Owen was equally pleased with the muffler I gave him, jauntily tossing it around his neck and over his shoulder even though the room was quite warm. I was even warmer, thanks to the way he smiled at me as he thanked me. The room temperature shot up a few more degrees when he gave me his gift to me.

It was a delicate locket, oval instead of heart-shaped like Ethelinda's, and the chain looked almost fragile. "Wow, it's beautiful," I said when I opened the box. And it was, but it was also a little uncomfortable opening something like that in front of his folks. Jewelry generally meant you'd moved pretty far along in a relationship.

Apparently, Owen was conscious of the same thing. He turned an impressive shade of red and hurried to say, "It's not the locket itself that's important. It does have some gold in it because that's essential for the spell to work, but the important part is the spell. If it works correctly, it should amplify your sensation of magic being in use nearby. Since you don't see illusion, you might not know that there are layers over reality that other people see. I know you're getting better about feeling the use of power, but this should help, and it doesn't matter whether you're immune or not. The locket reacts directly with the magic in use and responds in a way that you'll feel."

"That's kind of cool. I wouldn't dare wear it at work, though. I'd be buzzing all day."

"It shouldn't hurt," he clarified, "But yeah, you'd probably want to save it for times when you're away from the office or away from known magic users, in general."

James looked as fascinated by the idea as I was. "Was that something you found in—" he started to ask, but Gloria cut him off.

"Not now, dear. You and Owen can talk shop later. We're opening presents at the moment."

Owen leaned over and took the locket out of the box. "Here, put it on, and then we can test it." I lifted my hair from the back of my neck so he could fasten the clasp, and the touch of his fingers on that already sensitive spot sent the rest of my nerve endings into overdrive. It was a good thing that wasn't the kind of magic the locket amplified, or I'd have exploded on the spot. As it was, I was fairly sure there would be no more pretending to Gloria that we were nothing more than co-workers. She was sharp, and she had to have noticed the steam coming out of my ears and the way I couldn't help but squirm when he touched me.

When I opened James and Gloria's gift to me, I was sure Gloria had never been fooled. They gave me a basket of beautiful woolen yarns, and that meant Owen must have told them a lot about me. I may have mentioned once in passing during our morning commute that I sometimes liked to knit, so if he noticed and passed on that kind of detail, Gloria would have to have known there was something going on.

"This is gorgeous, and so soft," I said. "Thank you."

"Use it to make something for yourself," Gloria instructed. "That's why I got the rose color. I doubted you'd be tempted to use that to make a gift for anyone else." She glanced meaningfully at Owen as she said that, and I had to fight back a giggle at the thought of him wearing a rose sweater.

We'd barely done away with the wrapping paper and ribbons when the doorbell rang. Gloria insisted on answering the door herself. A moment later, she came back to the parlor with a young woman. "Owen, you remember Rebecca Middleton, don't you?"

He stood, and out of manners and curiosity I also rose. The guest was tall and thin, with the kind of build that probably had made her something of a beanpole in her teens. She held a loaf-shaped object wrapped in colored cellophane, and she wasn't the least bit shy about giving Owen the eye. "Here, I brought you some of Mom's banana bread for Christmas," she said. "And sorry about last night. I don't know what came over me."

Gloria thanked her for the bread, then very pointedly thanked her for stopping by before gently escorting her to the door. "At least that girl has finally filled out," she said as she returned to the parlor "She's improved, but she had a lot of room for improvement." I decided I quite liked Gloria.

"Please don't send that banana bread back with me," Owen said with a shudder. "She brought enough of it over when we were in school that I think I developed an allergy to it."

The next time the doorbell rang, Gloria was in the kitchen preparing Christmas dinner. Judging by the tingling around my neck, I suspected she was using a few magical shortcuts, and that was why she'd declined help. Owen answered the door and soon returned bearing a fruitcake tin and bright red cheeks. "It was Stephanie Heller," he said to James. "She asked me to tell you to have a merry Christmas, and she's sorry about last night."

"At this rate, we'll have baked goods to last us until Easter," James remarked drily. That only intensified the flush on Owen's cheeks.

I went along with Owen the next time the doorbell rang. Soon after he opened the door to reveal a mother and daughter, he put his arm around me and pulled me up against him like he was using me as a human shield. I could hardly blame him. That mother looked pretty scary. I recognized her as the one who'd thrown the first cookie in the fight. The way the daughter stood with her eyes cast to the ground, I got the impression that the mother had dragged her over by the ear. Mother seemed to be the one who was keen on her girl snagging the local hot catch. The chain around my neck throbbed, which made me wonder if she was attempting to use magic on him. No wonder he was using me as a shield.

"Mrs. Ellis," he said, his voice sounding tight. "How nice of you to stop by. I'm afraid James and Gloria are busy right now."

"Oh, that's okay," she simpered. In that moment she reminded me of Ethelinda. "I can see them anytime. They are neighbors. I'm just glad to see you." She elbowed her daughter, who thrust out a napkin-covered basket. Owen kept his arms tight around me, so I took the basket from her. Her mother elbowed her again.

"Are you going to be here long?" the daughter asked stiffly. As bashful as she looked, she might have been the perfect match for Owen, aside from the scary mother. I noted that neither of them had yet apologized for all but attacking Owen the night before.

"No, we're going back to the city tomorrow," Owen replied. "Thanks for coming by." He barely waited until they stepped back from the door before reaching around me and closing it. Then he shuddered. "That woman is scarier than any harpy I've faced. I'm amazed her daughter hasn't snapped yet."

"Who was it this time?" James asked from behind a book when we found him hiding in his study.

"Mrs. Ellis. And what was her daughter's name?"

"I have no earthly idea. She can barely get a word in edgewise with her mother around. What's our haul looking like?"

I checked under the napkin. "Blueberry muffins."

"We should have you to visit more often, my boy," James said.

We'd just sat down for Christmas dinner when the doorbell rang again. "I thought we were out of neighbors with marriageable daughters," Gloria muttered as she started to get up.

"I'll take care of this one," James said, motioning her to keep her seat. "I hope this time it's cookies."

But a moment later, he called, "Owen, Katie!" and there was an urgency to his voice that told me this wasn't about baked goods or over-eager women after Owen.

We got up and went to the foyer, where Sam sat perched on the banister newel. "You two have to get back to the city right away," he said.

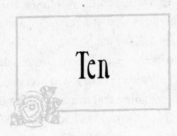

Ten

"What is it?" I asked.

Owen answered for Sam. "Idris. I knew it. I knew he'd hit on Christmas. Last night must have been just a diversion. I never should have left town."

"Whoa, hold your horses, kids," Sam said, holding his hands out with a "stop!" motion. "I didn't say it was a disaster, and I don't think you bein' in town would have made much of a difference. The boss just wants you back ASAP so you can get a read on things and start formulating a disaster-control plan first thing in the morning."

"So nobody's dead, bleeding, or in danger?" I asked to clarify things.

"Nothing scary yet, but it's a doozy, believe me."

"It's a couple of hours until the next train, since they're running on a holiday schedule," James said, checking his watch. "I suppose you could borrow our car."

"It's okay, Pops," Sam said. "We got it covered. Rolls is on the way."

I had a brief mental image of returning to the city in a chauffeur-driven

Rolls-Royce, but Sam's next statement shattered it. "In fact, I'm almost surprised he didn't beat me. He doesn't hold too much to things like speed limits. Come to think of it, even the laws of physics don't mean much to him." Apparently this Rolls was a person, not a car. Rats.

By this time, Gloria had joined us in the foyer. "Dinner's getting cold," she said. "What's the matter?"

Owen turned to her. "It's a situation back in the city. I don't know much more than that. They sent a car to get us back quickly."

"You don't have time to eat?"

" 'Fraid not, ma'am," Sam said. There was a loud screech of tires outside. "That'll be Rolls now."

"While you two get packed, I'll put together some dinner to take with you," Gloria said. "Now go! You need to hurry."

Owen and I ran up the stairs. I didn't have much to pack, so it didn't take long. When I got back down to the foyer, Owen was already there, getting our coats out of the closet. Gloria came from the direction of the kitchen, carrying a small hamper. She hustled us outside to where a silver Town Car waited in the driveway. On its hood perched two of the oddest gargoyles I'd ever seen—and most gargoyles are pretty odd, so that was really saying something. I recognized them as my guardians from the night before.

"Here are your passengers," Sam said to the waiting gargoyles. "Treat 'em nice. They're in tight with the big boss, and the boy there could zap you back to stone on a permanent basis. Katie, Mr. P., I'd like you to meet Rocky and Rollo."

"Otherwise known as Rock and Roll!" the two gargoyles chorused. They looked like something out of a Saturday-morning cartoon, all pop-eyed and funny-faced.

The taller one with a long, thin face added, "We met last night at the church, but we haven't been properly introduced. Oh, and Rocky's not my real name. It's just a nickname, on account of I'm made of stone." He and Rollo nearly fell off the hood of the car, laughing. Rocky coughed, got himself under control, then said, "Get it? Rocky? Stone?" He elbowed the other gargoyle in the ribs, and both of them fell to laughing again.

I turned to ask James if the offer to borrow his car still held, but Sam opened the door to the backseat for us and said, "Well, go on with you. I'll fly on ahead and let the boss know you're on the way."

"Last one there's a rotten egg," Rollo said. He was shorter and squatter than his buddy, and instead of having a separate pair of arms, his wings were his arms, with tiny hands at the ends.

With grave misgivings, I climbed into the backseat. Owen gave Arawn one last scratch behind the ears, then slid in next to me. Gloria reached into the car to hand him the hamper. "You can eat on the way. I put together two plates, some dessert, and some extra napkins. I wish you could have stayed longer, but I know duty calls. Katie, it was very nice to meet you. I hope you'll come again."

"Thank you for having me. I enjoyed myself."

"I'll give you a call when we get back and have things settled," Owen said. She gave him a quick kiss on the cheek before stepping back and letting Rocky close the door.

Neither gargoyle was big enough to see over the steering wheel while also reaching the pedals, so I wondered if gargoyles could adjust their size the way fairies could. The way Sam had talked, Rollo was apparently the driver, and he seemed the least likely to be able to see, steer, and hit the accelerator or brake at the same time. I soon learned how they worked it. Rocky clung to the steering wheel with his feet and used his hands to work the turn signals, gear shift, and horn, while Rollo sat on the floorboard and worked the pedals.

I instinctively reached for the seat belt, and Owen did the same. "Good idea, kids," Rocky said, looking over his shoulder. "Rolls here has got a stone foot." He nearly fell off the steering wheel from laughing so hard, and muffled laughter echoed up from under the dashboard. "Get it? It's supposed to be lead, but since Rolls is made of stone, it's a stone foot. Okay, Rolls, I've got her in reverse and nothing seems to be coming, so give her a nudge."

The car backed out of the driveway. When Rocky had steered the car into the street, he shifted into drive and said, "We're on the road. Give her some gas."

If I'd had any second thoughts about maybe waiting for the next train and letting Owen handle the crisis, there wouldn't have been much I could have done about it. Rollo really did have a stone foot. We all but flew down the neighborhood streets. If I'd tried to get out of the car, I'd have killed myself. I could only imagine what it would be like once we were on the open road.

"Brake!" Rocky yelled as we neared the intersection with the main road. The car screeched to a halt, fishtailing a little. After checking up and down the road, Rocky then called out, "Hit it," as he spun the steering wheel by shifting his weight. I wasn't sure the tires were actually in contact with road surface, we were going so fast.

"Aren't you worried about getting stopped for speeding?" I asked.

The two gargoyles went into hysterics. "Who can stop an invisible car?" Rocky said between bursts of laughter.

"Hey, Rocky," Rollo's voice came up from under the dash, "maybe you should let one catch us someday. Wouldn't it be funny to see how a cop would react to seein' a car driven by two gargoyles? Wouldn't it? Huh?"

"It'd be a scream."

"I wouldn't suggest it," Owen said mildly, even as he white-knuckled the edges of the seat. "You know the rules about exposing yourselves to outsiders."

"We wasn't talkin' 'bout exposing ourselves," Rocky said, sputtering with laughter. "Just lettin' 'em see we're gargoyles." He and Rollo found that highly amusing, providing their own laugh track once more. "Get it? Usually when you say you're exposing yourself, you're talking about the naughty bits."

"And gargoyles don't got naughty bits," Rollo added. "Hey, Rocky, we got room to go faster?"

"Yeah, give 'er some gas. Pedal to the metal!" As the car shot forward, both gargoyles gave a hearty, "Woo hoo!"

Owen turned to me. "So, lunch?"

I wasn't sure I could eat while we were breaking the sound barrier, but I needed something to distract myself from the speed at which the scenery blurred past. "Sure, why not?"

The hamper Gloria had packed turned out to contain individually packaged to-go type boxes full of Christmas dinner, still nice and warm. I was just about to dig in when I realized we were eating in front of our drivers. "I'm sorry, we should have offered you two something," I said. "Would you like a snack?"

"Don't worry about it," Rocky said. "At these speeds, I've got to keep my eyes on the road. Besides, we don't eat your kind of food. Unless you've got some pebbles in there?" He and Rollo found that highly amusing, as usual.

Rollo chimed in, "Or maybe some pecan sandies. Get it? Sand? Like we're made of stone?" That was apparently even funnier. Gargoyle humor must be a matter of taste, I thought.

Guiltlessly, I dug into the meal. In spite of the high rate of speed and two-gargoyle driving job, the ride was fairly smooth. The way my necklace buzzed around my neck, I was beginning to get the feeling that Owen's magic detector could turn out to be irritating.

"You won't hurt my feelings if you take it off," he said, and I only then realized that I'd been unconsciously touching it. "Remember, I told you it might be a problem around magical folk. Here, let me help you with that."

I braced myself for the usual meltdown as his fingers brushed the back of my neck. He seemed utterly oblivious to his effect on me as he handed me the necklace. I put it in my pocket while he dug in the hamper for dessert, which turned out to be slices of chocolate Yule log cake with chocolate filling and icing. "I think I really like Gloria," I said.

"I think she liked you, too. But I worry about how much she tries to do, keeping that big old house all by herself."

"She's not by herself. She's got a brownie helping her."

"She does? How did you find out?"

"I caught the brownie last night while she was cleaning my room. I guess she usually uses an illusion to keep people from seeing her at work. She gave me permission to tell you because I said it would make you feel better, but you can't let on to Gloria that you know."

"It does make me feel better. I wonder how long she's had help."

"Since you were little, from the sound of it."

In the front seat, the two gargoyles started singing Christmas carols with great enthusiasm, if very little talent. Rocky might have been one of the few beings in the universe with a worse sense of pitch than I had, and Rollo's attempts at harmony didn't work, but their joy was infectious. Before I knew what I was doing, I was singing along, my terrible voice fitting right in. When Owen grinned and joined the chorus, his ability to carry a tune made him seem to be the one out of place.

Soon, the singing had to stop because we'd reached the edges of the city proper and Rocky had to use his voice for shouting instructions to Rollo. Traffic was light on Christmas day, but this was New York, so "light" was a relative term. "Okay, start easing off the gas," Rocky instructed. "Brake. Inch forward a bit—a little more—not that much. Green light! Go! Go! Go! Wait a second, brake! BRAAAAAAAAAKE!"

I squeezed my eyes shut and turned my head because the rear of the truck in front of us was a little too close for comfort. When I didn't feel a jolt or hear the screaming of tearing metal, I cautiously opened my eyes, only to close them again. I'd have been a little unnerved at driving myself in city traffic, but being a passenger in these circumstances was almost enough to make me want to get out and walk the rest of the way. The only thing keeping me from it was the fact that this was an unfamiliar neighborhood. It was also pretty cold outside.

It only got worse as we made it into Manhattan proper, where driving down Broadway can be stop-and-go at the best of times. I had a feeling

I'd be hearing, "A bit more, no, brake! Go! BRAAAAAKE!" in my night-mares for the next few nights. Other cars had an uncanny way of swerving out of our path, so we made remarkably good time. Finally, the car screeched to a halt in the middle of Times Square, with one wheel up on a curb just inches from a lamppost.

"Okay, folks, here we are," Rocky announced as Rollo climbed up onto the driver's seat behind him. "And Sam's nowhere to be seen, so it looks like we win." He and Rollo started a victory dance. "We rocked and we rolled, we're Rock and Roll," they chanted.

"Guess again, boys," Sam said as he landed on the hood of the car. "Now, come on. You've got to see this."

Owen opened the car door and climbed out. I followed him. Merlin was already standing in the traffic island, looking up. As soon as I looked around and got my bearings, I realized why we'd been called back to New York. "Holy crap," I said under my breath.

My voice must not have been as soft as I'd thought, for Merlin turned to me. "I take it you see it, too. And that would mean it's real, not illusion."

"Yeah, it's real, all right."

All the brightly lit, giant billboards in Times Square were a glaring tribute to one Phelan Idris and his company, Spellworks. One billboard urged people to "Spell Different," and I doubted we were part of a spelling bee. "Not very original, though," I commented. "He's reusing an old Apple slogan that wasn't that great to begin with." Another billboard said, "Do magic your way." There were images of stodgy, gray conformists in suits being bested or shocked by colorful radicals.

"Now we know what he was up to," Owen said, staring up at the billboards.

"I'm assuming these ads are veiled to the rest of the world," I said. "Maybe the spell is filtered to target only people with magical ability?"

"That's probably it," Owen agreed. "He's definitely making a splash in a big way, and it appears to be that he's attempting to legitimize his company among the general magical population. No more photocopied spell instructions sold in hole-in-the-wall shops."

"I'm afraid the implications are bigger than that," I said, a sense of gloom filling me as the realization dawned on me. "Do you know how much this kind of thing costs? These ads are really physically here, which means he had to buy the ad space, and that costs millions. He's bound to have the space for at least a week because New Year's Eve is a prime high-traffic time here. And this probably isn't his only advertising. You wallpaper Times Square to make a splash, but you also have to follow it up with ads that everyone else will see. Odds are, this little display is for our benefit so we'll know he's gunning for us."

"He's got someone bankrolling him," Owen said grimly, finishing my thought. "He might have been able to raise some cash through magically underhanded means, but not at this level. So he's got someone rich—and presumably powerful—in league with him. Maybe that's where your friend's enemy comes in." He gave a quick recap about Philip and Mr. Bones to Merlin.

"That company certainly would have the capital to fund these activities," Merlin said. "They've been one of our larger corporate customers—mostly security and contract-enforcement spells. I haven't much liked Jackson Meredith in my few dealings with him, but I had no sense that he was unethical enough to be involved in this sort of thing."

"He's currently 'indisposed,' " I said, making air quotes. "His niece Sylvia is in charge now."

"Ah, yes, that would explain things. She quite clearly is evil."

"There's got to be something else going on," I said, staring at a larger-than-life image of Idris breaking a cement box with a karate chop. It looked like the hand breaking the box had been badly Photoshopped onto a picture of Idris striking a karate pose.

"What do you mean? Isn't this enough?" Owen asked.

"Has Idris ever done anything splashy when he wasn't there to see it?

That's his big downfall—he gets so sidetracked watching us react that he forgets to follow through on whatever advantage he's gained."

"And that is the reason I called you in," Merlin said. "I thought it would be a good time for a stakeout. He's sure to be nearby."

All of us then turned and looked around Times Square. The area wasn't quite as crowded as it was on most early evenings, but there were still enough people milling around that it would be hard to spot one unprepossessing wizard. "I don't think I see him," I said, well aware that I was probably the only one who would see him.

We settled in to wait. Owen conjured up cups of hot coffee for us, and Rocky, Rollo, and Sam took aerial patrol. I wasn't sure if there were any laws against loitering, but this didn't seem like the kind of place where it would be easy to enforce them. Still, I couldn't help but feel jumpy whenever a police officer went by. One finally did stop and ask us, "Are you folks waiting for something?"

"I'm fascinated by these billboards," Merlin said cheerfully. "Don't you think they're more entertaining than television?"

The cop gave us a funny look, and I took Merlin's arm. "Grandpa doesn't get away from the nursing home often," I said. "When he gets out for a holiday, we let him do some of his favorite things."

The cop nodded. "Ah, I see. Well, have a merry Christmas." Then he moved on, and Owen and I immediately broke down in laughter.

Merlin looked mildly amused. "I never thought I'd have to play the dotard in order to do my job," he said.

As I turned to reply to him, I thought I saw something out of the corner of my eye. "Is that—? No, rats, it's not," I said.

"Not what?" another voice asked. We all turned to see Rod. His hair still looked good, his skin was smoother, and if I wasn't mistaken, he'd had his teeth whitened. "I just got the message and thought I'd join you. Any action?"

"You mean other than convincing a cop that Grandpa's senile and likes to look at the pretty lights when we let him out of the nursing home?" I asked.

"So, no fight scenes yet, then." He looked up and around at all the billboards. "These are truly, spectacularly awful."

I opened my mouth to respond, but then I saw something, and this time I was sure it was Idris. He was lurking just inside the doorway to a nearby restaurant, and he had a few of his usual gang surrounding him. "There!" I said.

"Where?" Owen asked, then he said, "Oh, hell," and waved his hand. Nothing much changed for me. I still saw the same menagerie of magical creatures—both the good guys and the bad guys. But judging from the screams, I got the feeling that now everyone else could see Mr. Bones and the circling gargoyles. "That's not what I meant to do," Owen groaned. "Katie, you and Rod see if you can catch up with Idris." He and Merlin were already muttering magic spells, presumably to reveil all the magical folk who'd been revealed to the world.

Rod waved to the gargoyles, who zoomed in on Idris like they were on a bombing run. "I got 'em!" Rocky shouted, latching onto Idris's shoulder with his feet. A second later, he lost his grip. "Hey! Ow! That hurt! No fair!"

Rod and I nearly reached Idris, but just before we got to him, a clump of tourists moving in an eerie zombie lockstep got in our way. I wormed my way through them, but when I got to the other side, Idris was gone. I made a full circle turn to see if I could spot him, but all I saw was Rod fending off a couple of women. It seemed Idris knew just how to target him. It must have been the first time in a very long while that Rod had actually fought to get away from women. Even the ugly magical creatures were gone. On the bright side, the worst of the panic had been quelled, as Owen and Merlin had apparently reveiled all the magical stuff.

"He got away," I reported when I got back to them and Rod had escaped from his female admirers with a couple of phone numbers. "He must have used that influence spell of his to get the crowd to block us. Is everything okay here?"

"I think so," Owen said wearily. "Next time, I won't be so impatient and I'll try targeting the unveiling a little better. It shouldn't have hit the whole square like that, though. I thought it would only cover a short distance."

"There aren't many with the power to forcibly remove veiling spells from that many beings at once," Merlin said. "It was an impressive display, and there seems to have been little harm done. We put things right soon enough that most of these people will likely assume they just imagined it all. Not that you shouldn't be more prudent in the future, with that kind of power at your disposal." I remembered then what I'd overheard from James and Gloria. Merlin had a similar tone to his voice, a mixture of pride and concern.

"I guess that spell needs more work," Owen said with a shrug. His face was flushed, and he didn't look Merlin in the eye.

"I doubt Mr. Idris will make another appearance tonight," Merlin said. "Now, I've taken away enough of your holiday. Please enjoy the rest of the evening, but I would like to meet in the morning. Say ten at my office?"

Owen and I exchanged a look, then he said, "We'll be there."

"Rocky and Rollo will get you the rest of the way home," Sam told us. He then addressed the two goofy gargoyles, emphasizing each word. "In. One. Piece."

They saluted him. "Yes, sir, Sam, sir."

"Oh, off with you," Sam grumbled.

The drive from Times Square to my apartment near Union Square managed to be even more bizarre than the drive from the Eatons' house into Manhattan. Owen gave Rocky directions for each turn, and then Rocky told Rollo when to drive or brake, so the entire drive was a flurry of, "Turn left at the next intersection. Ease up on the gas. BRAAAAAKE. Okay, now you can go. Then make another left. Stop, stop, stop! Go!" and so forth.

When we finally stopped in front of my building—one tire up on the curb and the fender inches from a tree—Owen said, "I'm close enough to home. I can walk from here, and you guys can take the rest of the night off." He looked about as pale and shaky as I felt. Once we were safely on the sidewalk with our bags, I vowed never again to complain about New York taxi drivers. After the Town Car peeled out into traffic, to much honking of horns, and took the next corner on two wheels, Owen turned to me and said, "Do you want some help getting your bag upstairs?"

I was sorely tempted to say yes so I could then invite him in and try to salvage a little of what remained of Christmas, but my roommates would be getting home at any time now, and I knew he'd want to get home and study our latest problem. "No thanks," I said reluctantly, "I've got it. I guess I'll see you in the morning?"

"Yeah. I'll come by around nine-twenty."

"Okay." I unlocked the front door, then turned back to face him. "Merry Christmas. And thanks for inviting me to go with you. Aside from the last hour or so, I really enjoyed it."

"And I enjoyed having you there. It made things a lot easier."

I would have hoped for a kiss, but I could tell he was distracted again, brooding over whatever had happened with that unveiling spell. After seeing James and Gloria, I understood better why physical affection wasn't exactly second nature to him. I waved good-bye as he walked away, then picked up my bag and trudged up the stairs. The more time I spent around Owen and now his family, the dingier this stairwell seemed to me. I felt like I was entering a different world, or maybe going down to steerage on the *Titanic* after having been up on the first-class deck—and we know the steerage folks didn't come out of that situation too well.

It was hard to believe I'd only been gone a little more than a day, the apartment felt so foreign to me. It was stiflingly hot, which meant my downstairs neighbor must have spent the day complaining to the super about being cold, and he didn't want to be called again on a holiday. I opened every window in the apartment and traded Gemma's cashmere for a T-shirt before I unpacked. As much as I'd joked about enjoying the time alone and changing the lock before they got back, the apartment felt empty without my roommates.

That reminded me, they weren't expecting me to be home. I was supposed to have come back the next day. I needed an explanation for why I was already home and why I had to go to work the following day. And I needed it fast, considering I heard a key turning in the lock.

Gemma yelped when she opened the door and saw me. Marcia, coming in behind her, dropped the bags she was carrying and assumed a defensive posture at Gemma's yell.

"Gee, I didn't know I was that scary," I said.

"We weren't expecting anyone to be here," Gemma said. "Why are you here? Weren't you supposed to be with the hottie's folks until tomorrow? Nothing went wrong, did it?"

I followed them as they carried their bags back to the closet to unpack. "No, nothing went wrong. The visit was fine. I was apparently a big hit with the folks."

"Of course you were," Marcia said. "You're a mother's dream girlfriend for her son, unless she's one of those controlling mamas who can't handle the thought of turning her baby boy over to another woman."

"There was just a work crisis," I continued my story, "and he had to come back to the city. I even have to go in for a while tomorrow because the executive I work for is part of it."

"What kind of business crisis comes up on Christmas?" Marcia asked.

"It's the perfect time for a business crisis. Don't they often plan sneak attacks during wartime on Christmas, because they know your guard will be down?"

Even Marcia didn't have a good response to that. After they dumped their bags in the bedroom, Gemma ordered Chinese food, then we settled down to chat about our respective holidays while watching the last of the Christmas specials on TV until a commercial came on that almost made me spit rice across the room.

Eleven

Phelan Idris's face filled the TV screen, which in and of itself wasn't a pleasant sight, but the implications were disturbing beyond that. He'd definitely launched a serious ad campaign. The ad urged magic users to try new and different spells to help them break out of their humdrum lives. Or something like that. The music used as background for the ads gave me a headache and was very distracting. The real surprise was the announcement of a Spellworks store, opening the next day on Fifth Avenue.

I managed to cover up my shock at seeing the ad by going into a coughing fit and sputtering, "Oops, that went down the wrong way," but I watched my roommates for their reactions at the same time. I doubted they'd seen what I saw, or surely they'd have commented on someone opening a magic store and claiming to sell actual spells. It would have been nice if they'd done me the favor of saying anything that would have hinted at the cover ad nonmagical people saw—something like, "Hey, sale at Victoria's Secret!" or "Yeah, like a body spray really has that effect." Unfortunately, whatever they used to mask the ad for normal people, it didn't seem to be an ad worth noticing or snarking about. Once they were sure I wasn't going to choke to death, my roommates went back to eating and chatting.

The ad was the first thing I told Owen about when I met him on the sidewalk in front of my building the next morning. "I wish I could tell you what the rest of the world sees," I finished, "but I couldn't think of a way to ask my roommates what ad they saw on television without sounding like I'd lost my mind."

"This is not good," he said, shaking his head. He looked tired. If I knew him, he'd been up most of the night thinking and researching.

"No, it's not good," I agreed, "but hey, at least we know what he's up to now." He didn't rally to my attempt at good cheer. If anything, his frown got deeper. "Okay, is there something I should know that you're not telling me?" I asked, trying to interpret his mood.

It took him a while to answer, and I'd just started to think he hadn't heard me when he said, "No, not that I know of." And that, apparently, was that. He didn't say another word on the entire walk to the subway station, and I decided against pressing the point. Owen wasn't the kind of person you could make talk.

Most people had a holiday, so the crowds were a little lighter than normal and we actually got seats. That meant I had a rare chance to notice the advertising that ran overhead. I blinked, then elbowed Owen. Spellworks had blanketed the entire car. He closed his eyes and groaned.

As we walked from the subway station to the office, he finally spoke to me. "I'm sorry everything's been so messed up," he said. "Every date we've tried to have, the holiday. I guess we haven't made that great a start." He gave a bitter little laugh. "In fact, I couldn't blame you at all if you decided to cut your losses because this isn't working."

"Why would I do that?" I asked. "Whatever we've run into, it's had as much to do with me as it has with you. If I dumped you and tried getting together with someone normal, things would probably be even worse." My heart suddenly felt like it had been caught in a vise. "You don't want to end this, do you?"

"No. But you know it's not going to be easy, the two of us. I don't think it will ever be easy for me because of who I am, or what I am."

"Maybe it'll be easier if we take it on together." I tried to make my voice lighter. "Besides, if you knew my dating history, you'd know nothing's been easy for me. If we go out one more time, we'll be closing in on my record for the past year or so, whether or not we run into another disaster."

Some of the weight seemed to leave his shoulders. "Okay, then, if you insist."

"I do."

It looked like Merlin had come to the realization that this was too big for our little team to deal with, for when we got to his office for the meeting, there was a room full of people (and other beings). I recognized Sam and the heads of Sales and Accounting, as well as the chief seer from Prophets and Lost, the forecasting unit. Even Owen's direct boss was there, and he almost never left his own office.

I was especially surprised to see our corporate counsel, Ethan Wainwright, there. He was a magical immune, like I was, and we'd dated very, very briefly about a month ago. It was the first time since he'd dumped me that I'd had to deal with him on a business basis. You'd think that dating Owen would have made me feel better about that, but it still stung a little. Facing an ex in a situation like that can be challenging. Do you act like nothing ever happened, or do you acknowledge the past? I went with sitting on the other side of the room and trying to avoid him unless I had a specific reason to address him.

I glanced at Owen, who sat next to me, to see if he'd reacted to Ethan being there, and then I realized that this same dilemma could apply to Owen someday. What if it didn't work out, if he was right about what he'd said earlier, if all the disasters piled up and made one of us give up? Would we one day face each other across a conference table and try to decide if we should just pretend nothing happened? It was almost as sobering a thought as the implications of what Idris had unveiled the day before.

Merlin called the meeting to order by summarizing what we'd seen on Christmas. "As Miss Chandler pointed out to me, the real concern appears to be that Mr. Idris has the funding to operate like a legitimate, high-level business."

"It gets worse," Owen said. "Katie, tell them what you saw last night."

"Was anyone watching TV last night?" I asked. I was met with a room full of blank faces. I felt like I must have been the only loser with no life, but then I remembered the sheltered magical enclave Owen was from and realized that explained a lot about the things I took for granted that others at MSI didn't get.

Then Merlin said, "Are you referring to the television commercial?"

I turned to him in shock. Merlin, of all people, was the one watching TV? Then again, that could account for his rapid adaptation to modern life. "Yes, the commercial. If he's buying TV time, it means he's got even more resources than we realized, and he's trying to reach an even broader audience. The commercials must be masked to nonmagical people because my roommates didn't notice anything odd."

"According to the commercial, Mr. Idris and his company have now opened a retail establishment," Merlin added. "I believe our first order of business should be to investigate and determine what spells he is currently selling."

"We could send someone in undercover," Mr. Lansing, Owen's boss, said. "Otherwise, I'm pretty sure most of our staff would be recognized."

Owen shook his head. "Not a good idea. It's easy enough to screen out disguises, and then it would be even more obvious what we're up to. That person would either be thrown out or given something entirely different. I'm not even sure it's good for a magical person to go in. For all we know, he's using some of his darker-influence spells on his customers to get them to buy or to make them more agreeable to him. Remember, that's why we were fighting him in the first place. The storefront and the ads may all just be a way to get more people under his influence."

I was rather impressed that he'd dared contradict his boss, but the frog-man didn't seem to mind. "So we send in an immune? A regular nonmagical person probably wouldn't even see the store or be able to enter it."

He looked straight at me when he said it. It was my turn to shake my head. "No, he knows me too well. We'd have to send someone he's never met."

All heads in the room turned toward Ethan, who also shook his head. "Sorry, no can do. I was there for our first showdown, remember? He's not likely to forget a flying tackle."

"When he was working here, he shouldn't have run into anyone from Verification too often," Owen mused. "Surely we've got someone around here we can count on to get the job done who would also be anonymous."

I remembered the group of people I'd worked with in Verification before I got my current job, and I wasn't sure we could count on any of them. People who were immune to magic saw odd things they couldn't explain, which wasn't necessarily good for their mental health. If that didn't get them, knowing that their abilities were so unique and that magical people couldn't do anything to them tended to create champion slackers. There was one person I thought might be able to get the job done, as much as I hated to admit it.

"Kim could do it," I said, even though my stomach was already churning at the thought. "She's probably the sharpest verifier we've got." I reminded myself sternly that this was for the good of the company, possibly for the good of the magical world, maybe even for the good of the entire world. When I got back to my office, I was going to have to write, "It's for the greater good," a hundred times in my day planner to make sure that sank in. Maybe then it would counter my fears that she really was taking over my job.

Merlin nodded. "Yes, she is quite efficient. Very well, we will send her to investigate."

"I'll give her a list of what she should look for," Owen said, making a note in his lab book.

"It would be interesting to learn how he's disguising his operation from the rest of the world," Merlin said. "That may be more problematic. It would appear that his veiling spells filter for anyone with magical ability, so all of us see what's really there, as do our immunes. We have no one in our employ who is nonmagical and nonimmune, and I am hesitant to bring anyone from outside in on the secret. That is a step we take only in particular circumstances, and I don't believe that curiosity about what the rest of the world sees is yet that extreme."

I was glad he'd said that, as I was probably the one in the group who knew the most so-called normal people, since Ethan had that thing for weirdness and had likely ditched his old nonmagical friends, and I really didn't want to drag my friends into this. I figured they'd eventually see something I'd have to explain, but I preferred to wait for Merlin's extreme circumstances to face that. There was one other option, though.

I didn't want to bring it up. In fact, it made me queasy even to think about it. But I couldn't come up with a way around it. "You know, you can temporarily create a nonmagical, nonimmune person," I said.

Owen's head snapped toward me. "No, I don't think so. Not a good idea."

"I got through it the last time when I had no idea what was going on and hadn't told anyone. We could do it under more controlled circumstances, with people there to watch and make sure I'm okay. Don't tell me you haven't worked out the precise formula to temporarily dim immunity." He turned red and looked away from me, which was confirmation enough. "Besides, it's not like I'd be going on any major secret mission. It would be a walk through Times Square, a look at a few subway ads, and maybe a stroll past the store. If y'all can't keep me safe for that much, then you don't stand a chance of winning this."

"But, as you just pointed out, we have other immunes on staff," Owen said.

"But none who has experienced a loss of immunity," Merlin put in. "Miss Chandler has learned to recognize the differences and even compensate for them. We might want to consider training some of the other immunes that way in the future, but for now, she is the best suited for the assignment."

I turned to Owen with a smug "So, there!" look, but he didn't seem to see me. He was focused on Merlin. "But I need her!" he said, more forcibly than I'd ever heard him say much of anything. Then he seemed to realize how that sounded, and a flush crept upward from his shirt collar to his hairline. "I mean, I'll need her help analyzing the items we get from this Spellworks store so we can see if there's anything hidden in them. Finding out what the rest of the world sees in the advertising is surely a much lower priority."

Merlin nodded. "That much is true. Very well, we will wait before using Miss Chandler for that aspect of the investigation, but please make certain you're making decisions based on business reasons rather than your personal feelings." Owen, still blushing furiously, nodded as he kept his eyes on the table. Merlin acknowledged that with a nod of his own before continuing. "Now, those are the strategies for dealing with the potentially less-than-seemly aspects of our opponent. What can we do to face this from a business standpoint?"

Mr. Hartwell, the head of Sales, smiled his plastic smile. "Have we ever considered opening our own storefront or doing veiled advertising like that? Until now, our only way to promote ourselves has been through the products themselves, and we only recently started putting marketing messages on the packaging. Now that we appear to have real competition that's marketing at this level, I'm not sure we can afford not to step it up a notch or two."

"Or would that be playing into his hands by legitimizing his claims?" I asked, thinking out loud. "He seems to have cast us as IBM in the IBM versus Apple saga. He's even stealing old Apple advertising slogans. His company is fresh, new, and innovative, while we're old, stodgy, and resistant to change."

"That's not entirely untrue," Minerva Felps, the head seer, muttered under her breath.

"What was the outcome of this legendary battle?" Merlin asked.

I supposed in a sense that it really was a kind of modern warfare, so I didn't bother correcting his assumption. "Both companies are still in business. IBM changed its business model, but not really because of Apple. Apple still has a limited market share. The real victor in all of this was Microsoft, which has the dominant operating system. I'm not sure any of that applies to our scenario. Oh, and as far as I know, none of those companies was literally evil, destructive, or aiming for true world domination. Well, not that anyone's been able to prove."

"How would us responding to their efforts play into their hands?" Mr. Hartwell challenged, his arms crossed over his chest and his eyes narrowed.

"For one thing, it would take a lot of money, and if we try to compete on that level, it could just end up hurting us without helping much. I don't see how he can sustain this level of exposure for very long unless he rakes in some serious sales. He's got to have a big source of funding."

"If the connection you believe you've observed is correct," Merlin said to me, "we may know where he's getting his funding."

Every head in the room turned to look at me. "I was at the offices of Vandermeer and Company last week, helping a friend with something, and I noticed that they had one of the creatures I usually associate with Idris there, apparently working as some kind of bodyguard. I've seen that particular creature several times, always attacking me when I've been investigating Idris. It's possible that they're in league with Idris."

"Those Merediths never have been up to much good," Minerva Felps muttered. "I've always wondered what happened to the missing Vandermeer heir that allowed them to take over."

"He was turned into a frog, then disenchanted, and now he's dating my roommate," I answered. "But he's not a frog anymore. That's why I was at their offices. I was helping him scope out the situation so he could see about getting his family business back."

"I wonder if this is who's been pulling the strings all along," Owen mused.

Mr. Lansing spun his pen around, which was an impressive feat with frog flippers. "Possibly," he said. "Or else it's someone who saw Idris's potential."

"Minerva, have any of your people noticed anything?" Merlin asked.

"We've seen some portents, but we're still trying to analyze them. Things are hazy enough that I suspect we're being deliberately blocked. We may send someone to wander by the store to see if any of the signals are stronger there, and I'm planning a big meditation session tomorrow, but I don't anticipate any earth-shattering revelations to come from it. Still, you never know."

Ethan looked over at me. "It's Philip you're talking about, the one who was enchanted?" I nodded, and he said, "Maybe I should meet with him and see what we might be able to do legally. If we can prove who he is and get him back in charge of that investment firm, maybe we can cut off Idris's funding." He frowned for a moment, then added, "I'm assuming that there are magical channels for handling this sort of thing, where saying you were turned into a frog is actually a valid claim and won't land you in the loony bin."

"Yes, of course. We have to have our own ways of settling legal disputes involving magic," Mr. Hartwell said.

"Okay, then I'll look into the legal angle," Ethan said. "Fighting against evil schemers isn't my legal specialty, but it's becoming something of a hobby."

"While you guys are taking the thinkin' end of the plan, we're gonna send a few folk down to stake out the store," Sam said. "I doubt Idris'll be working the cash register himself, but you never know who you'll find popping by. There might be someone worth following. That is, if we can see past their disguise illusions. We probably shouldn't try simultaneously unveiling everyone in Times Square again." Owen turned bright red at that and became engrossed in the pattern of wood grain on the conference table.

Merlin nodded. "Very well, then. There isn't much we can do until we have more information. Tomorrow we'll send Kim to the store to obtain some samples of their merchandise, which we will then analyze. Based on that analysis we'll have a better sense of what the scheme seems to be, and we will also know how we should respond, businesswise. Now, I've asked you to give up enough of your holiday. Please feel free to enjoy the rest of your day. We will meet again in two days to discuss preliminary results."

As the meeting broke up, Owen went over to Merlin to talk, and that left me standing face-to-face with Ethan. "How's it going?" he asked, eliminating my option of pretending not to notice him.

"Pretty good," I said.

"I hear you and Owen are together now."

"Yeah."

"Good. He's a nice guy. And apparently not into chicks with wings." He glanced over his shoulder to where Trix's desk sat empty. "I guess you were right about that, after all."

It had been one of my better breakup lines, I had to admit. He'd said he thought I was a little too normal for him, and I'd accused him of really wanting to date chicks with wings. The fact that it turned out to be true made it even better. "Well, they do say I'm perceptive. And I'm glad things are working out for you."

"Thanks. No hard feelings?"

I was rather surprised to realize that there weren't any. He seemed to belong to another lifetime, even though it wasn't that long ago. "No hard feelings," I confirmed.

Owen wrapped up his business with Merlin and joined me. "Ready to go?" he asked.

"Sure. You're not staying to work?"

He sighed. "What do I have to work with? I'd be tempted to drop by that store and grab a few spells to start with, but he's probably got the place specifically warded against me."

"This isn't something we're going to fix with a few hours' work, and I doubt a few hours will make much of a difference."

"Unfortunately, that's probably true. However," he glanced around to make sure none of the stragglers were in earshot, "it might not hurt to walk by that store and see what's going on."

"No, it might not."

"We might just happen to be going to lunch somewhere in that area, and if we pass the store, then we could look through the windows."

"So, lunch, then?"

He did a great job of looking utterly innocent. "Yes, lunch. Are you free?"

"I'll have to check my calendar," I replied with a coy smile.

We got our coats at his lab, then headed out, taking the subway uptown to Times Square. From there, we headed over to Fifth Avenue and walked up a block or so. I spotted the store at the right address across the avenue from us right away. It wasn't nearly as splashy or impressive as the ads would have had us believe. Instead, it was in a narrow old building that didn't seem to have seen much remodeling. Then I realized that was the way I saw it. "What does it look like to you?" I asked Owen.

He shrugged. "A store. Too much neon for my taste. The strobe light might not be such a great idea. Just looking at the store gives me a headache."

"It seems like we've found one place he's cut corners. To me, this isn't too different from those ten-dollar clothing stores downtown."

"Maybe we should get a better look," he suggested, taking my arm and heading toward the nearest crosswalk.

But then I saw someone standing on the other side of the avenue—someone wearing what looked suspiciously like a flamingo-pink 1980s prom dress with her tarnished tiara. I couldn't see the back of her dress, but I'd have bet a week's pay that there was a big bow on the butt. Ethelinda waved her wand at me, and I immediately tugged on Owen's arm. "Let's get lunch first. Then we can catch the store on our way back."

"Okay. There are a lot of places for lunch back toward Times Square."

We hadn't made it half a block before I saw another familiar face, and this time it was someone I'd been looking for rather than someone I was trying to avoid. A fairy with curly blond hair wove her way through the crowds on the sidewalk across the street from us. I gripped Owen's arm. "Don't make any sudden moves, but Ari's across the street from us."

He kept walking but slowed his pace ever so slightly as he cast his eyes in that direction. "I don't see her, but she's probably disguised. Let's follow her and see where she goes."

"But won't she see us?"

"Two can play that game. Stick to me and she won't see a thing." With that, he reversed direction and took off. "Tell me which way she turns."

It was a challenge keeping up with Owen's brisk pace while not taking my eyes off Ari. I'd expected her to head straight to the store, but she turned in the opposite direction. I tugged on his arm to steer him the right way, feeling kind of like Rocky telling Rollo when to brake or hit the gas. "Do you think she might be heading to their secret headquarters?" I asked.

"We can only hope. Is she the one making a rude gesture at that cab she just stepped out in front of?"

"Yeah, that would be our girl."

"Okay, then, I've got her in my sights, too."

And that was a good thing, because I then spotted Ethelinda heading toward us, and it was all I could do to keep track of both of them. I wasn't sure how I could manage to avoid a fairy godmother while tracking an evil fairy. Fortunately, Ethelinda didn't seem to have much interest in contacting me. She just seemed to be following and watching, which meant she must have been able to see us. I supposed Owen was targeting his spell strictly to Ari. That made sense. You could get trampled

walking down a crowded city sidewalk when you were visible. Going totally invisible would have been practically suicidal.

"Looks like she's heading to Grand Central," Owen remarked, speeding his pace.

"Maybe their secret headquarters is out of town. That would explain
why we've been having trouble finding them."

"Somehow, I have trouble imagining a magic spell with 'Made in
Yonkers' on the label."

"That's why it's such a brilliant hiding place."

"Okay, she's definitely going into the station." He picked up his
pace, which put me at almost a run. "We'll have to get closer because it'll
be easier for her to lose us in there, even if she doesn't know we're following."

And he was right. In the cavernous main concourse, there were too
many people moving in too many different directions with no clear-cut
pathways for it to be easy to track any one person. Fortunately, there
weren't that many people with wings, which made it a little easier for me.
I wasn't sure how Owen was doing it, unless he'd locked in on the sense
of her magic or was using his precognitive abilities to anticipate her
moves. Meanwhile, I completely lost track of Ethelinda. Even in Grand
Central Station, I should have been able to spot a fairy godmother wearing a bad 1980s prom dress.

Ari headed down one of the side passageways that lead toward both
tracks and retail shops. I'd be really annoyed if she was just going to a
bookstore after we went to all that effort to follow her, but she turned in
the opposite direction, which seemed to lead to train tracks. I lost sight
of her for a split second, then Owen pulled my arm. "Come on, this way,"
he said.

"Are you sure? I thought I saw her turning the other way."

"No, she went right down toward this platform."

As he pulled me in that direction, I looked back over my shoulder,
but I didn't see any wings, so I gave in and followed him. He was proba-

bly right. Except, there was no train waiting at either of the tracks along the platform we were on. "She kept on going. See, there she is ahead."

"I don't see anything." Or did I? There was a hint of movement at the far end of the platform. "Are we supposed to be down here?"

"Relax, I fixed it so nobody can see us. We won't get in trouble."

We reached the end of the platform, and he stepped off onto the ground below, pausing to help me down. At this point, there were only the dimmest of lights. I supposed that was good because the bright light of an oncoming train wasn't what we wanted to see. The tracks led into a cavelike area where railroad supplies were stacked up against brick pillars. It was all very spooky. I halfway expected to come upon a candlelit underground lake with the Phantom of the Opera rowing himself across while singing love songs to a spellbound soprano.

By this time, we were well away from the tracks, and it was extremely dark, without even a few safety lights. Owen created a small, glowing sphere that hung in the air above his hand. It worked to guide his way, but it left me almost blind. I was glad he'd recognized Ari because I now couldn't see a thing.

I could hear something, though, and it didn't sound like a disgruntled fairy giving the secret password to the hidden headquarters. It was more like a roar that echoed through the cavern. The roar was followed by a burst of sulfur-scented flame that shot straight toward us.

"Uh-oh," Owen said just before he doused his light and pulled me out of the flame's path.

Twelve

The flame exposed far more detail than I really wanted to see: scaly skin, yellow eyes, and sharp, pointy teeth. I've never thought of myself as a shrinking violet or damsel in distress looking for a knight in shining armor to rescue me, but I couldn't stop myself from screaming and clinging to Owen. I figured I got a free pass on any girly behavior when it came to real, live dragons. And that's exactly what seemed to be facing us in this cavern. There were several of them, all looking like something out of a scary movie, complete with ugly horned heads, leathery wings, and spiked tails.

Owen angled himself to shield me while he raised his right hand, deflecting the next burst of flame and sending it to hover in a ball of fire just below the ceiling. Although Owen was reacting calmly and logically, especially considering the circumstances, when I looked at his face, I saw that he looked more unnerved than I'd ever seen him.

Dragons didn't seem to be all that bright, which was lucky for us. They were sidetracked by the ball of flame and didn't appear to understand what had happened. That bought us some time. One of the beasts was between us and the only way out we knew of, but there was a niche in a crumbling brick wall that offered a small degree of shelter. Owen shoved me into the back of the niche, then hid just inside it, shielding me.

I hoped he knew what he was doing, because those monsters were truly terrifying, and there were more of them than I'd initially realized. We must have stumbled into a nest—assuming dragons lived in nests—which wasn't the sort of thing I expected to find under Grand Central. They kept roaring and breathing fire at us, and Owen kept deflecting the flames. I knew he was pretty powerful and he could probably keep doing that all day, but we needed to get out of there eventually if we were going to survive this. If nothing else, food and water might become an issue. For us, not the dragons. If they caught us, they'd have food taken care of, and I didn't know if they needed water.

"I thought the dragons in the sewer system were an urban legend," Owen remarked as he deflected yet another burst of flame. By this point, there were enough fireballs hanging in the air to make this underground cavern look like a July afternoon in Texas. The first ones were dissipating in a shower of sparks.

"I thought it was alligators in the sewer system," I said, wincing and flinching at the next dragon attack. Eventually they were going to give up on the flames and go to Plan B, which would probably involve eating us without cooking us first.

"That's the cover story," Owen said.

"Oh. But this isn't the sewer system, is it?"

"If you were that powerful, would you stay in the sewers for long, or would you find another place to stay? I'm sure there's a hole in a sewer tunnel somewhere that leads into one of these forgotten railway tunnels."

"Good point." I tried to think of some way I could help. "Need me to throw a rock or two at them?" I felt I might as well fall back on my known strengths.

"No, thanks. Right now, I think they're guessing where we are, based on smell. I haven't dropped the invisibility spell. I'm varying the angles on my deflections, but a rock might help them pinpoint us."

"Okay, then, no rocks. Us talking might not be such a great idea, then, huh?"

"I doubt they can hear us over their own roaring, and sound bounces around in here. But yeah, we might want to limit conversation."

I supposed the situation could have been kind of romantic, in a bizarre way, what with my dashing hero rescuing me from the terrible dragons and all, but I doubted it would get too romantic until we were safely out of there. And then we'd both need a good shower before we'd want to go anywhere near each other for the dramatic "thank goodness you're okay" scene. I could tell my hair already reeked of smoke.

Soon, the dragons got a clue, which wasn't a good sign for us. The head dragon swiped the air with one giant clawed foot, like it was looking for the hidden intruders. "Not that I'm ungrateful for you deflecting the flames," I said as that foot got closer and closer to us, "but we probably ought to come up with a plan to get out of here. Maybe you could create a diversion, or something."

"I'm open to suggestions," he said, sending away another burst of flame that came close enough that I could have used it to toast marshmallows.

"The diversion *was* my suggestion."

"If you come up with any specifics beyond throwing a rock, feel free to share."

If this had been one of those movies about a dragonslayer hero rescuing a damsel in distress, we'd have been kissing and expressing our true feelings toward each other about now, fearing that we were about to die and not wanting our love to go unspoken. Instead, we were practically bickering, and we'd never had anything close to a fight before. I tried to tell myself that this was actually a healthy sign in the growth of our relationship because it meant we trusted each other enough to say what we really felt. No matter how cute I thought

Owen was, sweet nothings were not at the top of my mind at this particular moment.

"The one blocking the exit seems to be the problem," I pointed out. "If you could zap it, or whatever it is you do, that might help. We could sneak past the others and get away."

"I'm not sure I know a spell acute enough to get through a dragon's scales to kill it—not off the top of my head—but that does give me an idea," he said, never taking his eyes off the lead dragon, which was now sniffing along the ground like a bloodhound in a disturbingly accurate path following where we'd been. It wouldn't be long before it found us.

"I'm all ears," I said.

"It's a spell that might help, but I haven't tried it on dragons. Or, well, really tried it in the real world. It's just a theory. It may or may not work, and it could possibly backfire."

"I'm immune to magic. I'm okay with backfiring."

"It could make them angrier."

"Still not seeing how that makes our situation much worse. Trapped by angry dragons versus trapped by angrier dragons. There's not a significant difference."

"Okay, then. Be ready to react."

"React how?"

"I'm not sure. Maybe run. Or duck. This might be a good time to be ready to throw something. I'm going to have to lift the invisibility spell to do this because I don't have the power to do both at the same time and be sure it will work."

I knelt to pick up a brick and hefted it in my right hand. "Okay, I'm set. Go for it."

He raised both hands over his head and shouted some strange words in a louder voice than I'd ever heard him use. In the underground chamber, his words echoed and rang. With his arms raised, silhouetted against the dragons' unearthly flames, he truly looked the part of the powerful wizard. Suddenly, the dragons stopped shooting fire. They also stopped roaring and snarling. Instead they . . . whimpered?

The one in front even seemed to be wagging its tail, which was almost as dangerous as when it had been waving its claw. It lowered its head to the ground in a submissive posture, and if I wasn't mistaken, it was giving Owen puppy-dog eyes. In fact, it looked for all the world like a puppy begging its master to throw a stick for it to fetch.

"Was this what was supposed to happen?" I asked.

"I wasn't entirely sure what was supposed to happen," he admitted.

"Now you tell me."

"I did say it was untested."

"So, this is how you get Jake to follow your orders," I teased.

"You know, I've never thought of trying that." He paused, tilted his head, and grinned at the thought. "But actually, I was expecting it to subdue them, maybe even put them to sleep. I must have done something wrong. But they do seem to have become friendly enough. Want to try getting out of here?"

"I'm more than ready."

He took my hand, and together we edged our way around the chamber. The lead dragon whimpered again and moved as though to follow us. "I think it wants you to play fetch," I said.

"That is what it looks like." He raised his free hand and sent one of the railroad ties lying in a rotting pile in one corner flying across the chamber. The dragons all turned and happily chased it. We took advantage of the distraction to run toward the exit, but next thing we knew, there was a "thud" on the ground behind us. We turned to see a railroad tie lying there, covered in dragon slime, with a dragon sitting expectantly behind it. "Uh, good boy," Owen said before sending the tie flying again.

We managed to run a few more yards and even out of the chamber before the dragon brought its stick back to us. This time, Owen sent several of the railroad ties flying in different directions. That gave us a little extra time, as the dragons all collided while they ran after their sticks. We were just through the doorway out of the next chamber and into a narrower passageway when the dragons happily brought their sticks back to Owen, dropping them just inside the doorway.

The passageway was too small for the dragons to enter, so we were safe. The last thing I expected to hear as we escaped, though, was a mournful whimper. The sound was so sad it brought Owen up short. He turned around. "Stay. Be good," he told the dragons, who were shoving one another out of the way so they could each see him through the doorway. They settled down, resting their heads on their forearms and looking very much like Arawn had when he lay at the bottom of the stairs, waiting for Owen to come down. "We'll play again some other time," Owen told the dragons, looking rather guilty.

"You really do have a way with pets, don't you?" I said as we hurried back to the tunnel that would take us into the train station. "But I bet you won't feed those guys from the dinner table."

"Loony might get jealous, and I'd give her pretty good odds against them."

"You're not really going to go back and play with them, are you?"

"I might. I feel bad taming them that way and then leaving them lonely. Besides, you never know when a nest of friendly dragons might come in handy."

"I wonder if you could break any of them to a saddle so you could fly on them," I said, remembering a book I'd once read about people who rode dragons as a form of transportation. I'd always thought that sounded kind of cool.

"I imagine we'd first have to teach them to fly. These dragons seem to have never left the underground. Their wings might even be atrophied." When we reached the train platform—with no trains on either track, thank goodness—he said, "Don't worry, we're invisible again, and I think we'd better stay that way until we get home, considering the way we look." In the brighter light, I could see that his face and clothes were streaked with black soot. I probably didn't look much better. Neither of us smelled all that fresh, between the sweat, the soot, the dust from the tunnels, and the dragons' sulfur scent. In the New York subway system, our odor would probably blend in with all the other smells.

We slipped through the terminal, leaving traces of sooty footprints behind us, then made our way into the subway station to catch a downtown train. Nobody seemed to notice the turnstiles that turned on their own as we passed invisibly through them. I wasn't sure if the invisibility spell covered talking or not, so I didn't try to make conversation with Owen. He nodded at me and got up one station before Union Square. I guessed that meant we were going to his place to clean up.

Sure enough, once we'd made our way to a nearly empty sidewalk near Gramercy Park, he said, "I assume you'll want to clean up a bit before going home."

"Very good idea. I can't think of a single reasonable explanation for looking—and smelling—like this."

When we entered Owen's home, Loony took one whiff of him, then arched her back and hissed. "Yeah, yeah, I've been cheating on you with other pets," he said wearily. Then he turned to me and said, "By this time, you know the drill. Your usual emergency clothes are in the guest room, and you're welcome to use the shower there. I have a washer and dryer, so we can take care of your clothes before you go home, and I know a few cleaning spells that may help your coat. And I just realized, we never got around to having lunch. Want to order Chinese or a pizza or something?"

"Anything that's not a flambé," I said, shuddering.

As I rinsed the sulfurous soot out of my hair in Owen's guest bathroom shower, I realized that at least I'd broken my usual pattern. Instead of ending up at Owen's place cold and wet, I was hot and sooty. That wasn't much of an improvement. I wondered if there would ever be a time when I was at Owen's home just because he wanted me there with him and not in the aftermath of a disaster. Of course, that would mean having time with Owen without any disasters popping up, and the chances of that ever happening were beginning to look infinitesimal as long as we were in our current jobs.

The one thing missing in Owen's well-equipped guest bathroom was a blow dryer, but I made do by toweling my hair thoroughly, then combing it and toweling it again. I'd lathered, rinsed, and repeated enough times to get the sulfurous smell out of my hair, and I'd scrubbed a layer of skin off my face trying to get the soot off. Then I dressed in that same old sweat suit that Owen seemed to have designated as mine. In most relationships, keeping clothes at your boyfriend's place meant things were getting serious, and it might even be a first step toward moving in. In this relationship, it would mean giving myself a better-fitting option for the next time I found myself recovering from a disaster.

When I got downstairs, Owen was already showered and dressed. He was on the phone ordering Chinese food—in Chinese. I shouldn't have been surprised. As many languages as he could translate, it made sense he might speak a few. I sat on the sofa and allowed myself to admire him. Even with wet hair that looked like it had been toweled halfheartedly but not combed and with his glasses on, he was still gorgeous. I waited for that usual jolt of insecurity to hit me and make me wonder what a guy who looked like that who could tame dragons and then order in Chinese would want with someone like me, but it didn't come. He'd given me no reason to think he wanted anyone but me. Now, whether or not we could make things work was another story.

"I'm impressed," I said when he got off the phone.

As I expected, he turned a fetching shade of pink. He leaned against the edge of his desk like he was trying to look casual. "Oh, yeah, well, I do speak a little, and it was easier than making sure I was understood in English."

"You're full of surprises. Like whatever that was today with the dragons."

He brushed his damp hair out of his eyes, then frowned at the moisture left on his hand as if just noticing that his hair was still wet. "Remember when you first came to work at MSI, Rod gave you the grand tour, and when you were in my lab Jake came in with his pants shredded?"

I nodded. I was surprised he remembered it that vividly, considering it was just a vague recollection to me. "Yeah. He was testing a spell, wasn't he? Something to do with dogs?"

"The spell was supposed to soothe wild animals, only it obviously didn't work when Jake tried it on the dog that came at him. I've been tinkering with it since then to see how it really worked. I'm pretty sure it was a mistranslation on Jake's part, or maybe he left something out, because it seems to have worked for me."

"And on something much, much bigger than a stray dog. Do they even make Milk Bones that big? Or does Purina have a Dragon Chow? I know they make just about every other kind of chow because we sold it in our store back home."

It wasn't a great joke, but I'd hoped for at least a hint of a smile from him. Instead, he pounded his fist on his desk. "I can't believe I was stupid enough to walk into that trap."

"Trap?"

"Ari's trap. You don't think we accidentally stumbled on a nest of dragons while we were following her, do you?" He stood up and started pacing, the energy that usually bubbled just beneath his calm exterior now all at the surface. "I should have known better. What made me think that after our entire security force has spent more than a week combing the city for her, she'd happen to cross our path? And then I was dumb enough to fall for it and let her lead us into danger."

"I don't know that we could have seen that coming."

He stopped pacing and looked at me. "But you did, didn't you? I was the one who had to go into that tunnel. You wanted to go the other way. She had me totally fooled. I should know to always listen to you. I bet she sent an illusion for me to follow, right into her trap."

"I wasn't totally sure which way she went. I'd lost sight of her. I don't think either of us could have known, and we couldn't have risked missing the chance to follow her to their hideout. For all we know, the hideout could have been on the other side of the dragons, and they're using the dragons as watchdogs."

That calmed him somewhat. "True. I guess we'll never really know."

"Unless we want to do a little more exploring in that area and see if we can find what she might have been heading to, in case it wasn't a deliberate trap. You already have the dragons eating out of your hand. What other danger are you likely to stumble on down there?" The look on his face made me say, "Okay, scratch that. I don't want to know. But surely it can't be anything a pet dragon couldn't scare away for you. You know, we could have just made a wrong turn and stumbled into the dragons on our own," I added. "There is such a thing as coincidence."

He looked lost in thought while he pondered that, but before he could say anything the buzzer from the downstairs door sounded. "That'll be lunch. I'll be back in a second," he said, heading for the front door. He was back not long afterward with a giant paper bag.

"What army were you planning on feeding?" I asked.

"I like to plan on leftovers," he said. "And I like to make sure I have a couple of favorites I know I'll like, plus one new thing to try."

We went back to the kitchen table, where we barely had room for a couple of plates among all the take-out containers. "I may even be hungry enough to eat all of this," I said as I served myself. "Being attacked by dragons works up an appetite."

After we ate, we washed my clothes so I'd have something to go home in and continued discussing what we thought Ari might have been up to, Idris's new scheme, and what our next move might be. I'd given up on any non-work-related conversation. It wasn't like I could expect him to spend the day whispering sweet nothings into my ear when he was convinced our enemies had just tried to kill us.

By the time I made it home, my roommates were convinced my evil boss must have made me work all day. "Even Mimi, ex-boss from hell, didn't make you come in for a whole day on a holiday," Marcia said as I hung up my coat, which still smelled faintly of sulfur despite Owen's best efforts to clean it magically.

"I haven't been at work all day," I said, wishing I could summon one of Owen's blushes on command. I was too tired to pull off the bashful maiden routine at the moment. "I went out to lunch with Owen after work, and the day got away from us."

They both hooted, and I finally felt my face warming properly. At this point, I didn't care what they thought I'd been doing because that had to be preferable to the truth. "Time flies when you're having fun, doesn't it?" Gemma said.

"Yeah, it definitely does."

"Speaking of fun," Marcia said, "what do we have planned for New Year's Eve? Since we were apart at Christmas, we should all do something together."

"I'm barely recovering from the last holiday," I said. "I can't think that far ahead." For all I knew, I'd be engaged in a major magical battle that night. When you're part of the team trying to stop a rogue wizard, it's hard to make advance plans.

"Can you think as far ahead as dinner tonight?" Marcia asked. "I'm starving."

I wouldn't have thought I could eat anything after all that Chinese food I'd wolfed down that afternoon, but my stomach rumbled as soon as Marcia mentioned food. "I could eat something."

Gemma stretched lazily on the sofa. "I'll buy yours if you'll go to that sandwich shop down the street and pick something up. That's what I'm hungry for, and they don't deliver."

I collected orders and money, then got my coat and headed downstairs. Only after I was a block away from our building did it dawn on me that going out and about on my own might not have been the brightest idea. I did have enemies, after all. Or was I beneath Idris's notice now that he'd launched his company and, for all he knew, I couldn't do him much harm? At any rate, I made sure to keep my eyes open for anything that looked out of place.

I was still pondering angles we might be able to take against Idris as I left the sandwich shop with our dinner. I'd just rounded the corner onto our street when someone jumped out at me, shouting, "Wasn't that exciting?"

Thirteen

I had to juggle for a few seconds to keep from dropping my take-out bags. Only when I was absolutely certain Gemma's roast beef and brie sandwich wasn't going to go splat on the pavement did I look up and recognize Ethelinda. "Would you stop that?" I shouted. "Are you trying to give me a heart attack?"

"Sorry," she said with a giggle. She still wore that hideous reject prom dress, with bits of the fur from her Mrs. Claus outfit peeking out around the neckline. "Didn't mean to startle you."

"When you don't mean to startle someone, you don't appear out of thin air right in front of them. And what did you think was so exciting? I was just getting sandwiches."

She waved her wand in a dismissive gesture. "I wasn't referring to the sandwiches. I was talking about the dragons."

"You knew about the dragons?"

"I hear about things. There's very little that happens to you that I don't find out about."

"Oh." I wasn't sure I was crazy about that idea. There were reasons why I'd never auditioned to be on reality TV. I didn't like the idea of being watched. "Well, 'exciting' isn't quite the word I'd use to describe the dragons."

"Yes, but surviving an encounter with dragons and being rescued by such a brave young man must have been exciting."

"You'd think so, wouldn't you? But trust me, it doesn't work out that way in real life." It occurred to me then that Owen might have been right about the dragons being a trap. Ethelinda herself might have set it, not to put us in danger but because a hero rescuing a damsel in distress from a dragon was such a staple of romantic fantasy sagas. But surely she couldn't be that stupid. If she knew my entire relationship history and all that stuff about our destiny, she had to know what our work entailed and that dragons were pretty darn dangerous. It would be awfully hard to play matchmaker to a couple of piles of cinders. "You wouldn't have happened to arrange our meeting with the dragons, would you?" I asked.

"Moi?" She batted her eyelashes vigorously, as though she was both hurt and offended by my accusation, but she didn't exactly deny it. "Rescuing a maiden from a dragon is a sure way to generate romance. It's in all the stories. I can't begin to count the number of couples I've known who met that way. But that doesn't mean I had anything to do with it."

"You were there. I saw you."

"I was merely keeping an eye on my client. You were hard to keep up with when you were chasing your friend that way."

I wasn't entirely convinced of her innocence, but I could tell arguing would do no good. "Well, for the record, there's nothing romantic about dragons. They're ugly, loud, and smelly. And Owen thought someone was trying to lead us into a trap to kill us, so he spent the rest of the day wondering what our enemies might be up to. He probably wouldn't have noticed if I'd swooned into his arms."

"You didn't swoon into his arms?" For once, she sounded unsure.

"No. I'm not really the swooning type. I'm also not very good at being a damsel in distress. I don't like being rescued. I'd rather rescue myself. We already have a pretty skewed balance of power—literally—in this relationship. Him always having to rescue me doesn't help matters."

"It wasn't romantic, then?"

"No!" For once, I didn't play the good Southern girl and apologize when she looked hurt. I repositioned my bags and resumed walking toward home, making her flutter to keep up with me. "If you did have anything to do with it, or if you were thinking of doing something like that, please give it a rest. You're really not doing me a lot of favors in the romance department. Not that I recall asking you for any favors in the romance department, beyond one little, tiny bit of information, which you didn't have."

"So falling through the ice didn't give him the chance to warm you up?"

"Aha! I knew that was you! Yeah, there was some warming up and even snuggling, but it also ruined our date just when it was getting romantic. Who knows what might have happened if you'd let things play out naturally?"

"You think I had something to do with that? I'd never do anything to cause you harm."

She looked so hurt that I almost relented. "Look," I said, a little more gently, "things are complicated for us right now because of our work, so when something bad happens to us, neither of us is likely to think about romance as we rescue or comfort each other. Instead, we think that someone's out to get us, so we worry, which isn't too romantic, and since he's very, very dedicated to his work, he tends to go right into work mode to try to solve the problem, and that totally kills the romance."

She perked up. "Oh. Then I shall have to see what I can do to help you with that."

"No! You don't have to do anything!" I called out, but she disappeared before I got the "no" out. I could only begin to imagine what her next tactic might be if she was actually behind all the things that had happened to us lately.

. . .

The next morning, Kim reported bright and early to Owen's lab to get her assignment from him. Being sent out into the field undercover must have been the most excitement she'd had in a long time. Her sallow skin almost had a healthy flush to it and she'd lost that pinched look around her mouth. Maybe all she really wanted was to feel needed and important. Or maybe she was just excited about getting that much more of a grasp on my job.

While we waited for her to return with the spells, Owen buried himself in a book that was almost bigger than he was, and I searched the Internet for advertising case studies that might have some bearing on our situation. When Kim had been gone an hour, Owen gave up on reading and started pacing. He seemed on the verge of calling out the cavalry when she finally returned with two large Spellworks shopping bags.

"He's serious if he has good shopping bags," I said as Owen took them from her. They were almost on a par with what you'd find at a high-end boutique, with a shiny logo on the sides and ribbon handles.

"They are good shopping bags, aren't they?" Kim said. "Do you mind if I keep one when you're done with them?"

"We'll see," Owen said distractedly.

"Okay, just let me know if you need anything else. I'm only a phone call away." It was then that I realized her flushed look hadn't been excitement. It had been makeup. She'd dolled herself up to meet with Owen. She'd moved in on my job, and now was she moving in on my man? Fortunately, Owen was too focused on the problem at hand to even notice her or her attempts at fluttering eyelashes. There were times when his focus on work and obliviousness about other things worked in my favor.

We spent the rest of the day with me reading the spells out loud while Owen read over my shoulder so we could compare what he saw to what I saw. That was more than a bit distracting, and if Jake hadn't been hovering to see what we'd found, I might not have been able to stop myself from tackling Owen and throwing him down on one of the lab tables. After clearing it of clutter first, of course.

When I'd read at least six spells and had to take a break because my throat was raw, Owen buried his face in his hands with a groan. "We are in huge trouble," he declared.

"Why? Is there something dark hidden in there?"

He shook his head. "No. There's nothing veiled that I can tell. They're all perfectly legitimate, straightforward spells. Not particularly good ones, granted. They take far more energy than necessary to do that kind of work, and I don't see these spells as all that valuable for day-to-day life. But there's no reason here for us to stop him or go after him. I can't believe he's really trying to compete with us directly."

"Are we sure he is? Maybe he's just trying to establish credibility so his company will be more acceptable when he wants to introduce something else."

He leaned back in his chair and ran a hand through his hair. "You know, you could be right. He was able to get to the people who'd be looking for darker spells with his old way of selling through less reputable outlets, but he'd never gain any kind of market share if he went into business on this scale selling darker stuff. But this way, he gets customers, then he has a group of people who might be open to the next round of spells he offers."

"It's like boiling a frog," I said, nodding.

"What?"

"Well, supposedly you can't throw a frog into a pot of boiling water because it'll jump right out. But if you put it in a pot of cold water and gradually turn up the heat, it'll be boiling before it knows it needs to escape. Not that I've tried this myself, of course."

"I can see how the analogy works, even if it is kind of disgusting," he said with a grimace.

By the end of the day, Owen looked as tired as I felt. "Are you up for dinner?" he asked, coming around the side of the whiteboard that constituted my office wall. "Since our lunch yesterday got interrupted, I thought we could go out tonight."

"I know I'm not up to foraging for my own meal. Someone to bring it to me would be nice."

"Then do you want to go home, change clothes, and let me pick you up for a proper date, or do you just want to stop somewhere on the way home?"

"I couldn't begin to pick out an outfit. Let's just stop somewhere."

"Good, I'd hoped you'd say that," he replied with the first genuine smile I'd seen on his face all day. "There's a great Italian place near my house. I can call before we leave and make a reservation."

"That sounds ideal." While he moved all the sensitive material into his more secure office, I hurried down the hall to the bathroom to at least attempt to touch up my makeup and put on some lipstick. I might not have been dressing up, but that didn't mean I didn't want to inject a little glamour into the evening. Before I left the bathroom, I undid one more button on my blouse, taking the outfit from work-appropriate to just the least bit sexy. Well, as sexy as one of my work outfits ever could be.

When I got back to the lab, I saw that I wasn't the only one who'd loosened up for the evening. Owen was in the process of taking off his tie and stuffing it in his jacket pocket. "Ready to go?"

"Let me get my coat."

As we walked from the Union Square station up to the restaurant, he took my hand, which was a shock in and of itself. It was the kind of gesture I often hoped for from him but that he never seemed to think of. "Tonight, let's forget about work, okay?" he said. "I know it's hard for us to get away from, but let's try it for once."

"That's fine with me," I said, even as I wasn't sure we could pull it off. What were the odds that we could manage a few hours without something weird and work-related happening?

The restaurant was small and narrow, with crisp white tablecloths, frescoed walls, and heavenly scents coming from the kitchen. As soon as we stepped through the door, my mouth started watering. The host approached us and Owen said, "We have a reservation. The name's Palmer."

The host checked his reservation book, then frowned and said in heavily accented English, "My apologies, signore, but there has been a mistake. We should not have given you a reservation when you called."

"But there's a table open, right there. And my name is in your book." He pointed to the entry that very clearly showed a table for two reserved for Palmer at six.

"Ah, but that is because we moved your reservation to another restaurant to accommodate you."

Owen turned to me and gave me a confused look. I responded with a shrug, and Owen returned his attention to the host. "I don't understand. I made a reservation for two not too long ago. I spoke to you, if I'm not mistaken. And now you're telling me you moved my reservation to another restaurant—and that it's somehow to accommodate me?" His voice remained calm and even, so you would have had to know Owen to realize exactly how angry he was. The fact that he turned white instead of red was the only visible sign.

I put a hand on his arm. "It's okay. Maybe they can give us something to go and we can eat at home," I said. "That might be even better."

The host shook his head. "No, no, you do not understand. The new reservation, it is for a better restaurant. We will even arrange for a car to take you there. Make it a nicer evening, no?"

Owen again looked to me. "What the heck," I said with a shrug. "Just as long as the car isn't being driven by the same drivers we had the last time."

We went outside to wait for the car. "I don't get it," Owen said, still stewing. "I eat there regularly, but not to the point they'd go out of their way like this for me, and I've never heard of a restaurant sending business to another place. I know that me having a real date is a special occasion, but I didn't think they'd go nuts just because I made a reservation for two." After a moment of silence, he laughed. "Wait a second, I know what's going on. I bet Rod did it. I told him what I had in mind earlier in the day, and player that he is, he probably didn't think it was good enough. And maybe I do need dating lessons from the master."

"Just as long as you don't take too many lessons from him. You don't have a second date with someone else lined up for later this evening, do you?"

"One person at a time is all I can handle," he said as a white limousine pulled around the corner and stopped for us.

A uniformed chauffeur—who was fully human and not at all goofy-looking, thank goodness—got out of the car and came around to open the passenger door for us. "Mr. Palmer?" he said.

"Um, yeah. This is for us?"

"Yes, it is. Now, miss?" He held a hand out to me to help me into the limo. With a glance and shrug toward Owen, I stepped in and settled onto a plush leather seat. Owen then joined me. "Please enjoy the champagne during your ride," the driver said before closing the door.

"Yeah, this is definitely Rod," Owen said, eyeing the champagne in the ice bucket and the red rose lying on the seat between us. "It's very much his style. Shall we?" he asked, indicating the champagne.

"Sure, why not? We might as well enjoy this."

He popped the cork, then poured two glasses and handed me one. "Cheers," he said, clinking his glass against mine.

"To a work-free, stress-free evening," I said.

"Oh, I'll definitely drink to that."

As I leaned back in the seat and stretched my legs, I said, "This is the life." Never mind that in the rush-hour traffic, walking or the subway would have been much faster. Traffic jams weren't so bad when you weren't driving and when you had champagne.

"And he's a better driver than we had on our last trip," Owen added. "BRAAAAKE!"

His imitation of Rocky was so uncanny and so unexpected that I almost choked on my champagne. "Wow, when did you become a comedian?" I sputtered.

"There's a lot you don't know about me. Come to think of it, there's a lot I don't know about me." He sounded almost, well, bubbly, and then I realized the champagne must have gone straight to his head. I knew he wasn't much of a drinker, and I didn't remember him taking a break for lunch.

"You might want to ease up on that stuff," I warned, feeling my own head get a little fuzzy. But before we had a chance to get too tipsy, the car came to a stop and then the passenger door opened.

We'd arrived at a restaurant Gemma was always talking about because of someone famous having eaten there with some other famous person the night before, both of them wearing something fabulous by an equally famous designer. It was the kind of place where the paparazzi hide in the bushes nightly, just in case one of their usual targets happens to drop by. Even on a slow night they could probably get at least one tabloid-worthy photo of a socialite showing off the latest designer creation.

That made me suddenly self-conscious of my work clothes, which were nowhere near stylish and which probably bordered on frumpy. It was going to take a lot more than undoing one button to make me fit in here. In fact, I was fairly certain that this was all going to turn out to be one huge mistake and they wouldn't let us inside.

I wasn't the only one having such worries, apparently. Owen froze just inside the restaurant doorway and patted his pockets. "I bet I'll need my tie to be let in here," he said. "It looks like that kind of place."

That was when I noticed something different about Owen. It must have slipped my attention earlier because he was wearing a dark overcoat, but inside, with the coat unbuttoned, he was now wearing a different suit. It wasn't that much nicer than his work suit, since his work clothes were usually really nice, but instead of his usual white shirt he now wore a dark blue dress shirt with a bit of a sheen to it along with a silk tie in a similar shade. It was a look I recognized from some movie star at the previous year's Oscars.

"You've already got a tie on," I said, and to his credit, he actually checked instead of automatically telling me he thought I was wrong.

"This is weird," he said. "And I guess since you're seeing it, it's real." He then blinked as he looked at me. "I'm not the only one it happened to."

It was my turn to look down at myself. Instead of my frumpy work clothes, I had on a low-cut, flowing dress in a complicated print. I'd seen one very much like it—or possibly even the same dress—in one of Gemma's fashion magazines. If it was the same dress, I wouldn't want to take my coat off because then I'd feel naked. As it was, I kept wanting to pull the top up. I'd have to remember to sit up straight, or else the neckline would hit my waist.

The maître d' greeted Owen, then called someone over to take our coats. I considered putting up a fight for mine, but decided to be a big girl about it. Still, I couldn't help but cross my arms over my chest as we were escorted upstairs. The dress left my arms bare, so I hoped it was warm in the dining room.

In spite of our designer duds, we were nobodies for this kind of place. Owen might have looked like a movie star, but no one knew who he was. Meanwhile, if they had any idea who I was, they wouldn't have let me in the door for fear of damaging their cool rating. As a result, our table was strategically located behind a large potted plant. "Dr. Livingston, I presume," I quipped as we fought our way past the greenery to get into a banquette. I looked around the room at all the beautiful people making sure they were seen eating beautiful food and unconsciously straightened my spine. "Don't tell Rod because I wouldn't want to hurt his feelings, but I liked the original place better. This is nice, but that would have been more comfortable."

"I know. This wasn't quite what I had in mind for the evening. I was hoping we could relax." I noticed that he was sitting up straighter, too.

A waiter came and pushed back the palm fronds so he could hand us leather-bound menus before reciting a list of specials that sounded more like avant-garde poetry to me. Owen's face was about as blank as mine felt, and he just smiled and nodded at the waiter. I hoped the menu was a little more understandable. It was about the size of an abridged version of *War and Peace*. Owen had magical tomes in his office that were less intimidating.

"I may have to just point to something on the menu," I said. Most of the dishes seemed unnecessarily complicated to me. I was a pretty good cook, if I said so myself, so I recognized all the culinary terms and ingredients, but I'd never considered putting any of them together in quite this way. Aspects of some of the dishes sounded like they might be good, but then there would be some oddball ingredient thrown in, as though the chef had an uncontrollable urge to make the dish different. Like, they couldn't just serve beets as a side dish. It had to be beet froth, whatever that was.

I went with something that sounded like it might be a steak with sauce on it when the waiter reappeared to take our orders. If I didn't like the sauce, I could always scrape it off. Owen ordered the same thing. The waiter sniffed disapprovingly when we declined a meeting with the sommelier.

"I think I've had enough to drink for the evening," Owen said, rubbing his head, as soon as the waiter disappeared. "I'm still fuzzy from the champagne in the limo. But I guess that's terribly unsophisticated of us."

"Well, I am a hick from a small town in Texas," I drawled. "I don't know what your excuse is." I shoved aside a palm frond so I could look out into the rest of the restaurant. "If you had a machete with you, there might be good people-watching here. We could even get ourselves kicked out by asking for autographs. Wait'll the folks back home in the trailer park hear about this."

He must have still been feeling the champagne, given the way he laughed at what I didn't think was a very funny joke. "I think I like you a little bit drunk," I said.

He rubbed his temples again, like he was willing his wits to return fully. "Gloria would be disappointed in me. She's a confirmed teetotaler."

"No wonder you can't hold your liquor. Wait a second, how did you manage the champagne at the office party?"

"Did you see me drink much of it? Besides, I ate a full meal before I went. This is on an empty stomach. I think I forgot to eat lunch."

This may have been the most relaxed we'd ever been together as a couple. We weren't talking about work, and although the situation was far from normal, disaster hadn't yet struck. I was afraid to even think about it, lest I jinx us. "I don't think Gloria would expect you to turn down champagne in the back of a limo. She'd want you to have a little fun."

"Did you meet the same Gloria I know? No, you probably didn't. She was practically cuddly at Christmas. But she doesn't believe at all in losing control. With power like this at your beck and call, you must always be in absolute control of it. One slip can have serious consequences." Then he winced. "And I guess I blew that with my stunt in Times Square. I should know better than to act that rashly." There went the relaxation. I knew I shouldn't have thought about it.

I peered through the palm fronds again, trying to take note of any celebrities I saw and what they were wearing because I knew Gemma would be dying for details. Then I saw someone I recognized. Sylvia Meredith was sitting at a table on the other side of the room. The man she was with had his back to me, so I wasn't sure who he was. There was a bottle of champagne chilling in an ice bucket on a stand by their table, so they must have been celebrating something. Or maybe people who came to this kind of place regularly drank champagne like it was iced tea and didn't have to be celebrating anything.

I ducked back behind the camouflage. "Sylvia Meredith is here," I hissed to Owen, even though the room was noisy enough that I doubted anything I said would carry all the way to her table. "You know, the one we think is teamed up with Idris."

Owen immediately looked about as alert as he could manage with champagne still in his system. "Where?"

"Over on the far side of the room—the blonde who looks like she's got a touch of shark blood in her." He craned his neck to see, and I snapped, "Don't look! At least, don't be so obvious about it."

"Who is that with her?"

"I don't know. I don't recognize him from the back of his head."

An alarmingly skinny girl who I thought I recognized as the heiress to something, or maybe a pop star, or possibly both, walked past Sylvia's table. She wore a filmy blouse that gave her even less coverage than my dress did, and the spaghetti strap kept slipping off one of her shoulders. That wasn't too unexpected, since she was basically a hanger with legs and didn't really have shoulders to hold up straps. But then the strap went clear to elbow, so that she flashed the entire restaurant with her unspectacular but totally bare chest.

Sylvia's dining companion turned to watch as the girl struggled to pull her blouse back up, and I was then very glad I hadn't been eating anything or I might have choked. "It's Idris!" I said. He was dressed in a nice suit instead of his usual ratty black trench coat, and it looked like he'd had a haircut since I'd seen him last. No wonder I hadn't recognized him from behind.

"Yeah, and what do you bet he was the one who pulled that girl's blouse down?"

The waiter arrived then with our food, distracting us as he laid out plates with a flourish, then carefully arranged a bed of salad greens and finally added what looked like a small McDonald's hamburger in the middle of each plate, the top bun slightly askew to show the purplish sauce on top.

"This is it? It's a hamburger." I said when the waiter had gone. It didn't look like more than a mouthful of food. I guessed that was probably how the restaurant's patrons stayed so skinny.

Owen poked suspiciously at his burger with a fork. He looked up at me and opened his mouth to speak, but another voice interrupted him.

"Owen Palmer. Well, well, well. They'll let anyone in here these days." Of course, it was Phelan Idris. He must have come over to our table while the waiter was busy artistically arranging our hamburgers.

"I take it you're celebrating the launch of your new company," Owen said with the cool he usually showed under pressure. Meanwhile, I tried to shrink back into the banquette and hide behind the potted plant because Idris had brought Sylvia over with him. I hoped she wouldn't recognize me out of my disguise as Sue Ellen.

"Yep, it's been pretty successful," Idris said with a smug grin. In his nice suit he looked like a kid dressing up for his first dance. His sleeves weren't quite long enough for his arms, so his wrists showed. "And we're also celebrating the start of a profitable new partnership." He put a possessive arm around Sylvia, who looked like she would probably be burning her clothes as soon as she got home.

"So, how's Ari?" I asked.

He turned red in a blush worthy of Owen, and Sylvia turned even redder. "It's not that kind of partnership," she hurried to correct. "Strictly business." She took one step sideways away from Idris. Then she took another look at me. "Have we met?" she asked.

"I doubt it," I said, fighting to hide any trace of my Texas accent. The conversation had caught Idris's attention. He was looking at my low-cut neckline, and I remembered that magic could affect my clothes even if it couldn't affect me. I casually hooked a thumb through one of my dress straps so I could be sure to hold my top up. "I'm Kathleen Chandler, and you are?"

"Sylvia Meredith, Vandermeer and Company," she said stiffly, like I ought to have known.

"So, you're funding Idris?" Owen asked. "I'd think that would be a losing proposition."

I might have expected her to act smug, as though she was in on something we couldn't possibly know about. Instead, she got defensive—the kind of defensiveness that comes when you know you don't have much of a leg to stand on. "There are nuances I don't expect you to understand," she said, not meeting his eyes. There was also a trapped air about her. I halfway expected her to start blinking an SOS in Morse code. Then again, if I'd been out with Idris I'd have already written my "help!" message on the bathroom mirror in lipstick.

Idris, keen observer of social cues that he wasn't, puffed up what little chest he had and said, "Shows how much you know. She got really good advice about how important it was to back me." Both Owen and I leaned forward in anticipation that he was about to slip and reveal something good, but Sylvia elbowed him in the ribs so hard that he spun away and doubled over.

And then he promptly became sidetracked, as usual. The starlet/heiress/pop star he'd targeted earlier was walking past again, and again the strap of her blouse started moving down one arm. She clearly wasn't the sharpest knife in the drawer, or else she actually didn't feel too bad about flashing the restaurant, since she made no move to pull the strap back up. Just as her blouse fell to her waist, there was a flash from the potted palm behind me, and a rumpled photographer jumped out from behind the plant. That was when the screaming started.

Fourteen

All the other famous people in the place made a show of being horrified that the paparazzi were in their midst, but they managed to pose and show their good sides while acting outraged. Others immediately took cover. The flash going off repeatedly, practically in my face, blinded me. I looked away to preserve my eyesight, just in time to see Rocky and Rollo swooping down at us from above.

"It's okay, miss," Rocky said, "we're on the case."

"On what case?" I asked.

"Your mortal enemy is here, and we'll take care of him for you."

I pondered crawling under the table, or maybe crawling through the potted plant—now that the photographer was no longer lurking—and getting out of the restaurant. I knew Sam needed the occasional night off, but did the gargoyle world's answer to the Keystone Kops have to be the ones on duty when we were face-to-face with Idris?

Except, we weren't anymore. He was happily in the middle of the melee, posing alongside every famous person in the room while Sylvia hissed at him. He had to be loving the chaos, and he must have disguised himself because Rocky and Rollo were back to circling the room, as if they'd lost him. I wondered which male celebrities would unexpectedly have their pictures in the tabloids this week, and which tabloids would be sued for printing incriminating pictures that were supposedly taken in New York at a time when the celebrities were documented as being halfway around the world.

Owen flagged down a waiter who was on his way to nab the photographer. "Could we get the check, please?" he asked. The waiter nodded but didn't slow his stride as he and two other waiters caught the photographer and hauled him bodily out of the room, camera still flashing. Even with the photographer out of the picture, so to speak, the melee continued. I wouldn't have been surprised if food started flying. I looked down at my untouched plate and couldn't help but agree that my hamburger would make a better missile than dinner.

The waiter returned, straightening his jacket collar. "Your bill has already been taken care of, sir. Thank you, and have a nice evening."

We didn't waste any time verifying who'd paid for this ridiculous night as we hurried to escape from the restaurant. There wasn't anyone manning the coat check when we got there—probably upstairs helping break up the fight that had started between two pop princesses who'd stolen each other's boyfriends—so Owen waved a hand and our coats flew to join us. We then ran outside to the sidewalk.

When we'd caught our breath, I turned to Owen and said, "I can't take you anywhere."

He looked stunned for a second, and then he broke down in near-hysterical laughter, bending over and bracing his hands on his knees as he gasped for breath between laughs. I imagined he was still a little tipsy, and he was pretty tightly wound, so if he started letting his emotions out, there was bound to be a lot pent up. His laughter was infectious. Soon, I was laughing, too. With the kind of dating luck we seemed to have, we had to laugh at it, or else we'd go crazy.

When he caught his breath, Owen looked up and down the street. "I wonder if the limo is supposed to take us home, or if we're on our own. Where are we, anyway?"

"I don't see any familiar landmarks. We must be uptown somewhere. I guess we could start walking and see if a street name rings a bell." I wasn't too excited about that prospect. Our fancy clothes hadn't changed back to normal when we left the restaurant, so I wasn't exactly dressed for walking. I pulled my coat's collar as tightly closed as I could over my bare chest.

Owen continued looking up and down the street. "And then maybe we'd pass a burger joint or any other place that serves actual food. I think I may have to hit Rod tomorrow."

"You've already hit Rod. Please don't make it a habit. Besides, he did pay for the dinner."

Just then, the limo pulled up, and the driver hopped out and hurried to open the door for us. Owen and I looked at each other, shrugged, then climbed in.

Owen glanced at his watch as the limo took off, then winced. "I didn't realize it was so late. I thought time only flew when you were having fun."

"It was kind of fun, in retrospect."

"And we got some valuable information."

"Was it just me, or did Sylvia sound like she wasn't happy about having to work with Idris?" I asked.

"I can't say I blame her. Would you be happy to work with Idris?"

"But you may notice I'm not working with him. It almost seemed like she was being forced."

"So maybe she's the one funding him, but there's yet another person pulling the strings."

"Is there anyone you know of who'd be powerful enough to force someone like her to invest in Idris?"

"I have no idea, but James might know some names to start with."

The driver's voice came over a speaker into the back of the limo. "Where would you like me to take you?"

Owen turned to me. "Up for some leftover Chinese? I still have plenty."

I checked my watch. "You know, you're right. It is late, and it's a school night. I'd better just go home." We had to search to find the controls that allowed us to talk to the driver. When the limo came to a stop and the driver told us we were at our destination, Owen helped me out of the car. "Well, it was interesting," I said. "And no, it didn't entirely suck."

"Next time it'll be normal. I promise."

"Don't make promises you can't keep," I said before he got back into the limo. He rolled down the window and waved as the limo drove away. Only then did I realize that we'd both forgotten to kiss good night. So much for a grand, romantic evening. We weren't adapting well to this whole dating thing, though I had a feeling we'd do a lot better if the universe would just leave us alone for a little while. Maybe we should even give up on trying to date and just be friends until everything settled down. It certainly wouldn't change much about our time together, only the amount of frustration I felt after we were together.

When I unlocked the front door, I realized I was still wearing that designer dress. I wondered if I'd get to keep it, or if it was like Cinderella's ball gown, something that would vanish at midnight. But that wasn't the real question. The real question was how I'd explain the dress to Gemma, who'd flagged it in a magazine last month, and even more, how I'd explain when it wasn't there in the morning.

I braced myself as I came up the stairs and hoped Gemma and Marcia were out, or at least sidetracked. No such luck. They both stared at me as I stepped through the door. "Oh, my God," Gemma breathed. "Where did you get that?"

"It's a knockoff I found in Chinatown," I lied. "It'll probably disintegrate overnight, but I didn't pay that much for it, and it worked for this one date."

She was across the room in a heartbeat, fingering the material and inspecting the seams. "It's the best knockoff I've ever seen. This is couture detailing."

"Oh no!" I said, dredging up some tears, "I bet some poor little girl in a sweatshop made this by hand, and she got paid nothing, and by buying something like this, I helped oppress her. But all I wanted was a nice dress." With my tears in full force, I ran for the bedroom and shut the door behind me, then I took off the dress, wadded it up and hid it in my footlocker, where I was pretty sure I'd find my work skirt and blouse the next morning.

Then I remembered that's what had happened to the dress Ethelinda had given me for my first date with Owen. Could she have been up to her old tricks, engineering her idea of a romantic evening, or was Owen right about Rod's interference?

At work the next day, while Owen and Jake continued testing Idris's spells, I got caught up on my other work that Kim hadn't taken over from me. I was out taking care of some paperwork when I ran into Rod in the hallway. "Hey, I'm glad I caught you," he said.

"What's up?"

"I'm having a New Year's Eve soiree and I was hoping you and Owen might make it if you don't already have plans. I left Owen a message, but he hasn't gotten back to me yet. Bring your friends, too—anyone you can think of. It's an impromptu bash, but I'm trying to make it as big as possible."

"Do you really want them there? They aren't in on the magical secret."

"That's the brilliant part. It's a costume party. That way, nobody will think anything of us having fairies, elves, or anything else running around, in case they don't want to veil themselves."

"Okay, sounds fun. I'll check with Owen and my roommates and let you know." I realized then that this was my chance to figure out who was behind our adventures of the night before and added casually, "Oh, and thanks for last night. It really was a special evening."

"Last night?" he looked blank. "I thought you and Owen went out to dinner last night."

"We did. But didn't you upgrade his plans for him?"

"No. I know better than that. You don't shift Owen out of his comfort zone without fair warning. He doesn't take well to that. Why, what happened?"

"Nothing. Just a little misunderstanding." As in, a fairy godmother who failed to understand that we really did not need her meddling in our lives. I was going to have words with her, and I was going to do it before this nonsense went any further.

I went straight back to Owen's lab to get my coat. "I'm going out for lunch," I declared. "Want me to bring you anything?"

He looked up from his work. "I could conjure you whatever you want."

"No thanks. Not today. I've got errands to run. You know, post office and stuff like that. I may be awhile." I took off before he had a chance to respond.

Life would have been easier if I'd brought Ethelinda's locket with me to work, but as I hadn't been planning to summon her anytime soon, it was still locked in my nightstand. That meant I had to go back to my apartment. Fortunately, the subway trip was pretty quick, and I lucked out with a train coming almost as soon as I entered the station. I got off at Union Square and then ran the few blocks to my apartment. There I grabbed the locket.

Ethelinda had said all I had to do was open the locket, and then I'd know what to do. It sounded simple enough. I held the locket in my palm and flipped it open. Words scrolled across the lower portion of the locket, almost like text messaging on a cell phone. "Would you care to arrange a meeting with Ethelinda?" the words said, spelled out in a fancy, flowing script. "Press your thumb inside the lid to say yes."

I pressed my thumb on the inside of the locket's upper portion. Then more words appeared: "Welcome, Katie. Ethelinda will meet with you at her earliest possible convenience. Press your thumb again if this is agreeable." What do you know, fairy godmothers had the magical equivalent of a voice-mail system. This seemed almost like calling my bank. I pressed my thumb as directed, then the words "thank you" appeared before the locket went dark. I closed it, then slipped it into my purse, wondering when her earliest possible convenience would be. I hoped it would be soon.

I made a peanut butter sandwich and got a soda from the fridge, then went back to Union Square, where I sat in the park to eat my lunch and wait on my fairy godmother. I didn't care if it took all day, but I wasn't going back to work until I'd taken care of this.

I didn't have to wait long. She appeared within minutes, scaring the pigeons away when she suddenly popped into existence next to me on the park bench. Today's outfit looked a lot like Scarlett O'Hara's famous dress made out of the drapes, only after the drapes had been hanging for decades and a few generations of moths had made meals out of them. The hot-pink prom dress showing through the holes clashed horribly with the green of the outer dress. A strip of the tasseled border at the hem of the skirt had come undone, leaving the tassels to trail on the ground.

"Oh, I'm so glad you called me. I couldn't wait to talk to you," she said, her wings fluttering hopefully. "Now, you have to tell me how everything went last night."

"So, it was you. You changed the reservations, got the limo, changed our clothes, and all that?"

"Of course! I don't know what that boy was thinking, taking you to an ordinary place like that when he's supposed to be courting you. He should be wining and dining you, showing you the finer things. He should be making an effort. But that's where I step in, to correct those little mistakes. Tell me how it went! I want to hear everything."

"It was . . ." I started to go by habit and say "okay," but instead I decided to be honest. "Quite frankly, it bombed."

Her wings wilted. "No romance?"

"No romance. I guess it was fun, in a way, but it wasn't the least bit romantic."

"But it was supposed to be romantic—the limousine, the champagne, the rose, the nice restaurant. That's what young ladies these days want."

I got the sinking feeling that she'd studied up on non-dragon-slaying paths to romance by watching reality TV dating shows. Now that I thought about it, the whole date sounded like the kind of thing you'd see on *The Bachelor*. It was a fake, made-for-TV date.

"Romance isn't a one-size-fits-all thing," I tried to explain, realizing the irony of me trying to explain romance to the fairy godmother responsible for hooking up Cinderella with her handsome prince. "I'm sure there are some people who would have found all that very romantic, but not Owen and me. Things were actually going pretty well for us that night. He held my hand on the way to the restaurant, and he never seems to think of doing stuff like that. I liked the restaurant he chose. It was comfortable and cozy, and we'd probably have had a good meal we could have lingered over. He was finally letting his guard down, and we might have really talked. It wasn't all your fault that things didn't work out. It just so happened that one of our enemies was there, too, and that created some of our problems. We were too distracted by everything that happened to even remember to kiss good night."

She didn't look convinced. "Have you considered that my efforts to inspire romance haven't worked for you because you're not suited for each other?"

I had, but only deep down inside, and I wasn't ready to go there yet. "We haven't even been dating for two whole weeks. Isn't that too soon to tell?"

"Cinderella knew after three nights at a ball."

I'd actually always wondered how she could have known so quickly that this was the guy for her, and how he could have based his choice of wife on her shoe size, but I didn't want to get into that with Ethelinda right now. "Aren't we supposed to be destined for each other?"

"Perhaps you were only meant to work together and it was that kind of partnership." She drew herself up straighter. "My methods of instigating romance are time-tested and go back centuries. If I can't get a couple together, then they have no romantic possibilities."

"Yeah, 'cause if dragons don't do it for you, you don't stand a chance," I muttered under my breath.

She reached over and gave my hand a gentle pat. "Don't take this too hard, my dear. Do you realize how difficult a mixed marriage would be? I can't believe I ever allowed myself to think that a wizard of his caliber was meant for an immune like yourself. You two see the world in entirely different ways. I know he tries to act normal, but do you understand what it's like to have that kind of power? And if you don't understand that, there's no way you could ever really understand him."

I shook my head, refusing to believe that—but was it because I was in denial or because it wasn't true? "But . . . but the magical differences haven't been our problem," I said, thinking out loud. "Whatever problems we've had seem to have more to do with the fact that we work together and our work is challenging. We've got enemies who keep getting in our way." Now that I thought about it, that was absolutely true. I felt better already.

Unfortunately, I didn't seem to have convinced Ethelinda. "You just don't appreciate the differences. That might not be the problem now, but it was sure to be one down the line. Best you stop it now before anyone gets hurt."

"If that's the case, if someone like me can't find happiness with someone like him, then why were you even involved in the first place?"

"Perhaps my job was to keep you from being together. Destiny does tend to blur at times."

I got up from the bench. "Well, I don't want your help. Stay out of my life. I'll take things from here. However things work out, it's up to us."

Needless to say, I was still crabby when I got back to the office, and even though I knew I was taking out my anger on the wrong person, I couldn't stop myself from snapping at Owen when he commented on me being back. "Yes, I'm back. So?"

He looked confused, but merely said, "So, we had a meeting. I was worried about you."

It was only then that I remembered the meeting we had to discuss Idris's latest scheme. "Oh no! I'm sorry, I guess I got sidetracked." I thought for a moment about telling Owen about Ethelinda, but now that she'd given up on us and would probably be out of our hair, I figured he didn't need one more thing to worry about.

"It's okay, I think I know all that you know at this point, so I was able to fill everyone in. You'll just have to cover for me at the next meeting." He frowned as he looked at me, then asked, "Is something wrong?"

I had to fight the urge to laugh maniacally. Seriously, what wasn't wrong? Our enemy was apparently thriving, and there was nothing we seemed able to do about it. I had an incompetent fairy godmother who was interfering in my life and who had just declared that I wasn't suited for the man of my dreams, after all. Meanwhile, I had to admit that things with Owen did seem to have stalled out on the romantic front, and I wasn't sure how much of that was because circumstances kept getting in the way of us having a normal dating life and how much might be because we really weren't cut out to be anything more than friends. But I knew that wasn't what he meant. "No, nothing's wrong. Just frustrating lines and unhelpful people. I'm sorry I took it out on you."

"That's okay. We all have bad days." He reached as though to touch the side of my face and came back with a foil-wrapped piece of chocolate. "Maybe this will help."

As I unwrapped it, I said, "I hope you just conjured this because I'm not sure I want to eat chocolate that's been hiding up your sleeve or behind my ear." He gave me a vague, mysterious look, but I needed chocolate in the worst way, so I popped it into my mouth. "Anything interesting come out of the meeting?" I asked once the chocolate had made its way into my system and calmed me somewhat.

He rearranged a few of the piles on one of the lab tables. "Nothing much. We rehashed the same old theories. I did share your theory about boiling a frog—but with a metaphor slightly less frightening to Mr. Lansing—and what we noticed last night about Idris and Sylvia Meredith. Ethan's still working on Philip's claim against that company, but it's hard to prove a century-old enchantment." He shuffled, then straightened another pile. "Oh, and Mr. Mervyn wants you to try that other experiment."

"What other experiment?"

"The one to take away your immunity temporarily so you can see what the rest of the world sees. He thinks that could be helpful."

"Oh yeah, that." I knew I shouldn't be nervous about this; since I trusted Owen to do the potion the right way and I'd survived the last time when Idris and his people had tampered with the water supply going into my building. It had been my idea in the first place, but now that it looked like a reality, it was scarier than I'd anticipated.

Owen moved over to another lab table, where a beaker and a few vials sat. As he mixed things up, he said, "You probably won't see any effects until the second dose, which I'll give you in the morning. This is more concentrated than the formulation you were given before, so I expect it will hit you more suddenly. You'll know for sure it's happening."

"And then how long will it last?"

"That depends on how well it works and if we get what we want rather quickly. If we stop at three doses, which is what I think we'll need for maximum effect, it should have completely worn off after New Year's."

His mention of New Year's reminded me of the message Rod gave me back before I ran out to confront Ethelinda. "Oh, yeah, have you called Rod back yet? I ran into him and he said to remind you he's having a big New Year's Eve party and he wanted us there. He says it's a costume party, so he wants me to invite my friends. They'll never know who's magical and who's in costume."

He scowled as he stirred his potion in the beaker. "Costumes? Where are we going to come up with costumes at this time of year?"

"You could always go as a wizard."

"Very funny."

"Oh, come on, you'd look great in one of those flowing robes and a pointy hat with stars and moons on it. Maybe a white beard."

"Or Mickey Mouse ears," he said, raising an eyebrow. "What flavor do you want this to be?"

"What?"

"The potion. I can flavor it to taste. Chocolate?"

I eyed the fizzing potion suspiciously. "I don't think that looks like the right texture for chocolate. Can you make it taste like tea?"

"Tea I can do." He waved his hand over the beaker, whispering a few words, then handed it to me. "Here you go. Bottoms up."

I took a cautious sip. It really did taste like sweetened iced tea, so I drank the rest. He watched me the whole time, like he thought I might suddenly sprout rabbit ears. I was tempted to shake violently or fake a faint just to see how he'd react, but I suspected he wouldn't take well to that. He looked tense enough as it was. I knew he wasn't crazy about this plan and was only doing it under Merlin's orders. "Not bad," I said when I'd emptied the beaker.

"Are you feeling okay?"

"I'm fine. Am I supposed to feel something?"

He shook his head and brushed his hair off his forehead. "No, I guess I'm just worried. I can't help it. If they've been coming after us, I'm concerned about what might happen while you're affected."

"How will they know? I managed to fake you out the last time. They shouldn't know I've lost my immunity." Again, I wondered if telling him about Ethelinda might make him feel better, but then decided it might make him even more paranoid. "So, about that party," I said, changing the subject.

"Do you want to go?"

"It might be fun. If your estimate is right, I should still be slightly affected by the immunity loss, so I would see some of what my friends are seeing, which might help avoid any real weirdness."

"I should warn you, Rod's parties are rather notorious. They usually get a little wild for my taste, but it is certainly something you should experience at least once."

I wondered for a second if he'd made other plans for us. A quiet evening at home with the two of us sounded more like his idea of a celebration, but I did also want to be with my friends. This party would be the best of both worlds—ringing in the New Year with him and with my friends. "If you don't mind, I'd like to go," I said. "I haven't ever been to a big New Year's Eve party. I promise to keep my roommates from bothering you."

He smiled and nodded. "Okay, then. We'll go." He didn't sound too disappointed, so if he had thought about what he'd rather be doing, he didn't seem like he'd planned in detail. If I knew Owen, he might even have forgotten that New Year's tended to follow Christmas, he was so caught up in his work. "And if you like, we could have dinner tonight and talk about costumes. Maybe it'll be our lucky night, and we can have a normal dinner."

As much as I liked him, I didn't think I could face another one of our attempted dates. I didn't have the physical or emotional energy to deal with yet another disaster without having a total meltdown. "Can I take a rain check?" I asked. "I suspect we'll need to get together tomorrow night anyway so we can scope out Idris's ads and you can tell me what you see so we can compare."

"Oh, right. Good point. Tomorrow night, then?" If I hadn't come to know him as well as I had, I wouldn't have been able to see the disappointment in his eyes.

That night I told my roommates about the party, and they were both so enthusiastic that they spent most of the evening digging around in the closet to come up with costume ideas. "A masked ball for New Year's is genius," Gemma said, holding a red pashmina around her head, Little Red Riding Hood style. "You can try out being someone else as the calendar changes. There's all kinds of symbolism there."

"This is that really hot guy you know who's hosting it, right?" Marcia asked.

"Yeah, he's Owen's best friend."

"And what's his job again?"

"He's head of Personnel."

"Oh." There was something about the way she said it that made me wonder if she was going to bother passing the invitation on to her boyfriend, Jeff.

The next morning, I put on Owen's necklace as I got dressed. I might have to take it off once I got to the office, but if there was any chance my immunity might be dimmed, I wanted to be sure to know that magic was in use around me. Owen met me on the sidewalk in front of my building with a cup of take-out coffee. "Let me guess, this is your own special blend," I said as I took the cup from him.

"A very special blend, indeed. You're wearing the locket."

"Yes. I thought it might come in handy."

"That's not the purpose I intended it for, but it works, I suppose."

I took a sip of the coffee. It tasted like plain old coffee to me, the way I took it with cream and sugar. I couldn't detect whatever drug or potion he'd put in it. "So, this is the dose that's really going to do it, huh?" I asked.

"You probably won't notice the effects until late today. We'll give it a test this afternoon, then I'll give you a final dose before we leave work. Tonight I thought you could take a look at the subway ads, and then we could have dinner at my place and watch for TV ads. That is, if you don't have other plans?"

"No, nothing else planned."

"Great. Then tomorrow we can visit Times Square and run by the store."

My neck began to tingle from the necklace as we boarded the subway, and sure enough, there were the Spellworks ads. I still saw them the same way I had all week, so I must have been fully immune. Although I knew we needed me to do this, I couldn't help but feel relieved that I still had my immunity. It had been a scary, helpless feeling the last time. Maybe it wasn't too late to tell Owen I'd changed my mind. He'd be all for stopping the potion and coming up with a plan B, since he'd been opposed to this in the first place. But I knew it was important. We needed all the information we could get, and this was the quickest and easiest way to go about getting it.

When we approached the MSI office building, the necklace began to vibrate. I realized I wouldn't be able to wear it at work at all. By the time I decided to take it off, it was almost painful. I was ready to grab it and break the chain, just to get it off my neck, but Owen stepped in and unfastened it for me. "Sorry about that," he said. "I may need to rethink this. There may be a better approach. But for now, it would probably be best if you avoid wearing it around the office. Power is so amplified in this building that it will drive you crazy." He handed it to me, and I could still feel it buzzing in my hand, so I quickly dropped it into my purse.

We got to Owen's lab and then both of us stopped short. One of the largest bouquets of flowers I'd ever seen sat in the middle of one of the lab tables, the piles of papers shoved aside.

"I wonder if those are for you or for me," Owen said.

Fifteen

I stepped forward and dug through the foliage to find a card. There was one with my name on it, but the inside said merely, "Thank you for everything, with my deepest devotion." It wasn't signed.

"They're apparently for me," I said, "but it looks like I have a secret admirer. I don't know who sent them." I gave Owen a sidelong glance to gauge his reaction, but he just frowned. I knew he was physically incapable of playing it cool in a situation like this, so that was a good sign he hadn't sent the flowers. If he'd been involved at all, he'd have been blushing furiously and unable to look at me.

He half closed his eyes and walked around the table, holding his hands out. Then he shook his head. "There's no magic here. The flowers themselves aren't magical in origin, and I don't detect any hidden spells." He sneezed violently. "However, there does appear to be some pollen."

My eyes watered at the strong, sickeningly sweet scent of the stargazer lilies in the arrangement. I tended to think of those as funeral flowers. "Yeah, the lilies are going to make me queasy if we keep them in here. Maybe that was the dastardly plan of whoever sent them."

"If you don't mind, I can get rid of them."

"Please."

He waved a hand, mumbled a few words, and the flowers vanished. Then he set about putting the piles of papers that had been rearranged back into place. "I wonder who sent those," he mused out loud as he worked. "It wouldn't have been any of your friends, would it?"

"A huge bouquet sounds like Philip's style, though I would have expected a formal thank-you note along with it if he'd sent it to thank me for my help in getting his business back. And I haven't yet actually accomplished anything there other than hooking him up with a lawyer."

Only as Owen went off to his office to get to work and I went to my own desk did it occur to me that it also seemed like something Ethelinda might have done. The size and general tackiness of the bouquet certainly fit her taste. I'd hope Philip would have been more tasteful than that, though the Edwardian era wasn't exactly known for its restraint and subtlety. If Ethelinda had sent flowers anonymously, she either had to be trying to make Owen jealous or make me mad at Owen because he wasn't sending me flowers when someone else was, while also distracting me from Owen by raising the possibility of a secret admirer. If it was Ethelinda, that was the final proof of just how clueless she was. It hadn't seemed to cross Owen's mind to be jealous, and I wasn't the least bit interested in the fictional secret admirer. I also wasn't the kind of woman who'd want Owen to be jealous. I'd hope he'd trust me and my feelings for him. Besides, when in the past few weeks had I had time to meet someone who could admire me secretly?

Late in the afternoon, Owen came around the corner to my office, looking grave. "Are you ready to test your immunity?" he asked.

"I suppose it's too late to change my mind, huh?"

"This was your idea in the first place. I argued against it."

"Yeah, and I keep kicking myself. Well, let's see how effective your potion was."

He held out his left hand, palm open. Then he waved his right hand over it and a coin appeared in his palm. "What do you see?"

I leaned over to get a better look. "A quarter. You're not doing one of your stage magic tricks, are you?"

He passed his right hand over his left again, and that time I could feel the tingle of magic in use. If I'd been wearing the locket, it would have given me a jolt. "Okay, now what do you see?" he asked.

"A quarter," I replied with a shrug.

"That's all? Are you sure?"

"Sorry. It's one of the special state quarters, if that helps." I started to turn away, then saw something colorful out of the corner of my eye. I blinked and turned back slowly, but the image faded when I looked at it head-on. "Okay, wait a second, I saw something in my peripheral vision, but it's fading in and out."

"It looks like you need another dose. I don't know if it will have taken full effect by this evening, though."

I followed him back out into the main lab, where he mixed up the potion and handed me a glass. "If the magic thing doesn't work out for you, you've got a future as a bartender," I quipped before I drank the potion, which was tea-flavored again.

He looked worried as he watched me drink. "I hope I got the dosage right. I may have underestimated your body weight."

"Don't ever apologize to a woman for that."

He grinned. "I know. And notice that I was smart enough not to ask. I'm not entirely ignorant where women are concerned." He checked his watch. "Let's give that dose another hour to work, and then we'll test you again." I went back to my desk and tried to work, even though I was nervous about really losing my magical immunity. Part of me couldn't help hoping that the potion didn't work, after all, and it would turn out that I was no longer capable of being rendered susceptible to magic.

When Owen came back to my desk an hour later, I got a sick feeling in my stomach. "Here we go again," I said. "Give me your best shot, O great and powerful Oz."

"Oz wasn't a real wizard. I am," he said with his typical straightforwardness. This time, he didn't bother playing magic tricks. He simply held out the hand with a quarter in his palm, said a few words under his breath, and then asked, "Now what do you see?"

"A Sacagawea dollar?"

"What?"

"Just kidding. I see a quarter. Sorry." But then I caught another one of those glimpses out of the corner of my eye. If I squinted just right as I turned my head, I could keep that image in place instead of it fading back to a quarter. "It's one of those rainbow-colored bouncy balls, like you get in a gumball machine."

"That's it. But you can't see it without squinting like that?"

"Not really. I can't quite keep the image in focus. But it's better than the last time when I could only see it out of the corner of my eye."

"You're being a difficult case, you know."

"I had to pick some area in life to be high-maintenance. Maybe the drugs lose their potency on you after a while. Or maybe it's harder to lose your immunity each time." That could also mean it would take longer to get the immunity back. I didn't like the idea of essentially losing a sense for very long while we had enemies out to get us.

"Do you still want to give things a try tonight, or would it be a waste of time?"

I looked up at his worried blue eyes and remembered the feeling I got the first time I met him, when he'd been almost too shy to speak to me at all. "Being with you is never a waste of time," I said as butterflies formed in my stomach. "That is, if you don't care how much work gets done tonight."

He pinkened slightly, but he held my gaze instead of looking bashfully at the floor. "It's all just a ruse to get you alone with me, anyway. Anything we might accomplish is a bonus. The way I see it, if we're in my very heavily warded house, that makes it nearly impossible for anyone to put us in danger or tinker with our plans and we might actually be able to spend time together without too many distractions."

"So, we're both on the same page, then. That's good." Even better, if things went more smoothly for us this evening than on any of the occasions in which Ethelinda had interfered, then I'd know she was wrong about us not being suited for each other.

By the time I left the office, the butterflies in my stomach had spawned offshoot flocks that had taken up residence in my heart, my head, and my knees. I wasn't sure what had me so keyed up, facing the thought of being magically blind or looking forward to what might happen with Owen without any major disasters to mess things up—or to break the ice (in a figurative way this time, I hoped).

Owen walked me through the building corridors toward the exit with a protective hand at the small of my back. You'd have thought I'd been stricken suddenly ill or frail, the way he was acting. As much as I'd meant what I said to Ethelinda about not liking it when I needed to be rescued all the time, I rather enjoyed this protectiveness. Come to think of it, what I was really enjoying was his proximity. He wasn't a touchy person, so I was up for anything that gave him a reason to touch me.

On the stairs to the building lobby, we ran into Rod—or rather, the handsome man I'd learned to see as Rod the last time I'd lost my magical immunity. The fact that I now saw his illusion instead of his real face was a good sign that the potion had finally kicked in. "Hey, I'm glad I caught you two," Rod said. "I take it you'll be at the party?"

Owen glanced ever so slightly at me before replying, "Yeah, we'll be there. But you aren't serious about costumes, are you?"

"If you want to be boring, you can wear evening clothes and a mask, but I'd hope you have more imagination than that."

"I told my roommates, and they're excited about it," I said. "And don't worry, I'll see to it that he comes up with some kind of costume." That was awfully big talk coming from me when I had no idea what I was going to wear, but dressing me was Gemma's mission in life, and I figured I'd leave it to her.

"I can't wait to see what you come up with," Rod said with a laugh. "I should warn you, though, that you're dealing with the kid who wore the same Robin Hood costume for Halloween every year until he outgrew it. Getting him into a costume will be a real challenge."

When we'd said good-bye to him and continued on our way to the lobby, I couldn't resist asking, "Robin Hood?"

"I liked the movie."

"The one with Errol Flynn?"

"The Disney one, where Robin Hood's a fox. Gloria questioned the moral lesson of robbery ever being good, regardless of who was being robbed, but she thought the cartoon presentation was benign enough in its anthropomorphizing of the animal characters, as long as I also learned the true history of King Richard and Prince John." Then he gave a crooked, rueful grin. "I just wanted to be able to shoot a bow and arrow."

"I liked that one, too," I admitted. "I went as Maid Marian for Halloween one year, but nobody knew who I was supposed to be and I got very frustrated. And by the way, the immunity is gone. I saw Rod's illusion, full-strength." Now that I thought about it, I hadn't noticed the usual effects of his attraction spell. Either he hadn't wasted the effort of using it on me, or Owen's nonmagical spell on me was too strong for me to notice anyone else when he was around.

"That's good to know. I think." He stopped just inside the main entrance and said, "If you've got the necklace with you, maybe you should put it on now." I fished it out of my purse, and he took it from me to fasten around my neck while I held my hair up out of the way. It seemed to take him forever to get it fastened, and I couldn't tell if he was fumbling with the clasp or deliberately torturing me by touching me lightly on the back of my neck over and over again. When we left the building, he had a protective arm around my waist. I'd seen what he could do and knew without a doubt that he wouldn't allow anything to happen to me.

We got on the subway and staked out a pole, standing face-to-face on either side of it. As the train lurched forward, he looked over the top of my head at the ads that ran the length of the car, just under the ceiling, then he bent to speak directly into my ear. "Tell me what you see."

I looked up and straight into his eyes, close enough to see the slight color variations throughout the midnight blue. If I wasn't mistaken, there were flecks of silver in there. But I didn't think that was what he was talking about. "You mean the ads?" I forced myself to look away from his eyes and at the ads. "They're just the usual 'get your degree and have a better life' ads in Spanish."

"You read Spanish?"

"You're not the only one who knows other languages. I'm from Texas. We have to learn Spanish in school."

"And that's all you see?"

"Yeah."

"What's your necklace doing?"

I'd barely noticed its steady thrum against my neck when my body was tingling so much from all the physical proximity to Owen. "It's not going berserk, but it feels like there's a low level of steady activity. Let me guess, this car is full of those ads."

"Exactly. And quite frankly, I'm disappointed. I'd have hoped for more creativity in veiling them."

"It looks like he just stuck with whatever was there before he put his ads up," I agreed. "I hope he does better with the TV ads and doesn't mask them with something boring like ads for a mattress store. If he's got ads for Pepsi in Times Square, I'll know he's really lacking in imagination. He loses even more points if it's the latest celebrity campaign."

The silver flecks in his dark eyes sparkled as he grinned and asked, "What would you have had him do?"

"Hmm, I'll have to think about that. Something ironic, maybe? All kinds of companies use magic as a description for their products—like magically clean or magically delicious. He should have used something like that, where the veiling ad talked about magic while covering a real ad about real magic." It felt weird to talk like this on the subway, but we were close together and speaking almost directly into each other's ears, so I doubted anyone else could overhear us even if they weren't all plugged into iPods.

"That's good," he said, nodding. "You should be working in advertising."

"What, and give up saving the world?"

We reached our station, and he kept his arm around me until we got to the exit turnstiles, then he got his arm back around me as soon as we were both clear. The attention seemed so sudden after all those times I'd hoped for the slightest bit of physical contact from him.

"You know, I don't think anything's lurking in the bushes to jump out and grab me," I said.

"I've got you inside a protective field that shields me, too. I had this weird feeling . . ."

I shivered, knowing the way his weird feelings went. No wonder he was hustling me toward his house at full speed. "Does what you see always come true, or can you do something to stop it?"

"I usually just see the presence of danger, not the results. So all I know tonight is that there might be something dangerous that could affect us, not whether it will actually attack or harm us. And if you don't mind, we can order takeout instead of stopping to pick something up. After the last time, I'm afraid to take the chance."

"That doesn't mean we won't end up with oysters Rockefeller when we try to order burgers."

"We can always feed those to Loony, if we have to," he said with a mischievous smile.

His sense of relief once we were inside the front door of his town house was almost palpable. Whatever he'd sensed must have been a doozy. When we were inside, he turned on lights with a careless wave of his hand while picking up his loudly meowing cat. "Make yourself comfortable," he said. "I need to feed her before she drives us insane, and then we can get something for ourselves."

I took off my coat and draped it over the banister, then wandered after him into the kitchen, where he was opening a can of food for Loony as she practically danced in anticipation. "If you actually fed her every day, she wouldn't be quite that desperate," I remarked.

He looked up at me with a grin after he put the dish in front of her. "Yeah, you can tell she's deprived. You should have seen the poor, orphaned kitty look she gave me when I got home on Christmas. If I hadn't seen the empty cans, I might have thought Rod forgot to feed her. Now for us. You mentioned burgers. Does that sound good to you? Ever since the other night, that's what I've been hungry for—but the real thing, this time."

"That sounds wonderful."

He searched the take-out menus hung on the refrigerator by magnets, then took one and handed it to me. "Their burgers are pretty good. Let me know what you want." When I'd made my selection, he called the order in and we retreated to the living room, leaving Loony alone with her dinner. As we entered the room, he waved a hand at the fireplace and a fire sprang to life. "I refuse to feel guilty about that particular shortcut now that I know Gloria has a brownie," he said, settling down on the sofa. "Besides, I tend to burn myself when doing that the hard way."

I joined him on the sofa, trying to fight off the surge of self-consciousness I suddenly felt. He was acting far more relaxed than usual, and I was determined not to let this devolve into awkwardness. We really did need to get over the mutual bashfulness that tended to strike us in the rare situations when we weren't in danger or we'd never get beyond kissing. I tended to move slowly on the physical side of relationships, but one would hope sex would be on the menu eventually. Like, while we were still young enough to enjoy it and have any kind of stamina. "I won't tell on you," I said. "If I could light a fire by waving a hand, I totally would. It seems a waste to have that kind of power and not use it at all."

"I think she was mostly teaching me not to become so dependent on magic that I never learned how to do things the normal way. She also didn't want me to get in the habit of taking shortcuts or the easy way out, in general."

"She and my dad would really get along. He's all about learning big life lessons."

He slid out of his suit coat and threw it over the arm of the sofa, then took off his tie and unbuttoned the top button of his shirt. "I hope this establishment doesn't require neckties," he said, quirking an eyebrow at me.

"I'll make an exception in this case." I kept seeing him in situations where I thought he'd never looked better, and then he managed to top himself. At the moment, he probably looked sexier than I'd ever seen him, with his hair tousled, the slightest hint of five-o'clock shadow on his jaw, and his white dress shirt unbuttoned at the neck.

"Remind me to tip you extra." He picked up a remote control and turned on the television. "I guess we ought to start watching TV so we can make it worth your while to go through the immunity loss. Let's hope he's got an ad on tonight."

While we watched the first commercial break, Loony came in from the kitchen to join us, jumping up between us on the sofa. I scratched the back of her neck while Owen changed channels. "It was on one of the local channels, if that helps narrow it down," I said. There weren't any Spellworks ads during the next commercial break we found, either. "Maybe he's only advertising during prime time. That would mean we wouldn't see anything until eight."

"Let's hope there's something on that isn't too painful to watch— none of those reality TV dating shows or movie stars trying to dance, or anything like that."

I felt a surge of warmth at the realization we had that much in common. "I hate those kinds of shows, too." It was funny, I thought I knew him fairly well by now, but there was so much I didn't know about him, like what he watched on TV.

The buzzer sounded from downstairs, and he jumped up. "There's dinner, and fortunately, it didn't come during the commercials." He paused before leaving the living room. "I never thought I'd say that."

While he was gone, I kicked off my shoes and tucked my feet under me, grateful that I'd worn a fuller skirt that made it easy to sit comfortably. Loony rolled over onto her back and waved a paw at me in a fairly obvious command to rub her belly, so I obliged. "How do you think it's going so far?" I asked her in a whisper.

Owen returned with a couple of paper bags that had translucent grease spots forming on the sides—a sure sign our burgers hadn't been magically transformed into more highbrow food worthy of a romantic date. "Any commercials?" he asked.

"No, you only missed a story on the newscast."

"Good. Normally I'd suggest we eat at the table, but we do have a TV-watching mission tonight, so what do you say to a living room picnic?"

"I say it sounds great."

"I'll get us something to sit on if you'll go grab us some drinks. There should be some sodas in the refrigerator. Take whatever you want and grab something for me. There's nothing in there that I don't like."

When I returned with a couple of canned drinks, he had a red-and-white-checked blanket spread picnic style on the living room floor in front of the fireplace and television. I hadn't felt anything in my necklace, so that meant he must have had a picnic blanket handy. Interesting. He flattened the paper bags the food had come in and then laid the burgers and fries out on them. I handed him his drink before I sat down.

"This is more like it," he said after taking a bite of burger. "Much better than the other night." He suddenly looked concerned. "Isn't it? Or am I incorrectly assuming? You said you had fun."

"I had fun because I was with you. I'm not sure I'd have had fun with the kind of guy who'd have deliberately taken me to that kind of place. Burgers on the living room floor are much more my style." And, I realized, this indoor picnic in front of the fireplace was a lot more romantic than the limo ride and the fancy restaurant, with or without the weird disruption we'd had.

"Good. And I guess I didn't realize how little I know about you. I feel like I know the kind of person you are because we have been through some pretty extreme stuff together, but I honestly don't know what you like or what you do enjoy."

"It's hard to carry on a good conversation when every time you're together, you're escaping from a fire, falling through ice, fighting off dragons, working, fending off a mob, or anything else we've done together."

"I had to enchant that necklace to know what to give you for Christmas."

"I bought you a scarf. I think that's lamer."

"So, tell me, what would have been a good gift for me to give you?"

"I like the one you gave me. The necklace really has been useful."

"Okay, then, let's try this another way. You already know my favorite childhood movie was *Robin Hood*. What was yours?"

"Hmm. Let's see, I think I was partial to *Sleeping Beauty*. They re-released it in theaters when I was about five or six, and we made a special trip to the city to see it. Afterward, I thought that going to live in the forest with a group of wacky fairies seemed like a pretty good life. As an adult, I must admit to being drawn to the dashing prince who fights a dragon."

"Now, I would have got that one wrong. I saw you as more of a *Cinderella* girl. You don't lie around waiting for other people to take care of the situation. You pull yourself together and head out to the ball to get what you want."

"Yeah, I guess that does make sense, but I still liked Sleeping Beauty's prince better, and let's face it, the prince is the part we really like in those movies. It's your turn now. Let's see, what can I ask you? Favorite movie now?"

"I haven't been to the movies in so long that I couldn't begin to say."

"Okay, then, how about favorite grown-up movie?"

He worried his lower lip in his teeth while he thought, then said, "A lot of it depends on the mood I'm in. But *Casablanca* is a consistent favorite."

"Oh, so you're a romantic."

"Well, that's not the main thing," he said, even as he turned slightly pink. "I like the idea of knowing you're part of something bigger than you are, and at the same time, no matter how epic the scope of a situation is, it's still about people. Plus, Humphrey Bogart was incredibly cool, and he always knew just what to say in a situation. I'd love to be able to toss out smooth lines like that instead of thinking of them hours later or not having the nerve to say them even if I do think of them at the right time."

"Yeah, you're a romantic. And worse, you're an idealistic romantic.

You'd totally make the grand, sacrificial gesture for the greater good and then stride off into the fog."

He slipped his arm around my waist and pulled me against him. "Well, maybe I am a bit of a romantic. Enough so that I deliberately ordered our burgers without onions."

"And you think you're not smooth," I said just before he kissed me. It was even better than our very first kiss, which had been magically influenced. We'd kissed a few times since then, but not with the same kind of intensity. As in almost every other thing he did, he was thorough, meticulous, and quite skilled. Fortunately, this time he didn't withdraw in horror, like he had once before after realizing he was under magical influence. Instead, he kept kissing me, and I let myself relax enough to really kiss him back. After all our struggles of the past weeks, once we got over the initial awkwardness, it felt so very right between us.

Then just as I was getting into it, my necklace began vibrating furiously.

Sixteen

I should have known it was too good to last. "Um, Owen?" I said between kisses.

"Mmm hmm?"

"Unless you're working some serious mojo on me, there's magic going on."

He pulled away, keeping his arm around me, and we both turned to look at the television. "What do you see?" he asked.

"I was right. It's a mattress commercial."

"That's not what I'm seeing. But I don't think it's any better than the mattress commercial in production values."

"Yep, that would be the ad I saw the other night."

"And there's no indication that there's anything unusual about the ad you're seeing?"

"No. It's not even a new ad, just that same annoying mattress ad that's always on. It makes you wonder if he actually bought the airtime, or if he's hijacking it and the station thinks they're showing the same old ads."

"He still had to produce the ad and somehow get it on the air, since we know that there really is an ad there. It isn't an illusion." The ad ended and he picked up the remote to turn the TV off. "I guess that's mission accomplished for the night," he said. "Now, where were we?" He bent to kiss my temple, then my cheek, and then my neck.

I leaned back against him with a sigh of contentment. "I still feel like there's something we're missing. There's a connection we haven't seen yet between the funding and the person who seems to be running things. Like maybe why they're doing this when it doesn't look too profitable. And where did all this come from, anyway?"

"All what?"

I turned to face him. "You. For the last couple of weeks, you've barely touched me, even though we were supposedly dating, and now, well, wow. We're not under enchantment again, are we?"

He tapped the locket where it rested in the hollow of my throat. "What does this tell you?"

"That there's nothing magical going on nearby right now."

"So?"

"So, excuse me if my head is spinning."

"You said it yourself, there was Ari's escape, the fire that wasn't a fire, the ice, my family, the crisis of the day, the dragons, the messed-up dinner plans. This is the first time in a long time it's been just us with nothing crazy going on, and I was determined to make the most of it instead of panicking, getting nervous, or chickening out."

"You were channeling your inner Bogie," I said, resting my hand against his cheek. "I get it now. I like it."

He wrapped both arms around me and pulled me against him in a warm embrace. "Sometimes I wish we could forget about magic and saving the world and all of that and just be us for a while."

"But without the weirdness, would it still be us?"

"Good point. I guess we're stuck with it."

"I don't mind all that much." I rested my head on his chest and could hear his heart beating. "Now we know that all we have to do to have a successful relationship is never go out again."

"That sounds like one of your better plans."

But we did have to go out again, since the rest of the world was still spinning and we had things to do. After another hour or so of quality snuggling mixed with a kind of twenty questions quiz as we swapped lists of our favorite things, he walked me home and arranged to meet me the next morning to head over to Times Square. This time, I got my good-night kiss on the front steps. Things were definitely looking up.

I got home in time to catch my roommates in the middle of planning their costumes for the party. "Ooh, someone's all aglow," Gemma said when I walked into the bedroom. "We could turn out the lights in here and still find our way around, thanks to Miss Radiance USA."

"I take it you had a good date," Marcia said, raising one eyebrow.

"Yeah. Good date."

"What did you do?" Gemma asked, flipping through a carton of masks.

"We ate dinner on his living room floor and talked."

"Talked, huh?" She held up a black mask shaped like cat's-eye glasses frames. "What do you think of this one?"

"Very sexy," I said. "And, well, there might have been a little more than talking going on."

"Then you're home awfully early," Gemma remarked.

"It wasn't *that* much more than talking," I said.

Marcia came over and patted me on the head. "Our Katie is an old-fashioned girl. And a smart one. Better to be sure of the situation before you get in too deep."

Gemma rolled her eyes. "Just don't be so smart you miss the fun. Now, any costume plans for you?"

I shrugged. "I was thinking of using those red shoes, maybe doing a Dorothy outfit, assuming I can find a blue gingham pinafore."

Gemma and Marcia looked at each other. "Tell me she didn't just mention dressing as Dorothy," Gemma said. She then turned to me. "This is not a Halloween carnival. It's a New Year's Eve masked ball. You will not do anything cute or sweet. You're going to have one of the hottest guys there. You must do sexy. But good idea to use the red shoes. Let's see what else we can do with them. Oh, I have an idea."

She disappeared to the back of the closet. There were times when I wondered if our closet had a spell on it to expand it from within. It shouldn't have been able to hold Gemma's extensive wardrobe, let alone Marcia's and my clothes. Gemma returned with a red satin dress and one of my red shoes. "The reds aren't a perfect match, but it's not too bad." When she held the dress up against herself, I saw that it had a pointy tail coming off the back of it. "The horns that go with this should be in the accessories box over there."

"But if that's your dress, it won't fit me," I said. Gemma was taller than I was, and although she was slimmer, she also had more curves. It really wasn't fair.

"Try it on," she ordered.

It turned out to be good that I was several inches shorter than she was, for the dress came to mid-thigh on me. On Gemma it must have been indecently short. It was rather formfitting on me, except in the chest area, where there was extra fabric. "That's okay," Gemma said. "That's why they make Wonderbras." She stuck a horned headband on me and turned me to face the full-length mirror that hung on the back of the bedroom door. "And voilà, a she-devil. I can't decide if you should wear fishnets or seamed stockings. Maybe seamed fishnets. We'll have to see what we can find. You're gonna knock your guy's socks off."

As I twirled my tail and looked at myself in the mirror, I was almost looking forward to the party even though I was starting to have a nagging suspicion that it was a recipe for disaster.

. . .

Instead of heading to the office the next morning, Owen and I went straight uptown to Times Square. "How will I know that my immunity is still gone?" I asked him while we waited for an uptown train.

"Do you see anything odd?" he asked as my necklace hummed.

"No."

"Your immunity is gone."

He was remarkably chipper, which I chalked up to our first truly successful date. "I figured out my costume for the party," I told him, taking his hand and leaning against him. "Now we have to find something for you."

"Oh really, what is it?"

"It's a surprise." A train pulled into the station, and he ushered me on board.

We got off the train at the Times Square station, then made our way aboveground. The impact of all the giant signs and lights was somewhat diminished during the daytime, but it was still pretty splashy. My necklace had intensified its hum, but I couldn't be sure exactly what was causing it, as I'd noticed magical people in Times Square before. It was one of those parts of town where things were so crazy, magical people could do whatever they wanted and nobody would notice anything weird, so long as nobody dropped all the magical veils in the area at once on a relatively quiet night. The locals had on blinders and the tourists would think it was just another one of those odd New York things. Besides, some of the nonmagical things going on there were weirder than anything the magical world had to offer. No magical person would be crazy enough to stand outside playing guitar in just his underwear in the dead of winter, for example.

"What do you see?" Owen prodded when we reached the traffic island where we'd studied the Spellworks ads on Christmas night.

"It looks like Times Square, the way it usually is. Some soft drink ads, some computer ads. No magic ads."

"So it's like the other veilings he's done, hiding the magic behind the last ads that were there. That does make you wonder if he really is paying for the space."

"The billboards alone wouldn't be cheap, so he still needs money. But we might not be at multinational corporation levels of financing. Just one good backer—say, Sylvia—might be enough. Maybe things aren't as bad as we thought. Knowing Idris, I wouldn't be at all surprised if he gets bored with this in a week or two and moves on to something else."

"Let's hope so."

"You know, that may be the way to deal with this," I said as a thought crossed my mind.

"How?"

"Well, I'd imagine that whoever is making Sylvia bankroll him is doing so for a reason and isn't likely to lose interest. If Idris gets sidetracked and moves on to something else, his boss isn't going to be pleased. That's bound to disrupt their operation. What we need to do is come up with something sure to distract Idris."

Owen nodded and chewed on his lower lip, deep in thought. After he'd processed the thought, he broke out in a huge grin and grabbed me in an enthusiastic hug. "You're brilliant!" he said before bending me back in a dip and kissing me thoroughly. A flashbulb went off, and I turned to see a tourist taking our picture. That was when I realized we'd more or less mimicked the pose from that famous photo of a sailor kissing a nurse in Times Square at the end of World War II. The deep blush on Owen's face told me he'd just become aware of the same thing. He carefully pulled me back up to a proper standing position while I fought off a bad case of the giggles that I knew would only embarrass him worse.

"Let's check out the store now," he said, making a valiant attempt at looking calm. "I doubt we can get in, but we can see what's going on outside."

"Yeah, they probably have our pictures up behind the cash register, like they do with people known for writing bad checks."

We passed one of those kitschy Broadway souvenir shops, and I tugged on Owen's arm. "Let's go in here a second."

"Why?"

My main reason was to escape the tourists who were still giving us odd looks and to give him time to compose himself, but what I said was, "I need to get some postcards. Are you that desperate to get this over with and get back to the office? It's practically New Year's Eve. It's even a short day."

"Whatever makes you happy." He didn't say it in the resigned way that people usually said that sort of thing. He sounded more like he actually meant it.

I flipped through the posters and T-shirts for shows I hadn't seen, and then I spotted something hanging on the wall. "I have an idea for a costume for you," I told Owen, pointing to the white Phantom of the Opera mask. "You have a tux. All you do is wear that and the mask, and you've got a costume. You'd essentially be wearing evening clothes and a mask, but it would still count as a real costume. Rod would have nothing to complain about."

"I don't know," he hedged, looking at the mask.

"It doesn't involve wearing tights or makeup."

"Very good point." He bought the mask, and then we got coffee from a street vendor before wandering over to Fifth Avenue to stand across the street from the Spellworks store. I now saw nothing more than a vacant, boarded-up storefront. We stood there for a while, under a bus stop sign as though we were waiting for a bus, and watched the foot traffic around the store. I saw a few people stop to look in the window, and Owen said he saw them enter the store when they disappeared from my view, but the majority of pedestrians passed it by.

"Well, this is exciting," I said after a while. "For this, I gave up my immunity. I think our work here is done, if you want to head back to the office."

He turned as if to go, then did a double take. "Wait a second, isn't that Ari over there? That woman looks exactly like the illusion she was wearing the other day."

"I wouldn't know. I didn't see her illusion then, and I can't see any distinguishing Ari features now."

"Come on, let's see where she goes this time." He grabbed my hand as he took off, and I had no choice but to follow him.

"Are you sure that's a good idea?" I said as I hurried to keep up with him. "Remember what happened last time? And I can't look out for her if she decides to swap illusions or do something else to throw us off."

"But that's only if she notices we're following her." By the time we got across the street, though, it became apparent that she wasn't actually going anywhere. She looked like she was spying on the store, like we were.

Idris soon came running out of the store. "What are you doing here?" he shouted. "Don't you know it's dangerous for you to be out? You're supposed to be hiding."

She rolled her eyes. In the human disguise I saw, she looked like a club kid who wasn't used to being out in daylight. "Do you know how boring it is down there? I'm going crazy."

"You'll be even more bored if they get you. Then you won't have any visitors."

"Like they'll catch me. I'm in disguise."

"They have immunes, remember?"

"I thought you were taking care of that."

"It's not as easy as you think, and as I recall, you weren't even that successful at it. Now, go. I have work to do."

"You're no fun anymore. It's that Sylvia bitch, isn't it?"

He sighed in exasperation. "I'm not getting into this with you again." Then I had to blink because the woman I'd been watching talk to Idris had vanished. "Not a smart move!" Idris shouted. The pedestrians on the sidewalk just kept pushing around him.

Owen edged me away from the store. When we were a block away, I said, "Looks like there's trouble in paradise."

"I'm surprised at how businesslike he was," Owen said. "He's got to be exhausted at the end of the day from the effort of maintaining that."

"I bet it only lasts a few minutes at a time and we caught him during one of his spells of businesslike activity. In a few minutes, he'll be off playing video games or trying to think of ways to make his employees dance the can-can."

We headed back downtown, and as we crossed City Hall Plaza on our way to the office building, he asked, "Do you want to get together again tonight?" Before I could answer, he shook his head and added, "And I just realized how that sounded. I know I shouldn't assume you never have any other plans. I should think to ask you a few days in advance. But I didn't really mean it as a date. You don't have your immunity and I'd feel better if I could keep an eye on you."

"As I recall, you warded my place," I said. "And I'd eventually have to go home, like I did last night. I'll be okay."

He looked away for a second, and when he looked back at me there were bright pink spots on both of his cheeks. "Okay, then. It's not just for your safety. I'd like to see you. Last night may have been the first entirely uneventful time we've ever spent together, and I'd like more of it."

"That does sound tempting, but I do already have plans with my roommates. I'm sorry."

"It's okay," he said with a shrug, but his ears had turned pink. I hoped he didn't take it as a rejection, but I did have plans, and I didn't want to be the kind of girl who ditched my friends as soon as a man came into my life.

We dropped coats and his mask off in his office, and I took off the necklace before it drove me insane inside the magically charged office building, then we went upstairs to find Merlin. Unfortunately, we found Kim first, sitting at Trix's desk. She must have been filling in while Trix took the day off, but even so, she'd already made that area her own, much as she'd taken over my office. She'd moved her pictures and plants and had even put a nameplate with her name on it on the desk.

"Did you have an appointment?" she asked curtly as we approached the desk.

"No, but I imagine Mr. Mervyn is expecting us," Owen said with the calm he usually displayed in situations like that. He may have struggled with his inner Humphrey Bogart in his personal life, but at work he often managed to be just that cool.

"I'd better check with him, anyway," she said, attempting a flirtatious look at Owen, who remained utterly oblivious. In fact, he ignored her entirely, walking toward Merlin's office doors.

She was opening her mouth to protest when the doors opened and Merlin greeted us with a smile. "Ah, you must have a report for me," he said, ushering us inside. I resisted the impulse to throw a gloating look over my shoulder at Kim as we went inside. Merlin gestured us to take seats on his sofa before he went to the counter on the far side of the office. "I've just made a pot of tea, so your timing is excellent," he said as he poured. He solved the problem of having three cups and two hands by letting one hover alongside as he carried the other two over to us. The third cup settled itself on the small table next to the wing chair he took. "Now, what have you seen with your immunity gone?"

I described what I'd noticed about the subway ads, television commercials, and Times Square billboards, as well as the appearance of the store. "It's possible they haven't necessarily spent as much money on advertising as we thought because the media companies may not even have noticed that there are ads. Still, it would have been an impressive logistical operation just to get those ads up physically, and that would have taken money."

"So they're possibly not quite on the verge of taking over the world," Merlin surmised with a wry twinkle in his eyes.

"Katie also had an idea for a way to deal with Idris," Owen said.

I swallowed and hoped this sounded as good now as it had when I'd first brought it up. "We've noticed that Idris is a bit distractible. That seems to have been the main thing holding him back. Before he can bring any of his evil schemes to fruition, he's become bored and moved on to something else. For instance, he never really took advantage of all the turmoil he caused when we thought we had a mole in the company. I think he became so fascinated by watching us run around in a tizzy that he forgot to actually do anything with that opportunity."

"That also fits the way he used to work," Owen added. "He seldom finished projects. He'd dabble in one thing after another instead of sticking to a particular line of thought or research."

"But now that he's apparently got someone interested enough in what he's doing to bankroll him, he may not be able to get away with that," I continued. "His boss must have something planned, and he's not going to want to just move on to the next great idea. So if we could come up with a way to really distract Idris, it might mess him up with his boss or force the boss to show himself."

Merlin stroked his beard and nodded. "Yes, I could see how that might be effective. It might not stop the plan entirely, but it could buy us time. We'd still need to find a way to discover who is behind him and what he's trying to accomplish, but this could make that task somewhat easier. Very good thinking, Miss Chandler. It's almost a pity you're not magical, for I'd be interested in seeing how you might innovate in that respect."

"I guess we'll never know. And maybe I have to think outside the box because I don't have access to any powers. If I had magical powers, I might be a really boring wizard." I hesitated, then asked a question that weighed heavily on my mind. "How are things going up here? Is there anything you need me to take care of?"

"No, Kim is quite effective. A trifle overeager, perhaps, but she is getting her work done. You can focus on this project in good conscience."

"Good, good." I hoped my smile didn't look too obviously fake. I tried to remind myself that Kim getting my work done didn't mean I was out of a job. It only meant I could concentrate on stopping Idris, which meant far more to the company than typing memos and making sure no one pulled a fast one in meetings.

She was still there, sitting smugly at Trix's desk as we left Merlin's office, which undermined my mental pep talk. There are some people who just bug you, and Kim seemed to be my person of the moment. There was nothing she could do that wouldn't get under my skin.

"Next time, it would help if you'd schedule an appointment in advance," she said.

And a lot of the things she did seemed designed specifically to push my buttons. Fortunately, Owen had my back and I didn't have to stoop to her level to respond. "Mr. Mervyn seldom needs anyone to schedule appointments. He'll know before anything important happens," he said. "You may notice that there's never a conflict, even when something comes up unexpectedly."

"That does take some getting used to when you're managing his schedule," I added, trying very hard to avoid sounding patronizing. The stunned expression on her face was more gratifying than any gift I'd received for Christmas, and I hurried to get out of the office suite before she thought of a clever comeback that would diminish my triumph.

By the time we got back to Owen's lab, the short preholiday workday was almost over. "I'll see you home," he said. "I feel like I ought to do at least that much with your immunity gone."

I was starting to regret having made plans with my roommates. Going home with him would have been really nice. "I'm meeting Marcia down here to go to lunch. She works in the financial district. And then we're going uptown to meet Gemma for some shopping." I took his hand and gave it a squeeze. "But I do appreciate the offer. Normally, I'm all in favor of having you keep an eye on me."

He squeezed my hand in response, but his expression remained serious. "I don't like the idea of you being unprotected, especially after what happened this morning. They know we're onto them."

"Have you met Marcia? I'd like to see the magical creature that could take her on. And aren't there my usual bodyguards? I'll be fine. But I'd better get going. She's the punctual type, and I'm more afraid of her than of monsters if I'm ever late meeting her."

I decided to walk to meet Marcia at the restaurant she'd chosen rather than ride the subway to the next station. I'd only walked a couple of blocks when I noticed an elderly lady who seemed to be following me. I tried to ignore her and kept going on my way. That was one of the city survival lessons Marcia had taught me when I first moved to New York. I reached the restaurant and stepped inside to find Marcia already waiting in the foyer. "You're right on time," she said, greeting me with a hug. "They said our table should be ready in a moment."

I opened my mouth to respond, but then a voice at my elbow said, "Well, now, aren't you being rude today?"

I turned to see the lady who'd been following me. She stood next to me, looking at me as though she was astonished that I hadn't recognized her. I mentally ran through every place I might have met someone during my time in New York so I could figure out why I might know her. No bells rang.

"I know you were angry with me," she said, "but that's no reason to snub me entirely."

Only then did I notice her facial structure and put it together with her voice to recognize Ethelinda. So, that's what the rest of the world saw. Without her wings, tiara, and layers of out-of-date evening wear, she looked like an entirely different person. It would have been nice if I could have ignored her, but I was afraid Ethelinda would make a scene. "I'm sorry, I guess I didn't recognize you right away," I said, frantically scrambling for an excuse to get rid of her.

"Who's your friend?" Marcia asked.

"Oh, this is Ethel—" I cut myself off because Ethel was a perfectly reasonable, if a little old-fashioned, name, unlike Ethelinda. "She, uh, we . . ."

"I'm her fairy godmother," Ethelinda declared proudly, putting an arm around my shoulders.

Seventeen

I froze. This wasn't how I'd planned to tell my friends about magic. Then I tried to recover. "Ha, ha! Yeah, that's what we call her at work. She's like a fairy godmother to all of us in the office. She gives us such great advice on dating, relationships, and stuff like that."

Marcia didn't act like she'd noticed anything odd, which made me relax a little. "It's nice to meet you, and you must be doing a good job, from what I've heard. It seems like Katie has found a good man."

"The best," Ethelinda said, beaming proudly, as though she had anything at all to do with it. "Now, if only we can make sure things work out for those two."

"Yeah, well, everyone goes through that," I said with a forced smile.

"Why don't you join us for lunch?" Marcia asked. I groaned inwardly because there was nothing I could say to stop Ethelinda from joining us and it would have been rude to uninvite her.

The hostess returned to her station and glanced at us, then asked Marcia, "Wasn't it just two in your party?"

"Our friend's going to join us," Marcia said.

The hostess then swept us back to our table. She plunked menus down and said, "Enjoy your lunch."

Ethelinda grinned gleefully once we were all seated. "I haven't had lunch with the girls like this in ages. Now, what romantic problems do you want help with?"

Marcia giggled nervously, then lined her silverware up in precise rows. "Funny you should mention it, but I did want to get some advice about something."

"Isn't that Gemma's area?" I asked. I wasn't sure it was a good idea for Marcia to talk about her love life in front of Ethelinda, not if she didn't want it completely screwed up.

"I definitely don't want to talk to Gemma about this right now. Her view of relationships doesn't always match mine, and you, well, you seem to be pretty level-headed." She turned to Ethelinda and added with a smile, "And I'd appreciate any wisdom you've got, too."

"What did you want to talk about?" Ethelinda asked.

"My boyfriend, Jeff. I thought for a while that he helped balance me. He's a live-for-the-moment guy, and I'm Ms. Spreadsheet. I'm ambitious and driven. But there's balance and then there's functioning in different universes." She looked at me and said, "You knew him before I met him. What do you know?"

All I knew was that he'd been sitting naked in Central Park, thinking he'd been turned into a frog when it was only an illusion because of a practical joke spell, until I'd kissed him and broken the spell. Unfortunately, the next effect of the spell was that he became obsessed with me until he met Marcia and fell for her. "I don't really know much about him," I confessed. "I'd just run into him around town a few times."

"I don't think I'm a snob, and it's not like I'm ashamed to take him with me to work functions, but I'm not sure I can stay with him. I just think we're fundamentally incompatible on a long-term basis. I'm a grown-up, and he's like an overgrown frat boy. Do I sound horrible?"

"No. You sound sensible," Ethelinda said. "If you're not happy, then there's no need to keep at it. It's not as though you're married." Which was pretty much what I'd planned to say. Why could Ethelinda give such sane advice to my friend when she only messed things up for me?

"Gemma would say I'm avoiding intimacy, that I'm not letting anything into my life that's not in perfect order."

"Then Gemma can go out with him. It's your life," I said.

"I'm not convinced you're meant to be together," Ethelinda said.

Marcia sighed, and I could practically see the tension leaving her body. "I'm glad you see it that way, because I broke up with him last night. I guess that means I'm the fifth wheel for the New Year's Eve party, since I'll be going solo. But don't tell Gemma yet, okay? I know she'd say I should at least have a date for New Year's Eve." She chuckled. "It does make me sound like a man, breaking up right before a major holiday."

"But it also means you really didn't want to be with him, if you were willing to go dateless at New Year's," I said.

"True. And did you say that gorgeous friend of yours is going to be at the party?"

It took me a second to realize who she was talking about, since I normally didn't think of Rod as gorgeous. "Oh, yeah, he's the one hosting it."

"Is he seeing anyone?"

"Uh, Manhattan? And maybe even some of the outer boroughs. Oh, and definitely a few foreign airline flight crews. He's kind of a player. I love him to death as a friend, but I'm not sure I'd encourage anyone I cared about to date him. It would be a recipe for heartbreak if you actually liked him enough to want to go out with him more than once or twice."

"He's going through a phase," Ethelinda said. "A phase he should have outgrown by now, but I don't believe it reflects his true personality. Still, he may not be ready yet to move out of that phase." There she went again with the sane advice.

Marcia twirled her hair around her finger. "Hmm. Sounds like a challenge."

"Don't say I didn't warn you." I looked up, and wouldn't you know it, Rod was walking through the door. There had to be some unconscious spell that made the person you were talking about show up, it happened so often. "Speak of the devil," I muttered.

"Why, what a coincidence!" Ethelinda said gleefully. "Here that very young man is."

Marcia turned to look, and while her back was to the table, Ethelinda waved her hand and a soup-and-salad lunch for four appeared. Rod saw me and came straight to our table. "How are you ladies today?" he said smoothly. Marcia batted her eyelashes at him flirtatiously, and I tried not to gag.

"Just great. Marcia, you remember Rod, don't you? And this is Ethel. I was just telling Marcia that she's like the fairy godmother of the office." I gave the words "fairy godmother" particular stress and hoped he'd sense her magic and figure it out.

"Yeah, that's what we say," Rod said, giving me a sly wink and the barest hint of a nod.

"Won't you join us for lunch?" Ethelinda said. "We already have food for you."

"Hey, when did that get there?" Marcia asked.

I shrugged. "The waitress brought it when you weren't looking." At that moment, the waitress came out of the kitchen with a tray, saw our table, frowned, and went back into the kitchen. The sound of raised voices filtered into the dining room as the kitchen door swung in and out.

"What romantic advice have you been giving?" Rod asked Ethelinda. I wondered if it was my imagination, or if he'd done something to alter his illusion. He was still very handsome, but it didn't seem quite so over-the-top as it usually was. Maybe I was getting used to it, or maybe the contrast with his usual appearance wasn't so strong now that he was making an effort.

"Marcia here has decided to break up with her boyfriend," Ethelinda said smugly, as though it had been her idea. I was getting the feeling that Cinderella and her prince had already worked things out, and it was in spite of the glass slippers and pumpkin coach rather than because of these things that they got together, while Ethelinda took credit and coasted on that laurel for centuries.

"Oh, really?" Rod asked, raising an eyebrow and leaning closer to Marcia. If he'd been sitting next to me instead of across from me, I'd have kicked him in the ankle. Then I realized that I still wasn't getting any sense of his usual attraction spell. The last time I lost my immunity, it had taken all my willpower to keep from throwing myself at him. Now I didn't feel so much as a nudge. Had he really given that up, or was he just being a lot more focused about it now?

Marcia gave him a rueful smile. "Yeah, I guess so. Bad timing, huh? It looks like I'll be flying solo at your party. You don't mind me coming without a date, do you?"

"I don't have a date, either, and it's my party." Rod not having a date for New Year's Eve, when he had a date for just about every night of the other three hundred and sixty-four days of the year, was almost unbelievable. Then again, it probably meant he was hoping to hook up with someone there without an official date to get in the way. "You can keep me company."

Marcia blushed and looked flustered in a way I'd never seen with her before. She had to be under a spell, but Owen's necklace gave off only a low-level hum that was probably accounted for by Rod's illusion and Ethelinda's veiling. I hadn't felt anything stronger or any surges of magic, other than when Ethelinda conjured our lunches.

The waitress, still looking confused, dropped off our check. "This one's on me!" Ethelinda declared. Money appeared on the table. I hoped for the sake of the waitress that it was real money. "And I believe my work here is done. It was lovely meeting you. I hope things work out."

We thanked her for the lunch, then I held my breath, hoping she'd leave the normal way via the door instead of her usual vanishing act. If she vanished, I told myself I'd let Rod explain it. Fortunately, she did use the door. Rod soon excused himself to go take care of some final party-planning details.

Marcia and I then went uptown and met Gemma as she got off work in the garment district. "There's a huge Victoria's Secret nearby, so we can go over there and get all the accessories we need for our costumes," she said after greeting us.

Once we were inside the store, she headed straight for the bra section. She skimmed through the displays, then pulled one off a rack. "This should do the trick. It adds a full cup size. The red satin one would be really sexy and would work under that dress, but you'll probably get more use out of the nude one because you could wear it under other things. What size do you wear?"

I was just about to tell her when I looked up and found myself looking straight at Mimi, my evil boss from my last job. Her smirk told me she'd heard everything Gemma had just said. She had to be feeling smugly superior, for she'd never need a padded bra. That was one of the many ways she felt she was better than me. "Why, Katie, imagine seeing you here," she said, doing a fake air kiss that I didn't bother returning. "I thought you were too sweet and wholesome for this kind of thing."

"Too sweet and wholesome to wear underwear?" I asked with exaggerated innocence. I mentally high-fived myself for having a good comeback. There was something about Mimi that always made me feel about an inch tall, even if I was no longer working for her.

She laughed. "Very funny." Suddenly, she was acting like Good Mimi. That was part of what was so evil about her. She could change personalities at the drop of a hat. She'd start the day acting like your best friend, lull you into complacency, then pounce with claws bared. "Whatever did you do with that gorgeous guy you were with the last time I saw you?" The last time I'd run into her around town, I'd had Owen with me. He'd jumped valiantly to my defense when she'd gone on the attack.

"I'm giving him a break today to rest up for New Year's Eve," I said, then grabbed something sheer and naughty looking from a nearby display. "And that would be why I'm here."

She looked at what I was holding, then glanced over at the heavily padded bra Gemma still held. "Then, word of advice—you don't want to disappoint him by starting with all that padding and then showing him the sad reality that you can't hide in that." She'd made a good, stinging barb and she knew it, so while I was still thinking of a better comeback than "I know you are, but what am I?" she turned and headed to another part of the store.

As soon as she was gone, Gemma and Marcia said in stunned unison, "What a bitch!" Gemma then asked, "Who was that?"

"That was the infamous Mimi."

Marcia shook her head as she watched Mimi berating a sales clerk on the other side of the store. "And I always thought you were exaggerating when you talked about her. How did you survive that long without killing her?"

"I needed the job if you wanted me to pay my share of the rent." I put the sheer thing back on the rack, then said, "Okay, show me this miraculous bra."

"You're not going to get that?" Gemma asked, raising one eyebrow.

"That? Are you kidding? It would give him heart failure."

"That's the idea."

"No, when I'm ready for that kind of thing—and I mean after we've been going out for more than a few weeks—I'd need something a little more classy, less calculated and obvious."

"Okay, then, try the bra on," Gemma said, herding me toward the fitting rooms with Marcia at her side. They didn't give me much choice but to go with them.

That didn't stop me from protesting. "I know what size I wear," I insisted.

"It can be different in different styles. In fact, you should try a couple of different sizes."

I really dug my heels in when they followed me into the fitting room. "I can do this alone, thank you very much." Gemma and Marcia ignored me, barging into the small room with me.

I changed out of my top, and with my back turned I took off my bra and tried on the one Gemma handed me. Then I turned around to get their opinion and found that they were holding my blouse, my purse, and my coat. "Okay, since we're all here, we need to talk," Gemma said.

"What's going on?" I asked.

"We're having an intervention," Marcia said.

"A what?" I moved toward the door to get away from them, then realized that unless I wanted to go out in just a bra, I was stuck because they were holding my blouse and coat.

"We're worried about you," Gemma said. "You've been acting odd lately. And we've been getting the feeling that you're lying to us about something."

"You never used to lie to us," Marcia added. "You can't tell a good lie and not look like you're lying, which is why we know you're hiding something from us. But we want you to know that no matter how bad it is, you can talk to us. We'll try to understand, and we'll be here for you."

"I have no idea what you're talking about," I said, sure I was proving their point about looking like a liar. "And do we have to get into this here?"

"We planned to do this here," Marcia said. "At home, you could lock yourself in the bathroom or go out. But right now, you're stuck, and you have to listen to us."

"Y'all are blowing this out of proportion," I said, feeling frantic.

"You've got symptoms of drug abuse, or maybe mental illness," Gemma said. "I looked it up on the Internet. You're gone a lot with no ex-planation, you lie about where you've been, you're associating with dif-ferent people. You don't enjoy things you used to enjoy."

"I've got a new job," I pointed out. "Of course I'm associating with new people, and I'm gone more often because I have more responsi-bility."

"This job is on the up-and-up, isn't it?" Marcia asked. "And the new boyfriend, he's not a drug dealer or an abuser, or anything like that?"

"You met him. What do you think?"

"I spent about twenty seconds with him before you hustled him out the door. Hey, wait a second, you aren't ashamed of us with your new work friends, are you? You didn't seem crazy about your friends joining us for lunch today."

"No, it's not like that at all." I tried to think of an explanation, but I was afraid I'd only make matters worse since they were definitely onto my lies and cover-ups. As a last resort, I decided on telling the truth—well, some of it. "It's just weird to mix worlds like that, you know? I've always had my work friends and then y'all, and I never had to mix the two groups. I kept my personal life and my work life separate. Now that I'm dating someone from work and some of my coworkers have become real friends, it feels like my worlds are colliding, and it's taking some adjusting." Oh boy, was it. "I mean, look at how freaky it was to run into my old boss here. Lunch today was that kind of thing for me."

Gemma handed me my blouse. "We just want you to know we're here for you if you ever want to talk. And that bra fits you perfectly. You should take it."

"But we will be getting to know your boyfriend better at the party so we can be sure about him," Marcia added.

"I can assure you he doesn't have me under mind control, and he's not trying to recruit me into a dangerous cult and separate me from my friends and family. Now, can I have some privacy?"

They were waiting out in the store when I returned, fully dressed and my wits more or less about me. This had been possibly the closest call I'd yet had in hiding my magical double life. Gemma had picked out a pair of flesh-toned fishnet tights. Mimi was torturing a sales clerk by making her open and search through every drawer to make sure the bra she wanted wasn't hiding from her. I certainly felt the clerk's pain. I was sure that as soon as the salesgirl found the bra, Mimi would change her mind and want to find a different one.

I'd just checked out and was moving toward the store exit when Owen's necklace went nuts. It was vibrating so hard it was almost painful. That meant big magic was in use nearby. Even without the necklace I'd have felt the power flying around. Before I had a chance to react, someone grabbed me and pulled me toward the exit.

Gemma and Marcia flew into action, hitting the guy holding my arm with their shopping bags and purses. My attacker was probably my old friend, Mr. Bones. Under my roommates' assault, he let go of me, but I wasn't sure where to turn. I didn't want to run out of the store because there were likely more goons out there waiting for me. I threw a few good kicks into the mix, and soon he was the one running from the store.

But that didn't stop the chaos. When the door opened to let my would-be kidnapper out, something else seemed to come in. I still felt magic in use and wondered if my magical bodyguards had come on the scene. I hated being without my magical immunity because it meant I could only guess at what was going on. A negligee-clad mannequin toppled over, then tried to right itself before falling over on the other side, right on top of Mimi. This time, she was the one to shove the mannequin upright, but she didn't seem to notice that she had something lacy and filmy hanging off the back of her head. That sight alone made up for the scary moments earlier.

"Let's get out of here," Gemma said. She and Marcia each took one of my arms and marched me out of the store. "That was bizarre. See why we're worried about you?"

"Hey, you're not blaming me, are you?" I asked, trying to keep up with their longer strides. "Did you think I set that up?"

"Of course not, but that guy went straight for you," Marcia said.

"It was random. Crime often is, you know. I was the closest one, and maybe I looked distracted because my friends had just accused me of being crazy or doing drugs, so I was an easy target."

"But then all that other stuff started happening," Gemma said. "Things flying, mannequins falling over."

"Okay, I admit it," I said, pulling my arms out of their grasp and throwing my hands in the air in defeat. "I've got magical powers, and I used them to torment Mimi. Are you happy now?"

Gemma laughed. "Well, you might have a point there. We can't blame you for that. It was just typical New York weirdness. But you are okay, aren't you? You'd tell us if something was wrong?"

"I'm okay," I insisted, skipping over the part about telling them. They didn't seem to notice my omission as they nodded and put their arms around me. I still had a feeling they weren't going to stop worrying about me anytime soon.

As I sat New Year's Eve with a head full of hot rollers while Gemma painted what felt like an inch or more of makeup onto my face, I wished I'd gone for Owen's stay-at-home idea. "Hold still and don't blink," she ordered, waving an eyeliner brush at me. I was almost afraid to look at myself in the mirror when she was through.

When I did get the nerve to look, I didn't recognize myself. She'd done a cat's-eye effect with eyeliner and eyeshadow, and she'd managed to make my lips look plump and red. "Now, go get dressed," she said, "and then we'll do your hair."

By the time I got on the pneumatic bra, the fishnet tights, the red dress, and my red shoes, I felt I'd been transformed even more. With the help of the bra, I almost filled out the top of the dress so that it hugged every curve—natural and artificial. Gemma took out the hot rollers, instructed me to bend over and shake my head while running my fingers through my hair, then patted the tousled waves into place and sprayed thoroughly with hair spray before sticking on the horned headband. "There we go," she said, admiring her creation with satisfaction. "One she-devil."

I had to admit, I looked pretty good, though even with my hot red outfit I wasn't sure I was anywhere near as sexy as Gemma was in her skintight black catsuit and knee-high black stiletto boots. And then Marcia came out of the bathroom.

We almost didn't recognize our own roommate. She wore a Marilyn Monroe–style dress, and with her hair curled she looked very much like

Marilyn. It was more overtly sexy than I'd ever seen her. "What do you think?" she asked, sounding a little unsure.

"You'll have to walk over at least one subway grating," I said, and she grinned as she mimicked the famous pose.

The buzzer from downstairs sounded and Gemma ran to answer the intercom. A moment later, she opened the door to let Philip in. He was dressed like a storybook version of Prince Charming, complete with cape and crown. He gave all of us a sweeping bow, then put a green frog mask up to his face. I had to bite my lip to keep from laughing out loud. He gave me a sly wink as he took the mask away from his face. "Is my costume adequate?" he asked.

"It's great," Gemma said, stepping forward and giving him a quick kiss.

"Absolutely brilliant," I agreed.

The buzzer sounded again, and this time it was Owen. When he came upstairs, he was wearing a tux and a full-length opera cape. His eyes went huge when he saw me, and he'd just started to blush when Marcia asked him, "And what are you supposed to be?" With a sigh and a pained look at me, he put on a broad-brimmed black hat and the Phantom mask. Marcia nodded in approval. "Nice, but I think you might be a little too cute under that mask to be a proper Phantom of the Opera."

He turned one of his better shades of red. "I guess we're ready to go," I said, trying to direct attention away from him even as I wished Marcia had given him a chance to react fully. It wasn't often that a man looked at me that way, and I didn't get the full effect of that look when he had the mask on. "Shall we head downstairs and try to get a couple of cabs?"

"Wait a second," Gemma said, turning to Marcia. "Where's Jeff?"

"He's not coming tonight." Marcia picked up her coat. "Let's go."

Owen took his mask off. "I called for a car, if you don't mind."

"Not one bit," Gemma said, blowing him a kiss that made him turn pink again. "Thank you."

As we all trooped downstairs, I hung back with Owen. "Nice cape and hat," I said.

"I borrowed them from James. I headed up there for a short visit last night. I was scolded for not bringing you. And, by the way, I, um, like your costume. It's a little out of character, but maybe it's an entirely different side of you. One that could be fun for an evening, I suspect."

"Thank you. I think." I didn't dare look at him because I was sure I was turning redder than my dress. I couldn't help but wonder what he meant about my she-devil persona being fun. We got down to the sidewalk, and before we joined the others, I glanced at him. "When you said you ordered a car . . ." The look on his face said it all. "Oh, no, you didn't."

But the squealing tires of the car that came to a stop with one of its front wheels on the curb said it all. Instead of the two goofy gargoyles, though, one man got out of the driver's seat. He had bulging eyes and Rocky's long, thin face, but his legs were short and stocky. Owen and I sat in the front seat, with me in the middle next to the driver(s), and the others got in the backseat. "And, we're off!" Rocky's voice said as we shot out into traffic. My friends didn't seem to notice anything strange about the driving, but I clutched Owen's hand and squeezed my eyes shut during most of the trip.

The party turned out to be in a spacious SoHo loft with large arched windows overlooking the street many floors below and cast-iron columns throughout the room. Rod greeted us as we entered. He wore a purple frock coat that reminded me of the Gene Wilder version of Willy Wonka. "You remember my roommates Gemma and Marcia?" I said. "And this is Philip, Gemma's boyfriend."

Rod kissed the girls and me on the cheek and shook Philip's hand. Then he turned to Owen, who was back in full Phantom regalia, and did a mock double take. "And who are you, stranger?"

"Not Robin Hood this time," Owen said. "Now, if you'll excuse us, there are some shadows I need to haunt on the other side of the room." He swept me away with an arm around my waist.

"Don't get too deep into character," I teased him. "I mean, unless you

really want to drag me off into the basement away from all these people."
We were fairly early, but the place was already packed. With the costumes, it was hard to tell who was who. I'd left Owen's necklace at home, assuming the place would be full of magic, so I couldn't even tell how many people were wearing illusions instead of real costumes.

"The basement idea is tempting, but we should probably save it for later," he said, scanning the room. "Do you want something to drink?"

"Sure. Whatever you can get to easily."

He took off into the crowd, and while I waited for him, Gemma and Philip joined me. "I think that costume went to Marcia's head," Gemma said. "She's back there flirting with your friend." I glanced across the room to see Marcia doing the Marilyn over the subway grate pose in front of Rod.

"Isn't that the idea of a costume party? To leave yourself behind and have fun?" I asked.

"I just hope she doesn't regret this later."

While Gemma glared in Marcia's direction, Philip sidled up to my other side. I still had to fight off a fit of the giggles when I saw his frog mask. "I must thank you for your referral to the attorney," he said.

"You're welcome. And how are things going?"

"Ethan and I have a meeting with them to raise the issue after the holiday."

"Good luck with that."

A masked pirate with Tinkerbell at his side then joined us. I recognized the fairy as Trix, which meant the pirate had to be Ethan. He wore leather pants and a shirt open almost to his waist, and I didn't think the hoop earring he wore in one ear was a clip-on. When he decided to explore the wilder side of life, he didn't do things halfway.

"Katie? Is that you?" Trix asked, then gave a tinkling fairy laugh.

"Yeah, I'm expressing my inner self." I gave my pointy tail a swish for punctuation.

"You couldn't be evil if you tried," Ethan said.

Philip perked up when he heard Ethan's voice. "Mr. Wainwright?" The two of them then recognized each other and were soon lost in legal conversation.

"What's up with them?" Gemma asked.

"They're working together on some business thing. It's a very small world." And even smaller when you factored in magic. Then I remembered that Trix was still there, left stranded while her date talked shop. Ethan might have been interested in exploring the wilder side of life, but he was still a lawyer, first and foremost. "Gemma, you remember Trix, don't you?"

"Oh yeah. Hi. I almost didn't recognize you with the wings. Great costume!"

Owen showed up then with drinks. I couldn't see his face well behind the mask, but I could tell he was flustered. "You would not believe the wait at the bar," he said as he handed me a drink. "I'm not even sure what this is. I just grabbed what I could get my hands on."

"If it's wet, I'm happy."

Gemma slunk over to Philip and whispered in his ear. I wasn't sure what she said, but soon she was leading him to the dance floor. Trix and Ethan weren't far behind. "Do you want to dance?" Owen asked, with a tone to his voice that told me he'd love me forever if I said no.

"The only time I can remember dancing in public was when I was under a spell, and I don't intend to change that anytime soon."

"Thank you," he said. "It's actually more fun to watch everyone else make fools of themselves. Gloria taught me to waltz and foxtrot, of course, but I don't think you can do that to this music."

Philip certainly seemed to be trying. He had Gemma in a proper ballroom dance hold and moved her smoothly around the floor to the beat of the thumping house music. It worked better than I would have thought.

"What I'd really like to find is a place to sit down," I said, trying to wriggle my toes within my shoes. "These shoes aren't made for standing around for long periods of time." I was already losing feeling in my middle toes.

"There are some chairs over there. And they're even empty."

"You hurry over and grab them, and I'll hobble behind you." As hot as these shoes were, I never would have bought them if I hadn't been under an enchantment at the time, but now I was stuck with them. They were impressive, but they were best for occasions spent mostly seated. "Ah, that's better," I sighed as I sat down.

The room was getting more and more crowded by the minute, and though we were far from the main dance floor, the dancers were getting closer to us. That made for prime people-watching. I soon began to wonder if inviting my friends was a good idea. It would be hard for them to avoid noticing that there were some pretty odd things going on. Then again, would anyone really think that odd meant magical if they didn't know the truth?

"You'd better look out for your friend," Owen said, gesturing toward the dance floor. I followed his gesture until I saw Marcia dancing rather closely with Rod.

"She just broke up with someone, so he wouldn't even need to turn on the juice to lure her in. He may be just what she's looking for."

"And she may be more than he can handle, from what I can tell. This could be interesting."

I thought for a second that I saw Ethelinda on the dance floor, but it turned out to be Isabel, Rod's secretary, dressed as a fairy godmother. She looked much as Ethelinda must have looked a few centuries ago in her prime, but wearing only one outfit and about four times Ethelinda's size. I was pretty sure Isabel was part giant.

She danced up to us, waving what I hoped was a toy wand. "Hey, you two," she boomed. "Great costume, Katie, and I presume the mysterious gentleman with you is one Mr. Palmer."

Owen raised his mask slightly to verify his identity and gave her a smile.

"Why aren't you two on the dance floor?"

We looked at each other, then Owen said, "Watching everyone else is more fun for us."

"It gives us better office blackmail material for after the holidays," I added.

She fluttered her fake wings at us as she returned to the dance floor. Others might have considered us to be wallflowers, but I had a good time sitting with Owen and trying to guess the identities of the various party guests in their costumes. Marcia and Rod were still dancing together, and still quite close. From what I'd heard about Rod's social life, that may have been the longest he'd spent with any one woman in years. Philip had finally given up trying to ballroom dance in that crowd and was attempting to follow Gemma's more contemporary dance style, even as he seemed to be a bit distracted by that catsuit. At least one fairy was floating and spinning above the crowd, and if I saw it, that meant my friends could see it, so I hoped they were too busy dancing to notice.

"I'd say it's a successful party," I remarked to Owen.

"Rod does know how to throw a party," he said. He checked his watch. "It's not long until midnight. I'd better fight my way back to the bar to grab some champagne."

While he was gone, I slipped my feet out of my shoes and pointed and flexed my toes a few times to try to get the circulation going again. As I bent to put my shoes back on, a sudden wave of dizziness struck me. Maybe I should have asked Owen to grab some food before he got the champagne, I thought.

Owen returned more quickly than I expected. "They had the champagne all lined up on a table," he explained. After he handed me my glass, he reached into an inner pocket of his jacket and withdrew two of those party things you blow into and make uncurl. "And we have something to help us usher in the New Year," he said, handing me one of those. "I wasn't sure if you'd want one of these or one of the noise-makers, but I figured there's enough noise in here."

"Very good choice," I said, then blew it at him.

The band stopped playing and Rod took the microphone. "Are we ready for the countdown?" he asked.

Owen and I stood up and moved to join the rest of the crowd. Everyone counted down from ten together, then balloons and streamers floated down from the ceiling—where I hadn't noticed anything hanging previously—and everyone cheered. Owen and I clinked our glasses together, then he leaned forward to kiss me. "Happy New Year," he said.

"And happy New Year to you, too."

I drank my champagne, and then things started to get a little fuzzy. And then things went kind of blank.

The next thing I knew, I was waking up in my bed with a killer headache, in my bedroom, in our apartment, and still wearing the red satin dress and fishnet tights.

Eighteen

It was hard to tell what time of day it was from inside my bedroom because so little light came through the airshaft no matter what time of day it was, but this didn't look like morning sun. I had to squint and force my eyes to focus so I could read my bedside alarm clock. The clock had to be wrong. It said it was nearly three in the afternoon. That was impossible. It would mean I was missing about fifteen hours, since the last thing I remembered clearly was kissing Owen at midnight.

I reached to rub my aching head and found the horned headband, still clinging precariously. Removing it eased the headache a little bit, but not enough. With a supreme effort, I willed myself into a sitting position. Maybe a shower would help, I thought, if I could make it all the way to the bathroom. The wooden floor seemed to have turned to ice, it was so hard to keep my feet under me, and I had to hold my arms out like a tightrope walker to maintain my balance.

A long, hot shower didn't do as much to clear my head as I hoped. A large part of my brain was still out cold and the other part was having to lug it around like deadweight. My balance had improved some, so navigating the path back to the bedroom wasn't quite as difficult as the walk to the bathroom had been. I threw on a sweat suit, and then I ventured out into the living room. I wasn't yet sure I wanted to know what had happened during all those missing hours, but I was sure my roommates would tell me.

"It lives," Marcia said drily from her seat at the dining table when I shuffled in. Gemma glanced up from the fashion magazine she was reading with a grunt.

"Yeah, it lives. More or less," I said, sitting very carefully on the sofa to make sure it was where I thought it was. I felt like I had a skewed perception of the world, as though everything was just a bit off from where it seemed to me to be. I noticed as I sat down that one of my red stilettos lay on the floor in front of the door. There was no sign of the other one. Maybe Prince Charming had snagged it when I lost it while fleeing the ball and he'd use it to find me again. "Would anyone mind filling me in on what happened after midnight? 'Cause I'm drawing a blank."

"Oh, it's quite the saga," Gemma said. "I'm not sure we have time to tell the whole story."

"How about we start with what should be the easy part: How did I end up at home and in bed?"

Marcia got up from the table and came over to stand in front of me. "When things got out of hand at the party, Owen and Philip dragged you out of there. Owen called for a car to drive us home. Owen and Philip got you up the stairs between them, and then Gemma and I threw you in bed."

I nodded. "Okay. That makes sense. Well, the coming home part does. But what do you mean by things getting out of hand?"

"Ha!" Gemma's response was somewhere between a snort and a laugh.

"Come on, y'all. What happened? I'm missing a lot of time here, and I don't know why. I remember kissing Owen at midnight, and after that everything is a big blank."

"Let's just say I never had you pegged as a mean drunk." Marcia tossed her hair, which still held some of the Marilyn curl, and stalked off to the kitchen.

"But I wasn't drunk," I protested. "I had one cup of punch, which seemed pretty watered-down even to me, and then a glass of champagne at midnight, and I don't remember drinking all of that."

"I hope you were drunk," Gemma snapped. "Because if you weren't and you were acting that way, well, you aren't the person we thought you were."

"What did I do?"

"You got nasty. You said some really mean things to us and to Owen, and then after you told him how pathetic he was as a boyfriend, you came on to every other man in the place—especially those who were there with dates."

I moaned and buried my face in my hands. I'd only ever been truly drunk a few times in my life, and even then, never to the point of passing out, so it was hard for me to compare the experience. Still, it seemed like I should remember more than a couple of drinks if I'd had enough to pass out. Or was it like a concussion, where sometimes you forgot the whole day, even the time before you got conked on the head?

"What did I say to y'all?" My voice came out muffled from behind my hands.

"For one thing," Marcia said, "you told everyone about me breaking up with Jeff. How did you put it? Oh yeah, 'Like she thinks she's too good for him.' "

Still with my face behind my hands, I said, "You know that's not what I think. I told you that."

"Yeah, and I also recall asking you not to tell anyone."

I looked up to see her sitting once more at the kitchen table, a steaming cup of coffee in front of her. My mouth watered at the sight. Coffee, that was what I needed. If I got some caffeine into my system I was sure I'd be able to think straight. And would it have killed Marcia to offer me a cup while she was up? I recalled having brought many a cup of coffee to her when she was in a similar state.

"I don't remember saying that, honest. I didn't mean to blab."

"What was the big secret, anyway?" Gemma asked. "Why didn't you want me to know?"

"It's my business, isn't it?"

While Marcia and Gemma argued, I eased myself off the sofa and aimed for the kitchen, hoping there was still coffee in the pot. I nearly wept with joy when I saw that there were at least two cups left. I poured half a cup for myself, added some sugar and milk, then took a cautious sip. One thing I remembered from the few hangovers I'd experienced was such a strong nausea that the thought of food or drink made my stomach churn. But my stomach felt fine. I was able to drink the whole cup, and soon my head felt a lot clearer, even if the headache hadn't eased at all. Actually, it was even worse.

I wandered over to the front window while Gemma and Marcia argued. It was snowing outside, in the stage of a snowstorm when it's mostly flakes dancing to the ground from the sky, but before much has accumulated yet on the ground. At any other time, this would have been the perfect day to stay inside with my friends, watching old movies while eating popcorn and chatting. Apparently, today wasn't going to be one of those days. I tried to force my attention back to my roommates.

"It's not like you've had perfect relationships, yourself," Marcia said.

"What? Because I hit a rough patch with Philip? Well, we talked last night, and he said work was distracting him. He's going to try to be better because he misses me."

"That's great!" I said, trying to radiate enthusiasm for my friend's good fortune.

Both of them turned to glare at me, looking like they wished I'd just vanished. "You say that now," Gemma said, "but that's not what you said last night. I believe there was something about what a slut I was because I was thinking of dumping him for not sleeping with me yet."

I cringed, though to be fair, she had pretty much said something along the same lines, except for the part about her being a slut. It wasn't like I'd broken any new ground there.

Marcia chuckled. "Yeah, and ironic, wasn't it, considering she went from that to complaining about Owen doing the same thing with her? And then she must have been thinking of poor Philip's reputation by giving him a chance to show he wasn't a cold fish."

By this time I'd cringed so hard I nearly had a cramp. "How did Owen react to the things I did?" I asked. My heart clenched at the thought of what he must have felt.

Gemma shrugged. "It's hard to tell with that mask he had on. But he went really quiet, still-like. He made sure you were looked after. A lot of guys would have left you there to find your own way home, and he wanted to make sure you'd be okay. I think he really, really likes you. And he's a good guy."

I shook my head as though that would clear out some of the deadness. "I just don't get it. I don't know where that stuff could have come from."

"It had to have come from somewhere," Marcia said.

"We should have known that nice routine was too good to be true," Gemma added.

I went from contrite to angry. "Come on! How long have you known me? We've lived together at least five years, off and on, and you've seen me drunk more than once. You'd know by now if I had anything ugly hidden underneath the surface." I tried to think of an explanation for whatever had happened. The most obvious, of course, was that I'd been enchanted. I'd done some pretty out-of-character things not too long ago, the last time I'd lost my immunity, when I'd been enchanted. It would have been easy enough for someone in that crowd to have zapped me with a spell. Unfortunately, I couldn't tell them that. "Maybe it was one of those drugs people slip into drinks, like the news shows are always warning you about. My mom sent me a magazine clipping about that the other day."

My head finally cleared completely, although I still felt like my brain was too big for my skull, and I felt like I was truly, fully awake for the first time today—even more awake than usual. I could now assess the situation and see it for what it was. They were lying to me, a voice in my head said, winding me up to make me regret drinking too much. None of that stuff had really happened. I'd probably fallen asleep on a couch and missed the whole party.

I laughed. "Okay, I think your little prank has gone on long enough. You've run it into the ground, and it's not the least bit amusing."

It would have been nice if I could have grabbed a coat and stomped out of the apartment, but the snow was coming down hard and I didn't want to be out in it. Instead, I went back to the bedroom and slammed the door. I thought about calling Owen to get the real story of what happened at the party, but then I realized I didn't have his home phone number. That certainly said something about our relationship. I hoped he might call to make sure I was okay, but he didn't. I spent the rest of the day curled up on my bed and trying not to dream up revenge fantasies against my roommates. I had the light out and was pretending to sleep long before Gemma came to bed.

Because I'd gone to bed so early, I woke before my roommates did. I got up, got dressed, and left. I figured I'd let them worry about me and stew all day, and then maybe they'd be sorry enough to come clean and apologize that evening. Leaving early also meant that I might stand a chance of missing Owen. If he didn't care enough to call to see how I was doing after a night when he'd had to carry me home, I didn't want to see him. It would serve him right if he worried about me.

I picked up a sweet roll and coffee at a deli I passed on my way to the subway station, but when I got into the station, I found myself heading for the uptown platform instead of my more usual downtown platform. I noticed the mistake and tried to correct it, but nothing happened. I kept heading for the uptown platform, as though someone else controlled my body. I saw an elf pass me on the staircase, so I figured I had my immunity back and no one could be controlling me magically. Maybe my subconscious was trying to tell me something and I should just go with my gut.

I got on an uptown express train, then got off at Times Square and in-

stinctively made my way over to the Spellworks store. I stood on the corner across the street from the store, waiting and watching. After a while,
I got cold from standing still, and just waiting there seemed pointless,
but when I tried to move, something in me resisted. My subconscious
was being really, really stubborn. I put up an even stronger fight and finally succeeded in moving one leg, but then I saw Idris approaching the
store and decided to stay for a while.

Of course, the moment I decided to stay, my subconscious got other
ideas. I darted out across the street, dodging honking cars, to reach him.
It took him a moment to notice me, and then yet another to recognize
me. "What are you doing here?" he asked, his eyes bugging. He immediately scanned the area around me like he was looking for my magical
bodyguards. Come to think of it, I hadn't noticed them, myself. I must
have thrown them off by leaving so early, before Owen got there to walk
me to work.

I opened my mouth to answer him, but what came out was, "Are you
missing anything? Or have you been too busy with your lady friend to notice?" My subconscious was a very strange place. I had no idea what I was
talking about.

He rolled his eyes. "I am not dating Sylvia. She's my investor. You may
think I'm joking around with my business, but it's for real, and it's going
to take that dinosaur you work for down."

I glanced over at his single, tiny storefront, then back to him. "Yeah,
we're shaking."

"How big a task force do you have assigned to figure out what I'm
doing and bring me down?" he asked, crossing his arms over his chest
and taking a pose that made him look like a wannabe rap star. "Yeah,
you're running scared."

"We're not scared of you. We're scared about the mess you'll make
and the innocent people who'll be hurt along the way." That was me talking, I was sure.

"That's what you say." He glanced around me again, then asked with a smirk, "Where's your boyfriend this morning? I thought taunting me was his job."

"He's too busy to waste time on you." Part of me wanted desperately to stay there with him, which made me really worry about my subconscious, but I knew I needed to get to the office. It took all my will to drag myself away from him to get to the subway station. While I waited for a downtown train, I checked my watch. Unless a train came very soon, I'd be late. I stared up the tunnel, wishing for a train to get there right away. For once, it worked.

When I got to the office, Owen's lab was empty. That gave me a chance to focus on my own work. I had a revised marketing plan in response to the Spellworks threat to wrap up and get to Merlin, and that almost distracted me from obsessing over what might have happened at the party and whatever was going on with me this morning. I still didn't think my friends had told me the truth. After all, I never acted like that. I printed the final document, then headed to the departmental printer room to pick it up.

Trix greeted me with a worried frown when I got up to Merlin's office. "Are you okay?" she asked. "You were in really bad shape by the end of the party."

"What kind of shape?" I asked.

She shrugged her wings. "You weren't acting like yourself." Then she gave one of her tinkling fairy giggles. "For a moment, I even thought Ethan might have regretted breaking up with you."

"That bad, huh?" I asked, playing along, though I was sure she was in on my roommates' scheme.

"I've seen worse. Remember, I used to hang out with Ari." Her eyes flashed in anger for a second, then she was back to her perky self. "What brings you up here?"

"I've got this plan the boss wanted to see."

The intercom on Trix's desk buzzed. "Tell her to bring it to me," Kim's voice said.

Trix looked up at me and rolled her eyes. "Her majesty beckons."

This would have been the perfect time for Merlin to fling open his office doors and ask to see me, but he didn't, so I sighed, shrugged, and headed to what used to be my office. "You need to make sure Mr. Mervyn sees this as soon as possible," I said, trying to give my best impression of a superior speaking to a lowly office peon. "It's high priority."

She took the document from me, tossing it casually into a nearby in-box. "I'm sure he'll look at it when he has time."

That was the last straw. If I didn't still have the remnants of a killer headache, I'd have been up for an all-out hair-pulling and face-clawing catfight. Before I realized what I was doing, I'd snatched the plan back out of the in-box. "Look, I don't know what delusions of grandeur you have going on, but you're just filling in for my clerical tasks until I finish catching the bad guys yet again. Until you've been a big part of stopping the latest evil scheme a couple of times, you don't stand a chance of taking my job, so you can get over yourself."

She was struck speechless, which was rather satisfying. It would have been even more satisfying if her elbow had bumped the tall Starbucks cup next to her computer and sent her morning latte into her laptop's keyboard, but I couldn't ask for everything. While she was still trying to come up with a snappy comeback, I said, "Now, I'll give this to Trix to give to Mr. Mervyn." Then while I stood there watching, the coffee cup tipped over, seemingly of its own accord. It took her a second to realize what was happening, and then she shrieked as she grabbed the cup and then tried to mop up the coffee.

In spite of her frantic reaction, the results were less than spectacular. A minor explosion, or at least some sparks and noise, would have been more fun. Just then, the laptop keyboard blew up, shooting keys and sparks everywhere. Ah, that was more like it, I thought. "It looks like you're too busy to deal with this at the moment, anyway," I shot over my shoulder as I left her to damage control.

"That must have gone well," Trix remarked as I returned to her desk.

"Usually you look frustrated instead of satisfied when you get away from Kim."

"Have you ever had something you wish for really happen? I mean, where you think it would be great if something would happen, and then it does?"

"Of course I have. I can do magic."

"No, not with you making it happen. I mean like when someone passes you like you're sitting still on the freeway, and you think it would be terrific if there was a state trooper with a radar gun around the next bend, and then when you get around the next bend you see a state trooper with that guy pulled over. It gives you faith that there is some justice in the universe."

"I take it Kim just got pulled over?"

"In a way. She had a cup of coffee next to her computer, and her elbow was awfully close to it while she did her superior act with me. I couldn't help but think that it would be funny if while she was playing power games with me, her elbow hit that cup and knocked it over onto her keyboard. And then the cup fell over, just like that. She's still in there trying to salvage the computer, but it may be a lost cause, considering it blew up."

She sighed wistfully. "Oh, I wish I'd been there to see that. Too bad you couldn't get it on video, but I have a happy picture in my mind. That may be enough to get me through the rest of the day."

"While you're daydreaming, can you give this to the boss next time he emerges from his cave?" I handed her the plan.

"Sure thing. I owe you for giving me my daily dose of motivation."

On my way back down to R&D, I passed a man who gave me an appreciative leer. "Oh, drop dead," I muttered under my breath as I kept walking. A moment later, I heard a horrible choking sound behind me. I spun around to see that man doubled over, coughing and sputtering while his face turned redder and redder. A bag of cheddar popcorn lay spilled on the ground in front of him. I might not have liked the way he'd looked at me, but I couldn't leave him to die. I ran over, stood behind him, and whacked him on the back. He was still choking, so I wrapped my arms around him and did the Heimlich maneuver. Soon, he was breathing normally.

I let myself breathe more normally, as well, once the disaster was averted. Then I looked up and saw that a crowd had gathered. While the women rushed to check on the choker, the men all studied me intently. I overheard one whisper to another, "Well, she did act like she wanted to wrap herself around him."

I ignored it and turned away to head back to Owen's lab, then almost choked, myself, when I heard another one mutter, "You know, she's not nearly as cute out of costume. I guess I'd still do her if she threw herself at me, but I'm not gonna compete for her. Palmer can have her, but can you picture him keeping her after all that?"

Another one snorted, "Yeah, our resident boy scout isn't going to be into that stuff."

It took all my strength to act like I hadn't heard anything as I walked away. This was yet another one of those times when it would have been nice if the universe would have set things right for me, but the fact that the universe had allowed itself a rare moment of balance by getting back at Kim did not mean I suddenly was going to get everything I wished for. Still, I wouldn't have objected if the ceiling caved in on them. I then heard a thud and some screams, and I turned to see a hole in the ceiling in that part of the hallway, with ceiling tiles lying broken on the ground. Two men seemed dazed and had bits of tile in their hair. This was starting to get freaky. Aside from karma kicking into gear, I couldn't help but wonder about the things those men had said about me. Maybe Gemma and Marcia hadn't been playing games with me. And that meant that maybe Owen hadn't been neglecting me but rather had been hurt deeply. I needed to figure out what was going on, and there was one person I was sure I could trust to tell me the truth without judging me.

I headed straight for Rod's office. It was ironic that a guy who habitually wore a face that wasn't his own was the person I felt I could trust, but enough had happened between Rod and me that I was sure he'd be honest with me, and although he was Owen's best friend, I felt like he could be a neutral party in this.

Isabel was out when I got there, but Rod was at his desk. "Can I talk to you?" I asked.

"Sure," he said, gesturing me to a chair. "How are you feeling?"

"I have a splitting headache, but other than that I'm okay. I just wanted to ask you, what did I do at your party? For real. Don't exaggerate, and don't try to spare me. I need the truth."

"Are you sure about that?"

The unease on his face made me think twice, but I said, "You don't have to give me gory details. A big-picture overview will do."

"Soon after midnight, it was like you became another person. You were very, um, flirtatious. You were loud, and you said some mean things."

I groaned and sank back into the chair. "So, it's true. Gemma and Marcia told me, but I thought they were putting me on, since I never act like that. I kept waiting for them to say 'gotcha.' But they didn't."

"Your immunity was still down during the party, wasn't it?" I nodded. "It's possible you were under a spell. Someone other than your roommates may have been playing a prank on you."

"You think that's it?"

"I know it is. You're not mean. You'd never act that way if you were in control of yourself." He gave me a warm smile and added, "Don't worry, Owen knows that, too. He'll brood and sulk for a while, but he'll get over it. In fact, I bet he's researching possibilities right now."

When he smiled that way, he really looked nice—even nicer now that he was doing something with his hair and was taking care of his skin. I realized then that his real face and his illusion weren't all that different. His illusion just looked like someone had Photoshopped his real face to remove his worst flaws and make everything look just a little bit better.

With a deep sigh, I stood up. "I have a killer headache, and I'm feeling utterly humiliated, so I'm going to go home early. Would you mind telling anyone who needs to know? About the headache, I mean. Not about the humiliation, though I suppose that goes without saying. I want to make sure this has all worn off before I face the office again."

"Don't worry, I'll take care of it."

I gave him a quick hug before I left. "You're a real pal, you know? You might even be good enough for Marcia."

"I'm glad you approve, because I was going to ask her out anyway," he said with a pat on my back.

Owen was in his office when I went back to the lab for my purse and coat, so I didn't try talking to him. That could wait until I felt a bit better. I left the building and trudged across the park by City Hall to get to the subway station, my head feeling heavier with each step. When a train arrived, I boarded and managed to get a seat. The woman sitting across from me wore what had to have been the ugliest shoes ever. Although she was well dressed, her shoes were repulsive—and probably the expensive kind of repulsive. In other words, they looked like someone had pulled them out of the trash and patched them up, but they were designed to look that way. There were even silvery bands across them that were probably inspired by duct tape. Staring at the shoes, I wondered what she'd think if she had the real thing instead of the designer version. Real duct tape holding her shoes together wouldn't be nearly as nice, especially if she'd spent hundreds of dollars to buy faux-trashed shoes.

I glanced away for a moment, then when I looked back at her, I saw that her shoes looked even worse. The duct tape wrapping around them curled up around the edges, and the sole was coming off in places. I blinked to make sure I saw what I thought I saw. No, it was still the same way, and I was sure those shoes had been in better shape before I started thinking about them.

I could have written off a lot of stuff that had happened that day to chance. There were logical explanations for the train coming when I wanted it to, for Kim's computer, the choking guy, the ceiling falling.

But shoes didn't change right before your eyes just because you thought they should. That is, it didn't happen with me. I knew people who could do things like that, but I also knew I wasn't one of them. At least, I shouldn't have been.

If I wasn't mistaken, I had somehow developed magical powers.

Nineteen

I forced myself to take a couple of deep breaths and calm down before I had a panic attack on the subway. I knew there were a lot of magical people in the city. It was entirely possible that one of them was on the train and shared my taste in footwear. Just in case, though, I focused on the shoes, trying to remember what they'd looked like before. I was fairly certain I felt the tingle of power in use, but much stronger than anything I'd ever felt from others doing magic near me. I blinked, and the shoes were right back the way they'd been before. Their owner didn't seem to have noticed. She crossed her legs and kept her eyes on her book.

That sealed it for me. Even if I wasn't really doing magic, this was suspicious enough to have checked out. I'd learned the hard way not too long ago that telling Owen when something odd and potentially dangerous was going on could save me a lot of trouble. I got off the subway at the next stop and walked back down Broadway toward the office. I barely noticed where I was or the fact that it was cold and windy as I hurried down the sidewalk. The pedestrian lights all turned to "walk" just as I reached them, but I couldn't be sure that was because of magic. If you walked at the right pace and no one got in your way, you could hit the lights in synchronization like that. I was tempted to try something else to test my newfound powers, but I knew that doing magic where people might see it was forbidden, and I didn't know the first thing about veiling the effects of magic from public view.

I had a lot to learn if this was for real. I wondered what had happened. Was this a weird side effect of Owen's potion? Maybe it had backfired, not only making me susceptible to magic, but also able to do magic. Or it could have had something to do with whatever happened at the party. As much as I liked the idea of being able to get whatever I wanted with a wave of my hand, it was also a little frightening.

When I got to the MSI office building, I balked at the front door. It was like earlier in the morning when I'd felt compelled to go to the Spellworks store. My subconscious must have wanted to play around more with magic, but I overruled it and forced myself to open the door. I ran up the stairs and was breathing heavily by the time I got to Owen's lab. He and Jake were in there working. "We need to talk," I blurted as I burst through the doorway.

He looked up from the document he was reviewing with Jake, blinked, frowned, and then looked like he was having a root canal. "Can we have this discussion—"

"Now," I interrupted. "Don't worry, it's not a relationship talk, but it is pretty damn crucial. Your office, ASAP."

While he was still looking at me like I'd lost my mind—and maybe I had—I headed straight for his office. Only when I reached the doorway did I remember his wards. I could usually get into his private office because I was immune to magic, but what about now that I could do magic?

I was able to get through the door, but I thought my head would explode as I crossed the threshold. I couldn't help but scream in pain, and that brought Owen running. He caught me as I swayed, still holding my head in agony, and helped me into the nearest chair. "Katie, what is it?" Now he sounded gentle and concerned but still a little distant.

"Something very, very weird is happening," I said, choking back a sob. Before I could change my mind, I blurted, "I think I can do magic now."

That got his attention. "What? How long has this been going on?"

"Today. I don't know, maybe I'm imagining things. Maybe I'm going crazy, but it's too much for coincidence. This morning, the slightest thought that it would be funny if Kim's coffee turned over and spilled on her computer crossed my mind—and then it happened a few seconds later. I chalked that up to karma because she totally deserved it. Then some really strange stuff happened in the hallway on my way back here. I decided to go home because I had a headache that was getting worse, and on the train, there was this lady with really ugly shoes. I thought about changing them, and they changed, then changed back again when I wanted them back the way they were. So I got off the train at the next stop to come back here and see what was going on."

He studied me like he was looking at a laboratory specimen. "While there are certainly other possible explanations for everything you've described, the number of events in that short a time is highly unlikely. You've had a headache, you say?"

I nodded, then regretted it as that intensified the ache. "Yes, ever since I woke up on New Year's Day. At first I thought it was a hangover, but it wasn't the typical hangover headache. I felt like my brain was too big for my skull. It's not as bad now, but it's a constant ache. And just now, when I walked through your doorway, that was the worst."

"Hmm. Okay, I want you to try doing some magic."

"Like what?"

"Think about something you want to make happen. Something simple and obvious that isn't likely to happen on its own by coincidence."

I looked around his cluttered office. There was very little in there that didn't look like it was bound to topple over on its own at any moment. I finally pointed to the magnifying glass that lay on top of a pile of parchment on his desk. "I'm going to make that flip over."

He nodded. "Okay, go for it."

I concentrated, imagining the magnifying glass turning onto its side, and then falling over onto its other side. Slowly at first, and then more surely, it rose, turned over, and then landed again on the desk.

"Son of a bitch," Owen said as he stared at the magnifying glass. It was the closest I'd ever heard him come to swearing in a language I recognized. Gloria probably didn't approve of profanity.

"So it's for real," I said, just to confirm it.

"It's real, all right. I felt the power, myself."

"So, is this good or bad?"

"I don't know. It depends on how and why it happened. The headache has me worried, though. That part's not good, if it's related."

"How do we find out how and why it happened?"

"I don't know that, either." He shook his head, his forehead knit in a deep frown. "I've never heard of anyone spontaneously developing magical powers, especially not a magical immune. That should be absolutely impossible. If it is possible, then it changes everything we think we know about magical potential."

"Well, obviously it's possible because, well, hello!"

"Again, that comes back to how and why." He knelt next to me, closed his eyes, and held his hands out toward me. Then he frowned even deeper and sat back on his heels. "That's really odd."

"A lot is really odd. Care to narrow it down?"

"You don't feel like, well, you."

"That would actually explain a lot about the past day or so, as well as what happened at the party, but wouldn't I notice it if I'm not me?"

"As I told you earlier, every magical person has a sort of signature. You can learn to recognize magical people by the magic they emit once you get to know them and know their magic, even when they're not actually using magic."

"Like the magical equivalent of a signature perfume."

"Exactly. But because you're magically immune and have absolutely no magic in you, you're magically blank. If I lost all my other senses, I'd still be able to find and recognize a familiar magical person. You would be mostly invisible to me."

"Mostly?"

He turned red. "There are other things about you I've learned to recognize that aren't in the realm of the usual physical senses. Anyway, you've got a magical signature right now, and it's not the same as the slight hints of magic you get when we tinker with your immunity. I need you to do something else magical."

I looked at the water glass on his desk and decided to fill it. As I concentrated on it, I felt the stirrings of power within me, and then the glass filled. I turned to look at Owen, who had an absolutely horrified expression on his face. "Oh, God, you're Ari," he said, backing away from me.

"I'm what? No, I'm Katie. I know I've been acting odd, but I'd know if I was someone else, wouldn't I? I wouldn't have been able to get through your office door. You have her specifically warded out, don't you?"

He grabbed my wrist and stood up, tugging me with him. "Come on, we need to talk to the boss about this." He pulled so hard, I had no choice but to go with him. My head nearly exploded again as I passed back through the doorway, but he barely gave me a chance to get my feet under me again before he took off, dragging me behind him. Jake moved as though to ask a question as we passed, but Owen ignored him and kept going. His grip on my wrist made me feel like I was a prisoner in custody, and I guessed that if he thought I had somehow been switched with Ari, I probably was.

This was too weird for me to get my mind around. If I really was Ari and I'd managed to switch bodies with me, Katie Chandler, would I really think I was Katie? Wouldn't I be going around thinking like Ari and gloating about having fooled them all? It would ruin the point to think I was Katie. Meanwhile, where was Katie? If Ari was in my body, shouldn't I be getting all kinds of good insight into Idris and his company about now?

Another stab of pain hit my head, and next thing I knew, I was digging in my heels and resisting Owen's pull. "Oh, no, not so fast," I said.

He turned back to fix me with a glare. "Katie, now is not the time."

"You know, you're kind of hot when you get all forceful and manly like that. Do you ever do that in the bedroom?" I heard the words coming out of my mouth but I didn't remember forming them in my brain. It was like these things came from outside me. I seemed to have a little devil sitting on my shoulder and whispering in my ear, like in the old cartoons. Shaking my head, as though I thought I could shake that little devil off, I said, "No!" Then I looked at a beet-red Owen and whispered, "Sorry. I don't know what's happening, but I want it to stop."

He looked sympathetic, and shifted his grip on my wrist so that he held my hand, instead. "I know. And that's what we're going to do now, so come on."

The closer we got to Merlin's office, the harder I had to concentrate to force myself to go along with Owen and not resist him. I tasted blood in my mouth from biting my lip to keep myself from saying all the awful things that tried to come off my tongue. The pain in my head got worse and worse, to the point that tears came to my eyes.

Fortunately, Merlin's office doors opened as soon as we reached his suite, so we didn't have to do battle with Kim over scheduling an appointment. I might not have been able to resist whatever cruel things the little devil wanted me to say or do to her because I would have kind of wanted to do them, myself.

Merlin shut the doors behind us as Owen swept me over to an armchair and seated me there. He remained beside me with one hand on my shoulder in a gesture that was both supportive and restraining. Merlin took a seat opposite us and looked at us expectantly.

"Something's been done to Katie," Owen said. He ran through what I'd told him about my odd string of seeming coincidences. "Then I had her do something for me," he continued, "and it's true. She can do magic. I saw it, and I felt the power in use." I couldn't see his face from where I sat, but I heard the intake of breath as he steeled himself for the next thing he had to say. "And here's the odd part: She's got Ari's signature to her magic. If you blindfolded me and had Katie do magic near me, I'd think it was Ari."

"I'm also acting more like Ari than I'd like," I confessed. "I keep saying things I don't mean, really awful things intended to hurt people, and I can't seem to help myself. I don't remember a thing about what I did at Rod's New Year's Eve party, but what I've heard was really awful. My roommates are barely speaking to me."

"Whatever it was that happened must have been done at the party," Owen went on. "She was fine until soon after midnight and then . . ." His voice trailed off, and when he spoke again there was a roughness to it. "Well, it wasn't Katie."

Merlin nodded. "You're right, that is quite odd. I'd never heard of a magical immune developing powers, but Ari's signature could explain it."

"She also has a bad headache," Owen said.

"Hideously bad, like an alien is about to burst out of my skull," I added.

Merlin got out of his chair and came over to stand right in front of me. "Katie, I need you to do some magic now."

I glanced around his office, which was far neater than Owen's, and saw a teacup sitting on a nearby table. Concentrating with all my might, I tried to lift the teacup and turn it around. Although I had a better sense of what to do to make the magic happen, this time it was more of a struggle, like I was fighting against something within me that didn't want it to work. By the time the teacup finally rose from its saucer and turned around, I had beads of sweat dripping from my forehead and my underarm antiperspirant had given up the ghost.

I let the teacup fall a few inches into its saucer and collapsed back into my chair. Owen's hand on my shoulder tightened, and Merlin frowned and stroked his beard. "Very, very interesting," he said. He stepped forward and rested his hand on the top of my head. I felt a slight tingle of magic, and then he lifted his hand. "And that is even more interesting," he said. "When she's not actually using magic, there's another magical signature lingering."

Owen lifted his hand from my shoulder and placed it on top of my head, which sent shivers down my spine. I had to bite my tongue to keep from saying the words to that effect that popped into my head. "Some other fairy, but not the usual kind?" he asked, moving his hand back to my shoulder.

"That's my assessment, as well."

Suddenly, I had a feeling I knew exactly what was going on. "Ethelinda," I groaned.

"Who?" they both asked.

"A fairy godmother. A couple of weeks ago—right at the time Owen and I started dating—this crazy fairy lady showed up and told me she was my fairy godmother. She even had a book with my entire dating history in it. I told her I didn't want her help, but weird things kept happening that she took a little too much delight in, and she seemed to think they should have brought us closer together. And then she decided when those things didn't work that maybe we weren't meant for each other."

"That does sound like a fairy godmother," Merlin confirmed. He glanced over at Owen. "They're still active?"

"Apparently. I've known a couple of people who had to deal with them. They're not too good at keeping up with the times, so they're more annoying now than ever."

Merlin stroked his beard again. "I know there are rituals for summoning them, but I'll have to do some research about this particular one to see how to get to her directly."

It then dawned on me that I was still wearing my coat and still had my purse over my shoulder from when I'd been heading home. In all that had happened after I got back to the office, I'd totally forgotten to take the coat off or put my purse away. If I had my purse, that meant I still had Ethelinda's locket.

I unzipped my purse and found the heart-shaped locket inside the coin pocket. I pulled it out and held it up to Merlin. "Will this help? She gave this to me as a way of summoning her. I've only used it to read her the riot act."

His face brightened. "It should help immensely. Thank you."

While he did something with the locket, I shrugged out of my coat. Owen took it from me and hung it on the coatrack in the corner of the office. He'd just returned to my side when there was a loud crack in the air, followed by something hitting the nearby sofa with a thud and a cloud of silver sparkles.

The sparkles cleared, revealing a pair of bloomer-clad legs sticking out of a mass of fabric. The feet at the end of those legs wore pink terry-cloth house slippers. The mound of fabric stirred, and then the legs lowered to the ground while a head and torso emerged. It was Ethelinda, of course, dressed in what looked like a high-necked Victorian nightgown over all the other clothes. She had pink sponge curlers in her hair and thick, white cream all over her face.

She started to act indignant, but then she saw who stood in front of her and fell to her knees at Merlin's feet. "You summoned me, my lord?" she said, bending to touch her head to the ground.

"Yes, as a matter of fact, I did," he replied, ignoring her bowing and scraping. "You seem to have been bothering one of my people."

"Helping!" she insisted, tilting her head up slightly but still on her knees. "Not bothering. I never bother people. I only help them."

"Perhaps, then, you can explain the latest trauma to strike Miss Chandler. Do you understand how a magical immune is suddenly able to do magic? And don't deny that you've done something to her. I detected the traces of your spell."

She rose awkwardly to her feet, beaming with pride. "That's one of the most clever things I've ever done, if I do say so myself. Of course, she's not doing the magic herself, but while her immunity was gone, I was able to plant someone who could do magic within her."

I couldn't help but shudder. "Ewww! And why?"

"So you'd understand magic, silly. You weren't willing to listen when I told you that someone like you isn't compatible with a wizard, so I thought if you discovered what it was like to have power, you'd understand."

"That makes no sense whatsoever," Owen said.

Merlin cleared his throat. "At this point, the question at hand is not why this was done, but how, and who else was involved?"

Ethelinda tittered and batted her eyes at Merlin. "Of course, I can't take full credit." She turned to me. "Your friend had the initial idea, and she volunteered to help."

Considering what Owen and Merlin had already noted about my "magic," I knew exactly who that "friend" was. "Friend?" I asked, trying to keep from screeching.

"The friend you were trying to catch up with in the train station. I saw her at the party when we were both watching you. When I discussed your romance problems with her, she volunteered to help. It was very brave of her. Not many fairies like being shrunk to that size."

If it hadn't been for Owen's firm hand on my shoulder, I would have come out of my chair. "You mean I've got a fairy inside my skull? And you thought Ari was my friend and was volunteering out of the goodness of her heart? Are you insane?"

Owen's grip tightened on my shoulder, and I couldn't tell if that was because he was trying to restrain me or if it was because he'd become very tense. "You have to undo the spell," he said with the kind of icy calm in his voice that meant he was absolutely furious.

She shrugged and flounced down onto the sofa. "I can't."

"You can't?" This time, I did shriek. "You mean, this is irreversible?"

"I can't do magic on an immune. It won't work." She waved her wand at us teasingly. "Surely all of you are well aware of that. I didn't realize her immunity would return again so soon before I could undo it." She pointed her wand at Owen. "If you weren't so eager to get her away from the party, I would have had a chance to undo it before it was too late."

I couldn't help but whimper. Owen rubbed my shoulder gently, which made me feel a lot better. I had to bite my lip to keep from blurting out an Ari-like comment about how much better it made me feel. And then my sluggish brain caught up. "We know how to take care of the immunity issue," I said. "Could you get Ari out of my brain if we did that?"

Ethelinda blinked. "Oh. I suppose I could."

I sighed in a mixture of relief and resignation. I'd just barely regained my immunity, and now I had to give it up again. In this case, though, I was more than willing. Magic powers would be cool to have, but not at the price of having a psycho evil bitch fairy stuck in my head. As that thought crossed my mind, I was struck with another stabbing pain. That made me realize something. "While she's in my head, it's very possible that she can read my thoughts," I told the others.

Merlin turned his attention from Ethelinda to me. "Why do you think that?"

"Just now, I thought something about Ari that was, well, not very nice, and it felt like someone kicked me in the head right away. And one of my roommates told me the mean things I said to her at the party were things only I knew. There's no way Ari could have known, and I'm thinking that since I don't remember that time at all, she must have been totally in control then. She's possibly picking up on anything I think, which means she might also be getting anything anyone else says around me. We've got a spy all over again."

"That's easy enough to solve," Merlin said, walking over to the kitchenette area of his office. He took out a glass, then opened the cabinets, fiddled with a few jars, mixed something up in the glass, then brought it back to me. "Drink this. It's a sedative specific to fairies. As it doesn't rely on magic to work, it should still be effective, even with the current circumstances. You may notice some minor effects, but I'm afraid they can't be helped." I took the glass and downed it in one swallow, even though it tasted pretty nasty. Anything to get Ari out of my head.

Merlin then returned his attention to Ethelinda. "It will take a couple of days to remove Miss Chandler's immunity once more, and then we will have to call upon you to undo the spell. You will cooperate." He said it in a way that emphasized that he was Merlin, the greatest wizard who ever lived.

"Why, yes, of course!" she said. "Anytime you need me!" He waved a hand, and she vanished instantly.

I was beginning to feel light-headed. "Why do we have to drag her into it?" I asked, resting my elbow on the chair's arm and propping my head up against my hand. "We know she's incompetent. I'm not sure I trust her to do this right."

Merlin tucked the locket into his vest pocket. "Unfortunately, a fairy godmother's magic can only be undone by the godmother, herself. There are occasionally ways to counteract her spells, but not to actually undo them."

"Oh yeah, like in *Sleeping Beauty,* where they can't undo the curse about pricking her finger on the spindle and dying. They can only change it to sleeping."

"From what I've heard, that might not have been technically a fairy godmother situation," Owen said, sounding like he was veering dangerously close to launching into a scholarly lecture, "but the analogy is close enough to work."

I yawned. "You know, sleep sounds like a really good idea right now."

"Good, the sedative must be working," Merlin said. "Now Mr. Palmer, perhaps you should go prepare the immunity loss potion. We need to take care of this as soon as possible. I don't know what damage might be done by forcing magic into a person who has an immunity."

Owen took off, and I missed his reassuring presence, even if he was still being a little weird around me. Not that I could blame him. I must have scared him to death, based on what I'd heard. I wasn't sure I ever wanted details of what Ari had done at the party with my body.

I closed my eyes and let myself drift as my head grew heavier and heavier. Just when I thought I was going to conk out, my head suddenly cleared. For the first time since the year began, I could think straight, with no interference from within my head. "Oh yeah, that's better," I said, sitting upright. I saw then that Owen was back, holding a beaker of potion. I must have really dozed off for a while.

Owen handed me the beaker. "I don't suppose this would work faster if I took more of it at a time?" I asked after drinking it.

"No, sorry. It's something that has to build up in your system. I've tried to adjust it to be more effective, based on our experiences last time, but it will still probably take a day or two."

"In the meantime," Merlin said, "you should be watched carefully. We don't want our enemies taking further advantage of your lost immunity, and while we can continue dosing you with the sedative, I'm still concerned about what might happen."

"You should stay with me," Owen said. "My house is secured and private, and you wouldn't have to worry about explaining any oddities to your roommates. They've seen too much as it is."

I didn't feel like arguing with him. I knew he was right, and I also knew that this wasn't going to be the cozy snuggling in front of the fireplace we'd had not so long ago. This would be uncomfortable and tense in the worst way. "Okay," I said. "I'll invent a business trip I have to go on. We can go to my place and I can pack a bag and get over to your place before my roommates get home from work."

"Excellent plan," Merlin said. "And the two of you should stay there until this is resolved. I'd rather you not take any chances while going to and from the office."

Great. Even more forced togetherness with a guy who was looking at me like I'd grown a second head. He wouldn't touch me while there was any hint of Ari about me, even if he wasn't mad at me. Come to think of it, I didn't want to touch him while she was there and possibly eavesdropping. I was lucky she was such a bitch she couldn't resist showing herself. If she'd behaved herself at the party when she first got put in my head, it could have been a while before I figured it out, and then there was no telling what she might have seen—both work-related and personal.

I forced myself out of the chair. "I guess we'd better get going." Owen immediately went to my side, a protective hand at my back.

I felt like my fate had been taken out of my hands. Having magical powers, no matter how unorthodox and temporary they were, should have made me feel strong rather than vulnerable. Here I was, finally able to zap stuff for myself, and I had men rallying around me and treating me like I was made of glass.

Owen and I went down to the lab to collect the things we'd need to work from home until all this got fixed and then headed to my apartment. I threw a few things in a bag, then wrote a short note explaining that I'd had to go on an unexpected business trip where my boss needed my help. I didn't think they'd believe it. They'd think I'd run away to avoid them, but at least they wouldn't guess the truth.

When I was ready to go, Owen picked up my bag without a word, and we walked in silence from my building to his town house. Loony was waiting for him inside his front door, but instead of rubbing against my ankles in greeting as she usually did after first welcoming Owen, she hissed at me and arched her back. "Eluned!" Owen scolded. I supposed that using her real name instead of her nickname was the cat equivalent of when my mom called me Kathleen Elizabeth.

"It's okay," I said wearily. "She's probably confused. They say animals pick up different kinds of vibes and scents about people, and I must feel strange to her." I nodded my head toward the stairs. "The usual guest room?"

"Yeah. Make yourself at home."

While I climbed the stairs, he picked up his cat and took her back toward the kitchen. Up in the guest room, I changed out of my work clothes and into something more comfortable, but not the old sweat suit of his that still lay on the guest bed. As oddly strained as things currently were between us, it might have been weird to wear his clothes.

I got back downstairs to find that he'd removed his suit coat and tie, but otherwise was still wearing his work clothes. Loony lapped at her water in the far corner of the kitchen. She gave me the evil eye, then returned to her water. Owen poured boiling water into a teapot. "I thought I'd make some tea," he said. "That was always Gloria's cure for everything."

"I wish it could cure this," I said with a wistful sigh, leaning against the counter. "I'm sorry about all this."

"It's not your fault," he said, not turning to look at me. All I could see was his back. His shoulders looked stiff and tense. I wanted desperately to rub his back to get him to relax, but I doubted that would go over very well. It would only make him more tense.

"Well, none of this would have happened if I hadn't gone against your objections about removing my immunity so I could check out how the ads were veiled."

Still with his back to me, and his shoulders stiffer than ever, he said, "You didn't overrule me. Mr. Mervyn did, and he was right to do so. We needed that information, and can you imagine what a disaster it might have been if this had happened to another immune, one who didn't know how to recognize when something was wrong, and who didn't have the kind of mental control you've got?" He shook his head. "My objection was for purely personal reasons, not for the greater good."

"It was my idea to go to the party. I should have known that wasn't the smartest thing to do in the state I was in."

"And I was with you at the party, which means I was with you when it happened. I let this happen right under my nose." He laughed bitterly as he lifted the teaball from the teapot. "And I'm supposed to be the super-brilliant wizard."

There was nothing I could say to that. Not that I totally agreed with him. I wasn't sure how we could have prevented this, short of locking me in a tower where visitors had to climb up my hair to get inside and no magic could reach me, but I knew he wasn't ready to hear that. He'd rather take the blame than admit that there were things he couldn't control, no matter how powerful he was.

"Why didn't you tell me about the fairy godmother?" he asked after a while, his voice cool and distant.

I shrugged, even though he wasn't looking at me to see the gesture. "I didn't think it was important."

He finally turned around to face me. "Not important? When all those things were happening that could have got you—and sometimes us—killed, and I was trying to figure out how Idris was involved? Don't you think it would have helped me to know everything that was going on?"

I felt about the size Ari must have shrunk to when she was put in my head. "I thought I had it all under control. I kept telling her I didn't want her help, and I was never sure she was actually behind that stuff." I could feel my face growing warmer as I admitted, "And I didn't want you to think I was using a fairy godmother to get you. I was afraid that would make me look pathetic and desperate."

"I might have understood that. I know how those things work and that you'd have very little control if a fairy godmother did decide to intervene in your life. What I don't understand is why you didn't trust me enough to tell me. It affected me, too, you know."

"It didn't have anything to do with me not trusting you," I protested, but he'd already turned his back to me again. He arranged the teapot, a couple of cups, a creamer and sugar bowl, and a small plate of cookies onto a tray in a way that would have made Gloria proud. She'd probably drilled him for hours, just for an occasion such as this. I followed him to the living room and took a seat at the far end of the sofa. He poured tea for both of us, fixing mine the way I liked it without having to ask. Then he sat at the other end of the sofa.

The silence between us grew almost unbearable. "Are you mad at me?" I finally blurted. "I know I must have done and said some awful things, but that wasn't me. And I'm sorry about not telling you about the fairy godmother. I didn't think it mattered, and I really didn't want to worry you when you had so much else to worry about."

"I was more hurt and confused than mad. I knew something had to be wrong."

"Would it have killed you to say something to that effect? I spent the first day thinking my roommates were torturing me by telling me lies about what I'd done, and then when I finally figured it out, I thought everyone would hate me. That is the rumor going around the company, by the way. I think there's an office pool on how fast you'll dump me."

"I wasn't planning to dump you." He got a look in his eye that on anyone else would have looked almost roguish, but he couldn't quite carry off even the hint of naughtiness. His furious blush counteracted the glint in his eye. "I actually found some of your suggestions rather intriguing."

I noticed, though, that he didn't move any closer to me.

Loony joined us, hissing at me in passing, then curled up against Owen's leg and glared at me as if to warn me away from him. That was the last straw. Ari had tried to sabotage me with my roommates, the entire company, and with Owen, but making animals dislike me was too much, in spite of what I'd said earlier about understanding it. I wished for a moment that I could give Loony a good reason for hating me.

A split second later, she jumped up with a sharp yowl, took a flying leap off the sofa, and darted out of the room. "There goes psycho cat," Owen said, watching the doorway where she'd disappeared. "Sometimes I think this house is haunted, the way she reacts to things even I don't sense or see."

"Oh, cats do that kind of thing, for no good reason," I said, trying to keep my voice from shaking. I was not going to admit to Owen that I'd just zapped his cat. It looked like I still had access to magical powers, and I could see where having that kind of power offered some unpleasant temptations.

We passed the rest of the day without much interaction. He dug back into his magic books while I stared at my laptop screen and pretended to work on a report. I was just starting to think it might be late enough for me to get away with going to bed when Owen's doorbell rang. He got up and returned a moment later with Rod.

Rod looked stricken. There was no other way to describe the mingling of horror and worry on his face. "What is it?" I asked him.

"It's Marcia," he said.

Twenty

"What about Marcia?" I asked, my heart already hammering in my chest before I even heard what happened. People tended not to look or sound like he did when they had good news.

Rod paced in front of the fireplace, talking as he walked. "I called her at the office this afternoon to ask her out. Her receptionist said she wasn't in, and they didn't know where she was or when she'd be back. She'd gone out to lunch and hadn't returned. Then I tried her at your place, but there was no answer, and I tried her cell phone. It went straight to voice mail. I called your place again a little while ago, and your other roommate said she wasn't home yet. She sounded worried. I take it this is uncharacteristic of Marcia?"

"It's certainly uncharacteristic of you," Owen muttered. "You didn't just move on to the next candidate?"

Rod scowled at him. "I like her, okay? I want to go out with her, not with the next person on my list. Not that there is anyone else on the list right now."

"Yes, it is uncharacteristic of her," I said, stepping in before they could start squabbling. They weren't kidding when they said they were like brothers. "She's obsessive about keeping us posted on where she is and when she'll be somewhere, and if you leave her a message, she'll return your call the moment she gets it. Do you think she's been caught up in all this?"

Rod shrugged. He looked utterly miserable. "I don't know, but isn't it suspicious that she disappeared while we've got Ari?" It seemed like word of what was going on had already spread within the company.

A horrible thought struck me. "It may not have anything to do with Ari. Philip and Ethan were supposed to have a meeting with Sylvia Meredith today, and that was when they were going to tell her that Philip planned to press his claim to get his company back. She may have found out that Philip was dating one of my roommates—Ari knew that, which means Idris might have known—but they got the wrong roommate."

"I'll call Ethan," Owen said, heading over to his desk.

Before long, it seemed like we had half the magical people I knew gathered in Owen's dining room, which made Owen visibly uncomfortable. He'd spent the time after he made the necessary phone calls frantically moving his piles of junk around. I wasn't sure whether he was cleaning up for company or making sure people wouldn't accidentally rearrange anything.

Merlin, Philip, Ethan, Rod, Owen, and I gathered around Owen's unusually bare dining table over Chinese food to strategize. In spite of the food piled in front of us, none of us felt much like eating. Philip's lips were pressed into a thin, white line. Rod had lost even the pretense of cool. Owen paced the room, and even Merlin looked unusually tense. Ethan was the only one who seemed relatively at ease. The possibility of excitement was probably revving his engine.

"I realize that you value your friend," Merlin said to me once the situation had been outlined, "but we cannot allow Mr. Vandermeer to give up his claim. That appears to be the primary funding source for the Spellworks operation, so we must have it in less dangerous hands."

"Which is why they grabbed her in the first place," Ethan said. "It's an ironclad case. If it weren't for the frog factor, I bet I could even get a ruling in our favor from a regular judge. In a magical court, she doesn't stand a chance. She panicked, and then she resorted to kidnapping."

"You're not going to let them kill Marcia," Rod said, his voice cracking with emotion. He really must have liked her, I realized. Maybe he had finally met his match. I felt bad that I wasn't the one arguing for saving my friend, but I knew as well as anyone did what was at stake.

But then I realized something. "Wait a second—we've got our own hostage." They all turned to me, looking blank. I tapped my forehead. "Remember my fairy parasite? We've got something we can exchange."

"But do they care enough about Ari to be willing to exchange her?" Philip asked.

"They sprang her from our custody in the first place," I reminded them all, "and it didn't even seem like Idris knew about it, so his bosses must have done it, probably to keep her from talking. They must still be worried about what she might know and blab about, and if they aren't willing to free her, you know she'll be angry enough to talk."

Owen stopped pacing and leaned forward, resting his arms against the back of a dining chair. "She might also be good bait to help us catch someone who would be a valuable hostage for the higher-ups."

I knew exactly where he was going with that. "Yeah, Idris cares about her on some level, I think. We might be able to catch him by letting him know we have Ari, and then we can use him to free Marcia. If Ari knows enough to do damage, imagine what Idris could do, and he is their front man in all this. If they lost him, they'd at least have to make new ads."

"He is most likely the weak link in the chain," Merlin said thoughtfully. "We may not be able to determine who is ultimately directing this endeavor, but if we have Mr. Idris, we might be able to get information, or we could force them to make a trade if they worry he'll give information."

"Okay, it looks like we're agreed that we'll use Ari as leverage to eventually get Marcia back without Philip having to give up his claim," Ethan said. "But we'll need to find a few more ways to stack the deck in our favor."

"Meeting them in the right place could help," Owen said. "There are some abandoned railway tunnels under Grand Central that should be ideal. It's possible that they have some base of operations near there, so they'll think it's their territory, but we have other advantages."

Again, I was sure I knew where he was going. Being able to read him wasn't always reassuring, I was learning. "Oh no," I moaned. "Not that. Are you sure that's a good idea? It might not still be safe."

"It's safe." He didn't quite look me in the eye when he said it.

"You've gone back to check on them, haven't you?"

He turned red. "I felt bad about leaving them tame and then abandoning them."

"Owen, they'll find a way to follow you home someday, and your neighbors won't be happy about that."

"Would you mind filling the rest of us in?" Ethan asked.

"Dragons," I said. "We found a nest in those tunnels, and the dragon whisperer here seems to have made pets out of them."

"He's always been that way," Rod said. "You should have seen the things that followed him home when he was a kid."

"I don't exactly have them tamed," Owen said, still blushing, "but I think they will do what I ask, and I can make sure nobody gets away from there without my say-so. It gives us some benefit having an extra force on our side."

"Okay," Ethan said with a nod. "Now, how do we want to do the exchanges, in what order? Choreographing this thing should be interesting."

"We do them both at the same time," Owen said. "But they don't have to know they're all there. Rod, you're our master of illusion. You can keep them from seeing each other until we're all ready."

They went on strategizing, but my ever-increasing headache made it hard for me to concentrate. It sounded like my main role in all this was to stay out of the way with Ari in my brain until they absolutely needed me to prove we had her. I picked at the food on my plate, but it had gone cold. Then I remembered that I could temporarily do magic, so I concentrated on reheating my dinner. When I put a forkful of food in my mouth, it scorched my tongue. It seemed that there was a lot to learn in order to have the precise control Owen and the others had.

Finally, the others settled on the complex choreography of who would do what and when. All that was left was to set it up and see if the bad guys were willing to play along. "Mr. Wainwright," Merlin said to Ethan, "you will contact Miss Meredith in the morning to arrange that exchange. Make it sound like your client is planning to give in to her demands, but say nothing that sounds like it might be a pledge. Meanwhile, I will go to the Spellworks store and give them the message for Mr. Idris. Someone at the store has to know how to contact him, and under the circumstances, I'm sure they'll do so."

I'd have loved to be a fly on the wall for Merlin's visit to the store. Imagine being a magic store clerk and having the real Merlin walk into your store. It would be like Elvis walking into a neighborhood record store.

"What about Gemma?" I asked as the thought occurred to me. "If they figure out they have the wrong person, she could be in danger."

"We already have her guarded," Merlin said.

"She'll be worried sick, though. She's probably called the police by now."

"Why shouldn't she call the police?" Rod asked, his voice and face hard and grim. "Marcia is in danger."

"I have one more question," I said, raising my hand. "When do we deal with Ari?"

"After everything is secured, we will get you to a safe place where we know we can retain custody of her, and then we will summon your fairy godmother to do the spell," Merlin said. I tried not to groan at imagining any more time spent with Ari in my head.

Once everyone had synchronized their watches and verified their parts in the plan, the others went home. I helped Owen clear away the remains of the mostly uneaten Chinese food. "Do you think we have a prayer of making this work?" I asked.

"We'll find out tomorrow. I'm sorry your friends have been caught up in this." His voice had warmed a little toward me since our earlier conversation, but I still felt a bit of a chill.

"It's Ari's fault, really," I said, forcing a light tone into my voice in an attempt to ease the awkwardness. "She was the one who broke the spell on Philip in the first place, which left him wandering the park for Gemma to find when she decided jogging in the park on Saturday mornings was a good way to meet men."

"I assure you, I will do everything in my power to make sure your friend is returned safely." He said it like he meant it as a solemn vow, and I knew his power was considerable enough that he wasn't swearing anything lightly.

"Thank you," I whispered. He just nodded in response. I could have really used a hug, but he didn't look like he was in the mood, and I could practically feel the barrier between us.

Before we headed to bed, he gave me the immunity potion and the fairy sedative. I'd have to go through magical detox when all this was over, given the number of magical drugs I was taking.

I wasn't sure if it was the potions or my overall weariness, but I slept hard and woke feeling heavy and lethargic. When I'd showered and dressed, I found Owen in the kitchen, making breakfast. As soon as he noticed my presence, he gestured to the two glasses that sat on the table. "Ah, yes, the morning doses," I said.

"Drink those, and then you can have some coffee." He looked even more tired than I felt. I wouldn't have bet on him having slept at all. He certainly hadn't shaved, and he still wore his glasses.

I drank the fairy sedative first, then chased it with the tea-flavored potion. As I put the second glass down, Owen put a mug of coffee in my hand. "Bless you," I said before taking a good, long swallow.

He dished up scrambled eggs, bacon, and toast, and we ate in near silence. I didn't feel much like talking, and he wasn't one to talk just to fill silence, whether or not he was mad at me. Normally, I would have insisted on helping him wash dishes after breakfast, but this time I sat there and let him clear the table. "You know," I mused out loud while I watched him wash dishes, "when this is over, I think I want a vacation. I want to go somewhere quiet and lie in a hammock or sit on a front porch and read a big, juicy book—and have no magic anywhere around me. No fairies, gargoyles, elves, gnomes, none of it." I looked up to see him gazing at me. His eyes looked hurt. "Magical people would be okay," I assured him. "As long as you don't actually do magic. And it's not that I have anything against all the other species. It's just that they remind me of things that I'd prefer to forget while I'm on this hypothetical vacation."

"Maybe you ought to take it." I noticed he said "you" and not "we," even after I'd clarified myself to show he might be welcome.

"I don't have any vacation time accrued yet."

"I'm sure we could make an exception. Call it hazard pay or comp time."

I decided to start taking my comp time immediately. I knew I couldn't concentrate on work. Owen had his head buried in a stack of magical tomes, probably working out some wonder spell he could use in the big showdown. I discovered that he had an impressive collection of paperback spy thrillers, so I settled on the sofa and read while he worked.

Late that afternoon, he brought me another dose of the immunity potion. "I'm going to stop giving you the fairy sedative now," he said. "We'll need Ari awake and functioning in case you have to prove you have her. It'll be a few hours more before it all wears off, but we'll need to start being careful."

"Apologies in advance if I do or say anything particularly bitchy," I said after drinking the potion. "I'm not in the best of moods, myself, and with her influence I could be awful."

He gave me a crooked smile that was almost enough to warm my heart, since smiles of any kind had been rare lately. "I'm sure I can cope with it," he said.

. . .

By the time we were ready to leave for the big multihostage exchange, my headache was worse than ever. It felt like someone was kicking at my skull from the inside, and come to think of it, someone probably was.

We got to the tunnel first, so that Owen could get his dragons settled down. They were overjoyed to see him, and he had to play a game of fetch before they'd stand still. Merlin, Rod, Sam, Rocky, and Rollo soon showed up. Sam saluted Owen with one wing and said, "I've had my people watching all the comings and goings at the store. Anyone we're fairly sure is part of their outfit has a tail on them. That doesn't mean we've got everyone, but we've got a lot of ground covered."

Owen nodded. "Good. I don't know what else he might try to pull tonight, so I wanted to be prepared."

Ethan and Philip arrived next. Ethan was in full lawyer mode, suit, briefcase, and all. Owen directed them to the other side of the cavern. "Okay, Rod, do your thing," he said.

Rod rubbed his palms together. "I'll use a selective illusion. All of us should see everything, while they should only see their own side of the room until you give me the signal to drop or change it, and I can drop it in one direction either way."

"And none of it will work on me, so I can make sure everyone's being honest," Ethan said. Normally, that was my job, but I couldn't do it with my immunity to magic stripped away so we could get Ari out of my head. Whenever it happened, it wouldn't be soon enough. She'd thoroughly awakened from the sedative, and she was really pissed off. I had to bite my lip to keep my mouth shut so I wouldn't say all the things that came into my head.

Owen directed his dragons off to the sides of the room, then waved a hand, and they disappeared. "We're all set now," he said.

Merlin pulled out a pocket watch and checked it. "Mr. Idris should be here at any moment."

"He's here now," a voice said from the darkness. Phelan Idris stepped forward out of the shadows, along with a few of his henchmen, the ones who'd been with him in the big magical battle we'd fought a couple of months ago. They still looked more like they were on their way to a science fiction convention to meet up with a bunch of other people who'd seen *The Matrix* a few too many times than like anyone you'd expect to be on the cutting edge of magic.

Then again, our side didn't look all that intimidating unless you knew what they were capable of. Merlin looked like a little old man in a dapper suit, while Owen looked like an astonishingly good-looking version of the boy next door. Sam and his people could have starred in their own Disney cartoon.

"Let's make this happen," Idris said. "What is it you want? That is, if you really do have Ari."

"Oh, we've got her, all right," I said, rubbing my temple.

"We understand that one of your colleagues has taken custody of Miss Chandler's friend," Merlin said. "We would like you to secure her return."

Idris's eyes grew to the size of dinner plates. "What?" he squeaked, his voice going up about an octave. "Whoa, I had nothing to do with that! I may have mentioned that the dude trying to take back his company was dating one of Katie's friends, but it was just a conversation, you know? I didn't think she'd do anything about it."

"Nevertheless," Merlin replied, "we would like her safe return, and we do have someone who must have some meaning to your organization, or else she would not have been freed earlier. Your superiors will not be happy that she is in our custody."

"And you think I can do anything about that?"

"You will if you want Ari back," Owen said. "Unless you want to tell your bosses that you lost her."

Idris looked even more panicked. "I'll see what I—I'll try—this could take time, you know."

"Relax," I told him. "It's not like we're going to cut off one of her fingers every fifteen minutes or torture her." If there was any torture, it was the other way around. My head felt like she was throwing a hissy fit in there.

"And what if I don't care whether or not I get her back?" Idris switched tactics, which played beautifully into our plan. We were supposed to stall him until Sylvia and her crew showed up with Marcia.

"Then we keep her. She might not think so favorably of you at that point," Merlin said.

"Well, where is she?"

"Right in here," I said, tapping my head. "It's a long story involving a fairy godmother."

He laughed, long, loud, and hard. "You expect me to believe that?"

Reluctantly, I eased my tight control on my tongue and let the foreign thoughts that had been welling up in my brain spill out. "You moron! I bet you didn't even notice I was gone until they told you, did you? You were so busy with your precious business. I hate this! This wasn't what I signed up for!" It was weird to hear someone else's words coming out in my voice.

Idris wasn't convinced. "Anyone who's spent five minutes around Ari knows she'd say something like that."

Before I knew what was happening, I'd put my hands on my hips. "Oh yeah? Well, how about this: I know you've got a mole shaped like Mickey Mouse on your—"

"Okay, I believe you!" he shouted at exactly the same time I bit down hard on my tongue. I didn't want any more details like that about him. "What do you want me to do? I can't do anything to get your friend back. I don't have that kind of pull with these people."

"You need do nothing more than you already have," Merlin said. "Your presence is enough."

"So you're going to give Ari back, just because I'm here?"

"Not exactly," Owen said, his voice soft but still ringing through the cavern.

I glanced over to Ethan and Philip and saw that Sylvia and Mr. Bones were there, with Marcia. Marcia was blindfolded, much to my relief. I didn't want her seeing any of this. I couldn't begin to imagine the cover story I'd have to concoct.

"You see," Owen continued, "we just needed you as our prisoner. You're what we plan to exchange for Marcia." He signaled Rod, who made a waving motion with one hand. I assumed that meant Idris could then see the other side of the chamber.

"What if I don't want to stay and be your prisoner?"

"I wouldn't suggest you try running."

"What are you going to do, stop me?"

"No. They are." Owen snapped his fingers, and dragons appeared, blocking every exit. One of the dragons obliged us by shooting a mighty burst of flame at Idris.

Idris tried to act unimpressed, but there was fear in his eyes that he couldn't quite mask and he jumped as the flame got too close for comfort. "Illusion, right?" he said with a snort.

"If you'd like to test it, be my guest. Your friends are free to leave, however."

They didn't need much encouraging. Owen raised a hand, holding the dragons back, while the geek brigade took off, leaving Idris alone. He went pale, and his hands trembled, but he seemed to be trying to look brave, for which I had to give him the tiniest bit of respect. "So, you're trading me, huh?" he said. "I guess after I go over there, you'll let Ari go?"

"Whatever gave you that impression?" Merlin asked, his voice like ice. "You have no choice in the matter. You are our prisoner, and Ariel was our prisoner before she was illegally freed. We will merely be returning her to custody once we've removed her from Miss Chandler's head. Now, shall we make the exchange?"

He nodded at Rod, who did something complicated with his fingers. "Miss Meredith, I presume?" Merlin said.

She whirled to face him. "You!" she shouted, as if she'd just met her old nemesis.

"Yes, I am here, and I request that you release the young lady there. She has no part in this."

"Why should I do that?"

"Because I have two of your people in my custody, and I'm sure they could be persuaded to give us some interesting information on your operation."

Rod did something else with his fingers, and then Sylvia went white. "How did you get yourself involved in this?" she hissed at Idris. "You were told to refrain from contact."

For a split second he looked like a schoolboy being scolded, but then his posture relaxed and he said, "Don't worry, though, I've got it under control." He turned his head toward Owen. "You're not the only one who has a threat to make. I happen to have people placed all over the city. One word from me, and the illusions I have covering all of my ads are gone. The whole city will learn the truth about magic all at once. How do you like that?"

I couldn't help but laugh. The rest of them turned to look at me. "You have got to be kidding. Those ads won't convince anyone of anything. People will think it's a prank or publicity stunt, if they even see the ads. They once put a seventy-foot robot in Times Square to promote a movie, and not only did no one notice the robot, nobody saw the movie." I wasn't sure if the words were mine or Ari's. The tone was meaner than I'd like to think I ever sounded, but I agreed with the content.

I thought I saw a hint of worry cross his face, but then he put his usual sneer back on and said, "And my people are ready to demonstrate the magic to anyone who's there to see it. They'll act if they don't hear from me."

"You idiot!" Sylvia screeched. "You'll ruin everything if you reveal it all right now. We're not ready."

That deflated Idris. His shoulders slumping, he said, "Oh. Well. Never mind."

Owen and Merlin exchanged a worried look, then Sam nodded at them and took off, flying past the dragon in one of the doorways. The dragon made as though to try to play with Sam, but Owen called it back to attention.

"Very well, then," Sylvia said. "You can have the girl. But this isn't over." She addressed Philip. "You can't imagine I'll give up easily."

"I've waited a hundred years. I can be patient, but I will have what's mine," he said.

Sylvia nodded at Mr. Bones, who shoved Marcia forward. Rod moved to steady her. "What's going on?" she asked in a voice more frantic than anything I'd ever heard from her.

"It's okay, you're safe," Rod said. He removed her blindfold and started moving her toward the exit, Rocky and Rollo flanking them. I hoped for Marcia's sake that he was using illusion to hide the rest of the madness from her.

But before they were clear of the room, Sylvia launched a magical attack at Philip. All the good guys rushed in to help. Owen managed to deflect most of whatever she'd sent toward Philip, but Philip still froze, then slumped to the floor. Ethan put himself between her and Philip's motionless form. "He's alive, but out cold," he reported.

A scream rang out, echoing painfully in the chamber. I spun to see Marcia looking horrified. Rod must have dropped his illusions when he went to help Philip. "Marcia, it's okay, I'll explain later," I said, then I told Rod, "Get her away from here."

"I'm not leaving until I get some answers. Katie, what the hell is going on here?"

I knew her well enough to know that she'd dig in her heels and refuse to go until she was satisfied. "Okay, short version: Magic is real, the guys are all wizards. I'm not, but I work for a magical company. Those are the bad guys. We'll do the Q and A later. Now, Rod, get her out of here."

While I was talking to Marcia, Sylvia and Mr. Bones made a run for it, only to find themselves facing a roaring dragon. Owen brought it into view just before it got to roast Sylvia. Marcia screamed again.

"Oh yeah, there are dragons, too," I told her. "But these are good guys. They love Owen." I had to give her credit for not fainting. Marcia was made of pretty stern stuff.

"I demand you let me leave," Sylvia said to Merlin. "I gave you what you wanted."

"And with you here, I've gained even more of what I wanted. With you in our custody, we might even be able to find out who's directing you," Merlin said. His voice and bearing made him seem like he'd look a lot more appropriate in old-fashioned wizard's robes and a pointy hat than he did in his modern business suit. This was definitely the guy who'd put King Arthur on the throne.

"You may not allow me to leave, but I dare you to put your hands on me."

"Yeah, or me," Idris said, broadening his stance defiantly.

A magical battle of wills ensued. Enough power flew around to practically make my hair stand on end. Ari added to the uproar by throwing a few zaps of her own inside my head. I'd need a bottle of Advil when this was over. Apparently, though, Sylvia was right. We were at a standoff. I knew Owen could take out Idris, but Sylvia seemed to know her stuff. With Sam gone, Philip out, and Rod looking after Marcia, the two sides were evenly matched. I supposed we could leave them with the dragons until they begged for mercy, but that wasn't an ideal solution.

Then I remembered that I temporarily had Ari's power. I had to fight her to use it, but the next time Idris sent a burst of magic in Owen's direction, I focused as hard as I could on deflecting it, raising my hands as I'd seen wizards do. I was surprised to see sparks shooting from my fingertips and turning back Idris's magic. That gave Owen an opening, and he caught Idris in a spell that immobilized him. "Nice work," Owen said to me.

"I thought you said you weren't magical," Marcia said.

"It's temporary," I said before returning my attention to the standoff. The odds had moved in our favor. Keeping Idris was the goal, and Sylvia was a bonus.

A loud pop echoed in the chamber, and Ethelinda appeared in a burst of silver sparkles. She wore a Viking maiden's costume out of a low-budget production of a Wagner opera, complete with brass breastplate and horned helmet. The outfit looked funny with bits of ruffles, lace, tulle, taffeta, and velvet peeking out from under the brass. "My senses tell me you're ready for me," she said. "I'm here to relieve you of your burden."

Twenty-One

Before any of us could stop her, Ethelinda pulled back her wand and pointed it at me while saying some nonsensical-sounding words. If I'd thought I had a headache before, that was nothing compared to what I felt next. I couldn't stop myself from screaming, and I would have hit the ground if Owen hadn't caught me. Through the blinding red haze of pain I thought I saw a tiny spark floating in front of me. That spark grew until it was a human-sized fairy.

"There you go," Ethelinda said with satisfaction.

"Get her!" I shouted. Owen was closest, so he left my side and got a grip on Ari's arm before she could reach Idris. I moaned, and not just because of the headache. Ethelinda, bless her well-intentioned but incompetent heart, had really complicated matters. Ari had been our one sure bet in this whole situation, and now she was loose.

I had just got back to my feet when something grabbed me. "Hey, what is this?" I shouted. I couldn't see anything. An invisible force held me in place. With my immunity gone so I could be rid of Ari, and without access to Ari's magical powers, I was in real danger.

Idris leered at Owen. "Okay, then," he said, his tone full of smug superiority. "You've got my girlfriend hostage. I've got your girlfriend hostage. And I'd be willing to bet that you like yours better than I like mine, so I think I have the advantage."

"Hey!" Ari yelled. "Maybe I want to stay with them. I'll tell them everything. So, there."

Idris ignored her. "Either you call off your dragons and let Ari, Sylvia, and me leave, or I'll take care of your girlfriend. You might be able to protect her, but that would mean dropping your attention to me, even for a split second."

I struggled but couldn't move a muscle. For a moment, everyone else seemed stuck in the spell I was. They just stared at me. Then I noticed what they were staring at. A blue magical flame pooled around my feet, moving toward me. In moments, it would be on me, and I could already feel the heat. Meanwhile, Sylvia and her goons were taking off toward the exit that led deeper into the tunnels. Ethan tried to catch her in a tackle, but Mr. Bones shoved him aside, sending him sprawling. The dragons roared, but Sylvia did something with her hands, and I feared for the dragons' safety. "She's getting away!" I yelled. When the others still focused on me, I insisted, "It's just a little blue flame. No big deal. Go!"

When Idris grabbed Ari and made to follow Sylvia, the others finally jolted out of their shock and took action. Owen did something to counter whatever it was that Sylvia was doing to his dragons while Merlin took on Sylvia and Rod tried to stop Idris and Ari, with some dive-bombing from Rocky and Rollo.

Marcia ran to my side. "What's going on, Katie? Are you okay?"

"I don't think it's serious," I said. "I just can't move. Trust me, this guy doesn't ever do anything really serious, and he'll lose interest before long." The blue flame was coming closer to me, and growing in intensity. I had a feeling it wouldn't have done anything to me in my magical immune state. Now, there was no telling what might happen, and it didn't look like the kind of fire a fire extinguisher could put out. Marcia tried stomping on it, then she blew on it, like she was trying to blow out a candle.

"No!" I said to stop her. "It's not a candle. If you blow on a fire, it gets more intense."

The magical battle continued to rage. Marcia yelped as Rod was tossed aside and hit a wall, and I winced when Idris sent a chunk of rock flying toward Owen. Owen got out of the way in time to avoid all but a glancing blow, but it seemed to me he staggered a little.

The flame came closer and closer to me. I was sweating, and not just from the fear. It was getting awfully hot. I was all for saving the world from bad magic, but that didn't mean I wanted to pull a Joan of Arc. I'd like to think I'd be willing to sacrifice myself to save the world, but when you're staring at flames coming very close to making that a reality, it has a way of changing your perspective.

"You're awfully calm about this," Marcia said.

"All in a day's work, I'm afraid."

"I guess this is why you've been acting weird, huh?"

"Yeah. It was kind of hard to talk about, and I wasn't allowed to tell you about magic."

Just as I'd expected from my association with Idris, the flame started to die. I could move my fingers and toes, which wasn't very useful, but it was a good sign. He wasn't great at multitasking, so when he got sidetracked by fighting Owen, he couldn't sustain what he was doing to me.

Then suddenly the flame flared up again, and I couldn't help but scream. Marcia jumped back, yelling, "It's going to kill her!"

"Yes, it is," Sylvia said. "If you don't call off your dragons, she will die." Now, I was worried. Idris was a flake, but Sylvia was focused, powerful, and kind of a bitch. I had no doubt that she'd kill me to secure her own escape.

Owen whistled, and the dragons left the doorways to come to his side. "You're free to go," he said, his voice even softer than usual. It still carried clearly and echoed in the cavern. "Release Katie."

And then a lot of things happened very quickly. Sylvia shouted, "Release her yourself," and ran for the exit. Idris grabbed Ari's hand and ran after her. Ari pulled back at him, slowing his escape. Mr. Bones got ahead of them and took off down the tunnel while they struggled with one another. The fire singed the edges of my shoes, but then Owen whirled to do something to it. For the first time since I'd known him, there was real fear—panic, even—in his eyes.

Merlin went after Sylvia, Ari, Idris, and the henchmen, shooting spells to restrain them, but Owen called to him, "It's a layered spell, I can't stop it alone." Merlin hesitated only for a second, then spun to join Owen.

I'd barely felt the flames lick at my feet when they vanished entirely and I could move again. I swayed and for a moment thought my legs might buckle under me, but I caught myself, got my legs under me, and took off running. "Don't let them get away!" I shouted as I ran.

The dragons had tried to go after the bad guys but could only go so far before they were too large to get into the passages. I didn't have that problem. I could see Ari and Idris ahead of me, him dragging her behind him. Sylvia must have been ahead of them. Ari finally broke free, and that gave me the chance to catch up with her and tackle her. Owen caught up with me and sidestepped Ari and me on the ground as he ran after Idris and Sylvia.

I felt the tingle of magic while I tried to get a better hold on Ari. Merlin then reached Ari and me and said, "I have her. You may get up now, Miss Chandler." I stood shakily. Ari still lay on the ground, but she looked up at me in an odd way, with some of her usual hostility gone. That was more than a bit unnerving as I remembered that she'd had access to the inside of my head. How much did she know about me? Merlin waved at her, and she shrank back down to a point of light, like the way they depict Tinkerbell in stage productions of *Peter Pan*. Another wave of his hand sent the point of light to rest inside his vest pocket. "She should be safe there," he said, lightly patting the pocket. He then held out his arm to me and escorted me back into the main chamber, where the dragons hovered anxiously near the exit where Owen had disappeared.

Marcia was at Rod's side, helping him sit up. On the other side of the room, Ethan was stirring. Philip was still out cold. I opened my mouth to ask Merlin if he'd be okay, but a shock wave shook the whole underground chamber. I ducked instinctively as dust showered us from the ceiling. The dragons twitched and whimpered. Ethelinda—who'd stayed out of the fighting—took to the air, and Merlin looked alarmed.

A moment later, Owen returned. "I couldn't catch them," he said with a weary sigh. He had a red spot on one cheekbone that would probably develop into a bruise, and there was a bleeding cut on his temple. There was also a wildness in his eyes.

"You certainly tried," Merlin said, and there was an unusual degree of sternness to his voice. "That use of power was unnecessary and could have been dangerous. I expect you to have more control than that."

Owen ignored him, grabbing me in a fierce hug. He then shoved me out in front of him at arm's length. "Are you okay?" he asked. Before I could answer, he pulled me against him again and held me like he would never let go.

"I just love a happy ending." I looked over to see Ethelinda dabbing at her eyes with a yellowed lace handkerchief.

"Yeah, you really helped here tonight," I said, unable to hide my sarcasm. I figured I deserved a little snottiness, considering I'd practically been burned at the stake, thanks to her interference.

I expected her to deny messing up anything, but instead, she burst into sobs. "It was supposed to be an easy assignment. You can only go so long based on reputation, and Cinderella was centuries ago. They weren't even all that happy ever after, you know. They had nothing in common. Sure, the first few years were fine, but then he started going on more hunting trips and she got caught up with the children, and they were like strangers living in that enormous castle." She gave a big sniff, then blew her nose so loudly that it startled the dragons. "But now I can't seem to do anything right." With that, she dissolved into shuddering tears.

She'd just about ruined my life, and had come pretty close to ending it, but I couldn't stand to watch her cry. "Wait," I called out, tearing myself from Owen's embrace. "You know, those two—" I gestured toward Merlin's pocket and down the passage where Idris had disappeared "—seem like they could use some help. He doesn't appreciate her properly."

Her face lit up and her tears dried immediately. "Oh, yes, that young man does need to learn a lesson or two, and she would have better luck if she were more ladylike. Very good suggestion. I'm on the case!"

Merlin bowed to her. "Thank you for your assistance, but I would appreciate it if you'd leave my people alone in the future."

"Oh, I have no need to meddle further here. Things seem to be perfectly peachy. And now, if you'll excuse me, I have work to do." She vanished in her usual burst of silver sparkles, and I hoped that was the last I saw of her.

Owen squeezed my shoulder. "You never did tell me. Are you okay?"

"Yeah, I'm fine. I want to sleep for a week, but I seem to be mostly unsinged, except maybe the soles of my shoes. But why did you let them go in the first place? You had them."

He looked at me like I was crazy. "Because they were going to kill you!" he shouted. It was the first time I'd ever heard Owen Palmer really and truly yell at someone, and he was yelling at me.

"But you let them go. Now what're they going to do?"

He shook his head. "I don't know, but we've always managed to stop them before. We can stop them again."

"What about the whole saving the world from bad magic thing?"

"It's not like my choice was you or the fate of the free world."

I sighed and rubbed my still-aching head. "I know. I'm sorry. I'm glad you saved me. I really wasn't enjoying the idea of being a human torch, but I hate the idea of them getting away. They're still in business, and we haven't learned anything about who's really in control."

"We might be somewhat better off," Merlin said. "They seem to have acquired a major hindrance, due to your efforts. And we once again have our original prisoner. I honestly believe that Ari will be willing to cooperate now, even if it's only enough to make him suffer for insulting her. In addition, we have freed your friend and preserved Mr. Vandermeer's claim on his business, which may ultimately cut their funding."

Owen smiled then as he put an arm around my shoulder. "If that fairy godmother works with them the way she did with us, then they won't get anything done for weeks. We said we needed to distract Idris."

"And Ethelinda is the ultimate distraction," I said.

"Not such a bad day, after all, then," Owen said, giving my shoulder an extra squeeze.

"Speak for yourself," I groaned. "Can I take a break from being a victim for a while? I don't enjoy playing damsel in distress."

"Next time I'm in terrible danger, you're welcome to come to my rescue," Owen said with a teasing grin. He sounded almost giddy with relief. I guessed he wasn't mad at me anymore. All it took to make him get over his hurt feelings and restore our relationship was me nearly getting killed. It wasn't a relationship counseling technique I'd recommend.

"Count on it," I assured him. "But I wouldn't mind if we avoided terrible danger for a while. I'm looking forward to some typing and filing, maybe updating our marketing campaign. Just as long as I'm not being chased by anything or put under any spells. And in case anyone is wondering, I'd be happy to help train some other immunes to cope with immunity loss, but I am not going through that again."

"No, you're not," Owen said firmly.

"Now, I believe all of us need to rest and tend our wounds," Merlin said. Marcia helped Rod up, and I thought he looked steady enough to walk on his own, but he kept his arm tight around her. Ethan managed to get back on his feet, and then Merlin did something magical over Philip, who soon sat up, blinking. The weary lot of us headed out of the caverns, much to the dragons' dismay, and ran into Sam before we reached the train station.

"It turns out he was only bluffing partway," the gargoyle said. "He did have someone set up in Times Square to demonstrate magic, but we apprehended him under the code provision against public use of magic with intent to expose magic to outsiders. We also caught a few minor incidents around town that weren't too difficult to deal with. The secret still seems to be safe, and there's no buzz about the word being out."

"It's a gargoyle, and it's talking," Marcia said.

"Yes, it is, just like the other gargoyles back there, and can we talk about it later?" I replied, patting her on the arm.

The train station was deserted except for a few security guards who didn't seem to see us. Rocky and Rollo's car was still sitting in front of the station. "I'll get Katie home," Owen said. "She should probably stay with me until she gets her immunity back."

The others piled into the car. I heard Marcia ask, "Hey, how are the gargoyles going to drive?" as Owen turned me away and summoned a cab. I was not looking forward to the conversation I knew would be in my future.

I fell asleep on Owen's shoulder between the station and his house. He nudged me awake, then helped me out of the cab. He walked me up the steps and then guided me up the indoor stairs to his part of the town house. Loony met both of us at the door, and this time she rubbed against my ankles instead of hissing at me.

"Looks like I'm fully me again," I commented as I listened to her purring at my feet. "I just wish I felt more like myself."

"I think both of us could use a stiff drink."

"Oh, very good idea."

"As you know, I'm not much of a drinker, but I do have a medicinal bottle around." He winked. "Even Gloria approves of that."

I wished I could smile at his joke, but I didn't feel like joking at the moment. I wasn't sure what freaked me out more, nearly being magically burned at the stake, Marcia being in the middle of it all, Owen letting the bad guys go to save me, Owen having nearly blown up Grand Central in an attempt to catch the bad guys, or Owen having actually yelled at me, which was possibly a once-in-a-lifetime thing. Whatever it was, I felt deeply unsettled, like my universe had gone out of whack and I didn't know how to set it right.

In contrast to my dark mood, Owen was in bubbly overdrive. He practically bounced as I followed him back to the kitchen and watched him rummage in cabinets. He pulled a bottle out of the back of one cabinet. "I doubt you'd want to drink this straight, but I'm sure we could put it in something. Hot or cold?"

I blinked out of a stupor. "Huh?"

"Do you want a hot drink or a cold drink?"

You'd think that after almost being burned I wouldn't want anything hot for a while, but I realized I was shivering like I'd never be warm again. "Hot, please."

"Okay, then how about that hot toddy like I made when you fell through the ice?"

"Sounds good." While he made drinks, I sat wearily at the kitchen table. Loony jumped up into my lap and I stroked her fur automatically, letting her purring hypnotize me. I barely noticed when Owen put a drink in front of me. Loony put a paw on my hand and meowed to get my attention, and I blinked back to reality to see the drink.

Owen sat across from me and took a few sips of his own drink before saying, "The boss said we don't have to go to the office tomorrow. I think he wants to make sure your immunity returns, and we could all use some rest."

"So I guess you have to put up with me one more day."

"I wouldn't say I'm having to put up with you. I don't mind at all." He looked down into his drink and turned a rosy shade of pink. "I actually like having you around. You're good company."

"I take that to mean you're not mad at me anymore."

"I wasn't really mad. Just disappointed. I wish you'd trusted me enough to tell me what was going on. I thought I'd shown you before, the first time you lost your immunity, that I can deal with a lot."

"And you're going to have to get used to the fact that I'm stubbornly independent. If I think I can deal with it myself, I will. I don't like always having to run to others for help." I allowed myself a smile. "But I will admit that when it comes to magical things I don't know much about, I should probably try to get over that. And don't I get credit for going to you the moment I realized I was doing magic, even though I thought you were angry with me at the time?"

"We'll call it even," he said with a smile that lit up his eyes and warmed my heart. We were going to be okay, I was sure, in spite of a few little misgivings in the back of my mind that refused to give up.

"That's good, because it's entirely possible you'll be stuck with me for a while. When my 'business trip' ends we'll see if my roommates let me back in."

"I don't think you'll have any problems. Marcia should understand."

"If she doesn't hate me for getting her mixed up in all this." I hesitated, then added, "I am going to tell my roommates the truth, all of it. Will you back me up?"

He nodded. "Yes, especially after what happened tonight. They need to know, for their own safety as well as their acceptance of you."

"Okay, then. Tomorrow evening when they're home from work. You can take me home, and then we'll tell them the whole story." I drained my cup, then said, "But for now, I'm going to take a shower, then sleep until I can't sleep anymore."

I trudged up the stairs, took a long, hot shower, then put on my pajamas. Loony was waiting for me on the bed, and I was grateful for her presence. I didn't want to be alone, but I wasn't sure I wanted to be with Owen. It was dawning on me that I really must have meant something to him. He hadn't thought twice about letting his enemies escape because his sole priority had been saving me. It's the kind of thing it's fun to dream about when you put yourself in the place of a heroine in a book or movie, but in reality, it was unsettling.

While it was nice to know that Owen would do anything to keep me safe, I wasn't crazy about the feeling that I was in his way. He had to beat Idris and whoever was running this show. There was no doubt about it. I'd read enough magical history lately to know that when someone tried to use magic to gain real earthly power, things got really bad. They had to be stopped, and could Owen do that if his first concern was for me? In this case, being cherished that much was nicer in theory than reality. If anyone was harmed by their activities from now on, I wouldn't be able to help but feel responsible.

As tired as I was, it took me a good hour to fall into a deep sleep. I was sure I had nightmares, but they were too vague to recall when I woke. When I finally dragged myself out of bed, I felt weary. I sat on the side of the bed for a while before I could summon the energy to get up and get dressed. I found Owen lying sprawled on the sofa, a book in his hand and Loony draped across his chest.

"What time is it?" I asked.

He looked up from his book. "A little after two. I haven't been up long, myself, and I'd have probably slept longer, but a certain cat couldn't stand me being in bed one minute more." He put aside his book, then shifted Loony from his chest to his lap as he sat up. "Are you hungry for breakfast or lunch?"

My impulse was to say I wasn't hungry at all, but then my stomach growled. "Breakfast food would be good right now."

"Breakfast food I can do. That's my specialty." He moved Loony from his lap to the sofa, then stood up. "I've already made coffee if you want some."

I wasn't sure coffee would clear my head, but I was willing to give it a shot, so I went back to the kitchen with him. He poured the coffee for me and doctored it up with milk and sugar the way I liked it. "Are you okay?" he asked as he handed me the mug. "You don't look so good."

"Gee, thanks a lot," I muttered, then when he flushed bright red I hurried to add, "I'm sorry. I know what you meant. And I'm not feeling great."

"You've been through a lot."

I sat at the kitchen table. "Yeah, that week in a hammock or on the front porch is sounding better and better. But we have work to do, what with the bad guys on the loose and all."

He expertly cracked eggs, then beat them with more vigor than was probably necessary. "I'll take care of that. Idris and I are due for a good showdown one of these days."

"Is that something you've seen or just something you'd like to happen?"

"A little of both."

It was a showdown that I couldn't help but think would go more smoothly without me in the picture.

That evening I repacked my bag, and then Owen walked me over to my apartment. It was still a little early to expect Gemma and Marcia to be home, which was fine with me. I thought things might go better if I were already there instead of walking in on them. I was relieved and a bit surprised not to find my belongings sitting in the hallway. My keys still fit in the locks, and when I opened the front door the place looked pretty much the same way it always had.

"They haven't kicked you out," Owen said.

"Not yet."

"They won't."

"You've seen that, too, I suppose?"

"No. But you and your friends have been through a lot together. I don't think they'll give up on you so easily. Look at Rod and me. We're still speaking after all these years and some worse stuff than you know about."

"Really?"

"Remind me to tell you sometime."

Marcia was the first one home. She looked startled when she saw us there, and then she hugged me. "Are you okay?"

"I've felt better. I'm tired. I've been through a lot, but I'll be fine. How are you holding up?"

"I'm confused, but I presume you're here to explain?" She frowned. "It did really happen, didn't it? That wasn't all just a dream?"

"It was real." I paused, then asked, "Do you know if Gemma will be home anytime soon?"

"She didn't say anything about being out late. Why?"

"We need to tell her, too, and I only want to go through it once, so let's wait for Gemma, okay?"

All three of us jumped when the key turned in the lock and Gemma entered, with Philip right behind her. He was still pale, but looked like he was recovering from the night before. I was glad to see him. He'd be good for backing up my story as a neutral third party. "You're back," Gemma said. She sounded chilly, so Marcia must not have told her the full story yet.

"Get yourself a glass of wine," Marcia said. "Katie has something to talk to us about."

She went to the kitchen and got some wine, offered some to Philip, who declined, then joined Marcia at the table. Philip sat next to her. "Okay, what is it?" she asked.

Twenty-Two

I glanced at Owen, then faced my roommates and took a deep breath. "I have something to tell you. It's going to sound crazy at first, but it's absolutely true, and by the time I'm done, it'll explain a lot."

"Including New Year's Eve?" Gemma asked.

"Including New Year's Eve, but it goes back further than that." I had to pause then and think. As many times as I'd imagined how I'd tell my friends about everything going on with me, I hadn't ever come to a conclusion of the best way to go about it. Should I tell it like a story as it happened to me, or just launch into the part about magic being real?

I decided to fall somewhere in the middle. "The company I work for is a little unusual," I began. "It's not quite as boring as I let on. In fact, it's really rather interesting, but most of what goes on there is top secret." Philip's eyes went wide, and I could tell he'd figured out what I was going to tell them. He frowned, but Owen gave him a reassuring nod. "The product this company sells is magic, more or less."

"Like magic tricks?" Gemma asked.

"No. Real magic. Spells and stuff like that. For people with real magic powers."

Gemma laughed. "Good one, Katie. But there's no such thing."

"Uh, yes, there is," Marcia said.

Gemma whirled on her. "You know about this?"

"It has something to do with where I've been, but let them tell the story. I only know parts of it."

A vase of flowers appeared in the middle of the table, and Gemma jumped back. "Magic does exist," Owen said softly before making the vase disappear. He waved his hand, whispering some words, and Marcia's red wine turned to white, complete with beads of condensation dripping down the outside of the cool glass. Another wave, and the wine returned to red.

Gemma shook her head. "Nice tricks, but . . ." She shook her head again, unable to even form a question.

"It is real," Philip put in. "I can vouch for their truth."

She turned to him, openmouthed. "What, you're mixed up in this, too?"

"I am like he is." He gestured toward Owen. "However, at an entirely different level. I don't have his degree of power."

"How do you fit into that?" Marcia asked me.

"I'm immune to magic. Well, I normally am, but I'm not at the moment and that's a very long story. Remember back when we first met Rod and he was recruiting me? It was because they'd discovered I have this magic immunity, where nothing they do works on me. I don't see the illusions they use to hide magic from everyone else. That's a useful ability in their company."

They looked dazed. I couldn't be sure that they bought it or even understood it fully, but I forced myself to go on. "Meanwhile there's a bad guy using magic the wrong way, and our company is trying to stop him. Owen's in the thick of it. I got mixed up in it, and that's brought me to the attention of the bad guys. A lot of the strange stuff that's been going on with me in the past few months has been because of that."

"Including New Year's Eve?" Gemma asked.

"Especially New Year's Eve," I confirmed. "It's a really complicated explanation, but the simple version is that I was possessed by one of the bad guys, and all the stuff I said and did was really her. I just got rid of her last night."

"But I thought you were immune to magic."

Owen stepped forward. "We had to remove her immunity temporarily to check on something. They took advantage of the vulnerability."

"And all that stuff last night?" Marcia asked.

"I'm afraid that was because of me," Philip said. "One of their enemies is my enemy, as well, a descendant of the man who enchanted me to take over my family's business." I noticed that he left out the nature of the enchantment, but that was his secret to tell Gemma when he was ready for that level of sharing. "If I regained the business, they lost funding for their schemes. They seem to have known I had feelings for one of Katie's roommates, but when they took one of you hostage, they got the wrong one."

"We've spent the last couple of days trying to find a way to get Marcia back and get rid of our enemies," I wrapped up the story as simply as I could.

"You beat the bad guys, I take it?"

Owen and I looked at each other. "Not exactly," I said. "We haven't yet had the ultimate showdown, but we've managed to head off each of their evil schemes before it gets out of control. They're still out there, and that's why I wanted to tell you guys the truth. It may get even hairier in the future, and you need to know what's going on."

"Why haven't you told us before now?" Gemma asked.

"We're not supposed to let outsiders know," Owen said. "We could only tell you now because of what Marcia saw last night. If knowledge of the existence of magic and the fact that there are people with fantastic powers walking among you got out among the general public, the result would be chaos. The rule is to protect you as much as it is to protect us. If we're forbidden from showing our power, that makes it harder for us to use it against you. The problem with our current enemies is that they're not abiding by the rules. We're worried they might try to use their magic to gain real power."

Gemma nodded, glanced at Marcia, then said, "Okay, we're in. What do you need us to do?"

I'd been expecting to have to go into hours of explanation, lots of demonstrations, and even then face skepticism. This was almost too easy. "You mean, you believe me, really? You're not just humoring me to keep me calm while you go off and call the funny farm to reserve me a room?"

"I was there," Marcia said with a shrug. "It makes more sense than most of the stories you've told to cover it up."

"What do we need to do to help fight this bad guy?" Gemma asked. "Or is there something we need to do to protect ourselves? Hang garlic from the doorways? Wear crosses?"

Owen had to fight to keep a straight face. While he got himself under control, I said, "This isn't Buffy, and we're not dealing with vampires." I turned to Owen. "There aren't vampires, are there?"

"Not in this country, and they're not like in the movies."

"Okay, no vampires to worry about at the moment, so stakes, crosses, and garlic won't do you much good."

"Your apartment is warded against magical attack," Owen said. "No one can get in here using magical means or use magic to get anything else in here."

Philip nodded. "I thought I'd sensed a barrier here."

"Mostly, I just need you to keep alert," I said, "and give me the benefit of the doubt when things get weird. I seem to have made myself a favorite target of the bad guy. If anyone approaches you and claims to be my friend, assume they aren't unless you've met them with me, and even then, it's entirely possible that there are illusions at work."

"We'll need passwords," Marcia said. "Or questions to make sure everyone's who they say they are, something about you that nobody else would know. So if someone claiming to be you doesn't know your childhood pet's name, we'll know it isn't really you."

"That's actually a good idea," Owen said, nodding. "Other than that, though, it's best that you stay out of this as much as possible. You're especially vulnerable since you are susceptible to magic being used on you, yet you don't have any power of your own."

Marcia got up and went over to her briefcase, from which she took a notepad and pen. "Okay, let's get to work on passwords to start with. And I want a complete list of contact information for everyone."

While she grilled everyone on secret info to use for identity verification, Owen edged over to me and put his arm around me. "That went better than I hoped," he said.

"Yeah, I'm kind of surprised, but I guess I shouldn't have been. They seem to take everything in stride."

Once Marcia had her phone list and secret passwords, Owen took off for the night. I followed him out into the hallway. "Thanks for helping with this," I whispered so neither my roommates nor my neighbors would hear us.

"You handled it pretty well on your own. I just provided the proof."

"In your usual dramatic fashion."

He ducked his head and blushed. If I had to name a mannerism that defined him to me, that would have to be it. It had been one of the first things he'd done when we met, and it was still something I could count on him doing regularly, even though he did it less often as he grew more comfortable with me. Watching him, I felt my heart swell in my chest. I hadn't had the chance to prove definitively how strong my feelings for him were the way he'd proved it to me the night before, but I knew now that if our positions had been reversed, I'd have probably made the same choice he'd made. We could fight the bad guys again some other day, but I couldn't replace him. It might be early to start thinking along these lines, but I was pretty sure I was falling in love with him, if I hadn't already fallen.

"You should probably take tomorrow off," he said. "It's not quite your front porch or hammock, but it would be a chance to unwind and recover—and get your immunity back."

"Good idea," I said, nodding.

"Okay, then, I guess I'll be going." He turned to leave, but I caught his arm and pulled him back. Then I stood on my tiptoes and gave him a very thorough kiss. It took him a second to recover before he kissed me back. He wrapped his arms around me and held me like he had in those tunnels, after he'd saved me from the fire. "I'm glad you're okay," he whispered. "If something happened to you . . ."

"I'm glad I'm okay, too, thanks to you," I said. I forced myself to break away from his embrace. "Take care of yourself."

"I try," he said with a crooked grin before he turned to head down the stairs. I watched him until he disappeared to the floor below, then I went back into the apartment.

Philip was getting his coat on and preparing to leave as I entered. Once he was gone, I sank into one of the kitchen chairs next to my roommates. "So, magic, huh?" Gemma said after a while.

"Yeah, magic," I said, nodding.

"Wow."

"And your boyfriend turns out to be a grown-up Harry Potter," Gemma said.

"Nah, he's cuter than Harry," Marcia said.

"I don't know, Harry's pretty cute for a kid. You can tell he's going to be a knockout when he's all grown up."

"Movie Harry is cute, but I don't get the impression from the books that he's supposed to be all that gorgeous," Marcia argued. "Besides, Harry has green eyes in the books, and Owen definitely has blue eyes. Plus, Harry wears glasses."

"Owen wears glasses sometimes," I said. "But most of the time, he wears contacts. No scar, though."

"And didn't you say something about him being an orphan?" Marcia asked.

"Yeah, but he doesn't know who his parents were, so it doesn't look like they were killed by the bad guy. The people who brought him up were strict with him, but they're basically good people and it doesn't sound like they made him sleep under the stairs." I pondered it for a moment, then said, "I think he's more like Superman, except for the part about being an alien and the exact kinds of powers. And maybe being a bit shorter."

Gemma nodded. "Yeah, the dark hair and blue eyes fits that, as well as being brought up by good people who aren't his parents."

"And I'm his kryptonite," I said with a deep sigh.

"What makes you say that?" Marcia asked. "Is it something like your immunity cancels out his powers?"

I shook my head. "No, not like that. But I'm afraid I may be his weakness. Owen chose to rescue me instead of catching the bad guy."

"Well, of course," Gemma said. "He's crazy about you."

"But it was his big chance to catch this guy who's been causing all sorts of trouble and find out what he's up to. Because of me, he didn't."

"At least you know for sure how much you mean to him," Marcia said. "That's something very few people get to have demonstrated for them in such a vivid way."

"I'm afraid I'm holding him back, though. I don't want to be what stops him from doing what needs to be done. I'm his biggest weakness."

"I think you also give him strength," Gemma said. "Saving the world is an abstract concept, but making the world safe for you is something he can care about. That boy needs you, no matter how powerful he may be."

That thought made my head spin. It was a real paradox. How could I manage to be both Owen's greatest strength and his greatest weakness? It was too much for an ordinary girl like me to cope with.

I slept so hard that night I didn't notice my roommates leaving for work in the morning. When I finally woke up, I was as tired as if I'd stayed up all night.

I put on my robe and slippers and stumbled into the kitchen to make some coffee. While the coffeemaker went to work, I looked out the front window. It had snowed again during the night, but after the rush-hour traffic, the snow had already turned to gray slush that piled up in the gutters and on the edges of the sidewalks. The gray slush matched the gray brick of the buildings and the gray sky above. The only color I could see through the window was the yellow of taxis. Even the row of trees down the street looked gray, their winter-bare limbs bleak and silvery, with no sign of life.

This was the downside of winter in New York, once the Christmas lights were gone and everything returned to normal. As I recalled, I'd nearly packed it up and gone home at this time last year. Mimi had been going through a particularly nasty spell, and the grayness had been almost too much to bear when I saw on the weather report that it was sixty-five degrees and sunny back in Texas.

Now home sounded good for another reason. It was the most normal, safe place I could think of. I'd have my choice of front porch or hammock for plenty of relaxing and reading, and while we might have the odd cold, gray spell, it would only last a day or two before we saw the sun again.

I poured myself a cup of coffee, then went back to the window. I doubted my immunity had returned, so I had no way of knowing if the people I saw on the sidewalk below were what they seemed to be. Were there creatures lurking in the trees or hovering outside my window?

Were Idris's henchthings waiting for me outside, ready to grab me now that they knew I was Owen's Achilles' heel? If they'd bothered me before, I could only imagine what it would be like now that they knew Owen would do anything to keep me safe. That was bound to be a distraction for Owen. How could he focus on what he had to do if he had to worry about what the bad guys were doing to me? It figured. I finally found a great guy who liked me, and our relationship threw a monkey wrench into his life's work. And since his life's work was saving the world from bad magic, our relationship had bigger potential consequences than just keeping him off the corporate fast track.

That was when I knew what I had to do. Actually, I'd known the night before. It had just taken me awhile to convince myself. I got dressed, got my laptop bag, and headed out into the cold, gray day, taking the subway downtown to the office. Sam was in his usual spot at the front door. "Hey, doll," he said in greeting. "I didn't expect to see you here today."

"I just want to wrap up a few things," I told him. I then went straight up to Merlin's office, hoping desperately that I didn't run into anyone else I knew along the way. I knew it would be far too easy to be blown off course. To do this, I'd have to focus on my resolve, and I couldn't do that if I had to face anyone I really cared about.

"You're right on time," Trix said to me as I entered Merlin's tower suite. "Go right in." Merlin's office doors opened for me, and I took a deep breath before crossing the threshold.

"Good morning, Miss Chandler," Merlin said when he saw me. "How are you faring?"

"I'm okay. Still tired. My roommates took the news about magic pretty well, and they don't seem to have any grudges about what I did under Ari's influence."

"I'm pleased to hear that." He gestured me toward a chair, and then sat in the chair next to me. "I believe you handled the situation admirably, from determining the problem to helping find the solution. You even helped salvage the operation by capturing our prisoner."

"I was highly motivated. I'm just worried that Owen was willing to let them go."

His expression darkened. "Yes, that is a concern. He cares for you, and that can be dangerous under these circumstances if he puts his personal desires ahead of the greater good. I'm also worried about his loss of control. That isn't like him, from what I've seen."

It was exactly what I'd been thinking, but I didn't like hearing it confirmed. I had to take a couple of deep breaths before I could bring myself to say, "I think I might be in the way. Whatever I bring to the table in terms of magical immunity might be outweighed by the fact that the bad guys now know that Owen will choose to save me instead of choosing to stop them." I took another deep breath, hoping to get rid of the tremor that had taken over my voice, and threw out the idea that had been stewing in my head all morning. "Maybe I should take myself out of the picture for a while."

"That might be the best option," he replied somberly.

My breath caught in my throat. I hadn't really wanted him to take me up on the offer. I'd hoped he'd say it wasn't necessary, that he had a plan for dealing with the situation, and then I could stay, guilt-free. He wasn't supposed to agree with me. "If you think it's best," I hedged.

"I'm primarily concerned for your safety. Mr. Palmer can take care of himself, and I have full confidence that he will eventually prevail. But now that our enemies can be sure where you stand in his priorities, that makes you even more of a target in the future."

"Okay, then. I guess I could go back to Texas for a while, at least until things settle down here. My parents will be glad to see me."

He raised an eyebrow. "I'm not sure things will ever truly settle down. Not around here. I do hate to see you go, for I've found your input quite valuable, but you're right, it would be best for you to be away. Kim is handling your tasks well enough that I believe I can get by without you." And there she'd done it. She had my job. It was almost enough to make me change my mind and stay, regardless of the consequences.

But this was for the greater good, I reminded myself. It wasn't about how valuable I was. It was about beating the bad guys, once and for all. Maybe when that happened, I could come back. I'd managed to get from Texas to New York once before, when I hadn't known what I'd be facing in the city, and with nothing to draw me there other than my college roommates. I stood up. "It's been a pleasure working here—well, other than the various times I've been enchanted or attacked. Good luck fighting the bad guys, and all that. Uh, do I need to hand in a formal resignation?"

"That won't be necessary." He stood and gave me a formal nod. "Thank you for your contributions." I was glad he left it at that, without any long good-bye speech. I wouldn't have been able to hold off the tears much longer, and it's never a good idea to cry in front of your boss—or ex-boss. Lucky for me, Trix was on the phone when I left, so I just waved at her as I passed. I could send her an e-mail later, I knew.

But I didn't think I could brush off Owen that easily. I needed to let him know what was going on. No, what I had to do was end things definitively. What were we going to do, maintain a long-distance relationship between New York and Texas? While the idea of him pining for me and us keeping in touch via phone and the occasional weekend visit was fun to contemplate in a pink-tinged, romantic way, it sort of defeated the purpose of me removing myself from the potentially problematic situation. If we were still together in any way, I might still be in danger, and I'd still be a distraction.

I mustered up every ounce of resolve I possessed, even borrowing on future reserves of resolve, and marched straight to Owen's lab, mentally rehearsing what I'd say as I walked. Then some of my resolve wavered when the only person there was Jake, who was poring over an old book with a magnifying glass. "Is he in?" I asked.

"Meeting with Mr. Lansing," he said without looking up. "He just left. It could be awhile."

"Oh. Okay. Thanks. I can't stay that long, but I'll leave him a note." I hated to admit how relieved I was. I knew that telling Owen in person was the right thing to do, but I wasn't sure I could have gone through with it when I was actually looking at him. Just imagining the hurt I was sure I'd see in his gorgeous blue eyes was enough to almost make me turn around and tell Merlin I'd changed my mind. Leaving a note was probably the best way to handle things so I could be clear about what I was doing and still maintain my resolve.

I went into his office, found a blank piece of paper in the mess on the desk, and wrote him a terse note about how I didn't see a way things could work out between us with everything else that was going on. "You have a job to do," I wrote, borrowing from the ending of his favorite movie so that maybe he'd understand what I was trying to do. "What you've got to do, I can't be any part of—not without getting in the way." I hesitated over giving him my contact information back home, then decided not to. If he wanted to track me down, he knew enough people who'd know how to reach me, and leaving the info would make it look like I was hinting for him to track me down. I ended the note with an exhortation to beat the bad guys, wished him the best of luck, then signed it, threw it in an empty envelope I found on the floor under his desk, and sealed it before I could change my mind. I wrote his name on the outside of the envelope and left it in his chair, where I was sure he'd see it.

Then I went over to the cubicle he'd built for me and gathered my few office belongings. I left my laptop on my desk and filled my computer bag with my desk calendar, coffee mug, and the other little things I'd kept on my desk. "I'll tell him you stopped by," Jake said as I passed him on my way out.

"Thanks. And let him know there's a note on his chair."

And then I walked out of the building one last time, my head held high. To be totally honest, I couldn't help but feel a little proud of myself for going through with my noble sacrifice in the name of the greater good. The world was a crazier place than most people realized, and in the grand scheme of things, my problems didn't add up to much. I could practically hear the stirring music swell on the soundtrack as I let myself disappear into the fog of the crowds on the sidewalk.

After all, we'd always have Manhattan.

PHOTO: JULIAN NOEL

SHANNA SWENDSON is the author of *Enchanted, Inc.* and *Once Upon Stilettos*. She's also contributed essays to books on such pop-culture topics as *Pride and Prejudice, Desperate Housewives,* and *Battlestar Galactica.* When she's not writing or watching television and movies so she can write about them, she enjoys cooking, traveling, singing, and looking for new hobbies to make her author bio longer and more interesting. She lives in Texas, but loves to play Southern belle in New York as often as possible. For more information on Shanna and her books, visit her website at www.shanna swendson.com.